THE CALL OF THE RIFT
WAKE

JAE WALLER

ECW

Published by ECW Press
665 Gerrard Street East
Toronto, Ontario, Canada M4M 1Y2
416-694-3348 / info@ecwpress.com

Editor: Jen R. Albert
Copy editor: Crissy Calhoun
Cover illustration by Simon Carr
Cover design by Made by Emblem
World Map: Tiffany Munro/ www.feedthemultiverse.com
Map of Ingdanrad: Jae Waller
Author photo: © Rob Masson

LIBRARY AND ARCHIVES CANADA CATALOGUING
IN PUBLICATION

Title: Wake / Jae Waller.

Names: Waller, Jae, author.

Series: Waller, Jae. Call of the rift ; bk. 4.

Description: Series statement: The call of the rift

Identifiers: Canadiana (print) 20230146023 |
Canadiana (ebook) 20230146058

ISBN 978-1-77041-459-4 (softcover)
ISBN 978-1-77852-123-2 (ePub)
ISBN 978-1-77852-124-9 (PDF)
ISBN 978-1-77852-125-6 (Kindle)

Classification: LCC PS8645.A46783 W35 2023 |
DDC C813/.6—dc23

This book is funded in part by the Government of Canada. *Ce livre est financé en partie par le gouvernement du Canada.* We acknowledge the support of the Canada Council for the Arts. *Nous remercions le Conseil des arts du Canada de son soutien.* We acknowledge the funding support of the Ontario Arts Council (OAC), an agency of the Government of Ontario. We also acknowledge the support of the Government of Ontario through the Ontario Book Publishing Tax Credit, and through Ontario Creates.

PRINTED AND BOUND IN CANADA

PRINTING: FRIESENS   5   4   3   2   1

For my brother Fletcher,
who will always be part of my refuge.

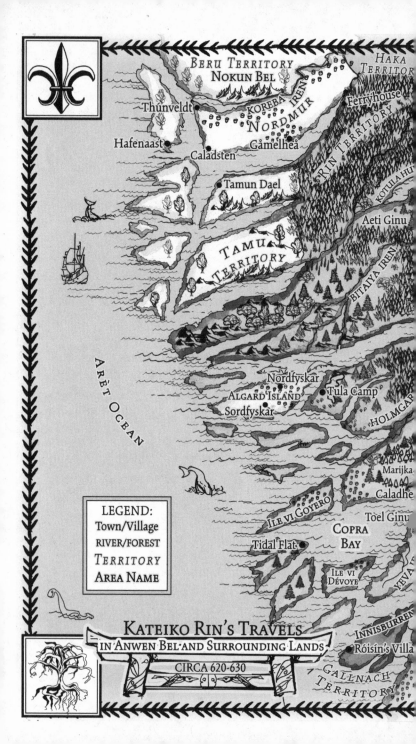

1.

AFTER THE BURIAL

"Come on, Kateiko. Focus." My cousin Emehein snapped his hand through the air. A whip of icy water shot from his fingertips and cracked against my ribs.

The cold wrenched me back to our sparring match. Our footprints formed a web across a snowy clearing. Sunlight glittered on a frozen brook. A crow cawed, its voice sharp in the thin air.

Waving at my shirt, I pulled out the water and flicked it away. "Sorry. Let's go again."

Emehein shook his head. "Maybe that's enough for today. We should head back for this wedding."

"One more round," I pleaded.

His face softened. Dozens of visitors had come from across the coastal rainforest for my parents' burials, then more had arrived for my cousin Malana's wedding. Strangers kept offering me sympathy as if they had any idea what I was going through. Some didn't even know *I* was a visitor here. My family had helped organize a mass desertion from our old jouyen, the Rin, then helped found a new one, the Tula, so people assumed I also lived here in the Tula settlement.

Emehein pushed up his sleeves, exposing a tattooed forearm. "One more."

He pulled water from the air, shaped it into a whip, and lashed out. I dodged. We spun in a dance, our braids whirling. I caught his whip and tried to snap it back toward him. We struggled for control. The whip split, twisting like octopus arms. My vision flickered. I tried to push through it, to focus—

The rainforest vanished. I floated above a wasteland. Scattered boulders cast shadows on cracked, blackened earth. Dust clouds wafted around me.

I stumbled and landed in snow. Colourful specks juddered across my sight.

"Kateiko?" Emehein crossed the clearing with long strides. "You all right?"

"Fine," I muttered, clambering up and brushing snow from my leggings. "Saw the wasteland again."

He frowned. "I thought you were getting better at controlling your visions."

I shrugged. There were all sorts of theories about seeing through the veil to other worlds, but I was in no mood to discuss the theological principles behind glimpsing a dead land. I was in no mood to discuss anything.

"Maybe it's a sign," he said. "How did it look?"

"Same as always. Flat, empty, and as dry as your sense of humour."

He gave me the look he used on his misbehaving toddlers. I waved my hand as if to say, *There you go.*

Not so long ago, I *was* better at controlling my visions. I'd learned to conjure them by focusing on the water inside sacred trees, which acted as conduits to other worlds. My first visions of the wasteland had felt like omens for the Battle of Tjarnnaast — scorched fields, ash falling like snow, smoke so thick that day seemed like night. My temal in his mountain cat form, riddled with arrows. My tema in her swan form, falling from the sky with a crossbow bolt in her chest. Rows of enemy Rúonbattai soldiers burned beyond recognition.

Now, a month after the battle, I kept seeing the wasteland every time I called water, usually in brief flickers. Occasionally the visions trapped me long enough that I burned dinner or boiled the kettle dry. I'd been practising blocking them out, and today decided to test myself by sparring with Emehein. Clearly *that* was a massive success.

He touched my neck, checking my pulse. "Are you sure you're up for this wedding?"

Absolutely not, I thought. I pushed his hand away. "I have to be. Malana's my cousin and Aoreli's my best friend's sister."

"Then we'd better go back and get this meat ready for the feast."

Sighing, I grabbed the rope handle of a sledge loaded with snowshoe hares and cloud weasels, the day's haul from my parents' trapline. We followed the brook into dense rainforest. Somehow the air was warmer in the shadows. It felt like if I were to peel moss off the trees, I'd uncover charred bark and petrified wood. Like this whole world was a mask over the land of the dead.

❋

Emehein and I took turns hauling the sledge up a mountain, climbing wooden steps overgrown with brambly underbrush. The temperature dropped as we rose. Soon after we crested the peak into the settlement of Nettle Ginu, two kids ran toward us on a shovelled path. Our half-Sverbian cousins stood out here with their blue eyes, foreign clothes, and faint accents.

"What'd you get?" eleven-year-old Hanaiko called, holding up her woollen skirts.

"Come see," Emehein said.

Eight-year-old Samulein bounded up and hugged me. His kitten, Stjarnå, poked her fluffy white head out of his leather jerkin. My uncle Yotolein followed with a wry smile. He'd tried to leave Stjarnå with our neighbours when they left the port city of Caladheå, but his son and the kitten were inseparable.

I pulled the sledge past rows of barren huckleberry bushes. At the tanning racks, we unloaded our haul. Hanaiko ran her fingers over the sleek hares and weasels, mottled with the start of their white winter coats. Stjarnå twitched her nose at the smell of blood, but Samulein stood back, biting his nails. He hated seeing dead animals.

"We'll skin these," Yotolein told me. "Go see Malana. She's inside getting ready."

"Can I come?" Hanaiko asked, bouncing on her heels.

"And me?" Samulein said, perking up at an excuse to leave.

Yotolein looked to me for an answer. They were from Tema's family, while Malana was from Temal's, so their only connection was through me.

I forced a smile and flicked one of Hanaiko's twin braids. "Sure. Malana will love having more people."

We wound through Nettle Ginu to the sod-roofed plank house where Temal's relatives lived with half a dozen other families. I paused in the doorway, its frame carved with the crests of everyone who lived here. Malana sat on a bark mat in the centre of the huge room, laughing while her older sister painted patterns on her hands. Aunts, cousins, and friends joked and gossiped. Men cooked lunch in flagstone hearths. Shrieking kids ran about, clambering over mattresses laid atop dirt platforms.

Tradition dictated that people grew up in their mother's plank house. Since returning from Tjarnnaast, though, unnerved by my parents' empty bed, I'd been staying with Temal's family. My grandmother Temal-tema had told me to treat it like home, but I didn't have formal rights to invite anyone in.

"Ai, Kako!" Malana cried, spotting me. "And Mister and Miss Blue Eyes. Get over here!"

I led my young cousins through the chaos. Malana wore black suede leggings and a black cottonspun tunic embroidered with red soapberries. The sleeveless shirt showed off her powerful javelin-thrower's arms. She'd braided her dark hair with glossy leaves, smudged charcoal around her eyes, and dusted glittering mica powder on her face.

Hanaiko stared in awe. "You look like a Sverbian goddess."

"Why, thank you." Malana kissed her fingertips and touched Hanaiko's forehead. "The Lady of Soapberries blesses you with bountiful forage and excellent hygiene."

Hanaiko giggled and plunked down on the dirt floor, sitting on Malana's right to speak toward her good ear. Samulein kept chewing his nails. Stjarnå mimicked him, biting her claws where she lay snug in his jerkin. A few kids eyed them curiously.

I'd been looking forward to this wedding for ages. In my daydreams, Tema's fierce expression stopped Tula kids from teasing Hanaiko and Samulein, while Temal told embarrassing stories about Malana's childhood, making everyone laugh until our sides ached. Biting back tears, I opened the purse on my belt and took out a macramé bracelet. Twined into the white cord were intricate flowers made of vibrant purple thread.

Malana gasped. "That must be Jonalin's handiwork. But he deployed with the navy months ago! When did he—"

"In spring, when you all came to Caladheå for the Ivy House mission. Nili bet that Aoreli would propose. I bet you'd do it first. Either way, I asked for Jona's help making your joining cord."

"Aeldu save me." Malana laughed, but she looked ready to cry. The mission had nearly killed her. A blow to the head had left her deaf in one ear and suffering balance problems.

"What's a joining cord?" Hanaiko asked, peering at it.

"It's an old tradition," I said. "We put our family crests in them to show we support a marriage. See, these flowers are my fireweed crest. Malana's family and friends each tie one on her wrists, then during the wedding, she and Aoreli will exchange cords, accepting each other's loved ones into their lives."

"Who wants the honours?" Malana asked, dangling the bracelet from her finger.

Samulein wrinkled his nose. "Not me. Weddings are for girls."

Malana threw her head back in laughter. "This one sure is. Then how about you, Miss Blue Eyes?"

Shyly, Hanaiko knotted the bracelet onto Malana's wrist. It hung with a cluster of others — leather and ropeweed and silk, strung with varnished seeds and nuts, resin-encased leaves and petals, and coloured glass beads that looked like berries. Malana shook her arm, making them rattle.

"Now we're honorary cousins," she told Hanaiko and Samulein. "And in a few hours, my wife's family will be your family."

Hanaiko beamed. Even Samulein gave a half smile, then we moved away as others came to see Malana. Temal's younger brother, Geniod, gave us mugs of cranberry-leaf tea and bowls of steaming salmon and duck potatoes. Samulein carefully plucked out the salmon bones and fed bits to Stjarnå.

Soon, Malana's mother called out that it was time to go. It was traditional for the couple to welcome their guests into the shrine grounds. As everyone began filing outside, Malana squeezed my hand and told me to catch up when I was ready. She seemed to know that the less time I spent at the shrine, the better.

My younger cousins helped me clean up lunch. Samulein let Stjarnå explore while he gathered dirty dishes for Hanaiko and me to wash. The house felt eerily quiet. Everyone had been cooking for days, making blood sausage, jam, compotes, and pickled mushrooms for the feast. Now the fires guttered as a breeze rustled down the smoke holes.

"Remember our first festival together?" Hanaiko asked me. "After Mamma died, and Temal brought Samu and me to live with the Rin?"

"I'll never forget." I finished scrubbing a bowl and passed it to her. "I gave you an arrowhead-leaf doll, not even knowing your name yet."

She paused, concentrating hard to call a stream of water to rinse the bowl. "Temal had told us about Rin festivals. Music, dancing, fancy clothes, tables piled with food. Mamma had never been to one, and I hoped we'd go together one day, but . . ."

I let a spoon slide into the wash basin, unsure what to say.

"Malana and Aoreli dressed you all pretty to dance with a boy. I was jealous of your outfit, sad you went without me, mad Temal wouldn't take me, scared of all the strangers, worried about Samu, miserable about Mamma, and . . . I had so many feelings I wanted to explode." She glanced up at me. "Sometimes I still feel like exploding. But not every day."

I hugged her, soapy hands and all. I appreciated her effort to cheer me up, but guilt still filled me like a sickness. I'd chosen a life in Caladheå, a city of foreign-born itherans, apprenticing at an apothecary and helping raise Hanaiko and Samulein. Not only had my medical training failed to keep my parents' blood from the ground, but I'd spent most of the last three years apart from them. Nothing could get that time back.

✳

Yotolein, his kids, and I walked to the shrine together, climbing an icy path to the highest part of the mountain. Weddings were a rare time that people from outside a jouyen were allowed onto sacred ground. Malana and Aoreli stood under a high gate carved with the Tula's kingfisher crest, welcoming the last arrivals. Aoreli kept smiling up at Malana, who stood a head taller. They made a stunning sight against the tiered wooden shrine and a backdrop of snowy mountains.

I greeted Aoreli with a hug. A white fur mantle draped over her tunic and leggings, which were dyed palest green and shimmered with pink embroidery of crabapple flowers. She looked like a spring day next to Malana's winter-night palette. Ribbons draped from her high tail of hair, stirring in an unusually warm breeze. It felt like the saidu, the nature spirits who controlled the weather, had woken from dormancy to join the celebration.

Aoreli beckoned Hanaiko over to see her joining cords. Hanaiko oohed and aahed, asking what the various flowers and berries were. Samulein stayed back with his hands in his pockets, sulking because Yotolein had made him leave Stjarnå behind. The last thing we needed was a kitten scampering through the wedding, tripping the dancers or eating the ritual salmon.

Yotolein coaxed Hanaiko away and we headed up the steps, through double doors and into the crowded shrine. Heat washed over us from hearth fires. Huge drums painted with kingfishers stood by a central stage. Garlands of pine cones hung from balconies.

Geniod, standing near a side door, beckoned to me. I wound toward him while Yotolein took his kids upstairs for a better view.

Geniod had always been my favourite uncle on Temal's side, partly because not having a partner or kids meant he always had time for me, but that felt like a curse these days. He'd fought the Rúonbattai in Tjarnnaast, too, and stuck to me like sap ever since. I was pretty sure my family had sworn a pact that someone would stay with me at all times. Apparently quitting medical work and sleeping on my parents' graves was "worrying behaviour."

"Here," Geniod whispered, slipping me a dusty envelope. "A Beru messenger just brought that. It's from Tiernan."

Elk sigils stamped in red ink marked its journey through numerous military camps. I tore open the pine-pitch seal. Written in smudged charcoal, the letter was dated about a month ago, mere days after we parted in Tjarnnaast. I read to *Dear Katja* before drumbeats vibrated the floorboards, rising through my bones and lodging in my skull. I grudgingly slipped the letter into my purse.

Malana and Aoreli entered hand in hand, bursting with smiles. Dancers twirled in after them, led by Nili, her father, and her younger brother, all holding kingfisher feathers and wearing slate-blue shawls that billowed through the air. People on the balconies tossed out handfuls of soapberry leaves and dried crabapple blossoms. They floated down, caught gusts from the dancers' shawls, and went spinning off. Some landed on the Tula's sacred trees, four rioden seedlings planted in clay pots and basking in afternoon sun.

After my parents' burials, desperate for an omen to guide me, I'd tapped into the seedlings' power and conjured a vision of the wasteland. A ghostly swan led me to a forest where a ghostly mountain cat waited outside a log cabin. Inside the cabin had been another me — making tea, laughing with another Tiernan. It had felt like my parents were telling me to find Tiernan. To trust him.

Colourful specks drifted across my sight like rainbows in river mist. I swore inwardly and blinked them away. When I could see again, Malana and Aoreli were kneeling on the stage. A wizened elder painted salmon blood on their throats, asking for blessings from our ancestral spirits, the aeldu.

My head throbbed. I felt like throwing up. Maybe if I let a vision come, it would be over soon. It was risky without protection, though. I fumbled through my purse, pulling out a swan carved from silver fir, then a mountain cat carved from pine. Closing my eyes, I sank into meditation, building a mental picture of the water in the shrine. Tracked-in snow stood out in white, while the timber walls and floor appeared in grey. I stretched my mind out toward the seedlings—

Pain shot through my skull. The shrine vanished. Phantom animals rolled and twisted in the sky above a scorched desert. *Shit*, I thought. This wasn't the usual wasteland. This was Aeldu-yan, the land of the dead.

A spectral fox stared at me. It drifted closer, sniffing. I tried to back away, but it was like swimming through sap. My floundering drew more attention. Bears and wolves prowled around me, baring translucent teeth. A shark grazed my arm, its rough skin scraping mine.

I looked at the reddish scrape in horror. If they could touch me, they could eat me. And they looked hungry.

Temal? I shouted. *Tema?*

A white streak shot through the sky. It grew into a swan, wings folded tight. The other animals scattered. I sighed in relief — but Tema was coming too fast, an arrow fired right at me. She shot through my chest, tearing the breath from my lungs. My scream ripped into shreds.

From the swirling mass of animals came a ghostly mountain cat, prowling on enormous paws. Temal yowled. The fine hair on my neck stood on end.

Fuck, I thought. *Nei, nei, nei, not you, too—*

Temal coiled his legs and leapt, slamming into me. Claws tore into my stomach. We tumbled through the air, tearing at each other, the horizon flipping. My guts slid out, a mess of slimy cords trailing through the sky —

The ghosts vanished. I woke screaming, thrashing, clawing at snow. Sunlight seared my eyes. Someone grabbed my shoulders, pinning me down.

"Kako, it's okay!" came Geniod's voice. "Breathe. You're okay."

I scrabbled at my stomach. No hole. No guts falling out.

Wedding guests leaned out the shrine's side door, looking shocked. Geniod ushered them back in, then knelt at my side. He picked up the carved swan and mountain cat from the snow. His voice turned hard. "Who made these?"

I snatched them back. "None of your business."

"Your temal never finished his apprenticeship. He wasn't allowed to carve makiri—"

"He made them to protect me," I snapped. "Not that you'd understand. *You* don't have children."

Geniod flinched. "Let me see. Their spirit fragments could've gotten corrupted—"

"Nei! I'm sick of you following me. I'm sick of people asking if I'm okay. No matter what I say, everyone treats me like a fucking glass doll!"

I scrambled up and ran, sliding down the icy path through the gate. I didn't know where I was going, only that I needed to escape the shrine, other worlds, the spectral animals, and everyone who acted like I'd already shattered.

2.

WEDDING FEAST

Deep in the forest, I slumped against a rioden trunk and slid down into a slushy pool. My stomach felt like a butter churn full of bad milk. I turned Tiernan's letter over in my hands, wondering what he'd think about my parents' spirits attacking me. Probably that I was beyond help. Sighing, I opened the envelope. He'd written in Coast Trader, the pidgin language we used with itherans. I couldn't read it fluently, but I muddled through.

> Dear Katja,
> We have made an important discovery. Recall that runed door outside Tjarnnaast, set in a cliff face under the Rúonbattai's painted oak and lilac crest? We suspect Liet's cleric escaped through it. I could not bypass the runes, so military sappers lit up blackpowder and blew the whole bloody cliff open. We found a tunnel leading into the

Turquoise Mountains. It appears to have been dug with earth magic.

We are not sure who created it. As far as we know, the Rúonbattai have no surviving earth mages. Perhaps they finally managed to wake a saidu. Then again, considering they intend for saidu to wreak chaos on Ferish lands down south, I doubt they would risk waking any here, this close to Sverbians in Nyhemur and Nordmur.

Regardless, Jorum and I volunteered to explore the tunnel. After two days' journey east, we surfaced in northern Nyhemur and found tracks in the snow. We plan to follow the trail. If we find the cleric, we will bring her to Caladheå to stand trial. You mentioned returning there after your cousin's wedding, so with luck, we will meet again soon.

Your devoted friend, Tiernan Heilind

P.S. Northern Nyhemur is stunning in winter. The snowy plains look infinite, as if one is floating among the clouds. Perhaps one day I can take you here.

"Fuck." I thumped my head against the rioden trunk. Slush fell onto my head. "God-fucking-damnit!"

In Tjarnnaast, we'd killed a golden-haired man matching the description of the Rúonbattai leader, Liet. The man's companion, a white-robed cleric, had vanished. Not until I'd returned to Nettle Ginu had I realized the cleric might've been their true leader, the temporal mage who could see through time and predict our moves. I'd sent a messenger to Eremur's military headquarters, but Tiernan and Jorumgard wouldn't have gotten the warning.

Had my parents known Tiernan surfaced in Nyhemur? I'd inter-preted that log cabin vision as them telling me to find him and rejoin the Fourth Elken War. Then again, maybe it hadn't been instructions from them at all. Maybe their spirits *were* corrupted. Maybe showing me a life with someone other than Jonalin had been deliberately cruel.

Fishing around in my purse, I found a gold coin marked with a leafy oak. Tiernan had forged the coin and told me to visit the Golden Oak in Caladheå if I needed him or Jorumgard. Now, I wondered if *they* needed *me*. I flipped the coin, reflecting a shaft of sunlight.

Something rustled in the canopy. I froze. A bald eagle was perched high on a pine, turning its head to avoid getting blinded by the reflection.

"Piss off!" I hurled a rock, falling short of the bird by an arm's length.

Geniod ruffled his wings, glaring as only an eagle could.

Groaning, I got up and brushed wet evergreen needles off my leggings. "I need to find Dune. Go back to the ceremony."

My cousin Dunehein, his Iyo wife Rikuja, my honorary Sverbian sister Kirbana, and her Dona husband Narun had offered to handle feast preparations while the Tula were at the wedding. I hiked back up the mountain and into Nettle Ginu, following plumes of smoke to firepits outside the gathering place. The smell of roasting meat made my stomach twist with the memory of burnt bodies in Tjarnnaast.

Dunehein whistled as he tended to two deer and five geese on spits. My hares and cloud weasels were skinned and ready. The heat was so intense that he wore a sleeveless shirt, damp with sweat and exposing his various tattoos. Inked on one bulky shoulder was the dolphin he'd gotten when he married into the Iyo-jouyen.

He looped his arm around me, crushing me in a hug. "I didn't expect you back yet, little cousin. Everything okay?"

"Not exactly." I read Tiernan's letter aloud, then said, "That was a month ago. He and Jorum could be lying dead on the plains, hidden under the snow. We wouldn't find them until spring."

"Ai, I'm sure those two are fine. They've faced the cleric before and survived."

"Yeah, but what if she led them into a trap? What if the Rúonbattai have another base in Nyhemur? What if—"

"Whoa. Slow down, jackrabbit." Dunehein rumpled my hair. "Tell you what. Go inside, get some veggies to peel, and we'll hammer out a plan."

❋

The wedding party hit the gathering place like a tidal wave. Temal-tema took over feast organization, barking instructions to light more fires, haul wood, and start an army's worth of trout roasting. Malana and Aoreli took their places of honour, sitting cross-legged on a platform in front of a kingfisher tapestry, while people spread bark mats on the floor for everyone else.

Dunehein and I had agreed to only tell a few people about Tiernan's letter, letting everyone else enjoy the wedding. Yotolein reacted to the news by swearing and smashing his fist against the log wall. Clearly his feelings for Jorumgard hadn't faded since their breakup. The Okorebai-Tula, Naneko, agreed to send scouts to Nyhemur. My visiting family agreed to move up our return trip to Caladheå to tomorrow. If Tiernan and Jorumgard hadn't made it there, then we'd know something was wrong.

I was tempted to go tonight, but the thought faded when Malana caught my eye and held her heart, grinning. I couldn't abandon my cousin's wedding. Thankfully, hardly anyone had noticed my outburst during the ceremony. Geniod had hauled me outside before I started thrashing, and the drums had drowned out my screams.

Midway through the gift-giving, as I hid in a shadowy corner with a mug of cranberry wine, someone sidled up. I blanched, thinking it was Temal until I noticed Geniod's cropped hair. I'd never realized how much they looked alike, with the same long nose and angular jaw.

"What now?" I asked. "Here to lecture me about drinking?"

Geniod flashed a dry smile. "You're seventeen. Old enough to make your own choices and young enough to survive the hang-over." He leaned against the wall, flipping his folding knife in the air and catching it. "I heard you're leaving tomorrow."

"Mm-hmm." I swigged wine.

"Your friends can handle themselves, you know. Tiernan and I examined that painted oak crest together. We both sensed living magic. He and Jorumgard know the temporal mage is still alive, even if they haven't realized it's the cleric."

"You mean I *shouldn't* look for them?"

"This war doesn't rest on your shoulders alone. You're allowed time to mourn."

I looked away, settling my gaze on a candle's flicker. Ghostly animals prowled through the shadows. "I don't belong here."

"You could." Geniod's voice almost faded into the chatter throughout the room. "You're right that I don't know what it's like to be a parent, and I'll never pretend I could replace your temal. But if you want an anchor here, someone who'll always have your back . . . I'd be honoured to adopt you."

I stared at him.

"It'll give you a formal place in our plank house," Geniod hurried on. "And since Malana's moving to Aoreli's house, you could take her bed. You don't have to keep using a spare mattress."

"Wow." I downed my wine and pushed off from the wall. "Now there's an offer I can't refuse."

I vanished into the crowd. People cleared away bark mats and replaced them with barrel-sized drums. The traditional wedding dances came first. I was surprised to see Malana's nineteen-year-old brother, Kotiod, among the dancers. He usually made fun of "all that stuffy old bearshit." The music sent colourful specks across my vision, so I perched on a table and watched, sipping throat-burning brånnvin.

Emehein, Kirbana, and Yotolein left one by one, taking their kids to bed. No one else came to bother me. Maybe my family had given up watching my every move. I thumbed my gold oak coin, wondering if I could slip off to pack for the trip tomorrow.

On cue, Nili plunked down beside me. I was getting passed along like hand-me-down boots. She started going on about how Tiernan and Jorumgard were surely fine, they were tough, I had nothing to worry about. So much for keeping things quiet. I tuned her out until she poked me. Kotiod flumped down on my other side and draped a bony arm around my shoulders, soaking me with sweat.

"Ai, mudskull," he said. "Mana's been asking where you are. Come dance."

I shrugged off his arm. "Not in the mood, Koti."

"One dance." Kotiod jabbed a finger in my face. "For Mana. Look, it's your moment!" He swept his hand toward the dance floor.

Everyone had gathered around an open circle. Antayul took turns spinning in and out, showing off their water-calling. If I was quick, maybe I could stave off a vision long enough for Malana to see me making an effort. I tossed back my brånnvin and pushed through the audience.

Kotiod's friend Riohem was inside the circle. Sheets of water flowed from his burly arms in a perfect imitation of a shawl dance, each droplet glittering in the candlelight. He dove and whirled with impressive grace for someone with such a husky build. Cheers rose across the room. Riohem grinned, letting his shawl fade into mist, and stepped back to give me the space.

I had no idea how to top that, but Kotiod was nudging me forward. Nili gave an encouraging whoop. As I caught the mist, inspiration struck. Rin shawl dances mimicked kinaru, our sacred bird.

I shaped the mist into an immense long-necked bird. Turning on my heel, I pulled the bird with me, curving it around my body, then sent it soaring up to the rafters. I called on the memory of riding a kinaru through glacial mountains. I spun as my bird twisted and rolled —

The floorboards vanished. Moonlight bathed dead earth far below me. I staggered, colliding with someone's broad chest.

"Whoa," came Riohem's startled voice. The sound brought the shrine rushing back. He steadied me before letting me go.

Nili caught my eye and mouthed, *He's lush!* Kotiod thumped my back and winked at Riohem. Across the circle, Malana and Aoreli clapped and hollered. Everyone seemed to think I'd run into him on purpose. Better than them knowing I'd hallucinated a wasteland.

Another antayul moved into the circle, drawing the attention from me. I slipped out through the audience. Only when I reached the wall did I realize Riohem had followed. He said something I didn't catch over the music, so I tapped my ear and shook my head. He held out a calloused hand. It took me a second to realize he was asking me to dance.

Growing up, I'd dismissed him as one of Kotiod's annoying friends, but he'd been friendly since my return to Nettle Ginu, always greeting me with a smile and never prying. The colourful specks faded, letting me see him properly. He had a solid face with a heavy brow and amber eyes. Maybe I needed a distraction. Hesitantly, I stepped toward him.

He slid his hands around my waist, careful not to graze my braid and touch my spirit without permission. I rested my palms on his chest, swaying to the drums. It felt familiar — the heat of his body, his firm muscles under his rough cottonspun shirt, his steady heartbeat. My forehead reached his chin, just like with Jonalin. And he wore his hair shaved like Jonalin had for naval training.

"Yan taku," I swore.

Riohem's brows creased. "What's wrong?"

"That scheming ass Koti—" I twisted, searching the crowd.

I spotted my cousin wrapped around a girl. A short girl with swaying hair ribbons. Kotiod bent down to whisper in Nili's ear, making her giggle.

"Seriously?" I yanked away from Riohem. "My cousin and best friend pawned me off so they could hook up?"

Riohem gaped at me. "Uh—"

It felt like the floor had vanished again. Cheeks burning, I strode off, grabbing my cloak and a bottle of brånnvin. I bit the cork and yanked as I emerged into the moonlit night. A hot wind stirred my hair. Either the wasteland was bleeding into this place or there really *was* a saidu here messing with the weather.

"Kateiko, wait," Riohem called, following me along a slushy path. "C'mon, it's not what you think!"

I swigged brånnvin and whirled on him. "I know what I saw—"

"I'm not talking about *them*." He jabbed his thumb at the gathering place. "Yeah, it's shitty they didn't tell you they're together, but they didn't send me to distract you. I liked your water kinaru and wanted to dance with you."

"Sure. From dozens of girls, you chose this." I plucked at my shirt, muddy from traipsing through the rainforest. My only adornments were a macramé necklace and a pair of sheathed knives. "The dishevelled fur trapper look has everyone swooning."

Riohem shrugged. "You'd look good in anything."

I narrowed my eyes. He sure had more confidence than Jonalin. Guilt rose in my throat upon realizing I liked it.

He drew forward, took the brännvin, and downed a mouthful. "Fuck everyone else. You deserve better."

On impulse, I stood on my toes and kissed him. He looked stunned, then cupped my jaw and pressed his lips to mine. I half expected him to smell like burnt clay from the Caladheå kilns.

"Not what I meant," he said after we broke apart. "But I'm game if you are."

I swallowed my guilt. "Wanna get out of here?"

Grinning, Riohem led me across a snowy field into the carpentry workshop. He set the brännvin on a shelf and kicked the door shut. Darkness enveloped the room. Moving by touch, we found each other's mouths and tumbled onto a pile of sawdust. His body felt familiar — big hands, thick arms, his weight on me — but he kissed me with unexpected fierceness, like a storm blowing in.

I fumbled at his shirt, but the haze of alcohol made my hands strange. Riohem pulled it off and tossed it aside. I wrapped my arms around him, digging my fingers into his back and feeling his muscles flex. He groaned and bit my lip, sending shockwaves through my body.

His hand had just reached my chest when we heard arguing. I batted him away, listening. Swinging lantern light appeared through a gap in the log wall as two familiar voices drew closer.

"You offered to adopt her?" Yotolein said, exasperated. "No wonder she took off!"

"I swore an oath in Tjarnnaast," Geniod snapped. "I held my dying brother and promised to protect his daughter."

"I promised my sister the same thing when Kako decided to stay in Caladheå. She *chose* that life."

"Kateiko stayed to help raise your children. That's not a life — it's being held hostage."

"Oh, don't start," Yotolein snarled. "As if living in a foreign city is a fate worse than death. That's the same racist bearshit the Rin-jouyen spouted."

Riohem shifted next to me, rustling the sawdust. "Are they looking for you?" he murmured.

I seized his arm. "Don't you dare tell them I'm here."

"Okay, okay. Gimme a sec."

He took a canvas tarp from a shelf and draped it across us. Sawdust billowed into my nose, forcing me to hold back a cough. Through the canvas came the faint glow of the nearing lantern.

"Things change," came Geniod's voice just outside the workshop. "Kateiko needs somewhere stable. She's not ready to fight again—"

Something hit the door, shaking the timbers. "Can't you see?" Yotolein demanded. "Kako's miserable here! She nearly killed herself in the shrine!"

Riohem sucked in a breath. The light sank as someone put the lantern down. The tarp felt suffocating.

"When?" Geniod asked in a hushed tone.

"After her parents' burials," Yotolein said wearily. "She had a vial of laudanum, the same medicine Jonalin overdosed on. Emehein says she keeps having visions of a wasteland, like she's slipping closer to Aeldu-yan. This place is *killing* her. And now she thinks Tiernan and Jorum are lying dead in Nyhemur."

"Aeldu save us. If you'd told me it was so bad, I would've watched her myself tonight."

The door latch rattled. Light spilled across us. I stayed still, heart juddering. Riohem's breathing was shallow. Too late I remembered we'd left the brånnvin on a shelf.

Someone called out in the distance. The door shut, the light faded, and my uncles' voices retreated.

I shoved off the tarp and got up. Fumbling in the dark, I cracked a window shutter to let in a wash of moonlight. Bad idea. Riohem's stricken face was suddenly too clear.

He heaved himself up and grabbed my elbow. "Kateiko—"

"Let go!" I yanked away.

Riohem backed up, hands raised. I found my cloak near the sawdust pile and pulled it on. I listened at the back door, making sure everyone was gone, then edged out. A snowy expanse lay between me and the forest. I ran for the trees, sweeping snow flat behind me to hide my tracks.

Nobody wanted me here. Geniod had only offered to adopt me out of some traumatized sense of duty. Nili and Kotiod couldn't get rid of me fast enough. Riohem never would've approached me if he'd known the truth. I was a burden, an infection, a walking disaster. It wasn't my parents' spirits that had gotten corrupted. It was mine.

I stopped at the treeline, stunned. Even the dead didn't want me. When I'd thought about overdosing, Tema led me away from the shrine. Today my parents chased me out. I couldn't live here, but I couldn't die here, either. Nettles snagged my cloak as I shoved through the dark woods. I hacked at them with my hunting knife, scratching my hands. I'd go find Tiernan and Jorumgard myself —

An owl hooted. Something swooshed overhead, ruffling my hair. I shrieked and ducked. The bushes ahead rustled and a human silhouette appeared. I backed up, wielding my knife.

"Yan kaid," came Kotiod's annoyed voice. "It's me, bludge-head! How many owls do you know?"

He whistled. A pinprick of firelight appeared in the trees, growing into a vellum lantern carried by Nili. She pushed through the path I'd wreaked through the nettles, her hair ribbons hanging loose on her shoulder.

"Of course," I said. "The happy couple."

"Kako," she said pleadingly. "We're sorry for not telling you. It's new for us, too. We spent a bunch of time together preparing for the wedding, and it kind of happened."

I snorted. "Right. And the second you got rid of me, you *happened* to fall onto each other."

Kotiod folded his arms and leaned against a rioden trunk. "Spare us the lecture. You looked happy with Rio, and we wanted to give you space. We didn't expect you to bolt and make us call a search party."

Nili frowned, taking in my rumpled braid and sawdust-covered clothes. "What happened? Where are you going?"

"To find Tiernan and Jorum. I'm not losing them, too."

She blew her cheeks out, then said, "Now that Aoreli and Malana are married, we're family. That means I have to tell you what no one else will. You're being selfish."

That shocked a laugh out of me. "*I* am?"

"Remember when your friend Akohin left town with no warning? Or you thought Nicoletta and Paolo eloped so he wouldn't get drafted into the military? Imagine how *we* felt when Riohem showed up in a panic and said you made a run for the woods, drunk and alone on a winter night."

"I watched my parents *die*! Sorry I don't want my friends to die, too!"

"Y'think you're the only one hurting?" Kotiod said. "We're cousins, mudskull. I loved your parents like my own. So did Mana. Want me to tell her that *you're* gone, too? That you left her wedding without saying goodbye and broke your idiot neck climbing down the mountain in the dark?"

"My parents told me to go," I snapped. "They don't want me here."

"When did they say that?" Nili asked. *"How?"*

"During the ceremony! Their spirits attacked me!"

The two of them exchanged a look. Kotiod said, "The whole Tula-jouyen was in the shrine. Dancers, drummers, our most spiritual people. Wouldn't someone have noticed your parents trying to hurt you?"

"Are you calling me a liar?"

"Nei. I just think it's stupid to run away without asking anyone about it."

Nili set the lantern in the snow. "I can't speak for the dead, but *we* want you, Kako." She drew forward and took my nettle-scratched hands. "Come back and get some sleep. Things will look better in the morning, I promise."

3.

PARTINGS

I woke to a throbbing skull. Blearily, I pushed blankets off me and sat up. Nili dozed next to me. For a second I thought we were in her plank house — but no, we were on my borrowed mattress in Temal's home. Kotiod slept on the floor, curled up under a caribou pelt. A few early risers moved about the room, lighting fires and starting breakfast.

Malana's bed looked dismal without her blankets. If she'd married a man, he would've moved here, but same-gender couples traditionally lived in the elder person's house. It seemed unfair that Aoreli being a few years older decided so much of their future — which routes they traded on, where they could trap and fish, whose family would help raise their children.

Guilt filled my throat like bile. It hadn't sunk in yesterday what Geniod's adoption offer meant. He was thirty-seven, still young enough to marry and start a family, but that might mean leaving our plank house, the Tula-jouyen, or the entire Aikoto Confederacy. Instead he'd offered to stay here with me.

I edged out from between Nili and Kotiod. Geniod beckoned me over to our hearth, where he handed me a vial of willowcloak tincture for my headache. He worked in silence, kneading brassroot dough into a circle and setting it to fry in fish oil.

Realizing he wasn't going to start, I took a deep breath. "Sorry for running away. Nili and Koti told me off for being selfish."

Geniod glanced at me. "Did you think we wouldn't care?"

I shrugged.

He pointed at the nearest window. "Look outside."

I prised open the shutter, letting in dawn light and a rush of chill air. This side of the house looked down the mountain. Icicle-covered buildings lined the slope, and beyond, snowy peaks faded into a misty grey sky.

"Will it look that way forever?" Geniod asked.

"Of course not. The snow will melt and everything will turn green again."

He nodded. "Every winter ends. Even when the saidu have been dormant for generations, you have faith that they'll create spring. So why don't you have faith in your family's love?"

"I . . ." My throat closed up. *Kianta kolo*, Temal always used to say — *the sap will flow*. "Something happened in the shrine yesterday."

"Kotiod told me. Is that the first time you've seen your parents' spirits?"

Reluctantly, I told him about spectral animals showing me the log cabin. Geniod's mouth pressed into a thin line, but he didn't tell me off for keeping it secret. When I finished, he said, "I don't know why your parents would turn on you. If you want answers, I have to ask their makiri."

I grimaced. There were so many potential *bad* answers. He'd realize my spirit was corrupted, or my parents' were, or they weren't in the figurines at all. My last trace of them might be gone. I couldn't keep living this way, though. I passed the carved swan and mountain cat to Geniod.

He took them like they were made of glass. Their polished edges caught the firelight, making their faces look alive. Holding one in each palm, he closed his eyes. He was still deep in meditation when I noticed the scent of burning flatbread. I yanked the pan from the fire, scalding my hand, and waved the smoke away.

Geniod's brows drew together. A shudder passed through him, followed by him biting his lip so hard a bead of blood appeared. Finally his brown eyes opened and he sighed. "That explains it."

"What?" I demanded.

He shifted both makiri into one hand and ran the other down his face. "Your parents know you've been shutting everyone out. They wanted to scare you into accepting help."

"I *am* getting help! I told people about Tiernan's letter!"

"That's not what I mean." Geniod set his hand on my knee. "We're trying to look after you, Kateiko, but you have to give people a chance."

I scowled at the makiri. "So scaring the shit out of me was the only way to convince me?"

"It's not easy for aeldu to communicate. Especially when being dead is new to them."

A hot flush passed through me. Here I was complaining when my parents had to learn an entirely new way of existing.

Geniod placed the carvings on the mantelpiece alongside our family's other makiri of bears and birds and wolves. I pushed down the memory of their ghosts stalking me through the sky. He cut the burnt flatbread into wedges while I chose a tea, browsing his homemade blends in varnished boxes. When I was young, his tea boxes had felt like treasure chests. Today I picked a blend with bits of dried crabapple. The golden-pink skins dyed the water the colour of a sunrise. Long ago, Geniod told me that whenever he had a bad night, he made this tea at breakfast.

Hesitantly, he said, "Since you don't want to stay, can I make a new offer? Seeing your parents in visions isn't the best mode of communication. If you want their guidance, you need someone who can read makiri. So if you can tolerate my company . . . I'll go with you. Not just to find Tiernan and Jorumgard, but wherever this war takes you."

I glanced at him in astonishment. "You're serious?"

"As serious as if you were my daughter."

Tears pricked my eyes. I wiped them away with my sleeve. "One condition. Teach me to read makiri myself. No offence, but I don't want to depend on a translator."

He frowned, the faint lines around his eyes crinkling. "Reading makiri isn't easy. Some people train for years and never get the hang of it."

"I know. But I have to try."

Geniod sipped his tea, steam wafting around his face. "All right. If you're sure."

✳

My last task in Nettle Ginu was sorting through my parents' belongings. Inside Tema's plank house, my family greeted me with unusually warm hugs. Samulein offered Stjarnå for kitten snuggles, which pried a smile from me. Geniod stepped aside to talk with Yotolein, giving me privacy.

I lay on my parents' bed and trailed my fingers over their blanket, embroidered with the fir branches of Tema's crest. I'd meant to leave it here as a memorial, but it was sinking in that they would never sleep here again. I buried my face in the cottonspun, breathing the familiar scents of woodsmoke and fish oil, before packing the blanket into a wicker carryframe.

Neither of my knives — one for hunting, one stolen from a sacrificial altar — were suitable for battle. I lifted Temal's sword from its mount, testing its weight. I'd never learned to wield a sword, but Geniod could teach me that, too. From my parents' rioden chest, I took Tema's spare winter clothes and a coppery fox fur mantle.

Emehein drifted over, carrying his baby boy. "Leave whatever you want here. I'll keep it safe."

I closed the chest. "I've got what I need. I want your family to have everything else. Tema's sewing kit, Temal's carpentry tools, their bed and mine. Their trapline's yours, too."

His eyebrows shot up. "Are you sure? That's valuable land."

"You've got five kids to feed. It's no use to me."

Emehein sank onto the chest, the end of his braid brushing the wood. "I'll take the meat and set aside the pelt money. You'll have a solid inheritance for the future."

Anything beyond the war felt too far away to plan for. I kissed his baby's dark hair, wondering how big his children would be when I saw them again. My musing was interrupted by Riohem calling my name. His brawny figure filled the doorway, hands in his pockets.

I crossed the plank house, trying to act casual with the unfamiliar weight of a sword at my side. "What do you want?"

"Can we talk?" His eyes flitted past me. "Alone?"

I turned and found my family watching. "Ugh. Let's go outside."

Flat grey clouds covered the sky. I went around the corner of the house and brushed snow off a bench. Riohem sat next to me, making the timber creak.

"I, uh . . ." He rubbed his neck. "Sorry about last night. I think we both went too hard on the brånnvin."

I scoffed. "You came to say you regret a drunken hookup? Thanks."

"That's not what I meant. I should've realized how upset you were—"

"Oh, so it *was* fine until you found out I'm a suicidal wreck."

"Nei!" His cheeks turned red. "Fuck, this is coming out all wrong."

Give people a chance, Geniod's voice echoed in my head. At least Riohem had started this conversation, which was more than Jonalin had ever done.

"I get it, you know," he said. "Missing people so much you're not sure how to go on. When I left the Rin-jouyen, I left my twin brother behind. He supports their alliance with the Rúonbattai. I don't. It feels like I've been walking around half-dead ever since."

"Oh," I said faintly. I'd been so lost in my misery I hadn't noticed his twin's absence.

"You always seem so strong," Riohem went on. "You're a healer *and* a warrior, off living in an itheran city. So the suicide stuff caught me off guard, but . . . I don't regret what we did. Last night just wasn't the best time."

"Aeldu save me," I muttered. "*I* should be apologizing. This wasn't ever going to work."

"Why? 'Cause we're both antayul?"

I laughed in spite of everything. I'd broken so many customs that the one restricting antayul from marrying each other felt trivial. I chewed my lip, debating. My parents wanted me to stop shutting people out, and Riohem's honesty deserved the same in return.

"An Iyo boy made this for me," I said, touching my macramé necklace studded with blue and green sea glass. "We broke up this summer. I think I danced with you because you look like him, and I kissed you because you act completely different."

"Yan kaid." Riohem's laugh had the shadow of a cringe. "You sure he wasn't my twin?"

I snorted. "Definitely not. He doesn't have a Rin tattoo."

"Sounds messy either way." He called a few snowflakes to him, twirling them through the air. "How about just parting as friends?"

Smiling, I kissed his cheek. "I'd like that."

"If things change, come find me." Riohem threw me a crooked grin and left, hands in his breeches pockets.

Geniod slipped out of the plank house. He must've been watching from a window, but he just said, "Everyone's coming to see you off."

I headed inside with a knot in my stomach. It took forever getting through Temal's family, caught between aunts and uncles wishing me blessings from the aeldu while toddlers clung to my legs. The way Malana and Aoreli chattered on, it was clear they had no idea I'd run away from their wedding.

"You need anything, call on us," Malana said, gripping my shoulders. "We'll be there."

"Are you sure?" I asked. "That head injury you got at Ivy House wasn't mild."

She waved that off. "My balance is getting better every day. Look!" She stepped back and twirled, her loose hair spinning.

Aoreli caught her, laughing. Standing on her toes, she pulled Malana into a deep kiss.

Nili rolled her eyes. "Now who's being gross in public?"

While they bickered, Kotiod slung his arm around me. "You okay?" he whispered.

My usual lie crumbled. "Nei," I admitted. "But Geniod's going to help me with these." I opened my purse to show him the makiri.

Kotiod's eyes widened. I put a finger to my lips and he nodded. Maybe he'd grown up in all the years I'd been gone.

"Be good to her," I said, tilting my head at Nili.

"I will." He ducked his head, blushing. "I don't deserve her. But she makes me wanna be better, y'know?"

I knew. The fear of my spirit being corrupted hadn't gone away, but my family and friends made me want to heal. I wanted to believe I deserved their love.

✳

We left Nettle Ginu in a convoy, bundled in furs and treading carefully on icy steps. Kirbana carried her one-year-old daughter, Sena, on her shoulders while Narun carried their three-year-old son, Kel. At the bottom of the mountain, we headed to a creek where we'd left our canoes upside down to keep out rain and snow. Ice covered the creek edges, but there was enough open water to paddle on.

Each canoe had been made from a sturdy, hollowed-out rioden log. The Tula prows were carved with kingfishers. Dunehein and Rikuja's had an Iyo dolphin, Narun's had a Dona seagull, and Yotolein's was unmarked. I hesitated by my parents' canoe. The last time I'd touched it was when lifting out their frozen, preserved bodies. Geniod, seeing my expression, suggested we take his canoe instead.

I had a general idea of the route ahead. We'd take the creek to Oberu Iren, the Tula's border river, which led to an ocean inlet. We'd follow that west, then turn south and wind around jagged peninsulas into Eremur, then head east across a bay into Caladheå. It was roundabout but easier and safer than hiking mountains in winter.

As we travelled, the adults pointed out wildlife to Hanaiko and Samulein, testing their knowledge of bird and fish species. I would've joined in, but I wasn't sure if the animals I saw were in this world or another. I kept getting mired in my thoughts, paddling without being aware of my arms, losing all sense of time and place.

Tiernan believed we existed in a shoirdryge, one of countless parallel worlds that had splintered off from each other. He thought the wasteland was in a world that had split from ours six or seven years ago. If that was true, then entire mountains had somehow been levelled flat. The only way I could imagine that happening was if an edim-saidu lost its mind and went on a rampage. Instead of that terrifying prospect, I rather would've not believed in shoirdrygen at all, but I didn't have a better explanation for my visions of another me — tattooed with a Rin kinaru I didn't have, lacking the scars I'd gotten from my attuning. I couldn't help wondering about her life. Wondering if *her* parents were still alive.

We camped on the riverbank, cutting back dead ferns and roping our tents to evergreen branches. Dinner was slabs of powdered meat and berries held together by elk fat. We set a schedule for keeping watch, but after Dunehein woke me for my shift, he only pretended to sleep. The lack of snoring from his tent gave him away.

Short winter days limited our travel time, and frequent stops to change Kel's and Sena's wraps slowed us up. On the third night we reached the Tula salmon camp and took shelter in my family's smokehouse, sweeping away burnt woodchips to make room on the ground. I lingered in the doorway, tracing the crests Temal had carved in the frame — fireweed for him and me, fir branches for Tema.

Spectral figures haunted my dreams. A pale woman floated through a snowy forest, wearing deer antlers on her head and a robe of white swan feathers. She carried a crossbow and a bloody knife. Guttural words poured from her mouth. A mountain cat paced forward, then its tawny fur blurred into a golden-haired man with tattoos on his face. He lifted a flaming battle axe, eyes fixed on me, and snarled.

I jerked awake. Sweaty hair stuck to my neck. Flickering firelight fell between gaps in the walls, casting an orange veil over my sleeping family. *It was just a dream*, I told myself. *We killed Liet. I saw him burn.*

A soft rustle caught my attention. Two thin antlers moved through the shadows. A pale hand reached for me.

I shrieked and swung, hitting something hard. A yelp erupted. The antlered figure collapsed. I scrambled backward, tangled in blankets, grasping for my knives or Temal's sword.

The door burst open, blinding me with firelight. I threw my arm over my eyes. Someone tackled me. I screamed, pinned down, writhing on the dirt floor.

"Kako!" came a deep voice. "Kako, it's okay. You're safe!"

Dunehein's face coalesced above me. I stilled, gasping from his crushing weight. He rolled away. Our family's shocked, ashen faces stared at us. Kirbana and Narun clutched their wailing toddlers. Stjarnå yowled in Samulein's arms. Hanaiko had one hand pressed to her mouth. When she lowered it, blood ran from her trembling lip.

"Someone was here," I said, my heart beating out of my ribs. "A spirit or something. I saw antlers."

"This?" Hanaiko picked up a headband with antlers and a deerskin fringe. "You made it, remember? You told me to put it on whenever I need to feel brave like the goddess Thymarai."

"That was *you?*" Iciness went down my spine. If I'd gotten hold of my weapons . . .

40

Yotolein pulled Hanaiko close, dabbing at her bloody lip with a handkerchief. He didn't even look at me.

Dunehein steered me outside into the night. My limbs didn't seem like mine. The ground felt foreign and the memory of bone hitting bone reverberated through my knuckles. Around the smokehouse, the skeletal branches of cottonwoods looked like thousands of antlers, lit up by the wavering light of our campfire.

Rikuja followed, carrying my parents' embroidered fir branch blanket. She draped it over my shoulders. "That wasn't your fault," she said gently.

I crumpled against her, chest heaving. I felt like crying and screaming and throwing up. All that came out were shallow gasps.

"Wala, wala," she soothed, rubbing my back. "Breathe. Take a walk, if you need to."

Dunehein lit a torch and led me down the riverbank. Our family's voices faded, leaving only the swish of flowing water and the crunch of pebbles under our boots. He propped the torch against a mossy boulder, sank onto the ground, and patted the spot next to him. I sat uneasily, clutching my blanket. The matte-black sky looked as empty as I felt.

"Rija's right," Dunehein said. "We know you'd never hurt Hako on purpose."

"It doesn't matter. I still hurt her."

"You're a war medic. You know the worst wounds can be in here." He tapped his chest over his heart. "I've been there myself."

I frowned at him. I'd lived with him most of my life and had never seen him wake up the way I just did. "When?"

"Years ago, after I got married and moved south. Things with the Rúonbattai were real bad then. I was afraid to sleep next to Rija in case I hurt her. She's tough, but I'm no sparrow." He linked his fingers and stretched out his burly arms.

"How'd you get over it?"

Dunehein chuckled dryly. "Who says I did? I've just had the same nightmares so many times that I recognize 'em. I can tell they ain't real."

"I have no idea what's real." The words slipped out before I could stop them. "Asleep or awake. I could've *killed* Hako."

"I know." He said it simply, with so much pain in his dark eyes.

My insides heaved. I jerked to my feet and vomited in the river, splattering myself with icy water. Dizzy, spitting to clear my mouth, I flopped back on the bank. "I can't go back there. I can't risk that again."

"Okay."

"That's it? You're not going to say I'm selfish for leaving?"

"Taking off without telling anyone is selfish. Listening to advice isn't." Dunehein gave me a pointed look.

I sighed. "What's your advice?"

"That time away from the kids might be good. Rija and I can travel ahead with you to Caladheä. We'll track down Tiernan and Jorumgard, and the others will catch up later."

This place is killing her, Yotolein had said. Maybe the farther I got from Nettle Ginu — from the memory of my parents' spirits attacking me in the shrine, the terror of my spirit being corrupted, and the visions of the wasteland that I only saw in this sickly forest — the more I'd heal.

"I should go with Geniod," I said. "He's here just for me. And . . . tell Hako I'm sorry."

4.

HOLY FLAMES

Geniod and I left at first light. Half a league from the salmon camp, the river opened up into the ocean inlet. I sensed salt in the water as we canoed into the swelling tide. The hours blurred together as we followed the coastline west. Only the occasional seabird or surfacing whale broke the monotony of grey sky, grey waves, enormous salt spruces lining the shore, and forested mountains fading into mist.

That evening, Geniod asked if I still wanted to learn to read makiri. He seemed to think studying the dead would make my nightmares worse, but I needed to get things under control somehow. So, starting with the basics, Geniod got me to analyze pieces of driftwood — the colour, grain, and smell of the wood, the way the ocean had smoothed their splintered ends, the stories the world had written on them. I spent the next day examining his canoe's kingfisher prow as we paddled.

We turned south at Algard Island, a Sverbian fishing colony with cod-drying racks on the shore, and headed into a winding set of channels. Freezing fog rolled in and stuck around for days. Ice coated the canoe and crackled on our clothes. I had to navigate by water-calling, searching the blank whiteness for solid land. Mournful foghorns sounded in the distance, borne from ships that faded in and out of the fog. I had no idea which were here and which were in the shoirdryge. A few times, we ran into floating logs that I swore hadn't been there before.

A lighthouse guided us to Caladheå. We paddled into the northwest district, Shawnaast, and landed near the navy piers late at night. Two grey-armoured Elkhound soldiers demanded our identification. I held out my elk-sigil card proving I was a legal resident. Geniod had a trade permit to bring supplies for the war effort, but too late I realized we hadn't brought any trade goods. I was thinking up excuses when a moustached Elkhound glanced at my card again.

"Kateiko Leniere," he read, butchering my first name but saying my Ferish surname perfectly. In Coast Trader, he said, "You're that viirelei medic who served in Tjarnnaast, right? You helped my brother through a nasty amputation."

The other Elkhound looked up from Geniod's permit. "Oh, the apothecary girl. I didn't recognize you dressed like that. Sorry."

"It's fine," I muttered, pulling my cloak tight to hide my leggings. Better to not mention I was quitting my apothecary job.

The moustached soldier tapped two fingers to his forehead in salute. "I'm afraid you have to go straight home, Miss Leniere. There's a curfew from sundown to sunrise."

"Curfew?" Geniod echoed. "What for?"

"You'll see. Show this if you get stopped again." The man handed me a wooden coin. One side was painted with Eremur's elk sigil, while the other had today's date.

Geniod and I buckled our swords onto our belts, shouldered our carryframes, and headed into the misty docklands. Beyond a warehouse, we saw it — a row of torched workshops. I'd passed the workshops countless times, seeing Sverbians weave sailcloth on huge looms. Now the blackened doors hung like loose teeth, revealing gutted interiors. Someone had scrawled *sacro incendo* across a wall in scarlet paint.

"Holy flames," I read, translating from Ferish. My stomach twisted.

Continuing inland, we passed more Ferish writing on fences and brick walls. *Burn them all. For god and glory. Tjarnnaast — 1 fire, 500 dead heathens.* Underneath were replies painted in white. Most were in Sverbian, which I couldn't read, but I understood ones in Coast Trader. *Kill the killers. Death is coming.* They were tagged with the Rúonbattai's sigil of a raven over crossed swords.

Unnerved, we kept to the main roads where street lamps formed chains of golden light. Elkhounds stopped us again twice. They let us pass after seeing our wooden coin, but I felt their eyes follow us. Near home, I picked up a frosty newspaper discarded on a bench. The *Sol vi Caladheå* was usually trash, but it was the only local paper published in Ferish, which I could read better than Trader.

My family's rowhouse looked abandoned, the windows shuttered, my garden black with frost. Hanaiko's and Samulein's sleds had frozen to the ground in the tiny yard. I climbed the rusty stairs to the one-room flat I shared with Dunehein and Rikuja, turned my key in the lock, and shouldered the door to break the seal of ice.

Dust coated the furniture and a musty smell had settled in. Geniod built a fire in the iron stove while I spread newspaper pages on the floor. The ink had run. All I learned was that Antoch Parr, the captain who led the razing of Tjarnnaast, hadn't been seen in weeks. The article suggested he'd fallen victim to demonic possession. There was no mention of his son, Lieutenant Nerio Parr.

"Useful as always," I said, tossing the pages into the stove. "The *Sol* once claimed the Rúonbattai were hexing everyone, and it turned out people had just gotten sick from rotten crabmeat."

Geniod chuckled. "Do you want to look into Captain Parr? Or just focus on Tiernan and Jorumgard?"

"Definitely just them. Parr's blood could be in the ground for all I care."

"You don't mean that," he said reprovingly. "Imagine how Nerio would feel."

I shrugged. Of course I didn't want my friend orphaned like me, but I wouldn't shed any tears for his father, who'd threatened my family and blackmailed me into doing his dirty work. If I never saw Antoch Parr again, it'd be too soon.

In the morning, we cobbled brassroot flour and salted sardines into a half-decent breakfast. I dressed in my layered city clothes — chemise, corset, petticoats, black dress, bonnet, wool coat. It was a short walk over the river into the old Sverbian quarter. A lumber mill had been burned down, leaving a black gash in the snowy yard. A few blocks on was the Golden Oak, a long timber building with icicles hanging from its eaves. I held up the gold coin Tiernan had given me. The etched oak perfectly matched the inn's sign, complete with birds nesting in the leafy branches and a dog snoozing underneath.

Inside, the fog dimmed the place so much that the candles had been lit. A handful of pale-skinned itherans sat at long tables, chatting over bowls of rye porridge. The aroma of baking bread wafted from the kitchen. Nhys, the yellow-bearded innkeeper, stood behind the bar, fashioned from a split log with the bark still attached.

"Katja!" He waved me over. "Nerio said you might show up."

"You've seen him?" I asked.

"Aye, for better or worse." Nhys leaned in and lowered his voice. "Trouble be afoot. Go upstairs to the sitting room. I'll be up in two shakes."

I led Geniod up the narrow stairs, making way for a woman coming down. In the sitting room, I paced by shelves of dusty books, my boots sinking into the woven rug. Geniod opened the faded curtains and checked the street, then leaned against the wall, arms folded.

Nhys came up a few minutes later, carrying a pot of steaming mead. "I didn't catch your name," he said to Geniod. "Katja's relative, I'm guessing?"

Geniod nodded. "I'm her uncle, Geniod Tula."

"Nhyskander Svarind, but only my mother and the gods call me that. Speaking of which, Katja, Nerio told me about your parents. All my love to you."

I cast him a grateful smile and sank onto a padded chair. Nhys took three mugs from a cabinet and poured the mead, filling the room with the scent of spiced honey. Geniod eyed the cloudy golden liquid skeptically, but at his first sip, his brows lifted with pleasant surprise.

Nhys settled on a chair, adjusting his apron. "Well, now. Where to start. You've seen the graffiti and torched buildings?"

"Hard to miss them," I said. "It's because of Tjarnnaast, right?"

"And this." He took a folded leaflet from his apron and smoothed it out on a table. "These turned up all over the city, supposedly written by Captain Parr. They call on Ferish citizens to take up arms in a holy war against heathens — not just the Rúonbattai but all Sverbians, plus you viirelei and anyone else who doesn't obey the Ferish god. Parr says he had nothing to do with it, but he got demoted anyway. Removed from command."

"Really?" I picked up the leaflet, astonished. "What's he doing now?"

"Stewing in his own rage, I expect. He's on 'indefinite leave' at Parr Manor. Too valuable to kick out, too dangerous to keep in."

"Who took over from him?" Geniod asked.

"Fedos Valrose, the infantry captain from the Battle of Tjarnnaast. A cautious, by-the-book man. Parr wanted it to be Nerio, but the Caladheå Council overrode him."

"What about Tiernan and Jorum?" I asked. "Have you heard anything?"

"Not recently. Nerio said they headed into Nyhemur about five weeks ago, tracking some Rúonbattai cleric."

Something heavy turned over in my chest. I'd been telling myself for days that everything would be okay once we reached the Golden Oak.

"I'm sure they're fine," Nhys reassured me. "They've gone away for months and always returned with stories to dazzle the gods."

"I know, but . . ." I slid my etched coin across the table, the nine-branched oak facing up. "Tiernan told me to come here if I need him or Jorum. Instead it sounds like *they* need *us*."

Nhys chuckled. "'Course he sent you here. That man thinks I know everything." He examined the coin, then slid it back to me. "Any news would go to Captain Valrose, but last I heard, he's up north fighting the Rúonbattai occupation of Nordmur. Parr might be your best bet."

Geniod raised an eyebrow. "The man who wants to kill us for heathenry?"

"I reckon you're safe," Nhys said. "Even if Parr started this holy war, I doubt he *believes* in it. He hired Tiernan and Jorum, two of the most pagan mercenaries around — a mage and a former guard for the Sverbian queen. Parr's not known for being pious."

"He also tried blackmailing my niece," Geniod countered. "I'll talk to him myself. Kateiko, you wait here."

For once, I would've gladly let him be overprotective, but it wouldn't work. I heaved a sigh. "Parr Manor's being used as a military hospital. They won't let a stranger in alone. Luckily, I volunteered there this summer."

❊

On the plains southeast of town stood Parr Manor, busier than ever. Men unloaded sleighs, a stablehand pushed a wheelbarrow through the snow, a postal carrier unloaded envelopes from her horse's saddlebags. Pigeons roosted in the mat of fire-red blazebine covering the brick walls. The door guard looked skeptical when Geniod and I asked to see Parr, but he fetched a porter to take us in.

Bleach and camphor stung my nose as I entered the lobby. Memories flashed across my vision — scorched fields, dead soldiers in rows, a blue-eyed man coughing blood. I forced myself not to look into the adjoining room where wounded men lay on cots. The porter led us down a portrait-filled corridor and knocked on a door with a trembling hand.

"Enter," came Parr's muffled voice.

Geniod went first, hand on his sword hilt. A chill hit me as I stepped inside. The windows were thrown open. Plants in huge ceramic pots ringed the room. Parr stood barefoot on a canvas mat, twirling a wooden practice sword. His black hair hung loose past his shoulders, and he wore only breeches and a damp shirt. It felt unnatural to see him out of uniform.

"Miss Leniere," he greeted me. "And your uncle Geniod, correct? Is this a diplomatic visit, or have you come to gloat?"

"Neither," Geniod said. "We're looking for Tiernan and Jorumgard."

"I see." Parr set his sword on a wall mount and wiped his forehead with a handkerchief. "Then your visit is in vain. I have no idea where they are."

"You mean they're missing?" I asked.

"Not at all. I am sure *they* know their location."

I stared at him in disbelief. "They were tracking a cleric who wants to kill them. A cleric who can see the future. Don't you care about finding them?"

"Care?" Parr's voice cracked as he laughed. "Of course. Heilind and Tømasind are my friends, my comrades. Yet thanks to that traitorous bastard Fedos Valrose, I am condemned to suffer in my own home, tortured by the moans of dying men I should be avenging."

Geniod and I exchanged a look. I could see why the military blamed Parr for the holy war. The man looked deeply unwell — dark half moons under his eyes, bruises on his hands, stubble shadowing his jaw.

Parr crossed to a table surrounded by rubbery plants, poured a glass of ice water, and downed it. He stared out a window across the misty grounds, swirling the ice in his glass. It tinkled like windchimes. "I had plans, contingencies, alliances in progress. Thousands of men under my command. Now I have nothing. Not even my son."

"Nerio? What happened?" I asked.

"Valrose sent him away. Deployed to some backwater post down south. No doubt the military is reading our letters, too. And I need to send him an urgent message, but—" He whirled, locking eyes with me. "You. *You* can take it."

I backed up, unnerved. "What message?"

Parr deliberated, then drew his hands apart as if unrolling an invisible banner. "'The strawberry winters in the bathhouse.'"

Geniod choked with laughter. He covered his mouth, feigning a cough.

"What does that mean?" I asked.

"It will lead Nerio to one of my informants. She has contacts in Nyhemur and may know what happened to Heilind and Tømasind." Parr abandoned his glass on the windowsill, crossed the room, and opened a door. "Come."

We followed him into the library where he'd once blackmailed me. Comforting. Empty wine bottles and stacks of books littered the tables. Parr padded barefoot across a thick rug to a gilt-labelled map covering one wall. He pointed at Ile vi Dévoye, an island to the southwest where Jonalin had done his naval training.

"Go first to the Dévoye camp," he said. "The man in charge, Captain Baccini, is a family friend. He will tell you where to find Nerio."

"How do I get *into* the camp?" I asked.

"You are a war medic. That should get you access." Parr collapsed into a gilt chair and propped his bare feet on his cluttered desk. "I did not sell you out, you know. Valrose knows nothing of your secrets. Your family is safe."

Geniod scoffed. "From everyone except you."

Parr's mouth twisted in a smile. He tapped two fingers to his forehead in salute. "Good luck, Miss Leniere."

I turned to leave, then took Nhys's crumpled leaflet from my purse and set it on the desk. "Did you do it? Launch a holy war?"

A muscle twitched in Parr's jaw. "If I deny it, would you believe me?"

I held my chin high, looking down into his dark eyes. "No. I wouldn't."

✳

"We don't have to go," Geniod said once we were back home, sorting through groceries. He tipped a bag of turnips and rutabaga into the vegetable bin. "This informant sounds like a long shot."

"I know." I collapsed onto my mattress and planted my face in Tema's fir branch blanket. "But my parents sent me to find Tiernan, right? Maybe this is the way."

"Why don't we ask?" Geniod took down their makiri from a shelf over the stove, where I'd placed them alongside a pair of dolphins from Rikuja's parents and a coal newt from Tiernan. "See if you can sense anything."

I sat up and closed my hand around the carved swan. Voices out in the street kept distracting me. Tema's makiri felt smooth, cold, and lifeless. "Nothing."

"I'd be shocked if you could," he said. "Most makiri-readers learn as children. Training a teenager is like throwing a fish into the air and telling it to fly."

I snorted. "Thanks."

Geniod ruffled my hair, knocking the pins askew. "Give it time. Right now, you've got me."

He balanced the mountain cat on his palm and closed his eyes. I waited, flipping my gold oak coin, reminding myself what he'd said about aeldu having trouble communicating. The setting sun lit up my stained-glass butterfly in the window, casting rainbows across the walls.

Geniod blinked like he was coming out of a dream. "I saw . . . you and your temal sparring by a lake at dawn. It looked like the Rin training grounds. The cottonwoods were turning yellow."

I paused, thinking. "That sounds like — Wait. You can see dead people's *memories*?"

"Only if they show me. I can't dig through someone's past against their will."

"Yan taku," I muttered. "That was the autumn the Rúonbattai crossed through our land to Tjarnnaast. Temal switched my dawn antayul lessons to combat training. He said I should be prepared."

"Ah." Geniod smiled wryly. "There's your answer."

"Be prepared? I don't even know what Nerio's doing down south."

"Maybe we're meant to figure that out." Geniod glanced out the window at the twilit street. "We'll have to start tomorrow, though. Curfew's upon us."

5.

LAVENDER

After another night of bad dreams, I woke to Geniod humming as he fried flatbread. His cheerfulness was grating. Worse yet, he insisted on walking me to the apothecary. I finally escaped him in the back alley. Ice-encrusted laundry hung on a cord between the brick walls, and greenish slime filled the gutters. Nicoletta's stub-nosed cat, Luna, meowed and curled around my skirts. I scooped her up and buried my face in her white fur, then headed into the steamy kitchen.

The sharp scent of ammonia assaulted my nose. Memories of dying soldiers washed over me. *Help*, they'd cried, reaching out as I hurried past. I could still feel their clammy fingers brushing my hands. By the time I came back to treat them, their fingers had gone limp.

"Kateiko?"

Agata's sixteen-year-old grandson, Matéo, stood with a broom in hand, staring at me. A mess of damp auburn curls fell across his eyes. He'd hit a growth spurt. Instead of his school uniform, he wore an apron over a faded shirt, the collar undone and sleeves rolled up.

"You okay?" Matéo reached out, making me flinch.

Heat flooded my cheeks. I hung my coat and bonnet near strings of onions dangling from the rafters. "Since when do you work here?"

"Since you left." He shrugged, leaning on his broom. "Grandmera couldn't keep up without you. She's out at a military hospital right now."

"Matéo?" came a sharp voice. Nicoletta swept in from the front room, skirts swishing. "Who are — Oh!"

She flung her arms around me. I hugged her curvy frame, resting my chin against her forehead. *She* hadn't changed, still wearing the same gingham dress, the same brass hairpins in her curls. I inhaled her familiar scent of ginger and lye soap.

"We heard about your parents," Nicoletta said, pulling back. "I'm so sorry. I've had a letter from Paolo, though. He and Jonalin are fine. Still deployed in the Beru nation's territory."

I sagged with relief. "Thank the aeldu."

"Of course the military's in chaos since Captain Valrose took over, but—" Nicoletta whirled toward the brick hearth where murky liquid simmered in a pot. "Matéo, I told you to stir that! If it boils over, so help me god—"

"God's your only hope," Matéo grumbled, picking up a wooden spoon.

Nicoletta rounded on me. "Please say you're back for work. Somehow my brother's hung around for months without learning anything."

Behind her, Matéo mimed hanging himself with a noose. I held back a snicker.

"Sorry," I said. "Captain Parr's sending me south with a message for his son. Speaking of which, I need to see the naval captain at Ile vi Dévoye. Any idea how I can reach him?"

Nicoletta looked taken aback. "Not offhand. Our only business there is with other medics, and delivering medicine would only get you to the quartermaster. Though . . ." She heaved a flour sack off a pile of newspapers. "I saw something about the island in the *Sol vi Caladheå* a couple weeks ago. I figured you'd want to know what you missed, so I bought a paper every day since you left."

It was one of the few thoughtful things she'd ever done for me. Matéo made room on the huge oak table, pushing aside bowls of diced roots and slimy animal offal. Nicoletta dropped several papers onto it with a *whump*. We each pulled up a stool and began skimming. Most recent war news was about the front lines in Nordmur. Valrose had laid siege to Gåmelheå, the last town held by the Rúonbattai.

"Found it," Matéo said, jabbing at a page. "A crew of undead pirates has been torching cottages near Ile vi Dévoye."

"Near?" I repeated. "What, in the ocean?"

"*That's* the part you're questioning?" he said. "Dunno. Could be the mainland, could be surrounding islands."

"Sounds like the arsonists here," Nicoletta huffed. "I've never treated so many burns in my life."

I groaned. "Nica, you're right. That 'undead pirate crew' must be part of Parr's holy war."

"Then why's Nerio there?" Matéo asked, getting up to stir the simmering pot. "Is he one of 'em?"

"Nei. Captain Valrose sent him there, probably to hunt down the arsonists. Which means Valrose is using Nerio as a pawn against his own father."

"If you're heading into a war zone, you'll need supplies." Nicoletta started pulling jars and bottles from the shelves. "Let's see. Camphor, beeswax salve, salt of hartshorn — Matéo, get some laudanum from the surgery—"

"Wait, wait," I interrupted. "I'm not going as a healer."

"What?"

"I quit. I'm done with medicine."

Nicoletta turned. She pursed her lips, tapping a bottle. "No."

"No?"

"Grandmera and I didn't teach you all this just for you to throw it away. We're at war. People need you."

"I'm not throwing it away," I said indignantly. "I can't *do* it anymore. You weren't in Tjarnnaast — you didn't see—"

"Oh, don't give me that," she retorted. "You know where those wounded soldiers got sent? Here. I've spent weeks treating my friends and neighbours. Amputations, gangrene, men burned past recognition. I could fill a book with the horrible things I've seen, but I keep going. So does Matéo. You have no idea what he sacrificed to be here."

Matéo winced. "Nica, it doesn't matter—"

"Of course it does! It's your whole life!"

I looked between them, frowning. "What are you talking about?"

He sighed and ran a hand through his curls. "Our parents want me to enlist. That's how it works in the Solus family. The boys go to war, and if they make it home, the girls patch 'em up. I compromised by joining the student military club, but then I dropped out of school to help here, and . . . our parents told me not to come home again unless I'm in uniform."

I clapped a hand to my mouth. "They kicked you out?"

"Yes," Nicoletta cried. "Sent their eldest son away without a goodbye. Matéo's been sleeping on our couch upstairs. But *he's* still working here because *he* knows how important this job is."

"It's not the same!" I snapped. "I *can't do it*. I open my medicine satchel and can't breathe. I call water and it disappears. I pick up a scalpel and my hands start shaking. I'll kill someone by accident!"

"You'll kill them by doing nothing!" She smacked the table. "I'm not saying you have to work here. But promise me — *promise* — if you come across someone in need, you won't turn your back on them."

A lump filled my throat. I couldn't get the words out, so I just nodded.

"Good. Then I'll get you supplies." Nicoletta strode into the front room.

Matéo rubbed his temples, muttering. He took a vial of amber liquid from a rack. "You'd better take this, too."

"What?" I said distantly, feeling like I'd been run over by a cart.

"Contrary to what Nica says, I know some medicine. Like that lavender oil calms the nerves." He poured a droplet on his fingertip, then dabbed it above my upper lip. "Breathe in. Slowly, remember."

The floral scent filled my nose. He corked the vial and took the stool next to me, resting his feet on the cross-brace.

"Sorry," I said. "Earlier, I didn't mean . . . It's different, your parents and mine, but it's still awful."

Matéo looked down, his lashes covering his moss-green eyes. "Yeah."

He looked faded. Flattened. His family was everything to him. When we were younger, his parents had given him an ultimatum — break up with me or get sent to boarding school away from his siblings. He'd broken up with me and never looked back. As much as it hurt, I'd understood. This, though, getting torn between two sides of his family — this was breaking *him*.

❋

I spent half an hour flipping through newspapers, trying to learn who'd been attacked near Ile vi Dévoye. I hadn't found anything by the time Geniod came to get me. We went to the navy piers to ask around, then paddled his canoe down the shore, trying the fish market, the southern docklands, and the Iyo docks. No one had answers.

All we could do was prepare in other ways. The Iyo sold us elk jerky and smoked salmon for travel food. One of their carvers agreed to repair Geniod's canoe. The floating logs we'd hit on the way here had cracked the resin coating. Water had seeped into the cracks, frozen, and expanded, splintering the hull. The repairs would take a few days, but without them, one bad storm could sink us.

In a park near home, Geniod gave me my first sword-fighting lesson, sparring with long sticks. Temal's sword used to be too long and heavy for me, so he'd trained me with a spiked flail, which I'd lost years ago when Elkhounds detained me as an illegal immigrant. I was taller and stronger now, but a real sword fight would drain me. To Geniod's credit, he didn't suggest using a lighter blade. Instead he drilled me on strength-building exercises, from lifting bricks to hauling flour sacks around the block.

Curled up in bed, aching in muscles I didn't know I had, I reread Tiernan's letter. I hadn't paid attention to the postscript until now. *Northern Nyhemur is stunning in winter. The snowy plains look infinite, as if one is floating among the clouds. Perhaps one day I can take you here.* It was an odd thought to have while chasing a murderous cleric, but Tiernan had always been like that, finding joy in unexpected places.

We'd once ridden through southern Nyhemur in spring. Clouds of pollen, blowing grass, damp earth. It had all looked the same. Tiernan told me to view it through the lens of my trapping skills. I'd begun noticing tiny gopher footprints, shorter grass where bison had grazed, duck eggs hidden in creek-side reeds. All that life blooming under the surface, and now he and Jorumgard might be lying dead among it.

Alongside my worry about them grew another concern. Yotolein and the others should've been close behind us. Maybe they'd gotten shipwrecked, or attacked, or detained by the navy. Maybe they'd decided not to come home, too horrified by me hurting Hanaiko. I didn't want to leave town without knowing they were okay, so I began leaving notes in our flats telling them where to find us.

Midway through a sword-fighting lesson in the park, Dunehein and Rikuja appeared, their cloaks and fur mantles glittering with sea spray. They beamed. Dunehein lifted me clear off the ground and spun me through the air, my braid flying out behind me.

"Have we got news," he said, plunking me back into the snow. "Our little cousin Hako ain't so little anymore. She's now officially an adult."

I gasped. "She *attuned*?"

"Yes," Rikuja said with delight, clapping her mittens together. "We've all been so worried it might never happen. Instead she did it early."

Two years ago, after we rescued Hanaiko and Samulein from the Sarteres — a Ferish couple who'd adopted them and refused to give them back — Yotolein and I had discussed if half itherans could attune. He thought it depended whether they grew up knowing their Aikoto heritage, our beliefs and sacred legends. That conversation had convinced me to stay here to help raise his kids. A thousand emotions tangled inside me. I should've been delirious with relief, yet . . .

"Where's Hako?" I asked. "Does she not want to see me?"

"Of course she does," Dunehein reassured me. "She knows you panicked at her antler headband and didn't mean to hurt her. But we figured we'd better warn you."

"Warn me? What about?"

"Well . . . she attuned to a deer."

"She—" My voice faltered. "Yan taku."

My lungs stuttered like a dying butterfly. The wintery park tilted. I dug through my purse, yanked the cork from my lavender oil, and stuck it against my nose. *Breathe in*, Matéo's voice echoed. Just in case, I gave my obsidian-handled knife to Geniod.

We found Yotolein and his kids across the park having a snowball fight. Samulein spotted us first and squealed, making Stjarnå poke her furry head out of his jerkin. Hanaiko spun, her face lighting up. At a wave from Dunehein, she bounded toward us, tripping on her skirts and slipping in the snow.

"Kako!" she exclaimed. "I did it! I'm grown up!"

She barrelled into me, knocking me off-kilter. A laugh bubbled up from my chest. I bent down and kissed her hair. Touching her spirit was the closest I could get to being sure this was real.

"Can I show you?" Hanaiko asked, bouncing on her heels.

"Not here," Yotolein called, catching up. "Try the hedge garden."

Hanaiko dragged me away. Countless games of hide-and-seek in the park had taught us every secluded nook, including a memorial garden surrounded by a hedge wall. We passed through an arched gateway, finding the garden empty except for dead flower beds. Our family filed in after us. Geniod took up post by the gate to stop strangers from entering.

"Go on then," I told Hanaiko. "I'm watching."

She screwed up her face as if trying to remember something. Antlers erupted from her head. Sleek brown hair rippled across her skin. She shuddered and fell forward onto cloven hooves. A second later she was gambolling across the garden, kicking up clouds of snow. A flock of birds took to the sky squawking.

Hanaiko's attuned form was a coastal deer, smaller than the inland types. She bounded over and rubbed her nose against me.

Her antlers barely reached my shoulders. I sank to my knees and wrapped my arms around her neck. Everything I'd suffered and sacrificed for her and Samulein, all the time lost with my parents, had been for this.

6.

WHAT MAKES A HOME

We threw together a hasty celebration dinner in Kirbana and Narun's flat. Most of our gatherings were there since their two-room home had the most space, though with eleven people, we kept knocking elbows. Narun took Kel and Sena to play in the bedroom while the rest of us talked in the kitchen. I expected Samulein to tease his sister about attuning to a male deer. Instead he was quiet, clutching Stjarnå even as she squirmed to go free. I knew that feeling. I'd spent years watching my cousins and friends attune, wondering when I'd catch up.

Curfew meant we couldn't cross the street to go back home, so we spread blankets on the floor. I'd just finished pulling out my hair-pins when Yotolein beckoned to me. Hesitantly, I followed him into the hallway connecting the upper-level flats. Golden light from a street lamp filtered through a frosty window.

Yotolein brushed dry mud from the top of the staircase and sat down. I hiked up my skirts and settled next to him. He produced a flask from inside his jerkin, took a swig, and offered it to me. Recognizing the fennel scent of brännvin, I shook my head.

"I keep thinking about the night we rescued Hako and Samu," he said. "Disguising you as a Sverbian goddess, breaking into the Sarteres' home, scaring those arrogant takuran into giving my kids back. It felt like a fever dream. The next morning, you and I sat on the stairs like this, drinking tea and watching the sunrise."

I touched a smooth scar on my scalp. Kirbana had glued antlers to my head for part of my disguise as Thymarai, Lady of the Woods. My scalp had bled when we pulled them off. A few months ago, I'd sewn those same antlers onto a headband and gave them to Hanaiko, telling her to be brave while I was away at Tjarnnaast.

Yotolein nudged me. "Pann for your thoughts?"

"Save your money."

He arched an eyebrow.

"What do you want me to say?" I snapped. "I fucked up the most sacred part of your daughter's life. Every time she attunes, she'll remember me hurting her. You want to sit here and act senti-mental, pretending you're not furious?"

Yotolein held out the flask again. This time I took it, sputtering as the brännvin seared my throat. Lavender wasn't strong enough for this conversation.

"You know why Hako wears those antlers?" he said. "To be like you. You're Thymarai to her, someone who'd walk through fire for our family. I think she decided to take over so you have time to heal. *That's* why she attuned."

"But—" My reply faltered. "She's only eleven. I thought I'd have years to sort my shit out. I wanted to be there when it happened."

"Who says you weren't?"

I frowned, wondering if he really had been suffering fever dreams.

Yotolein pulled a leather cord out from under his tunic. Hooked onto it was a limestone carving of a tundra wolf, the makiri I'd given my cousins before I left for Tjarnnaast. "Your spirit's always with us. No matter what happens or where you end up."

I touched the wolf's smooth head, warm from Yotolein's body heat. I was staring down my own mortality. If I died, my only way of communicating would be through this wolf, passing on confusing visions.

"If . . ." I bit my lip and started over. "*When* I find Jorum, do you want me to tell him anything?"

"Other than 'You're a bastard for leaving me'?"

I snorted. "I already told him that in Tjarnnaast."

"Atta girl." Yotolein thumped my back, then sighed. "I used to dream of a life with Jorum. Marriage, a family, retiring to a cottage by the sea. Hako and Samu would call him Pappa, the Sverbian way. But Jorum doesn't want any of that."

"He does. He told me he fucked up by leaving. I think he'd give anything for another chance."

"Mm." Yotolein took his flask back and swigged brännvin. "If that's true . . . he knows where to find me."

*

In the morning, while Geniod retrieved our canoe from the Iyo carver, I returned to my flat with Dunehein and Rikuja. Our rusty postal box held leaflets advertising charity events. Every time I checked the mail, I hoped to find another letter from Tiernan, and every time I was disappointed. I wondered if I should leave a note at the Golden Oak in case he and Jorumgard turned up while I was away.

"Where's the kettle?" Rikuja asked, moving dishes around with loud clanks and scrapes.

"Not sure," I said, perching on a stool by my tiny writing desk. "Geniod moved stuff around."

Dunehein cleared his throat as he built a fire in the iron stove. "So, Kako . . . Rija and me are thinking about going with you. You'll need all the help you can get finding Tiernan and Jorum."

"Really?" I opened a varnished wooden box and began setting out quill, ink, and paper.

"Really. Problem is, if we're not here working and paying rent . . . we'll lose our flat."

"Oh." I smoothed a paper across my desk. "I can get our mail redirected to Yotolein."

Dunehein blew out a noisy breath. "That's all you have to say?"

Irritation flared inside me. I was sick of people interrogating me, poking and prodding. In my peripheral vision, I glimpsed Rikuja, holding the kettle and a watering can. Her mouth was drawn tight in an odd look.

"C'mon." Dunehein set a huge hand on my shoulder. "It's a big decision. We need to know how you feel—"

"I don't care! Can't I write a damned letter in peace?"

Rikuja burst into tears. I swung on my stool, mouth agape. Dunehein lunged across the room and wrapped her in a bear hug.

"Never mind me," she gasped, wiping her eyes. "It's silly. I . . ."

"Deep breaths, love." Dunehein kissed her hair, put the watering can atop the firewood box, and set the kettle to heat.

Rikuja took a steadying breath. "I wondered if your potted herbs need water, Kako. So I looked over and they were gone. I forgot you gave them to Nicoletta before leaving for Tjarnnaast. Then I noticed how bare the room looks without them, and . . ."

My pots had left water stains and a yellow dusting of pollen on the windowsill. Our presence had marked this place — sawdust in the cracks, a lingering scent of fish oil, stained floorboards from a disaster with laundry bluing. Rikuja and I had laughed so hard that day we cried. Memories lived in the wood and bricks.

"Aeldu save me," I said. "Sorry. I didn't even think—"

"It's fine," Rikuja interrupted. "*I'm* fine."

"Right. Just like me."

She managed a watery smile. When the kettle whistled, I got up to fetch it. Geniod had made a few of his favourite tea blends. I chose a rosehip one that made a rich red tea, then added lavender oil to each mug. The three of us settled side by side on their bed, our backs to the wall.

"Are you serious about coming with me?" I said.

"Of course," Dunehein said. "You matter more than this old pile of bricks. But . . . we want you to have somewhere to come back to."

"What if I don't come back?"

His gaze shot to my leather medicine satchel.

"Not like that," I said hastily. "I mean if I move to Nettle Ginu or whatever. Would you keep living here?"

"Probably," Rikuja said. "It's not the life we expected, but I like having Yotolein's family just downstairs. I like glancing across the street and instantly knowing if it's okay to visit Kirbana and Narun. Curtains open, it's fine. Curtains closed, the toddlers are asleep. If we lose this flat, we might never get another place so close to them."

I hadn't thought about that. This flat wasn't just *our* home. It was somewhere dry for Yotolein and his kids when their place flooded, a safe spot for Kirbana to leave her toddlers while doing errands, a refuge for Hanaiko or Samulein when they bickered and needed to be apart. We had no idea who might move in after us. The way this holy war was going, it could be someone dangerous.

The simple solution was for Dunehein and Rikuja to stay here, but I did need their help. Ile vi Dévoye was part of the Iyo-jouyen's traditional territory. Neither Geniod nor I had been there, whereas Dunehein and Rikuja had canoed past it on trading trips. Beyond that, I wanted their company. I wasn't sure I'd survive weeks or months with only Geniod to talk to.

I jerked upright, spilling tea across my lap. "I have an idea."

✳

I found Matéo on his knees in the apothecary surgery, scrubbing bloodstains from the floor. A bucket of reddish water sat nearby. I emptied it in the alley, brought it back, and filled it with clean water, earning a grateful smile from him.

"So," I said, leaning against the wall next to a rack of sharp metal tools. "Still sleeping on the couch?"

"*Sleeping* is a generous term," he said. "I keep waking up to Nica's cat on my face. Pretty sure she told that fluffy mongrel to suffocate me."

"Then how would you feel about renting my flat?"

He stopped scrubbing and looked up. "You're joking."

"Dead serious." I set my key on a table next to a stack of bandages. "Our landlord said we can sublet it until we return. It's a bit of a walk from here, but it's the cheapest rent you'll find in Shawnaast, and you won't be stuck with Nica every waking hour."

"Hard to argue with that." He got up and dried his hands on his apron. "But we've barely talked in ages. You're okay with me living in your home?"

I picked dirt from my nails. "Better you than some stranger."

Matéo didn't reply. When I mustered the nerve to glance up, he had my key in his open palm as if it were a butterfly about to take off. I curled his fingers shut. He tensed at my touch. I had the impulse to kiss him, to run my fingers through his loose auburn curls, to breathe his scent of soap and ginger.

"I, uh . . ." A blush spread to his ears. He backed away. "I'm seeing someone. A Ferish girl."

"Oh." I clapped my hand to my mouth. Embarrassment seared through me. "Oh, no—"

"Sorry. I didn't mean to make you think—"

"It's fine," I cut in. "*I'm* sorry. I'm a fucking mess."

"So am I." Matéo gave me a crooked smile. "If it's too weird — if you don't want me in your home—"

"Nei. Don't worry about it. I mean, as long as your new girl's not part of this holy war or something."

"If she is, I don't want anything to do with her." He slid my key into his apron pocket. "I'll take care of your place. Just promise you'll take care of yourself."

On my way out, passing through the steamy kitchen, a familiar voice barked my name. Startled, I turned to see Agata. I hadn't expected to see her before leaving town. I hugged her, and she thumped my back and pushed me off, a rare smile on her wrinkled face.

"I hear you want to see Captain Baccini." She rummaged in a drawer and produced an envelope sealed with red wax. "You'll need this."

"What is it?"

"A writ requesting an audience with him. Another navy captain signed it in exchange for me not telling anyone that he knocked up his mistress. And I attend the same sancte as his wife, so . . ." Agata waved the envelope. "This better be worth it, missy."

7.

INNISBURREN

Waking to thick frost on the windows, I decided to swap my dress for the wool shirt and leggings I'd taken from Tema's belongings. I packed my Ferish clothes into my carryframe. If I wound up in another itheran city, I'd need to blend in. Draping my fox fur mantle over my shoulders, I gave one last look at our flat. It was Matéo's now.

The sun had crested the shingle roofs by the time we reached Shawnaast's docklands. I said silent thanks to the dormant saidu for blessing us with a calm, clear day. We paddled south along the coast past rugged cliffs, stopping briefly in the Iyo settlement, Toel Ginu, to see Rikuja's family. I studied each passing ship, half expecting them to vanish as they had on our last canoe trip, but my vision seemed fixed in this world.

That changed at night. We camped at a river delta where Rikuja's family had their traditional fishing grounds. I was pulling water out of kindling, drying it for a campfire, when the twilit shore flickered. The ankle-deep snow I'd been standing in was now up to my knees, but the tangle of salt spruce and ferns looked the same. It was reassuring that not all of the shoirdryge was devastated like the wasteland up north.

From the delta, we crossed a channel to Ile vi Dévoye, passing ships flying Eremur's naval flag. Dunehein and Rikuja guided us to the training camp. Piers lined the shore like the teeth of a comb. Above a muddy beach stood a cluster of brick barracks and workshops, nestled against snowy forest. As we tied our canoes at a low dock, naval soldiers came forward, dressed in red cloth over leather breastplates. They checked our identification, read the writ Agata had procured, and showed us to Captain Baccini's office.

The captain was a balding man with rough, wind-worn skin. Normally I'd trust a Parr family friend as far as I could throw them, but Jonalin had always spoken of Baccini with respect. He asked several questions about how we knew the Parrs and why we were looking for Nerio. Seeming convinced, he leaned forward, hands folded on his desk.

"This holy war has spread," he said. "Ferish naval recruits have been harassing Sverbian and viirelei recruits, picking fights and such. They are also taking aim at other races. An entire crew has gone rogue and started razing cottages on Innisburren. Do you know the island?"

"The Gallnach colony?" Rikuja said. "We've canoed past it, but we don't trade there. It's in Kae-jouyen territory."

Baccini nodded. "It is also independent, not part of Eremur. These arsons have shattered our fragile peace with them. Lieutenant Parr is trying to identify the rogue crew. Last we spoke, he was heading west of the island. You will know his ship, the *Cavalo ven Cielo*, by its figurehead of a winged horse. And by god, if you can help restore peace, please do. The last thing we need is a war with the Gallnach."

✳

In the remaining daylight, we paddled south to Burren Inlet, the border between Iyo and Kae territory. We camped on the Iyo side. Across the broad inlet, Innisburren looked like a bright smudge on the horizon, its snowy expanses dyed orange by the sunset.

Huddled in our tent under my embroidered fir branch blanket, I tried to remember everything I knew about the Gallnach. All I'd learned growing up was they came from Gallun, a group of islands far overseas. They'd been the first itherans to settle in these lands. None had come as far north as Rin territory, though. I'd never given them much thought until Hanaiko studied them in history lessons.

According to her schoolteacher, Gallun was once a wild, dangerous land of druids and cave-dwellers. Six centuries ago, the Sverbian queen "tamed" the Gallnach, stamped out druidism, and absorbed the islands into her empire. The place had become safe and prosperous. Hanaiko had shown us pictures in her textbook of smiling Gallnach farmers and white-robed Sverbian clerics feasting together at harvest.

"Well, that's birdshit," Narun had scoffed.

We'd all gaped at him. He never swore with the kids in earshot.

He'd explained that he had once worked with a Gallnach fishing crew. As he started the story, Kirbana flung down her dishrag and declared it wasn't appropriate for children. Narun gave her a hard look before leaving to "get some air." It was the closest I'd ever seen them get to arguing. We'd never spoken about the Gallnach again — until now.

Strong waves rocked our canoes as we crossed Burren Inlet. From afar, the morning light made the snowy hills of Innisburren look pristine, divided into pastures by ribbons of trees. Up close, everything changed. Blackened and crumbling cottages speckled the white beaches like ink spills. Seagulls pecked at the wreckage of vegetable gardens. An icy breeze sent eddies of ash into the water.

"Holy flames," Geniod said from the canoe seat behind me.

I shuddered, remembering the Ferish graffiti in Caladheå. *Burn them all. For god and glory.*

Dunehein pulled up his paddle so their canoe drifted to a stop. "Wonder where the Gallnach druids were. They ain't ones to back down from a fight."

"Druids still exist?" I asked, surprised. "Hako's teacher said Sverba stamped them out."

"They tried," Rikuja said. "A few druids escaped. We have carvings about it in the Toel Ginu shrine."

"Ai, here we go." Dunehein heaved a sigh. "Never get a shrine carver started on history."

She flicked water at him, smiling. "The Iyo and Kae let Gallnach druids build refugee settlements along Burren Inlet. Only two survived the Elken Wars. This here on Innisburren is one. The other, way up the inlet to the east, is the mage city Ingdanrad."

"*Druids* built Ingdanrad?" I said. "Tiernan never mentioned that, and he lived there for a year. He just said it's full of mages and scholars."

Rikuja's smile faded. "I'm not surprised. Sverbians either spout some bleached-linen version of what they did to the Gallnach, or they turn themselves inside out to avoid mentioning it. Remember how Kirbana wouldn't let Narun talk about his crewmates?"

"Well, we all have something in common now." Geniod pointed his paddle at the razed cottages. "Looks like the Ferish want to set us all on fire."

The first sign of life was a herring drifter, its ochre-red sails billowing, a net dragging through the water behind it. In a sheltered cove, we found a village harbour. Pale-skinned people hauled crates, repaired boats, and hung fish to dry in the salty wind. Everyone wore draping jewel-toned skirts called woolwraps, according to Hanaiko's textbook. The men wore them over trousers, while the women wore them over longer skirts.

Boulders painted with white symbols dotted the shore. The snow around them had melted as if they gave off heat. When I looked away, they shimmered in my peripheral vision. Protective runes, I realized. The work of druids.

As we paddled close, several people on the docks picked up crossbows. A bearded man in an amber woolwrap stepped forward, shielding his eyes from the sun. He looked wary of Dunehein and Rikuja's dolphin prow and surprised by Geniod's kingfisher prow.

"You here to trade?" he called in a thick accent.

"Just to talk," I called back. "We're looking for a ship called the *Cavalo ven Cielo*."

"Haven't seen it. And if you know what's good for you, lass, you'll leave now."

I started, taken aback. "But—"

"Hush," Dunehein whispered. "They're grieving. Look at the flagpole."

A black and red flag fluttered at half-mast. Like a punch to the gut, I realized the burning of those cottages wasn't just arson. It was murder.

*

Beyond the village, all we found was wild coastline. Shore pines grew at odd angles, bent by the ocean wind. Sea spray soaked our clothes. When we went ashore for lunch, Geniod suggested he scout in his eagle body for Nerio's ship. We fully expected he might not return for a day or two. Innisburren was enormous and Geniod would have to search every ship along its coast for the winged horse figurehead.

To our surprise, he returned within hours and said the *Cavalo ven Cielo* was on its way. The ship arrived at twilight, its white sails and rapier-like bowsprit silhouetted against a fiery sunset. We paddled out to meet it, and the sailors lowered rope ladders to us. I climbed up first, met by Nerio's haggard face.

"Katja," he greeted me hoarsely, helping me clamber over the bulwark. "What a place to see you again."

His skin was raw and chapped, his long dark hair escaping its ribbon. His breath had frozen onto his tangled beard while his black uniform reeked of mouldering wet wool. I hardly recognized him except for the yellow silk lieutenant's band around his arm.

"Look how far you've come," I teased. "From the 5th Mounted Archers to sailing the Sky Horse."

Nerio grimaced. "Hardly a triumph. This is one of the navy's oldest, slowest brigs."

He instructed his men to haul up our canoes, sent a deckhand to fetch us dinner, then took us into the great cabin in the aftcastle. The last rays of sunshine fell through frosty windows, casting shafts of light across a table covered in nautical charts. Behind a curtain, I glimpsed a nook with a rumpled bed. Fire was too dangerous on a wooden ship, so I dried everyone's clothes, earning a grateful smile from Nerio.

"I hear my father has a message for me," he said, collapsing onto the window seat. "Geniod said you'd want to tell me yourself, Katja."

I scowled at my uncle. He probably couldn't say it without laughing. I perched on a wooden bench, bracing my feet against the ship's rocking. "Parr wants you to find one of his informants. In his exact words, 'The strawberry winters in the bathhouse.'"

Nerio raised his eyebrows. "Interesting. And, at present, useless."

"Why? Who's the informant?"

"Neve Lisehl, a gem merchant with strawberry-blonde hair. Wealthy, well connected, and a shameless gossip. She must be wintering in Port Alios, a spa town up Burren Inlet. Unfortunately, I am stuck here on this mission, and Neve refuses to pass information through strangers."

"So we came here for nothing? Parr said it would help us find Tiernan and Jorum!"

Nerio rubbed his temples wearily. "I apologize. My father became slightly . . . unhinged after that Rúonbattai cleric slipped through our grasp."

I scoffed. "That's a polite way of saying he launched a holy war on us."

"Contrary to popular belief, he had nothing to do with that."

"He practically admitted it! I gave him a chance to deny it, and he didn't!"

"I suppose he thought claiming innocence was a waste of breath. But no matter how ruthless he gets, he would never endanger me. Whoever put the Parr name on those leaflets wanted us to take the blame."

Dunehein chuckled bitterly. "That doesn't narrow it down. Your family's list of enemies must be taller than me."

I pressed my fingers to my lips, thinking. "What if we help with your mission, Nerio? Once it's done, can you track down Neve Lisehl?"

"With any luck, yes. I can make up some excuse to visit Port Alios. And to be honest, I could use the help."

Dunehein and Rikuja traded a look. The Okorebai-Iyo was keeping their jouyen out of the war, so they weren't meant to get involved, but they nodded their agreement.

"Very well then." Nerio pointed at a map of Innisburren on the wall. Clusters of red-ribboned tacks speckled the island's coast. "Those are all the razed cottages I have found. There is no discernible pattern, no way to predict where will get hit next. The Gallnach say every attack comes from a schooner with a sea serpent figurehead, but half a dozen ships by that description operate from Ile vi Dévoye alone."

"It's a Ferish crew, right?" Geniod asked. "Captain Baccini said they're part of this holy war."

"Right. Every naval ship flies a secondary flag to show the crew's nationality. The Gallnach survivors reported seeing the flag of Ferland, a white three-blossom flower on an emerald background."

"How isn't this bigger news?" I asked, counting tacks on the map. "This crew torched more than thirty homes, and injured or killed who knows how many people, but the *Sol vi Caladheå* wrote some bearshit about undead pirates. They didn't even mention Innisburren by name."

Nerio shrugged. "Maybe the Caladheå Council is censoring the papers. More likely, people do not care. How much do you ever hear about the Gallnach?"

"Not much," I said with a twinge of guilt. I was only here because Captain Parr had sent me.

A deckhand arrived with a tray of cold food — ham, cheese, wheat biscuits, and spiced jam. Nerio must've dipped into his officer's rations for us. I bit into a piece of hard cheese, my stomach grumbling. Dunehein tucked into the ham, groaning with satisfaction.

"Captain Valrose has set me an impossible task," Nerio continued. "We have glimpsed ships that fit the description, but they are too fast to catch. When we returned to Ile vi Dévoye to resupply, I sent Valrose a letter begging for help. None has arrived. He wants me stuck here, out of the way, and the people of Innisburren are dying for it."

"Well, you've got us now," I said. "Although I don't know how to help."

"You may have already discovered a way." He leaned forward, steepling his fingers. "I have had little success speaking with the Gallnach. Every time we sail into a port here, they open fire. I tried going alone in a longboat and got the same reception. Not surprisingly, they distrust anyone Ferish. *You*, however, managed to exchange a few words. Perhaps you can reach the druids in charge."

I scoffed. "I just found out that druids still exist. I don't know the first thing about them."

"Honestly, I know very little myself. Druidism is banned in Eremur. I believe earth magic is a fundamental part of the religion, but its usage varies. Some druids are scholars or botanists. Some are warriors."

"Excellent," Dunehein said through a mouthful of ham. "So we've got equal chances of dying by boredom, poison, or a rock to the head."

Rikuja elbowed him, smiling. "We might have a way in. That village seemed potentially open to trade. The only furs we've got are our own clothes, though."

"Sounds familiar," I muttered. "Geniod's only allowed into Caladheå because he's got a trade permit, and we forgot to bring—"

I cut myself off, struck by a thought. The Elkhounds let Geniod in because they recognized me as the "apothecary girl." Me, who'd been forced by Nicoletta into taking medical supplies on this trip. Me, who held our ticket to negotiating with the Gallnach.

*

The moment Gallnach villagers saw our canoes again, they picked up crossbows. The bearded man I'd spoken with strode forward, his amber woolwrap swishing around his knees.

"We have medicine," I called. "Ointment, painkillers, bandages. We're willing to trade."

He paused, his finger on his crossbow trigger. "What d'ya want for it?"

"We'd settle for a hot meal by a fire. But we'd like to speak with your druids, too."

The man beckoned. A few Gallnach helped pull our canoes onto land. Heat radiated from the protective rune boulders. I slung my medicine satchel over my shoulder, and our guide led us up an icy track, our boots crunching on the snow.

Every building in the village was made of weathered sandstone, covered by vines and feathery lichen. People bustled past in narrow lanes, their bright woolwraps forming an ever-shifting rainbow. An Aikoto woman shepherded a flock of chickens along. Her moss-green woolwrap matched the Kae-jouyen's heron crest. Kids having a snowball war shouted and shrieked in a tangle of languages.

"The Kae and Gallnach have been intermarrying for generations," Rikuja whispered. "A lot of people on the island are of mixed blood."

Near a fenced pasture of mountain sheep with curling horns and shaggy coats, our guide heaved open a barn door. The stinging scent of camphor assaulted me. I grit my teeth, fighting off the memory of a blue-eyed man spitting blood. Inside the barn, bandaged figures lay on blankets and sheets spread over piles of straw. Several were small enough to be children.

"Kaid," Dunehein swore under his breath.

Rikuja clapped a hand to her mouth as if she was about to be sick. I uncorked my vial of lavender oil and inhaled its floral scent. *Breathe in*, came Matéo's voice.

Healers moved among the victims, washing wounds and passing out porridge. A grey-haired, scowling woman seemed to be in charge. Our guide explained our offer, then the healer thrust her hand out for my medicine satchel. She began pulling out vials and jars labelled with Nicoletta's neat handwriting.

"Iodine, belladonna, wormwood," she read, setting them on a table strewn with surgical tools. She stopped on a flask of reddish-brown liquid. "Má sí. We haven't been able to get laudanum since the Fourth Elken War broke out. Did you rob the navy, lass?"

I bit my lip, settling on a half-truth. "I have connections to an apothecary in Caladheå. There's more where this came from."

The healer snapped her fingers at our guide and spoke in Gallnach. Without waiting for an answer, she turned away to keep sorting through my supplies. Once more, our guide beckoned for us to follow.

Behind the barn, a hooded figure in loose burlap robes stood by a bonfire, hands clasped. A woman's voice drifted from within the hood, quiet and steady. It sounded like a prayer. Only after she fell silent did our guide clear his throat. The woman turned, lowering her hood to reveal a mane of curly red hair. Around her neck hung a pendant of scarlet wool, knotted into an intricate diamond shape.

"I felt your arrival through the ground," she said. "Two canoes, four pairs of boots. Traders?"

"Kind of," I stuttered.

The woman's green eyes were almost as pale as her skin. Her gaze floated across us, then over my shoulder. I turned, finding just the barn wall. When I turned back, she and our guide were speaking in Gallnach. The man nodded and left.

"Join me," the woman told us, sweeping a hand toward log sections set out as makeshift stools. "I'm Róisín ó Conn, the chief druid in these parts. Who are you, strangers?"

"Kateiko Leniere," I said, sitting by the bonfire's welcome heat. "This is my cousin and his wife, Dunehein and Rikuja Iyo, and my uncle, Geniod Tula."

"Ah yes, the new kingfisher nation." Róisín looked to each side of Geniod as if he had invisible wings. "What brings you to Innisburren?"

"We want to help," I said. "We know a Ferish naval crew's been attacking your people."

"And what do *you* get out of helping us?"

"We . . ." I faltered, clutching my gold oak coin inside my cloak pocket. "I'm a healer. I don't like seeing people suffer."

Róisín's gaze drifted over my pocket. "You're lying."

"What?"

"Ferish and Sverbian holy fanatics are warring on the mainland. Plenty of people there could've used your medicine."

I turned to my family, desperate. Geniod tilted his head toward Róisín as if to say, *Go on. Tell her the truth.*

Bracing myself, I said, "Eremur only sent one lieutenant to deal with these rogue soldiers. I need him to finish this mission so he can help find our friends. They went missing up north while fighting the Rúonbattai."

Róisín nodded, fingering her wool pendant. "I appreciate your candour. Too many people have come to our shores offering false promises. What do you know about Sverba's invasion of Gallun?"

"Pretty much nothing," I admitted.

She nodded again. "A druid assembly used to oversee Gallun. Rånyl Sigrunnehl, the first queen of Sverba, met with the assembly on the promise of discussing trade. Instead she murdered every druid present, then burned and pillaged her way through our homeland. My kin there have been rebelling ever since. Six centuries of flames. They never end in Gallun, and now they're here, too." The pain in her voice was sharp as broken glass.

Dunehein leaned forward, resting his elbows on the worn knees of his breeches. "We're trying to stop these attacks, but all we know to look for is a schooner with a Ferish flag and a sea serpent figurehead. Can you tell us more?"

Róisín's gaze dropped to the bonfire. "The ship only comes on foggy nights. Dark-haired men in uniform shoot flaming arrows, then vanish like ghosts. Filthy cowards. They know if they set foot on the island, we'll open the ground to swallow them whole. They'll waste away deep inside the earth, forgetting the feel of sun and wind on their skin."

I winced. Apparently Róisín was the warrior type of druid.

"We saw some Kae in the village," Rikuja said. "Some must attune to birds or sea animals. Have they tried following the ship?"

"A couple, but they lost it in the fog. The rest stayed to rescue their families from their burning homes." Róisín's glance flickered from Rikuja to Dunehein. "You don't understand yet. But you will."

The couple exchanged startled looks. Dunehein took Rikuja's hand in his huge one.

"Do you mean . . ." Rikuja had gone pale. "The Rúonbattai have a mage who can see the future. Is that what you do?"

"No. Temporal magic is the domain of Sverbians, a gift from their gods. I don't see what was or will be. I see what *is*."

"Then how do you know—"

"That," Róisín interrupted, "is the domain of druids."

Geniod cleared his throat. "Róisín, how's this for a plan? Send out as many Kae scouts as possible, all at once, to find every schooner in the region that fits the description. Have them note the ships' directions, crew size, and so on. Then we'll take that info to the navy and compare it with their deployment records."

Róisín fixed her pale green eyes on Geniod's collarbones. "Will you join the scouts, eagle?"

He blanched. "You can see that, too?"

Her mouth twitched with a smile. She got to her feet, brushing ash off her burlap robes. "I hear you were promised a hot meal. Come. We Gallnach make an excellent mutton stew."

8.

BELOW WATER

While Geniod was away with the Kae scouts, the rest of us waited on the anchored *Cavalo ven Cielo*. Nerio had given us space in the crew quarters. I passed time by playing cards and sparring with off-duty soldiers. In the semi-privacy of my hammock, I tried reading my parents' makiri, but they felt cold and lifeless. I couldn't sense their spirits in the wood, just as I couldn't see whatever Róisín had seen in us.

At dawn, I woke to find Rikuja's hammock empty. I climbed the ladder to the deck and found her leaning against the bulwark, gazing across choppy waves at Innisburren. She said she was thinking. But when I found her there again the next morning, her face grey and clammy, I pressed her to tell me what was wrong.

"Seasickness," Rikuja said, wiping her brow. "I prefer canoes."

"Is that all?" I asked, surprised. "I'll ask Nerio if there's any ginger in the ship's stores—"

"No, no," she interrupted. "I'm sure he's busy."

I glanced at the forecastle, where Nerio was throwing bread-crumbs to squawking seagulls. "He's clearly not."

Rikuja bit her lip. "It's not just the sea," she admitted. "I've felt sick for weeks. I've been sneaking off whenever I have to throw up, but it's getting worse."

"And you didn't tell me?"

"Well . . . you quit being a healer. I didn't want to guilt you into treating me."

"You—" I slumped against the bulwark, folding my arms over my head. "Aeldu save us."

I couldn't believe I'd missed it. Rikuja had been weirdly emotional lately, sobbing about my potted plants. She'd eaten pickled herring on Innisburren, which she normally hated. And Róisín had seen something about her and Dunehein. Something that was now but also the future.

"Rija," I said tentatively. "When was your last bloodflow?"

"What?" She frowned. "You don't mean — oh. Oh, *no*."

We stared at each other.

"I stopped using bloodweed months ago," she said. "It made me so sick, but I did everything else you taught me, everything you learned from Agata. I must've made a mistake, or—"

She burst into tears. Startled, I flung my arms around her. Rikuja buried her face into my fox fur mantle. A sailor nearby looked away, giving us privacy.

"I don't want this now," she choked out. "Not during a war—"

"Wala, wala," I soothed, kissing her hair. "Everything will be okay."

I fished a handkerchief from my cloak pocket while my mind raced. If her nausea was peaking now, she was probably about two months pregnant. Early enough to end it. It'd be easy to get pennyroyal or tansy for an infusion. I didn't want any part in that, though. If I made the infusion right, Rikuja might resent me forever. If I made it wrong . . . well, she wouldn't be alive to resent me.

※

Geniod returned with a Kae man who'd led their scouting party. They'd sent scouts who'd learned to read so they could report the names painted on ship hulls. In Nerio's cabin, we pored over the list, comparing it to the navy's deployment records. Every ship matched up except one — the *Marla*. It had been deployed north to fight the Rúonbattai occupation of Nordmur. Instead it was here, drifting west of Innisburren on the open ocean. The Kae woman who found it had noticed crude patchwork on the hull, probably signs of recent battle. When she tried flying closer as a tealhead duck, a sailor shot arrows at her, driving her off.

Nerio shook his head in disgust. "Seems we have mutineers on our hands."

"*Stupid* mutineers," I said. "Why not pull down their flags?"

"I have no idea. Maybe they want this holy war to seem bigger than it is, as if the whole navy is behind it."

Since the *Marla* was too swift for us to catch, I took Nerio to meet Róisín and make a proposal. We'd go after the schooner, spooking them into fleeing. Then we'd chase them into a fleet of Gallnach fishing ships, trapping them from all sides. With any luck, they'd surrender. Róisín agreed, although her bleak smile made me wonder if she was hoping to get revenge in battle.

Waiting for her to assemble a fleet of ships, druids, archers, and Kae warriors meant more boredom on the *Cavalo ven Cielo*. I asked Rikuja if she wanted to go home, but she insisted on staying. Reminding her the Okorebai-Iyo banned them from fighting in the

Fourth Elken War didn't sway her. Technically, she argued, this was part of a different war. We both knew it was a bearshit argument.

On our chosen day for battle, a Kae man flew to our brig and gave me a gift from Róisín — a bronze ring engraved with runes that would amplify my water-calling. I stammered my thanks and put it in my leggings pocket, not sure how much I trusted the druid. Only after the Kae man left did I realize I hadn't told Róisín I was an antayul. I didn't have the fan-shaped tattoo on my chest, and no one from Innisburren had seen me call water.

"Ready?" Nerio asked me, strapping his arrow quiver to his back.

I tapped two fingers to my forehead in salute. "Ready, Lieutenant."

Although he was formally in command, he'd put his more experienced first mate in charge of sailing. The mate called orders to heave anchor and unfurl the sails. A westerly gale filled the canvas sheets. Since we couldn't sail directly into the wind, we tacked back and forth, zigzagging from northwest to southwest.

Geniod scouted from the sky in his eagle body. With his sharp vision, he saw the *Marla* first and guided us toward it. Nerio lent me his spyglass for a better look. I searched the glittering blue waves, spotting a two-masted schooner with the figurehead of a coiled sea serpent. The warship drifted idly. They hadn't noticed us yet — or at least hadn't deemed us a threat.

"Are the Gallnach in position?" Nerio called up to Geniod.

My uncle flew off west. On his return, he trilled a high-pitched whistle to confirm he'd seen the Gallnach fleet. It was time.

Sea spray plumed around our bowsprit as we plunged onward. We'd gained a decent lead by the time the *Marla*'s white sails unfurled and billowed out. They veered away south, catching the wind sideward. We plowed after their foaming wake. Far ahead, the ochre-red sails of Gallnach fishing ships appeared on the horizon. The *Marla* didn't slow.

"That doesn't look like surrender," Dunehein said, watching with his arm around Rikuja.

If anything, the *Marla* was gaining speed. Yet the Gallnach fleet grew larger in our sight, closing in. I expected the *Marla* to try to dodge them, cutting an escape route between ships. Instead they veered straight toward a herring drifter.

"What are they doing?" I asked, worry blooming under my skin.

"Merdo," Nerio swore. "They are going to ram it. A warship that size will crush a drifter."

"Not on my watch." I cupped my hands around my mouth and shouted at the bald eagle perched on the mainmast. "Ai, Geniod! Get word to the Kae antayul. We have to stop the *Marla*!"

He whistled and took off. I tossed my mantle and cloak on the deck, unbuckled the belt holding my purse and weapon sheaths, then climbed the frosty ratlines for a better view. This high up, the brig's pitching made me dizzy. I stretched my mind across the vast expanse of ocean, trying to reach the *Marla*. It was no good. I couldn't call water from this far away.

Róisín's ring. I held the ratlines with one hand, used my teeth to pull off my mitten, and took the ring from my pocket. Bracing myself, I slid it onto my finger. Its engraved runes flared with white light, searing my eyes.

Suddenly I was aware of the water in a way I'd never been. My arms were immense wings and every droplet was a feather. I arced my hand through the air, flinging a wave against the *Marla*'s starboard. The schooner rocked, its masts tilting dangerously.

"Katja, aim for the stern!" Nerio shouted from below.

I flung another wave at the schooner's back, nudging it off course. *It's working*, I thought, ignoring spots flickering across my vision. I had no time to deal with the shoirdryge. I lifted my arm again—

—and the ships vanished. I screamed, hanging from invisible ratlines above the roiling ocean. A gust slammed into me, flinging me into the ether. *Shit* was my last thought as I fell.

The ocean cracked against me. Blinding cold enveloped my body. Dazed, I sank into endless blue, choking on salt water. My limbs didn't work. My lungs burned. Darkness crept into my vision.

Let go, a tiny voice whispered. The same voice that told me to keep a vial of laudanum. The same voice that promised Jonalin it could end his pain.

A cluster of white lights gleamed through the murky depths. Mica sparkling in tunnel walls, snowflakes falling into a lake, moonlight rippling on dark water. Tiernan's hands gliding through the air, leaving glowing trails in the shape of protective runes. Stars glittering over vast plains.

Northern Nyhemur is stunning in winter, came his voice. *The snowy plains look infinite, as if one is floating among the clouds. Perhaps one day I can take you here.*

I reached for the stars, grasping, finding nothing. The white lights floating above me weren't stars. They shone from the runed ring around my finger. A beacon, an underwater lighthouse.

A lithe shape shot through the dark water. It grabbed my shirt in its teeth. My hand brushed smooth rubbery skin. A dolphin — no, a porpoise. Rikuja's fins and tail beat against me as she dragged me upward.

We crested the surface into brilliant sunlight. Hardly had I drawn breath before a wave crashed over us. Rikuja thrashed, trying to keep us afloat. If my weight tired her out, we'd both go down. *Nei, not both*, I remembered. *All three of us.*

"Lass!" a deep voice shouted. "Over here!"

I turned my head, blinking away seawater. A Gallnach man stood aboard a little red-sailed cutter, whirling a lasso. It landed near us with a splash. I hooked my arm through it, clumsy from cold. The man pulled Rikuja and me close, straining from our combined weight. He stretched over the gunwale, grabbed my wrists, and hauled me into the cutter.

I collapsed on the deck, coughing up water and shivering. Coughing turned into vomiting. Pain shot through me with each heave. My rescuer threw his teal woolwrap over my shoulders, leaving him in only a jerkin and trousers. Figures bustled around us, their shouts blurring together.

"Rija," I sputtered through chattering teeth. "The porpoise—"

"I'm here." Rikuja knelt at my side and untangled kelp strands from my braid. "Oh, love, you scared the life out of me."

A Kae man waved his hands over me, drawing the icy water from my clothes. I stuttered my thanks. Frostbite tinged my hands grey, but getting dry would keep me alive. Probably. The Kae man dried Rikuja next, then lent her his moss-green woolwrap.

It took me a minute to remember there was a battle going on. Rubbing salt from my eyes, I peered across the ocean. The *Marla* and the *Cavalo ven Cielo* circled each other like hungry dogs angling for scraps. Smaller Gallnach ships surrounded the two Ferish warships, barricading them in.

"We followed your lead," the Kae antayul told me. "Knocked the *Marla* off course, then managed to sail around them. Any second now, I bet—" A cheer interrupted him.

"What?" Rikuja cried. "What is it?"

"They're striking the colours!" Our Gallnach rescuer jabbed his finger toward the *Marla*, where soldiers were lowering their flags. "The bastards are surrendering!"

First down was the emerald crew flag with the Ferish three-blossom flower, then the Eremur naval flag with rearing red elk over an anchor. They replaced them with a white flag, then reefed their sails to slow their pace.

"We . . ." I gestured at the *Cavalo ven Cielo*, struggling to put a sentence together. "Nerio."

Rikuja understood. The cutter's crew sailed us back to the brig. I could barely stand, let alone climb a ladder, so Nerio's men lowered a longboat for me to tumble into. They hauled it up and helped me over the bulwark.

Dunehein wrapped me in a hug. "Thank the aeldu," he said gruffly. "I didn't — of course Rija had you, but—" He broke off, swallowing hard.

Geniod brought my outer clothes. My frostbitten fingers felt thick and clumsy, so he pinned my cloak and draped my fox fur mantle over my shoulders. I felt like a child being dressed by their parent.

"Lieutenant Parr!" came a sharp voice. Róisín swung over the far bulwark, holding her burlap robes above the knee. Her damp red curls stuck to her face. She spotted Nerio on the quarterdeck and strode toward him. "That's no surrender. I can feel it."

Nerio made a sound of disbelief. "With respect, that is a regiment of the Royal Eremur Naval Forces. I cannot ignore a surrender based on a druid's feeling—"

"Wait," I cut in. "False promises. Right?"

Róisín's lip curled with disgust. "Exactly."

Nerio frowned, probably remembering the times I'd been right and saved his life. "Fine," he relented. "We get as close as possible. At my command, we attack. Agreed?"

Róisín studied the yellow lieutenant's band around his sleeve. She nodded, then turned away to signal Kae birds circling overhead.

"As for you," Nerio added, grabbing my elbow. "Keep back during the battle. You are in no shape to fight."

I didn't argue. Needles shot through my limbs as they regained feeling, and Geniod hadn't brought my sword anyway.

Nerio began issuing commands. Armoured infantry lined up along our bulwark, ready with grappling hooks. Dunehein joined them, towering over most of the men. Archers climbed the stairs onto the forecastle and aftcastle. Geniod took to the air, circling in his eagle body.

The first mate sailed us toward the *Marla*'s starboard side. Nerio stared at the schooner, tapping his thigh. I imagined calculations swirling inside his head — the wind, our speed, the archers' range. Every second was a chance for our opponents to get the first shot. We were close enough to see black elk embroidered on their red sleeves when Nerio swung his longbow off his shoulder.

"Nock!" he shouted to his archers. "Draw! Loose!"

A volley of arrows shot toward the *Marla*. They tore through the schooner's sails and slammed into its timbers. Splinters exploded everywhere. Two soldiers went down. The rest of the crew scrambled back, meeting a rain of crossbow bolts from Gallnach ships on the other side.

"Hooks ready!" Nerio shouted as we drew level with the *Marla*. "Throw!"

His infantry flung their grappling hooks. They snagged on the *Marla*'s rigging and timbers, anchoring us to the schooner. Our archers kept firing volleys. As the other side started to shoot back, an eagle dropped from the sky and shifted, landing next to Rikuja and me.

"Fire," Geniod gasped. "They—"

He yanked us down. Something bright whistled overhead. I straightened up and saw a burning hole in one of our sails.

"Kaid," I swore. I pulled a wave from the ocean and flung it at the sail. Steam bloomed into the air. Another flaming arrow, another wave. "I can't keep up—" The ships vanished. I shrieked, suspended over the ocean again.

An invisible hand grabbed my arm. "I'm here," came Rikuja's voice. "You're safe."

The ships flickered back into view. I rubbed my eyes, dazed.

Róisín appeared, burlap robes swishing. "Anchor yourself. The fires are only in this world. Focus on the heat, light, smoke. Like this."

She whirled a slingshot over her head. A stone whipped through the air and struck a *Marla* archer in the head. He dropped along with his burning arrow. Geniod whistled appreciatively.

Róisín and I fought side by side, her taking down archers, me putting out fires. Our infantry leapt onto the *Marla*'s deck, meeting their forces with a clash of blades. With both sides in red uniforms, it was hard to tell who was who. Dunehein shifted into his grizzly form and bounded across the gap. Snarling and roaring, he used his huge paws to bat men aside.

I couldn't mark the point that we won. It was more of a slow realization, a fading of screams and clangs and whooshing arrows. Nerio shouldered his longbow and crossed over to the schooner, followed by Róisín. They spoke for a moment, examining dead bodies littering the deck. Róisín shook her head, curls flying. Nerio frowned and beckoned to me.

"Fucking hell," I muttered.

Geniod helped me over the roiling water between the two ships. Dunehein rubbed his huge furry nose against me before shifting back to human. Blood covered the *Marla*'s deck, slippery under our feet, flowing back and forth with the rocking ocean.

"Something's off," Róisín said. "There is falsehood here."

Nerio crossed to the dead captain, marked by a black silk band around his sleeve, and searched under the man's collar. Frowning, he tried another man, then another. "None are wearing identification tags."

Róisín pulled the captain's eyelids open. His sky-blue irises looked oddly pale against his tanned skin. She pulled his dark hair away from his scalp, revealing straw-coloured roots. I crouched down and sniffed his head. Under the tang of blood and salt was the fresh, peppery scent of sage.

"Herbal dye." Struck by a thought, I slid a ring off his finger, exposing a band of white skin. "He's naturally pale, too. Is he even Ferish?"

"No." Róisín bent over another soldier and pulled up his sleeve. Tattooed on his inner arm was a raven over crossed swords. She spat on him and backed away. "Má sí. This, my friends, is a shipload of Sverbian Rúonbattai."

9.

CÉILÍDH

Nerio leapt into action. He commanded his men to search the *Marla*, bring out anyone in hiding, and leave anything that seemed magical or spiritual to Róisín and Geniod. Seeing me sway on my feet, he ordered Dunehein to take me back to the *Cavalo ven Cielo* to see the ship's medic. I got as far as the main deck before collapsing.

I came to in my hammock, buried under so many blankets I couldn't move. Rikuja noticed me stir and fetched hot broth from the galley. As well as hypothermia, frostbite, and shock from drowning, I had bruised ribs from hitting the ocean. Secretly I was glad to have an excuse not to help the medic treat our injured soldiers. Dunehein was helping instead, bandaging wounds the way he'd seen me do.

Nerio's men had found several wounded Sverbians hiding aboard the *Marla*, as well as three Ferish captives from the ship's original crew, the 15th Royal Eremur Naval Forces. The captives wept with relief at being rescued. Two months ago, during their deployment in Nordmur, they'd stopped to help a Sverbian cod trawler in distress. It was a trap. The Sverbians killed the *Marla*'s crew, only sparing the men whose skills they needed — the cook, carpenter, and medic. They donned the victims' uniforms, dyed their hair dark to look Ferish, and sailed under the flags of the massacred 15th Naval Forces.

"The newspaper was right," I said in disbelief. "It *is* an undead pirate crew."

It wasn't the first time the Rúonbattai had masqueraded as Eremur soldiers. Yotolein's wife used to mend the uniforms of fallen men for Rúonbattai spies to wear as disguises. They'd never pulled it off at this scale, though. It seemed like they'd relied on the chaos of the holy war, and of Fedos Valrose replacing Antoch Parr, to keep anyone from noticing the *Marla*'s plight.

During a brief respite from treating the wounded, Dunehein came by to check on me and change his bloody clothes. It was Aikoto tradition to return dead people's blood to the earth so their spirits could pass into Aeldu-yan. His boots could be scrubbed clean, but his cloak, shirt, and breeches would have to be burned. Rikuja kissed him with a look of sympathy. She didn't come from a warrior family. Dealing with the dead wasn't something she often had to do.

More news trickled down to my hammock overnight. Nerio's men had scoured the *Marla* and found no other links to the Rúonbattai. No other raven sigils, no suspicious documents, no oak and lilac crests that made time feel strange. Geniod knew the feeling from examining the painted crest in Tjarnnaast, but he hadn't sensed anything on the *Marla*. The only proof the Sverbians were Rúonbattai was the dead man's raven tattoo and Róisín's word.

That had caused an argument. Róisín wanted to execute the surviving Sverbians, while Nerio insisted they ought to stand trial in Eremur. Geniod negotiated a compromise. Róisín could execute whichever soldier she believed had done the most harm to her people. The others would go to trial.

If the *Marla*'s captors weren't part of the Ferish holy war after all, the real mystery was why they'd attacked Innisburren. It seemed bizarre for Rúonbattai soldiers to abandon the front lines in Nordmur and firebomb an island that had no involvement in the Fourth Elken War. Maybe they'd gone rogue. Maybe it was part of some greater plan we'd only started to unravel.

✳

Warm light fell across my face. I squinted and tried to sit up, hindered by the crush of blankets. Geniod sat cross-legged by my hammock, half in shadow, half in a sunbeam falling through a porthole. Temal's makiri balanced on his open palm. I waited until he finished his reverie and closed his fingers over the carved mountain cat.

"What were you talking about?" I asked.

Geniod looked up, a tired smile floating across his face. "Just telling him you're alive."

The last word stung. Not only because my temal wasn't alive, but because that was the best anyone could say about me.

"Nerio will be busy for several days," Geniod said. "Taking those Sverbians to Caladheå for trial, reporting to military head-quarters, visiting Port Alios, and tracking down Neve Lisehl. I think we should spend that time on land. Róisín says we're welcome in her village."

"This again?" I said, my temper flaring. "You and Jorum did this in Tjarnnaast, plotting to send me away."

"I know," he soothed. "It's not about that. I mean, you *do* need rest, but . . . today's the winter solstice."

I paused, taken aback. "Oh."

Geniod ran his thumb over the smooth edges of Temal's makiri. "We gave up a lot of traditions when we left the Rin. We haven't decided which to keep in the Tula-jouyen, but it'd be nice to light the beacons for the dead tonight."

We'd left our canoes on Innisburren, so we hitched a ride on a Gallnach cutter. Róisín's village had cleared out a boat workshop to make shelter for people whose homes had been razed. The harbour master showed us where to line up for meals and introduced us to a Kae-Gallnach family. The Kae had different traditions for Yanben, but the family agreed to drop us off in the countryside so we could do our rites in private.

We rode in their wagon, juddering along an icy track up into the hills, and slid off near a copse of salt spruce. A breeze lifted eddies of snow from the trees. It was a moonless night, the stars showing off their twinkling plumage. Traditionally on Yanben, we'd climb high into the forest and fling torches into the canopy, igniting the treetops to guide our lost loved ones from Aeldu-yan to Eredu-yan, the land of the living.

My bruised ribs hurt with every breath, so we'd brought a Gallnach crossbow and a flask of highly flammable herring oil. Geniod loaded a bolt, ignited its tip, and held the bow for me. I murmured Tema's name and pulled the trigger. The flaming bolt shot through the air and hit the top of a salt spruce. Geniod lit another beacon for Temal, Dunehein lit one for his father, and Rikuja lit one for her grandmother.

There was always so much I wanted to say to my parents without relying on Geniod. Sometimes I wanted advice. Sometimes I just wanted to tell them an inside joke. Tonight, all I could think about was drowning. How easy it would've been to slip into Aeldu-yan, how much I'd understood Jonalin's desperation to let go. How the one thing that gave me hope, the thought of visiting Nyhemur with Tiernan, was out of reach.

I wrapped my arms around myself, craning my neck to look at the burning treetops. "Tell me to hold on," I whispered. "I keep losing people. You, Jona, Tiernan and Jorum, everyone who stayed with the Rin. Tell me there's something worth holding on for."

Silence. The flames went on crackling.

Gradually, though, I noticed heat against my thigh. I slipped my hand into my cloak pocket and drew out Tema's swan makiri. The wood felt warm through my mitten. I stared at it in astonishment. "Okay," I whispered and kissed the swan's head. "I'll keep trying."

❉

We kept to the boat workshop for the next few days. The Gallnach were mourning soldiers lost in the battle, so we didn't want to stumble into a funeral. A constant grey drizzle made me glad to be indoors. We put out buckets to catch water dripping through the roof, and I did my best to help the refugees, drying their clothes and warming their drinks.

When the rain cleared, someone suggested lifting our spirits with a céilídh, a night of feasting and dancing. A farmer agreed to butcher a sheep for a roast. We tacked spruce boughs to the walls, pushed crates together for tables, and dragged in hay bales for seating. The brewer brought whisky bottles and ale casks. Around dusk, villagers arrived with platters of fish, sausage, blue-veined cheese, root vegetables, and pastries. The air filled with the savoury smell of meat and onion.

"I heard someone mention stuffed cod heads," Dunehein teased Rikuja. "Want some? You've gotten quite the taste for strange food."

She bit her lip and looked at me. I held up my hands, staying out of things.

Rikuja linked her arm through Dunehein's. Voice wavering, she told him, "Let's go for a walk."

Geniod watched them leave. "What was that about?"

"Dunno," I lied. Casting about for a distraction, I said, "I wonder if there *are* stuffed cod heads. It sounds kind of good."

"Really?" He frowned as if he thought I was joking. "I'll check. You stay here and rest."

I perched on a hay bale. A cluster of Gallnach youths were greeting each other, laughing and chatting in their language. The boys wore sashes over one shoulder in the same jewel tones as their woolwraps. The girls wore shawls woven with floral patterns. A few had sewn bells onto their skirts so they jingled with each step. I kept my cloak shut tight over my leggings, contemplating if I could fashion one of my Ferish petticoats into a woolwrap.

"Bread?" came a voice.

Róisín appeared, holding two slices of buttered bread. She passed me one and settled on the hay bale, adjusting her burlap robes.

"I've always seen bread as the great uniter," she said. "Every culture has their preferences, of course — we use barley, Sverbians use rye, Ferish use wheat, and you Aikoto use brassroot — but I've never met anyone who didn't enjoy warm fresh bread."

I stammered my thanks. The chief druid surely had better places to be. I wondered if she knew I'd been wanting to talk to her — this living, breathing treasure chest of knowledge.

"During the battle—" I paused, wondering how to ask. "You saw that other world, too, right? The shoirdryge?"

"I don't use the Sverbian word, but yes. I see it often."

"Really? How—"

"Save your questions," she interrupted. "The answers are the business of the druids."

"But . . ." I faltered.

Róisín cast me a knowing smile. "There is something that concerns us all, though. Both worlds are . . . changing. Growing further apart."

"What do you mean?"

"That fall into the ocean should've killed you. Cold shock hits faster than drowning. These last few winters have been oddly mild, though. Too warm, too little rain and snow. I'm curious how the weather looks in your visions."

Most of my visions were of the wasteland or the Rúonbattai's oak crests, neither of which I wanted to admit to seeing. "That," I said, trying to keep my voice level, "is the business of the Aikoto Confederacy."

Róisín chuckled. "Excellent answer." She finished her bread and sucked a bit of butter off her thumb. "It's not my place to advise you about magic, but I can tell you something else that might be helpful."

"What's that?"

"Your uncle's a good man." She nodded at Geniod, who was still searching for stuffed cod heads. "An eagle to his core. Quiet birds for their size, but powerful and attentive. He's always watching over you."

I rolled my eyes. "Even when I don't want him to."

"A normal feeling at your age." She winked. "Tell you what. No young lass wants to spend a céilídh with adults. If you promise to stay out of trouble, I'll find you some better company and persuade your uncle to leave you alone for a few hours."

"Really?" I looked sideways at her, not sure which part was weirder — that she was so sure of swaying Geniod or that she cared enough to try.

Either way, she'd know if I made a false promise. I thought it over. Talking to my parents on Yanben had soothed my spirit enough that I wasn't about to run off and leap into the ocean. A night away from Geniod, away from feeling like the fucked-up niece he'd sworn to look after, sounded . . . nice.

"Fine," I said. "I promise."

Róisín called out to the group of youths. A petite girl in a rust-orange woolwrap bounded over. I'd seen her around the workshop. Her soft open face had faded burns along her cheek and down her neck. Róisín introduced me in rapid Gallnach. The girl brightened with understanding.

"I'm Aoife," she told me, dropping into a curtsy. "Come eat with us girls. The boys always pull nonsense like seeing how many kippers they can shove in their mouths."

I snorted. "What's the record?"

"Honestly, you don't want to know. You'll never look at herring the same way."

She steered me over to a cluster of girls. They introduced themselves with warm smiles, switching into Coast Trader so I could understand. I half listened, distracted by Róisín. The druid intercepted Geniod as he started heading my way with a plate of cod heads. I couldn't hear them over the tide of voices and clattering dishes. Geniod looked caught off guard, rubbing his neck. Róisín leaned in and whispered something that made him laugh. Her eyes drifted over his chest. It looked like she was . . . *flirting* with him.

Aoife followed my gaze and burst into giggles. "Is that your father?"

"My uncle," I said, heat flooding my cheeks. "I guess Róisín can tell he's single."

"Well, what's the point of a céilídh except having some fun?" Aoife poked my bruised ribs.

I winced. "He won't . . ."

Geniod turned my way. I smiled through the pain and tried to look like I was having fun. With perfect timing, Aoife's friends noticed my macramé necklace and crowded around me, admiring Jonalin's intricate handwork. When I looked back across the workshop, Geniod and Róisín were gone.

Aoife sat by my side throughout the feast so she could explain what all the dishes were. She seemed to know everyone, too. She explained that her family lived up the coast — or had, until Sverbians razed their cottage — and travelled into the village each season to attend religious rites. As she spoke, she touched the faded burns on her cheek.

"Everyone's been so generous," she said. "Donating food, clothes, toys for the wee kids. Róisín said your family brought medicine *and* fought in the battle. I wish we could thank you properly."

"I bet Róisín is thanking Kateiko's uncle," said another girl, sending gasps and giggles around our makeshift crate table.

Aoife slapped a crate in mock outrage. "Wanna gossip, aye? Curly haired wench. Weren't you behind the granary with some lad's hand up your skirt?"

The other girls roared with laughter. They started guessing who the mysterious lad was, casting not-so-subtle looks at the boys. Aoife fetched a whisky bottle to pass around. Of all the itheran gatherings I'd been to, this felt the most like an Aikoto feast, warm and loud and cozy.

I'd started noticing patterns among the colourful array of woolwraps. Aoife's family all wore rust orange. She explained it was the colour of their clan, basically a huge extended family. Her father had grabbed their spare woolwraps as they fled their burning home. The garments were some of their last surviving ties to their ancestors in Gallun.

I was hesitant to pry further, but Aoife seemed proud of her history. Their chief druid had been killed fending off Sverbian invaders. The rest of her clan had splintered. A few made it here to Innisburren, where they banded together with refugees from dozens of other clans. The people who settled along this stretch of the island had chosen a new chief druid to guide and protect them. That tradition had continued for the last two centuries, leading up to Róisín's ascension a few years ago.

"She's amazing, isn't she?" Aoife said with awe. "It's rare, her gift of sight. Not even anyone in Ingdanrad can do it."

Once everyone was comfortably stuffed, we pushed the crates and hay bales aside to make room for dancing. Musicians set up along one wall. Among the fiddles, flutes, tin whistles, and flat hand-held drums was a Kae woman with a larger drum strapped to her waist. A Gallnach man held a leather bag fitted with steel pipes. Its wild, shivering tune stirred feelings in me I couldn't name.

My bruised ribs meant I had to watch from the sidelines, but I soon got swept away by it all. The dancers wove amongst each other, clapping and stomping and swirling in intricate patterns. With their colourful woolwraps, they looked like rainbow trout leaping up a creek. The smell of sweat and the heat of bodies filled the workshop.

One dance looked surprisingly familiar. The men formed two lines, facing each other across a broad gap. The women darted into the gap one at a time. They linked arms with a man and spun, getting flung across to the far line, where they spun again and got flung back. The sight of them zigzagging up the lines made me dizzy. Aoife joined in, so I couldn't ask her about it until she collapsed next to me, red-faced and panting.

"I've seen that dance in Caladheå," I said. "At the new year festival, I think. But all the dancers were Sverbian."

Aoife snorted, brushing curls of brown hair off her damp brow. "Oh, aye. One of many things the Sverbs stole from us."

"Stole? How do you steal a dance?"

"Same way they stole our magic, medicine, and mother of mountains knows what else. Copied it, stripped out the meaning, and pretended it was theirs all along. Haven't they done it to your people?"

Now that she said it, I knew what she meant. The Rúonbattai's temporal mage had copied Aikoto crests to design their oak and lilac crest, then used the oaks to spy on us. I didn't want to bring that up now, though. Not when the music and flowing whisky were distracting people from what the Rúonbattai had done to them.

The dancing went on for hours. When people started to tire, the musicians switched to calmer pieces. Soft, floaty feelings stirred in me as I watched figures twirl in the lantern light. In my warm whisky haze, I wondered if I could manage a slow dance. As if the mere thought of ruining my fun summoned him, Geniod plunked down next to me.

I groaned. "Wherever you've been, please go back."

He smiled dryly. "I've been in Róisín's greenhouse."

"Ew. No one calls it that—"

"Ai, grow up. I mean an actual greenhouse." Geniod opened a paper packet of leaves and blossoms, bursting with scent. "Apparently earth magic is a lot more than slinging rocks around. Róisín grows all sorts of herbs native to Gallun. She let me pick some for tea blends."

I shook my head in disbelief. It was such an uncle-ish way to spend an evening that I almost wished he *had* hooked up with Róisín. Then again, I wasn't doing any better. I got up, deciding to swallow my fear and ask someone to dance.

Halfway across the workshop floor, a huge figure grabbed me around the ribs. I shrieked in pain as Dunehein swung me through the air.

"Sorry!" he cried, setting me down. "I forgot — it's just — ai, Kako, I can't believe it!"

"Believe what?" I wheezed, eyes watering.

"This." Rikuja appeared behind him, laughing. She set one hand on her stomach. "Guess we're having a baby."

10.

A PROPOSAL

Next morning, when Geniod and Dunehein lined up with the refugees to get our rations of oat porridge, I got a chance to talk to Rikuja alone. We hunkered in a quiet corner with blankets over our shoulders. The boat workshop's only heating was a few stoves meant for steaming timber, and our breath puffed out in frosty clouds.

"What changed?" I asked. "When we first talked about it, you seemed . . ."

Rikuja laughed. "Terrified. I know." She fiddled with a loose thread on a blanket. "It took me a bit to realize *what* I was terrified of. The war, obviously, but you've seen Dune in battle. He'll fight off anyone who threatens our child. I was scared I couldn't live up to that."

"No one expects you to," I said. "You're not a warrior."

"Sure, but . . ." She scrunched up her face. "Mothers are supposed to have this protective instinct, right? Róisín told us about her people rescuing their families from their burning homes. What if I didn't have that instinct? How would I know until I wound up in a situation like that?"

"Oh," I said, realization washing over me. "Then I fell from the ratlines."

Rikuja took my hand, tears welling in her eyes. "It didn't matter that we were on the brink of battle. I just jumped. It felt like — that's why the aeldu blessed me with a porpoise body, so I could—"

She broke into sobs. I hugged her, murmuring soothing sounds. We stayed like that until her crying eased. She fumbled a handkerchief from her pocket and blew her nose.

"We'll ask the Gallnach healers to look you over," I said. "When you get back to Caladheå, Agata can give you some herbal supplements."

"I'm not going anywhere," Rikuja interrupted. "Dune and I promised to help you."

"Don't be stupid. That was before we knew the *Marla* crew were Rúonbattai."

"Exactly." Rikuja stared me down, looking unnervingly like a mother bear. "Remember what you told Jorumgard in Tjarnnaast?"

"I — what?"

"He told Geniod, who told me. You said you want Jorum in our family. Well, so do I. He's kind, brave, wonderful with kids. I want him as an uncle to my baby. But he and Tiernan are still missing, so we're going to do *whatever* it takes to find them."

✳

On a blustery day, as wind rattled the workshop roof and drove snow through cracks in the walls, a naval cutter brought a message. Nerio summoned us back to Ile vi Dévoye. This trip was a world apart from our first. Instead of checking our papers, the soldiers at the docks saluted and helped tie up our canoes. They accompanied us up the hill to Captain Baccini's home, a red-brick cottage overlooking the camp. Dunehein had to duck to get through the doorway. Baccini's sitting room was small and sparse, decorated with model ships and macramé hangings.

Nerio rose to greet us. He'd trimmed his beard, making him look more like his twenty-one years, but he still looked exhausted. He handed me a folded letter. "From your family. The children are on school holidays, so they went to stay with Rikuja's parents in Toel Ginu. It is safer there."

The letter was in Kirbana's delicate handwriting. I skimmed it, then pocketed it to read properly later. The sitting room only had two armchairs, so Baccini brought stools from the kitchen, then excused himself to make tea. Geniod perched by the window. *Always watching*, Róisín had said, though gusting snow obscured most of the camp.

"What did Neve Lisehl say?" I asked, settling near the roaring fire. "Any word of Tiernan and Jorum?"

"I never made it to Port Alios to ask her." Nerio rubbed the dark circles under his eyes. "Valrose is back from Nordmur and watching my every move, yet he barely listened to my report on the *Marla*."

Dunehein growled. "We took down a shipload of Rúonbattai and he couldn't muster a 'thank you'?"

"He refuses to label them as Rúonbattai without proof. I agree in principle. In practice, though, Valrose is wasting valuable time. He sent me back here to search for, as he phrased it, 'better evidence than the heretical nonsense of a backwater druid.'"

Geniod scoffed. "He should try saying that to Róisín's face."

"I would give a purse of silver to see that." Nerio paced the small room, grinding his fist into his palm. "Naive fool. Valrose does not see the whole picture. Leaflets with the Parr name appear across Caladheå, declaring a holy war against pagans? It is clear who is responsible."

"Wait," I cut in. "You think the Rúonbattai launched a holy war on their own people?"

"Look what it achieved. My father removed from command, me banished to this post, our capital full of riled-up fanatics. Sverbians have started retaliating, burning down Ferish homes and businesses. The Rúonbattai are breeding a militia. And, I suspect, trying to sway Innisburren to their side. They went to great lengths to pin these attacks on a Ferish crew."

"Six centuries of flames," Geniod said in an odd voice. "That's how Róisín described the invasion of Gallun. The Rúonbattai are using the Gallnach's worst fear against them."

"Why bother?" Rikuja asked. "The druids are powerful, but there's only a few on Innisburren. Everyone else is farmers or fishermen."

"That's it," I said, eyes widening. "They need druids for food." Dunehein snorted. "What, like cannibalism?"

"*For* food, not *as* food. My friend Akohin explained it when I found him living with Ainu-Seru. The Rúonbattai's big plan is to wake the saidu, right? They expect the saidu to go on a rampage, destroying farmland and causing a famine. Once all the Ferish flee, the Rúonbattai will get earth mages to build new farms — sustainable ones that are better for the environment, so the saidu will tolerate them. I thought Akohin meant Sverbian mages because I didn't know druids still existed."

"Of course," Geniod said, cottoning on. "Róisín said Sverbian magic is a watered-down version of druidism. I thought she was being arrogant until I saw her greenhouse."

"Sacro dios," Nerio muttered. "So the Rúonbattai are preparing to launch an apocalypse."

"Innisburren will never agree," Rikuja said. "They hate Sverbians above all else. Plus, they've stayed neutral through every Elken War."

Nerio shrugged. "The Rúonbattai can predict the future. I have learned not to underestimate them."

"May I offer a suggestion?" Captain Baccini said, returning from the kitchen with a tray. His porcelain tea set looked out of place in his gnarled sailor's hands. "I know your father well, Lieutenant. Just because he was forced out of command does not make him useless. Ask him for help."

"Nei," I said. "No way. Last time I saw Parr, he was a barefoot drunk talking to himself."

"The man still has his wits about him." Baccini passed me a steaming teacup. "We can choose to find the good in people."

I grit my teeth. "With respect, sir, you'd have to dig pretty fucking deep to find any good in Antoch Parr."

Nerio cast me a sour look. "That is my father you are describing. Besides, he may be ruthless, but he gets results."

"*Results?*" I put my cup down too hard, spilling tea. "Like taking down Councillor Halvarind? He got that by blackmailing me into the Ivy House mission."

"I recall," Nerio said testily. "*You* might recall, I executed Halvarind myself. But without Tiernan and Jorumgard, we need whatever help we can get."

Geniod cleared his throat and set down his empty cup. The twist of his mouth made me suspect he'd forced the tea down to be polite. "Kateiko, your parents gave good advice last time we had this debate. We could ask again."

"Your parents?" Nerio looked between us, frowning. "Are they not . . ."

"Dead, yeah," I snapped. "Thanks for the reminder."

"We can step outside," Geniod offered, just as a gust struck the cottage, driving snow against the windowpanes.

"Ask them here." I thrust my parents' makiri at him.

He balanced the figurines on his palms. Nerio and Baccini watched with apprehension as my uncle closed his eyes and sank into a reverie. The howling wind filled the silence. While everyone else was distracted, I added a drop of soothing lavender oil to my tea.

Geniod looked up, blinking. "That's rare. They both showed me the same thing."

"What was it?" I asked, leaning forward.

"The Okorebai-Tula. That's all."

I sipped my tea, thinking. The Okorebai-Tula had heard my proposal to ally with Parr for the Battle of Tjarnnaast, then spent days discussing it with her advisors before agreeing. When she met Parr face to face, she'd looked him in the eye and declared her terms. No fear, no anger, no bearshit.

"Fine," I told Nerio. "Talk to your father."

✳

Baccini set aside rooms for us in the officers' barracks. He'd been giving latrine duty to any recruits causing trouble as part of this holy war, and whippings to anyone caught doing it again. Between that and our discovery that the *Marla* wasn't part of the war at all, support for it had died down enough in the camp that we could safely stay.

Alone in my room, I read Kirbana's letter. It was short and simple, reassuring us that our family was fine. Matéo and the girl he was courting had joined them for dinner. I'd borrowed ink, paper, and a quill to write a reply but wasn't sure what to say. Would mentioning the Gallnach upset Kirbana? Did she hate them, or did she feel guilty about what her people had done to them?

This is stupid, I told myself, staring at a blank paper. *Kirbana's practically your sister. Just ask her.* But the earth had shifted, opening a chasm between us. It wasn't just that she'd grown up with a different perspective. It was that she'd hidden it from me. I didn't even know how angry I should be.

A tear hit the paper. I pulled the water back out and flicked it away, but more tears kept falling. I knocked the paper off the desk and collapsed onto my bunk. This was all too much — strange visions by day, horrible dreams by night, clinging to brief moments with my parents' spirits. Every minute was a battle to keep my head above water.

The endless travel didn't help. I trailed my fingers over the embroidered fir branches on my blanket. Every few days, I laid it somewhere new. The thought of finding someone to share it with, a warm body to hold me through the nightmares, seemed laughable. I was never in the same place long enough to forge that kind of bond with someone.

Tiernan would understand. As a mercenary always on the move, he lived with this same loneliness. I pulled his letter from the envelope, shedding grit on my bed. Once again, the postscript drew my attention. *Northern Nyhemur is stunning in winter. The snowy plains look infinite, as if one is floating among the clouds. Perhaps one day I can take you here.*

Those last words tumbled around in my head. *I* can take *you* here. Just us. Is that what he wanted? He'd written this days after I sobbed on his shoulder in Tjarnnaast, after he let me touch his hair to feel his spirit. I remembered his strong arms around me, the steady thump of his heart, the scent of smoke. It would've been easy for him to tip my chin up and kiss me.

I yanked that image from my mind like weeding a garden. Way too weird. Tiernan was twice my age and had never shown a hint of attraction to me. He'd clearly written this letter in a hurry, smudging the charcoal, more focused on tracking the cleric than the nuance of his words. Now finding the cleric was our responsibility, as well as finding him and Jorumgard — and our only lead was a strawberry-blonde gem merchant who didn't deal with strangers.

✳

In the end, I wrote a short reply to Kirbana announcing Rikuja's pregnancy. We sent it along with Nerio's letter to Parr on the next ship heading to Caladheå. Awaiting Parr's response gave me time to get back into combat training with Geniod. My ribs still hurt too much to wield Temal's sword, but I could spar with a long stick. In poor weather we practised in the training hall alongside naval recruits, and in good weather we walked up the coast to a secluded beach.

We were sparring outdoors when two figures approached through the ocean mist. I recognized Nerio by his yellow lieutenant's armband. The taller figure wore a long black coat and a triangular hat pulled low over his eyes. Not until they drew close did I realize it was Captain Parr. He looked like his old self again — clean-shaven, his hair neatly tied back, his spine straight, and shoulders square.

"I thought you were on house arrest," I said. "Did the military stop blaming you for the holy war?"

"Not yet," Parr said coolly. "If Valrose admits the Rúonbattai are behind it, he loses his justification for replacing me. The bastard would rather cling to power than see sense."

"My father managed to . . . slip out of Caladheå," Nerio said.

The stiffness of his posture told me he hadn't expected this, either. "We need to talk somewhere private."

"How about right here?" Geniod said. "I'm sure Captain Parr will enjoy the fresh air after being cooped up inside for months."

Parr studied him, tapping his sword hilt. Geniod was forcing this onto our terms. The two men were squaring off, fighting for ground.

"Certainly." Parr set his hat on a frosty log and drew his sword. "In that case, shall we spar? I could use the practice."

Geniod tossed aside his stick and drew his blade. Nerio and I retreated into the snow among the shoreline trees. Parr rolled his shoulders and started warming up with practice swings.

"I am glad you called on me," he said. "Valrose has his head stuck in the sand. He does not believe saidu exist, let alone that the Rúonbattai could use them as a weapon. If he will not act, we must take matters into our own hands."

Parr lunged. Geniod parried with a clash of steel. They fell back, angling at each other again.

"Where do you suggest we start?" Geniod asked.

"The strawberry in the bathhouse," Parr said. "Neve Lisehl may be useful for more than just finding Heilind and Tømasind. She has connections in, shall we say, high and low places."

Geniod snorted. "Are you blackmailing *her*, too?"

Parr's lip curled. "Such a bleak way of seeing things."

He lunged again. Geniod dodged, swinging past Parr. They whirled. The ringing of metal filled the misty shore. The two were closely matched — tall muscular men in their late thirties, both with decades of combat training. Neither could get an edge. Then in a flash, Geniod kicked Parr's ankle, tripping him. Parr went down hard. His sword clattered onto the rocks.

"You were right," Geniod said, sheathing his blade. "You do need practice."

Parr got up, wincing. "Miss Lisehl and I have an understanding. Her true name is Níamh ó Lónan, which you might recognize as Gallnach. That tends to raise eyebrows, so she floats through high society under a false name. She finds it an easier way to live. I have no desire to take that from her."

"Wait," I interrupted. "She pretends to be Sverbian?"

"It is more common than you might think," Nerio said. "The Gallnach have spent six centuries under foreign rule, forced to learn Sverbian language and religion. Some people turn that to their advantage."

"Aeldu save us," I muttered. "First the *Marla*, now this. Nobody's who they say they are."

Parr's smile didn't reach his eyes. "Miss Lisehl may be our key to figuring out the Rúonbattai's plans. The problem is reaching her. I cannot be seen in Port Alios while I am on house arrest, and Nerio is still stuck here on Valrose's orders."

Nerio frowned, shifting his weight. "I could request medical leave. Valrose is suspicious of me, though. He would want proof of illness or injury."

"I could poison you," I offered. "Remember the coal newts?"

He shuddered. "All too well."

"I am sure we can find a better option." Parr spun his sword. "How about a rematch, Geniod? I think best on my feet."

My uncle drew his sword again. Whatever the game was, neither man wanted to back down.

Parr struck. Geniod parried, grunting at the blow. Their blades sang in a flurry of strikes. This round was nothing like the first. No pauses, no banter. Parr kept pushing Geniod back, gaining ground. The ocean lapped at their boots.

"What's your father doing?" I hissed.

Nerio shook his head wearily. "Winning."

Parr struck with the flat of his blade. Geniod staggered, slipping on the wet rocks. Parr kicked my uncle in the chest. Geniod toppled back, hitting the water with a splash. I cringed.

"Seems I do not need practice after all," Parr said, panting. "Just warming up."

Geniod got up with a wince. "Was that worth it, *Captain*?" He spat the title like a curse. "You come up with some brilliant idea?"

"Actually, yes." Parr's lips edged into a cool smile. "There is another reason for Nerio to request leave. Marriage."

"Marriage?" Nerio said incredulously. "Where am I supposed to find a wife?"

"Right here." Parr pointed his sword at me.

"*What?*" Nerio and I cried.

"Hear me out," Parr said, raising a hand. "None of it will be real. Nerio, as a lieutenant, you are allowed one week's leave for your wedding. Say you want a quiet ceremony in Port Alios, away from the burning streets of Caladheå. You will have a week to track down Neve Lisehl. Wring everything you can out of her, then invent some excuse to end the engagement."

Nerio and I looked at each other like it was our first time noticing the other was human-shaped. We could barely go ten minutes without bickering.

"Valrose will not fall for it," Nerio said. "He will never believe Katja and I are in love."

"No, but he will believe I arranged the wedding." Parr staked his sword into the beach, leaning on it. "Miss Leniere is becoming a respected military asset. Serving as a war medic, capturing Councillor Halvarind, forging alliances with Innisburren and the Tula nation. It would be an auspicious match. A way to solidify ties with the viirelei nations."

"I don't *have* a nation," I protested. "I'm practically an exile."

Parr shrugged. "Valrose does not know that. You are registered as Rin in Eremur's birth records."

"Yeah, but—" I fumbled for another reason to refuse. "I'm not old enough. Not by Aikoto law."

"You are." Geniod's voice sounded strained. "You were born half a month after Yanben. Your eighteenth birthday is . . . now, give or take."

I sucked in a breath. He was right.

"We can make it work, Katja." Nerio fiddled with a button on his cuff, not quite meeting my eyes. "If you trust me."

I did genuinely trust him. I *didn't* trust his father, who'd probably planned this before setting foot on the island. I touched the sea glass in my macramé necklace. How far would news of my engagement to Lieutenant Nerio Parr spread? Would Jonalin believe I'd moved on? Would Tiernan and Jorumgard think Nerio and I had been hiding some secret romance?

Geniod set his hand on my arm. Quietly, he said, "You don't have to agree this second. Remember what your parents said."

I lifted my chin, trying to channel the Okorebai-Tula's confidence, and met Parr's eye. "I'll consider it. And if you breathe a word of this before I agree, I'll tell Valrose you left house arrest to arrange it. I'll tell him you're trying to pin this holy war on the Rúonbattai so you can take back command. Let's see whose side he takes."

11.

PORT ALIOS

My family and I discussed the plan late into the night. There were dozens of ways it could go wrong, but it *was* better than poisoning Nerio. I didn't trust myself to make an antidote correctly, and of all possible missions, going to a spa town was a good one. Even if Parr was stringing me along with his talk of finding Tiernan and Jorumgard, I wasn't willing to lose that chance.

There turned out to be an astonishing amount of preparation for a pretend engagement. Nerio took one look at the Ferish clothes I'd packed and said they wouldn't do. Port Alios was where Eremur's wealthy went to wash off the stench of the cities. Parr, who was returning to Caladheå, said he'd get money to Nicoletta. She knew high fashion from browsing Shawnaast's markets even though she could never afford anything herself.

For now, Nerio had to feign following Valrose's orders, so he sent the *Cavalo ven Cielo* out on patrol under his first mate's command. The two of us hunkered down in the naval camp's war room, surrounded by maps and reports. Our first task was getting our story straight — how the marriage got arranged, whether we'd live in Parr Manor, what I'd do as a military wife. Our next task was planning a way out of the engagement. Through all that, Nerio taught me as much high society etiquette as he could cram in.

We announced our engagement in the officers' mess, responding to everyone's congratulations with the resigned shrugs of a young couple getting forced into a loveless marriage. Nerio sent one letter to Valrose requesting leave and another to the *Sol vi Caladheä*. The newspaper announcement would emphasize it was a family-only ceremony so people didn't start planning to attend. I wasn't wholly surprised when Captain Parr arrived on the same ship as Valrose's reply.

"The bastard cannot ban me from my son's wedding," he said, clapping Nerio on the back. "Besides, I wanted to deliver a family heirloom in person."

He undid the drawstring of a silk bag. Inside was a gold filigree ring set with smoky brown quartz. My engagement ring.

"It matches your eyes," Parr said, making me want to chuck it in the ocean.

He'd also brought a trunk of clothes and a letter from Nicoletta. *Of course!* she began, followed by scathing comments about how nice it would be to visit a spa town instead of treating burn victims. She went on with *Kirbana and I talked it over. You'll never pass as a typical officer's wife, so there's no point trying. Go for silent and mysterious. Scare people out of asking questions.*

She'd sent a high-collared black dress with bell sleeves, pearl buttons, and cascades of gauzy muslin. The other clothing was also black — petticoats, stockings, heeled boots, mittens, and a hooded fur cape. Velvet cases held perfume bottles, cosmetics, and jewellery borrowed from Parr's dead wife. There were black clothes for my family, too. Rikuja had a silk dress patterned with shimmering grey brocade. Geniod and Dunehein had matching coats, breeches, and high-collared shirts.

"You're Thymarai again," Dunehein said, slinging an arm over my shoulders. "A pagan goddess terrifying itherans into submission. Rija's your spectral attendant, me and Geniod are your bjørnbattai bodyguards."

We left on a naval cutter crewed by Nerio's men. I spent most of the trip on deck, enduring the biting wind to watch villages pass on either side of Burren Inlet. We were sailing between the two halves of Eremur. Peering north through a spyglass, I glimpsed Sverbian log cabins and Iyo smokehouses. South were Ferish farmhouses and half-submerged boulder walls where the Kae had built clam gardens. It was eerie knowing the Rúonbattai wanted to have saidu destroy the entire south side.

Once night fell, the only sign of land was the occasional twinkling light. We slept in shifts in the tiny cabin. Early the next morning, we veered south into a fjord framed by forested mountains. Port Alios was at the far end. The white-sailed ships in the harbour looked like snow-birds nesting among the glittering water. On shore stood sandstone buildings rich with arches, towers, gables, and red-brick highlights.

"The mountains here have hot springs," Nerio told me. "Decades ago, a gold-seeker fell into a pond and was shocked by its warmth. He used his gold to build a bathhouse, and lo, Port Alios was born."

At the piers, dockhands loaded our luggage onto a carriage, which took us to a hotel overlooking the harbour. Dunehein gave a low whistle as we stepped into the lobby. Sandstone pillars rose to a mosaic ceiling. Everything was gilded — chandeliers laden with white candles, filigree mouldings on the walls, obsidian tables with vases of exotic flowers. I dried the slush from our boots before we stepped onto an immense woven rug.

Captain Parr approached a clerk behind a marble desk. After a brief conversation in gliding Ferish, he slid a full purse across the desk. The clerk passed over our keys and snapped his fingers. A porter in a starched uniform beckoned us up a sweeping staircase. Nerio and I weren't meant to share a room until after the wedding, so Rikuja and I were sharing. It seemed reasonable until we discovered our suite was *four* lavish rooms.

I didn't dare comment until we were alone, which took ages. First a maid built a hearth fire in the sitting room, furnished with velvet armchairs and glossy oak furniture. Next she pumped hot water for the bath, which was in a white-painted room decorated with bowls of dried rose petals. The porter carried our luggage into the bedroom. A kitchen girl brought a tray of tea and cake. She set it in the dining room, where she tied back the curtains, revealing tall windows overlooking the harbour. I remembered just in time to tip them each an iron pann.

After they left, Rikuja let out a disbelieving laugh. "Can you marry Nerio for real?"

"Honestly, I'm tempted." I bit into a square of cake, savouring the blend of cream and cloves. "Aeldu save me. I would marry Captain Parr for this cake."

"Speaking of marriage, we have work to do." Rikuja pointed at the bathroom. "Go get clean. I'll unpack your clothes."

I spent as long as possible luxuriating in the wash basin. Even the soap smelled like roses. By the time I dragged myself out, Rikuja had planned every detail of my Thymarai look. "Rich witch," she proclaimed, giggling.

She pulled my corset tight, pinned up my hair and wrapped it in black lace, then smudged charcoal around my eyes. For jewellery,

I had a ruby pendant, my quartz engagement ring, and Róisín's runed bronze ring. Removing my macramé necklace felt like a last goodbye to Jonalin. The final touch was my obsidian-handled knife on my belt.

"Right," I said, adjusting my skirt. "Your turn."

"Nei, nei," Rikuja protested. "You're the bride—"

"And *you're* going to be a mother," I countered. "That's worth celebrating."

✳

A porter knocked on our door near sunset and said the others would meet us in the lobby. Walking downstairs in heeled boots was my first ordeal of the night. When I reached the ground floor, I caught Nerio staring. Both Parrs were in dress uniform, starched and pressed with braided red cord on their shoulders. Apparently Parr Senior had decided to assert his role as a captain.

I'd chosen a subtler look for Rikuja, dusting her skin with sparkling mica powder. Instead of the bark cord she always wore in her braid to signify her as a shrine carver, I'd woven a ribbon into her glossy brown plait. The moment she left the stairs, Dunehein swept her into a kiss. A passing Ferish woman gave them a dirty look. I glared back. She squeaked and hurried off.

Parr watched with amusement. "Shall we head to dinner? It is close enough to walk."

He nudged Nerio, who held out his arm to me. I burned with awkwardness as we linked elbows, although the moment we stepped onto the icy street, I was glad to have someone to help balance me. Lantern posts around the harbour cast broken-up reflections on the dark, shifting ocean. Couples strolled along the boardwalk, the men in fur hats and the women in elaborate ruffled bonnets.

Our destination was the Mariners' Guild, a sandstone complex on the waterfront. Colourful flags snapped on poles lining the front. Neve Lisehl was registered in the guild as a gem merchant and often had dinner in the salon. The Parrs weren't guild members, but a burly gate guard glanced at their uniforms and waved us inside. I stepped through the salon door and gasped. In the centre of a dim, cavernous hall floated the skeleton of some huge, monstrous creature.

"What *is* that?" I whispered.

Nerio chuckled. "A whale. Terrifying without flesh, is it not?"

An intricate system of iron posts held up each bone. Wires affixed them to the ceiling for extra support. I was so fascinated that it took me a few minutes to notice anything else. Around the hall's perimeter, itherans sat at tables draped in white cloth, filling the place with the hum of conversation. Glass lamps on the walls cast long shadows across the sandstone floor.

"Remember how to spot Neve?" Nerio murmured.

I nodded. "Small, pale, early twenties. Strawberry-blonde hair and expensive clothes."

We walked arm in arm around the whale skeleton, studying it from every angle as an excuse to search the crowd. Most patrons were Ferish. About a quarter looked Sverbian, though I wondered how many were Gallnach in disguise. I kept catching people staring at us. I stared back, chin up and spine straight, imagining Thymarai's antlers atop my head.

Finding no sign of Neve, we joined our family at a table. An aproned man came with a bottle of white wine. As he filled our crystal goblets, he spoke in rapid Ferish. Before I could mentally translate, Captain Parr turned to us.

"Swordfish, mountain lamb, or glissetto?" he asked. "The latter is quite rustic, but the chefs here do an excellent job."

At every pub I'd been to, I got whatever was served that day. Glissetto contained animal heart, which my people didn't eat, so I chose swordfish. To my surprise, the server returned with bowls of clear broth. Then I remembered Nerio had said dinners here had several courses. I'd asked how that was legal, since the Caladheå Council was stockpiling food in preparation for the Rúonbattai causing a famine. Nerio had said dryly that wealthy people could always find ways around trifling issues like war rations.

Halfway through a course of spiced root vegetables, an older Ferish couple approached. The moustached man was in a grey coat and breeches. The woman's vivid pink dress, adorned with hundreds of ruffles, reminded me of tropical flowers I'd seen in botany books.

"Antoch!" the man cried, thumping Parr's back. "Heard you got strung up for some nonsense in Caladheå. What brings you to Port Alios?"

Smiling, Parr rose to greet the couple. "A delightful occasion. My son's wedding."

The woman gasped. "Goodness me. Nerio, I remember you as a babe toddling after your father. You've grown into such a fine young man. And your bride—" Her smile froze as she looked between Rikuja and me.

Parr set his hand on my shoulder. "Miss Leniere has been working as a war medic and liaison for the viirelei nations. We are honoured to welcome her into the Parr family."

"Oh, how wonderful." The woman beamed down at me. "What a stunning bride. Lovely as a painted vase."

Nerio flinched. Parr's grip tightened on my shoulder. Even the moustached man looked uncomfortable, fiddling with his cufflinks.

"Come along, dear," he said. "Let's leave them to their dinner."

He steered his wife away. Parr returned to his seat, his mouth pressed into a thin line. I gave Nerio a confused look. He shook his head. I glared, refusing to let it go.

Sighing, Nerio leaned over to whisper in my ear. His short beard tickled my cheek. "That woman insulted you. It means, well . . . no matter how beautifully you paint a vase, it is still just clay. Essentially dirt."

I recoiled. "And you didn't say anything?"

Nerio frowned, spearing a turnip. "How is this my fault?"

"We're engaged! You're supposed to defend your wife!"

"You think this is easy for me?" he hissed. "These people will gossip about this engagement for the rest of my life. *You* never have to see them again—"

Geniod rapped his knuckles on the table. Nerio and I broke off, scowling. I rubbed my cheek, trying to wipe away the feel of his beard.

Neve, Geniod mouthed, tilting his head toward the door.

A young woman was brushing snowflakes off her white fur coat, which had the speckled markings of a snowcat. Her strawberry-blonde hair was pinned up in an elaborate braided bun. She twisted her hips back and forth, shaking snow off her white silk skirt.

"Who's that with her?" Rikuja asked quietly.

"Her bodyguard," Parr said. "She has kept the same one for years."

I dropped my napkin as an excuse to turn for a proper look. Behind Neve stood a bored teenage girl in black leather armour. A curved dagger hung from each hip. She looked vaguely Aikoto, tall and thin with high cheekbones and bronze skin, though her wavy black hair was cropped to her chin. Aikoto women never cut our hair. It framed her perfectly oval face, dark eyes, full lips . . .

Wonderful. Here I was, celebrating my engagement to an irritable soldier, and I'd just found the most beautiful girl in existence.

The girl caught me staring. She nudged Neve, who looked to me first, then Parr. Neve spun on her heel and walked out, skirt swishing. Her bodyguard followed.

"Ah." A slow smile crossed Parr's face. "So she wants to play it that way."

I resisted the urge to throw my fork at him. Instead I whispered, "Should we go after them?"

"No. Too many eyes here." Parr picked up his goblet and sipped his wine. "Neve will talk when she is ready."

✻

I didn't blame Neve for fleeing. It made my skin crawl to stalk another girl getting blackmailed by Parr. I half wondered if he was the reason she had a bodyguard. Until she decided to talk, though, we had to keep up our wedding preparations. While Parr arranged the ceremony and a small family celebration, I started my bridal trousseau.

Rikuja and I left our hotel with a purse of gold sovereigns and a list of shops. We spent hours visiting tailors, furriers, jewellers, cobblers, and embroiderers. I didn't buy anything, playing the indecisive bride, but my clinking purse made the craftsmen tolerate us. At the harbour market, we browsed imported spices, cloth, nuts, and dried fruit. I glimpsed a few people slide over extra coins to buy more than wartime rations allowed.

Flashes of red hair kept appearing in the crowd, but if it was Neve, she didn't approach us. In the evenings, we went to various places she liked to visit — the theatre to watch a play, a pub to listen to Sverbian fiddlers, a vineyard for wine tastings. Port Alios was surprisingly busy for midwinter. Nerio's guess was Eremur's wealthy elites had fled here to escape the holy war. Everyone knew

Captain Parr had been blamed for it, but few people seemed to think he'd really started it.

"People always get restless in wartime," a balding man proclaimed at the wine tasting, waving his glass. "They're tired of rationing and long lines at the post office. Eventually they'll get tired of torching each other's homes. Then we'll charge them through the nose to rebuild!"

Laughter went up from the surrounding people. Nerio turned away with a look of disgust. On seeing my matching look, he turned back.

"Your construction business must be thriving," Nerio told the man, "if you could afford to bribe the military clerks to strike your son's name off the draft list. How much was it? A hundred sovs? Two hundred?"

The balding man sputtered. Nerio pulled me outside into the moonlit vineyard. He muttered as we followed an icy track past rows of bare vines. On an arched stone bridge over a frozen creek, he relinquished me and slumped onto the railing.

"I can't believe you did that," I said.

He shook his head. "My father will be upset. I wasted valuable leverage."

"Fuck leverage. It was worth the look on that takuran's face."

Nerio's mouth twitched into a smile. "I loathe people like that. Hiding behind golden shields while a war rages around them. My father tolerates them because their money is useful, but . . ." He looked up at stars scattered across the black sky. "I want no part of his underhanded dealings. I want to be better than that."

"You are better." I leaned on the frosty railing. "I wouldn't be here as your bride otherwise."

He glanced at me, hesitating. "May I tell you a secret?"

"Yeah. Of course."

"I . . ." Nerio sighed, drumming his fingers on the railing. "The military has been my life since I was fifteen. This is the closest I have ever gotten to courting a woman. I fear I may die in battle without so much as my first kiss."

I looked at him sideways. He was attractive, I supposed, with a sharp jaw and dark eyes that glinted in the moonlight. The faint musk of his cologne wafted through the thin winter air. I wondered how it felt to kiss someone with a beard. My stomach twisted as I realized he was close enough to find out. Our eyes met.

"No," we said together and cracked up laughing.

When I caught my breath, I said, "*You* want to know a secret? Strangers keep telling me how lucky I am. 'Oh, Lieutenant Parr's so handsome. Wasn't he with the Mounted Archers? *I'd* like to mount that archer.'"

Nerio's jaw dropped. "Nobody is saying that."

"Not in those words, but the feeling's there." I elbowed him, smiling. "You'll find the right person. I'm sure of it."

12.

SMOKESCREEN

After days of avoiding the Mariners' Guild, Neve Lisehl swept into the salon, adorned in a coppery fox fur mantle that matched her hair. She strode around the whale skeleton, her bodyguard in tow. The two women disappeared through a door across the hall.

Parr eyed the door, twisting one of his rings. "Interesting choice."

"What?" I asked. "Where'd she go?"

"The tea room. Women congregate there after dinner while men smoke in the pipe room. Perhaps she wants to talk with you ladies alone."

Entering the tea room felt like stepping into a vast spiderweb. Pearly white curtains separated the place into dim alcoves, each lit by wrought-iron candelabras. Women of all ages lounged on horse-hair couches, talking in low voices and sipping clear liquid from crystal glasses.

"That's not tea," Rikuja whispered.

An aproned girl offered us each a glass. I sniffed it, breathing in a smoky scent. Mezcale. Jonalin had been carrying a flask of it when he overdosed. Once the serving girl turned away, I poured Rikuja's glass into mine and called water from the air to refill hers.

"You're safer with that," I told her.

We drifted through the room, glancing into each alcove as if looking for somewhere to sit. A few women did double takes, then leaned in to whisper to each other. I kept my head high, balancing imaginary antlers. At the room's far end, Neve sprawled across a couch, her fox fur mantle draped over the back. It was astonishing how someone so small could take up so much space. She sure looked like a Sverbian gem merchant, decked out in diamond jewellery and a pale pink bodice over a white muslin gown.

I stepped toward Neve's alcove. Her bodyguard moved forward, blocking the entrance through the curtains. The girl was taller than even me, giving me an intimate view of her elegant chin and full lips. Her black leather spaulders made her shoulders look unnervingly broad.

"We're not here to fight," I said. "Just talk."

"That's a shame." The bodyguard eyed my obsidian-handled knife. "I was hoping for a fight."

Despite her Aikoto appearance, her lilting accent sounded closer to Ferish. She rested her hands on her sheathed daggers like a cat flaunting its claws. Neve ignored us, swirling her glass of mezcale. There was no way to reach her without causing a commotion. I backed away, frustrated.

"Now what?" Rikuja murmured.

"Dunno." I took a swig of mezcale and sputtered. "Guess we—"

"Excuse me," a breathless voice interrupted. "Aren't you Kateiko Leniere?"

I turned. Two girls in dark muslin gowns had appeared behind us. They looked about my age, wide-eyed and giggling.

"We heard about your engagement," said the breathless girl. "We wanted to congratulate you."

"Uh — thanks," I stammered.

The girl spoke in Ferish to her friend, who laughed. Fury flooded through me. Clearly she hadn't expected me to understand. I'd slapped Nicoletta for saying less about Matéo and me, but slapping this girl, whoever she was, might well get me arrested.

"You're wrong," I replied icily. "But even if I *were* a knocked-up whore, at least I'm not a gossiping bitch."

The girls gaped. They spun, skirts whirling, and fled the tea room. Rikuja stared after them in astonishment.

I downed my mezcale, wincing at the burn. "Let's go—"

Someone tapped my shoulder. I turned and found myself face to face with Neve's bodyguard. She leaned in, her breath warm on my cheek. The rich scent of oiled leather wreathed me.

"Tomorrow morning," she whispered. "Nine o'clock at the women's bathhouse. Come alone."

✳

Tomorrow, as it turned out, was the Ferish holy day. Most of Port Alios would be attending weekly rites at the sancte. I was glad for an excuse not to go with Nerio, partly out of fear his god might strike me down for heathenry, partly because my absence would make our coming breakup more believable. My family weren't thrilled about me going off alone, but Parr insisted Neve was "harmless, if a bit difficult."

A horse-drawn sleigh took me out of town, gliding along a snowy road through dense forest. I climbed off in front of a long sandstone building. Silence weighed heavy on the place. I pushed open thick oak doors and stepped into a bright, airy lobby. Potted trees and hanging plants basked in sunbeams falling through glass skylights.

"Miss Leniere?" A pale girl with a blonde braid curtsied. "I'm Miss Lisehl's handmaiden, Júni. She's awaiting you in the hot spring. Is this your first time here?"

"Yes," I said, trying to keep my voice level.

Júni smiled reassuringly. "Then I'll guide you through. Miss Lisehl already paid your entry fee."

She led me into a stiflingly warm room. Two Sverbians were undressing at the far end. Itheran women rarely even bared their arms in public, but here they didn't seem to care. Júni showed me niches in the stone wall where I could stow my belongings. She looked away while I undressed. Keeping her gaze averted, she led me into a steamy room with mosaic basins. The nude women ahead of me were scrubbing themselves with damp cloths.

"Everyone has to bathe first," Júni explained. "It's to keep the hot spring pure."

Following the women's example, I washed my hair and body with rose-scented soap, then scooped water over myself to rinse off. The suds flowed away into grates in the floor. Júni used a cloth to wipe the charcoal from my eyes. She gave me a wool robe and lambskin slippers, picked up a stack of towels, and beckoned me outside.

A shock of cold hit me. At first glance, the place looked like a flooded courtyard. Steam rose from a rectangular turquoise pool. The only dry ground was a narrow loggia around the perimeter, its roof supported by thick sandstone pillars. I scanned the nude women in the pool and spotted Neve's strawberry-blonde hair. She lounged in neck-deep water, one arm draped over the pool wall.

"Finally," she drawled as I approached. "I thought you'd refused my invitation." She spoke with a perfect Sverbian accent, musical but jagged, like falling pebbles.

I sat on the pool edge, tucking in my legs. A faint smell of sulphur wafted from the water. "I was surprised you invited me. Captain Parr said you don't deal with strangers."

"You're not a stranger, are you? You're joining the Parr family." Neve peered up at me. Her deep brown eyes were stark against her pale skin. "Get in. You'll freeze with wet hair."

Only then did I realize why she'd chosen this spot. She'd stripped away the clothes and makeup I'd worn like armour in Port Alios. Akohin had done the same when I found him living in the mountains with Ainu-Seru. That had been about baring our spirits to old friends, but this . . .

Neve clicked her tongue. "So modest. I won't look until you get in." She made a show of clamping a hand over her eyes.

I got up and untied my robe, letting it fall from my shoulders. Too late, I noticed Neve's bodyguard watching from the loggia. She smirked, brushing her gaze over my body, lingering on every curve. My pulse skipped. I couldn't tell if she was flirting or messing with me. If she was Aikoto, she'd know how strange it was that I had no tattoos. She might not want anything to do with me.

Worry about that later, I scolded myself. I kicked off my slippers and slid into the pool, gasping at the heat. Neck-deep water on Neve was only chest-deep on me.

"Lovely, isn't it?" Neve uncovered her eyes. "I've heard the men's bathhouse is bigger, though I don't trust men who brag about the size of things."

I choked on my spit. "Much as I'd love to discuss that, I'm looking for information."

"Straight to business? How boring." She sighed and waved her hand. "Go on, then. What do the Parrs want this time?"

I gave her the short version of our Innisburren mission, from hunting the *Marla* to uncovering the Rúonbattai's plans of recruiting Gallnach druids. Neve half listened, trailing her fingers through the water.

"I can tell you one thing," she said. "You played right into the Rúonbattai's hands."

"What? How?"

"The *Marla*, the holy war — it's all a smokescreen. The Rúonbattai know they'll never sway Innisburren. The real prize is ..." Neve glanced at the sun hanging over the mountains and pointed northeast. "That way."

"What's that way?"

A smile played across her face. "Tell me a secret and I'll tell you mine."

I wondered if this was what Parr meant by Neve being difficult. "What do you want to know?"

"Tell me about Nerio. Is he a good kisser?" She walked her fingers up my bare arm. "Do you think about him at night?"

I squirmed away. "He — we're—"

"Not getting married, right?" Her smile faded. "I knew it. Only Antoch Parr would fake his own son's engagement just to track me down."

"We were desperate." I felt sick at defending Parr. "If you tell us what you know, we'll leave you alone. I promise."

"I don't know anything for sure." Neve propped her elbows on the pool's edge, floating there. "But if the Rúonbattai have half a brain, they won't waste their time with Innisburren. They'll go for Ingdanrad."

"The mage city? Why?"

"Because it's half Sverbian these days. The Rúonbattai already have supporters there. They'll spread their lies like poison, convincing Gallnach druids to turn against the Ferish."

I fell silent, thinking. At Ivy House, searching Councillor Halvarind's belongings, we'd discovered hundreds of letters from the Rúonbattai's temporal mage. They were deliberately vague, not mentioning people or places by name, but we'd concluded the first decade of letters had been written in Ingdanrad. At the time, we thought the mage was the tattooed, golden-haired warrior Liet. Tiernan had written to his contacts in Ingdanrad asking if they could identify the man. No one could.

Now we knew why. Evidence pointed to the mage being the furious, silver-haired cleric who haunted my dreams. On getting my message about it, Nerio had passed the news to Tiernan's Ingdanrad contacts. None had responded with the mention of a cleric returning home after a long absence, but she likely still had family or friends in the city. They could be rallying support this very moment.

"How would we get into Ingdanrad?" I asked. "I heard they cut off diplomacy with Eremur after the Third Elken War."

"You mean after those Sverbian mages got murdered in Caladheå's prison? Throats slit midway through their court trials? Yes, that *was* rather upsetting to a mage city."

It seemed like a bad time to mention the mages were Rúonbattai. Yotolein, a courier for them at the time, had said so himself. Plus we'd found an oak and lilac crest carved inside the prison, meaning the cleric herself must've gotten arrested. I wasn't sure how *she* survived the murders.

"There must be some way into Ingdanrad," I pressed. "Maybe as a trader?"

"Sure, if you want one day in the market. If you want to stay long enough to do anything . . ." Neve shrugged. "Claim you only care about studying magic, then swear neutrality in all current and future wars. That's how most non-Gallnach get in."

"Is that what Tiernan Heilind did?"

"The Sverbian fire mage? Ask him yourself." She looked at me sideways. "Unless he's still missing?"

My breath caught. "You heard about that?"

"Mm-hmm." Neve twirled a lock of wet hair around her finger.

"You know something, don't you? What do you want? Another secret?"

"Oh, I'm not sure," she said airily. "Tell me something fun. Surprise me."

I pressed my fingers to my lips, wondering what would interest a shameless gossip, as Nerio had described her. "If you want a surprise, come to the Mariners' Guild tonight."

"Really?" Neve perked up. "I don't usually settle for promises, but fine. I'll spill. Two months ago, Jorumgard Tømasind returned to Caladheå alone. No sign of Heilind."

"They split up? Why?"

"Who knows?" she said, examining her manicured fingernails. "It's not like I can ask Tømasind. The Elkhounds arrested him on sight."

"*Arrested?* What for?"

"Royal desertion. Kånehlbattai are sworn to protect the Sverbian queen for life. And since this is a province of Sverba . . ."

"Jorum left years ago," I protested. "He's spent half his life fighting for Eremur."

"Under Antoch Parr. Now Captain Valrose is cleaning house, quietly removing Parr's 'untrustworthy allies.' I heard a rumour — who told me?" Neve tapped her chin. "Oh yes, a handsome naval soldier. Quite talkative after a few mugs of brånnvin, and goodness, the mouth on him—"

"What was the rumour?" I interrupted.

She huffed. "Valrose planned to arrest both your mercenary friends. He was rather irked when only one showed up. *Supposedly* he offered a deal. Tømasind can walk free if he reveals where Heilind is. If he refuses, he'll get deported to Sverba to face the queen's justice. Which means" — Neve mimed hanging herself — "bye-bye to your Kånehlbattai."

✳

"He did *what*?!" Parr bellowed.

"Keep your voice down," I hissed. "I'm not supposed to be in here before the wedding."

"Cingari sia mera. I will skin Valrose alive." Parr paced the sitting room he shared with Nerio, his heavy steps muffled by the rug. "Filthy hypocrite. He dragged *me* through the war council for making underhanded deals. If he truly cared about the law, he would hang Tømasind himself."

Nerio had gone pale. He closed the curtains, casting a shadow over the room. "That explains why Valrose keeps sending me away. He did not want me to find out — Ow. Goddamn it." He grimaced, rubbing the shin he'd banged in the dim light.

Geniod took a tinderbox from the mantelpiece and began lighting candles. Rikuja sank into a velvet armchair, holding her stomach. Just a few weeks ago, she'd talked about wanting Jorumgard as an uncle to her baby. Yotolein had told me about his dream of marrying the mercenary, of raising Hanaiko and Samulein together. No wonder Jorumgard had kept his distance from us. He'd known something like this would happen.

And where in Aeldu-yan was Tiernan? He and Jorumgard were brothers-in-arms, a pair like gloves or boot laces or knitting needles. Had he been arrested elsewhere? Captured by the Rúonbattai cleric? Killed? Colourful specks flitted across my vision. I pressed his gold oak coin to my lips, clinging to its solidness.

"One thing I'm stuck on," Dunehein said. "Why wouldn't Jorum admit where Tiernan is? *He's* not a criminal. Valrose has nothing to arrest him for."

Parr gave a barking laugh. "He would make up some excuse. Treason, leaking military secrets, aiding the cleric's escape — anything to get Heilind out of our ranks. Valrose thinks all mages are dangerous and untrustworthy." He flexed his hands, pacing away into the dining room.

"We have to go back," Nerio said. "Maybe we can talk sense into Valrose."

"*You* have to go back," I said. "Our wedding's tomorrow. After that, your leave is over and your father's back on house arrest. *I* have to go east."

He gazed at me across the room. A thin strip of light from between the curtains lit up his cheekbone. "Ah," he said quietly. "You are going to Ingdanrad."

Rikuja looked surprised. "Really, Kako? I figured you'd go after Jorum. That's our best chance of finding Tiernan."

"I know. But that's in Nerio's hands now." I slumped onto a couch and rested my forehead on my palms. "The Rúonbattai's whole plan hinges on druids. The cleric needs them to rebuild Eremur for Sverbians, to mend whatever damage the saidu cause. We have to keep the druids from allying with her."

"Agreed," Nerio said. "But how do you propose getting into Ingdanrad without Tiernan?"

The bedroom door swung open, making me jump. Parr strode

in. I wasn't sure how he'd gotten there until I realized he'd paced a lap around the suite.

"Miss Lisehl can help," he said. "I believe she has family there."

"We're not asking Neve," I said. "I promised to leave her alone."

Parr scoffed. "She *likes* her little games. Lounging about the salon, flaunting her jewels and secrets, baiting us into chasing her. The girl is asking for people to come after her. She *wants* it."

"Don't you dare blame her." I leapt up, reaching for my knife. "Don't you fucking *dare*—"

Geniod caught my arm. "No murder indoors."

Rikuja rose to her feet. She smoothed her skirt, crossed the room, and slapped Parr. He reeled, stumbling into a cabinet. An angry red mark bloomed across his cheek.

"Not gonna fight back?" she snapped. "You'll happily torment young women, but you won't hit a pregnant lady. That's the line, ai?"

He looked between us, all staring at him with loathing. Even his own son looked disgusted. Parr straightened his collar and walked out.

"Right then." Rikuja's nostrils flared. "Kako and I are going to dress for dinner. It's time to end this engagement."

✳

Entering the Mariners' Guild, I spotted Neve through the whale skeleton, dining across the hall. She lifted her wine glass with a smile. Her bodyguard tapped two fingers to her forehead in mocking salute. Great. As if being naked in front of a gorgeous stranger hadn't been awkward enough, she was about to witness me dramatically fall apart in public.

Nerio and I had rehearsed our breakup countless times. It would tarnish our reputations, but with luck, it'd keep Valrose from suspecting the engagement was a sham. The problem was our planned breakup started with an argument. We'd expected to get into one during dinner, but our table was silent except for the clink of dishes.

Help arrived in the form of mezcale. Our aproned server set two flaming glasses down in front of Nerio and me. "A gift from the bride's friend, Neve Lisehl," he said with a bow. "To wish you luck for tomorrow."

A murmur ran through nearby tables, the flames drawing attention. It was the perfect chance. Heart thudding, I rose and threw my napkin on the table. "I can't do it."

Nerio frowned up at me. "Do what?"

"I'm sorry. I thought—" I thrust a dusty letter at him. "I'm so sorry."

He read aloud. "'Northern Nyhemur is stunning in winter. The snowy plains look infinite, as if one is floating among the clouds. Perhaps one day I can take you here.'" He looked up sharply. "What is this, Katja? Who wrote this?"

"Tiernan," I said breathlessly.

"Tiernan *Heilind*? My best friend? My mentor?" Nerio gave a harsh laugh. He got to his feet and turned away. "Sacro dios. A fine time to tell me, the night before our wedding."

"I didn't realize how I felt! I haven't seen him in months. That's the last thing he sent me before he went missing—"

"Clearly you did realize! You were trading love letters with a mercenary!"

Our shouting carried throughout the room. I sensed eyes watching us, ears taking in every word. Unbidden tears pricked at me.

Captain Parr cleared his throat. "Miss Leniere," he said in a dangerous voice, "what is the meaning of this?"

"It means I'm done." I pulled off my quartz ring and tossed it on the table.

Gasps went up around us. I walked out, wiping my eyes, ignoring my family's calls.

Only when the night air hit did I realize I'd forgotten my fur cape and mittens. I hugged my chest and headed for the harbour. Snow floated through the orbs of lantern light, falling away into darkness. On the boardwalk, I collapsed on a wooden bench, my teeth chattering. A slow clap sounded behind me.

"Wonderful," Neve crooned. "A performance for the ages."

"Glad you enjoyed it," I muttered.

"Antoch Parr humiliated in public? I could live on that joy. Oh, but darling—" Her voice softened. "Are those real tears?"

I shrugged.

Neve sat next to me and draped her white snowcat coat over our shoulders. "Are your feelings for Heilind real, too?"

"Sort of," I scraped out. "I love him as a friend. He's the kindest man I've ever met, and . . ."

It was like I'd spent all day watching a tidal wave roll in. Now it struck. Every time Tiernan left for battle, I was afraid he wouldn't come back, and this time he hadn't. That along with missing my parents, learning about Jorumgard's arrest, fighting with Parr — everything felt so bruisingly real. I curled into Neve and sobbed.

"Amja, amja," she soothed. She patted her coat pocket and hummed. "Seems I've lost my handkerchief. Tsiala, do you . . ."

Her bodyguard drew forward from the shadows and held out a white square. Neve wiped my tears away with the soft linen. I hated strangers seeing me like this, shaky and snotty and pathetic, but my body insisted on crying until it ran dry.

"Well now," Neve said, "this fire mage must be quite something. You can tell me all about him on the way to Ingdanrad."

"On the—" I straightened up, sniffling. "You're coming?"

"No, sweet pea. I'm going home. *You're* coming."

13.

COMMON GROUND

Rikuja and I were having breakfast in our suite when Nerio knocked. He was in his usual uniform, just like I'd switched to my black work dress. I'd packed my family's expensive clothes back into the trunk, although I'd left out the jewellery case.

"You should take this back," I said, patting the case. "I don't want to risk losing your mother's jewellery. Oh, and I've written a letter to Jorum, if you can get it to him."

Nerio inclined his head. "I will find a way."

"And our canoes — we left them on Ile vi Dévoye. Can you take them to my family in Caladheå? Neve's arranging transportation to Ingdanrad."

"Of course. Speaking of which, you may need this." He held out a purse heavy with coins.

"I'm not taking your money—" I protested.

"Consider it military funding." He set it on the dining table.

"I know this trip feels like turning your back on our friends. But I swear to god, I will free Jorumgard and find Tiernan. We will get you help as soon as possible."

"You've got six months," Rikuja said wryly. "Then I need to get home to pop out a baby."

Nerio returned her smile. "I wish you and Dunehein all the best. Your child will have wonderful parents."

"Ai, you flatterer." She hugged him then gripped his shoulders. "Stay strong. Keep standing up to your father. Speaking as a future tema, I'm sure your mother's spirit is proud of you."

He nodded, his lips pressed together. I swore he blinked back tears.

A hug didn't feel like enough for him and me. I hesitated, then placed my hands on either side of his head. Nerio tensed. He'd spent enough time around me to know what touching someone's hair meant in my culture.

He leaned his forehead against mine and pressed his palms to my pinned-up hair. "Go with grace," he murmured. "May we meet again on the other side."

❋

From our window, we watched Nerio and his father board a naval cutter in the harbour. Parr cast one last look back at the hotel. He saluted before stepping onto the gangplank. I responded with a two-hand salute, thrusting my right fist up and slapping my other hand twice against my shoulder. In a pub, it would've landed me in a fight.

As I wrenched the curtain shut, another knock came, followed by a paper slid under the door. The bold handwriting adorned with loops and swirls had to be Neve's. *Fourth floor, second door on the left. Come alone.*

I climbed the sweeping staircases and paused outside Neve's door. She always caught me off-kilter. For once I wanted to be composed around her — not sobbing, naked, or fumbling through itheran high society. I took a whiff of lavender oil and spent a moment in meditation, sensing the humidity in the air, the weight of the ocean outside.

Júni, the blonde handmaiden, answered my knock. Neve's sitting room had the same furniture as ours, but it felt vastly more lived-in. Scarves, shawls, and blankets hung over the velvet armchairs. The wine rack was half-full of bottles. A rack of petticoats was drying by the hearth, which had built up a solid layer of soot. A sweet, woody scent filled the air.

"Morning, Kateiko," Neve called from the dining room. "I'm in here."

I followed her voice. Halfway there, my water-calling senses flared. I spun and lashed out, shattering an ice spike in midair. A rain of shards tinkled onto the floorboards.

"Thought so." Tsiala, the bodyguard, lowered her arm. She'd been standing behind the door.

"You—" I sputtered. "What was that for?"

Tsiala arched an annoyingly perfect eyebrow and tapped between my collarbones. "You don't have an antayul tattoo. I had to be sure."

Neve appeared in the dining room doorway, dressed in a silk robe over a linen chemise. "Nothing personal, sweet pea. I just like to know who I'm dealing with."

I took a deep breath, silently thanking Róisín for her lesson on anchoring myself. A vision of the shoirdryge would be the last thing I needed right now. "How'd you guess?"

"That." Neve pointed at my runed ring, which had flashed with white light when I called water. "I know Gallnach smithing inside and out. Come through and you'll see."

Spread across her dining table was a mine's worth of gold jewellery — rings, brooches, earrings, hairpins, necklaces, and bracelets with a dozen types of delicate chains, all set with a rainbow of gemstones. They looked like bright berries growing on golden vines.

Neve dangled a diamond bracelet from her fingertip. "My family are goldsmiths. I travel the coast wearing their work around high society. Women ask about it, their husbands ask where to buy it — then I tell them I'm the only supplier."

"I wish I'd met you a week ago. I wouldn't have had to wear Asmalah Parr's jewellery."

"Oh, darling, I would've loved to dress you. Shame you're not getting married today." She put a sapphire pendant to my throat, hummed, and set it aside. "Which brings me to why I invited you up. I have a proposal."

"Another one?" Tsiala asked, leaning against the doorframe. "My, the girl's popular."

"Tsiala thinks she's funny," Neve said dismissively. "Though this *is* about a wedding. I've been invited to one in Ingdanrad. I wasn't going to leave for it yet, but I think you can help me, Kateiko."

I folded my arms on a chair back. "How?"

"Oh, just a teensy favour." She held a rose gold chain against me. "I want you to look into the betrothed."

"You mean spy on them?"

Neve waved her hand. "You say burn wine, I say brånnvin."

"*Everyone* says brånnvin."

"It's a figure of speech," she said impatiently. "This will help you, too. Cozy up to the bride and groom. You'll need connections to influence the druids."

It felt like trading favours with Parr, except I didn't have the faintest idea what Neve got out of this. Maybe it was a matter of high politics. Maybe she was a jilted lover. "With respect," I said, "I'm not fond of spying on strangers. Especially *for* strangers."

"Is that all we are?" Neve held an emerald chandelier earring up to me. "You should pierce your ears, sweet pea. These would look so elegant on you."

"Can we focus, please?" I pushed the earring away.

She huffed. "Fine. I see your point. Antoch Parr has made us both paranoid, hasn't he?"

"A little," I admitted.

Neve tilted her head, studying me. "How about this? I'll be busy today, selling off jewellery before we leave. If one of your brawny companions is willing to be my bodyguard, I'll leave Tsiala with you. She'll tell you whatever you want to know."

I thought that over. Ever since the céilídh on Innisburren, Geniod had been better about giving me space. I could persuade him to escort Neve, giving Dunehein and Rikuja some rare time alone together. Which left me alone with a beautiful armoured girl who'd just hurled an ice spike at my back.

Tsiala gave me a bored shrug. "I won't bite if you don't."

✳

A short time later, I went down to the hotel lobby, pulling on my wool coat. Tsiala was already there, leaning against a pillar with her arms folded. Her lips had a raspberry tint that hadn't been there earlier. She nodded in greeting and headed outside. Thick grey clouds covered the sky, turning the ocean dark and opaque.

"You okay with street food?" Tsiala asked. "We can grab lunch and head somewhere private to talk."

"Sure," I said, hurrying to keep up with her long strides.

She led me south along the harbour, away from the huge sandstone buildings. The familiar scent of fish drifted toward us. Under a long timber shelter, itherans hawked the day's catch — stacks of cod and rockfish, baskets of oysters, tubs of scuttling purple crabs. A man gutted a halibut that took up an entire table. Tsiala kept eyeing me as we passed through the market. It felt like she was testing me.

"I've been in fish markets, you know," I said. "Worked in one myself."

"Really?" She glanced at my obsidian-handled knife. "That's a ceremonial blade if I've ever seen one."

Irritation flooded through me. With it and Temal's sword taking up space on my belt, I'd stopped carrying my hunting knife. Spotting a man cleaning a bucket of surfperch, I said, "Ai. I'll give you five pann to borrow your knife."

He handed it over, bemused. I slit open a surfperch's stomach, pulled out the guts, and tossed them in a bait bucket. The fisherman nodded his approval and added the fish to his pile.

Tsiala smirked. "That desperate to impress me, huh?"

I grit my teeth. Whatever the test was, I felt pretty sure I'd failed.

Past the fish market was a cluster of food stalls radiating so much heat that the snow around them had melted into slushy pools. A handful of burly sailors were eating lunch, sitting on a low flagstone wall along the boardwalk. I bought a hollow wheat bun filled with steaming beans. Tsiala studied a baker's goods and asked for a glissetto.

I squirmed. As she took the roll, I burst out, "You know that has chicken heart, right?"

Tsiala looked me dead in the eye. She tossed the roll into the air, caught it on a dagger point, and took a bite. I gasped.

"You—" I stammered. "You're *not* Aikoto, are you?"

"Full-blooded Sverbian," she said as she chewed. "Can't you tell?"

I stared blankly until I realized she was joking. Neve put me off-kilter, but Tsiala kept flipping me upside down.

She swallowed her mouthful. "I'm from the Kowichelk Confederacy. My full name's Tsi'alha Makōpa, but if you can't pronounce it, Tsiala will do."

Now it all made sense — her chin-length hair, unnerving height, and lilting Ferish accent. The Kowichelk's territory had been overrun by Ferish immigrants. Most people just called it "the southern colonies" now. I'd heard enough about the place to know I shouldn't pry into how or why Tsiala came here.

The boardwalk took us to the southwest edge of town. We continued along a road, moving aside into deep snow whenever jingling bells signalled an approaching sleigh. The road wound up into the mountains. Swaths of dense rainforest rose on either side. Tsiala stopped by a faded timber sign marking a path to a clifftop lookout.

"Up for a hike?" she asked, lifting her arm. Snow melted from the path, exposing a carpet of rotten evergreen needles. Rivulets of water trickled down the slope.

Wishing I hadn't worn a dress, I started to climb. The path zigzagged upward, sheltered by bluish-green branches of salt spruce. While I melted the snow ahead, Tsiala reformed ice behind us.

"So nobody follows," she explained. "We can talk openly here."

A good strategy, I thought reluctantly. "Tell me about this wedding Neve mentioned."

"Merdo, where to start. Do you know about the founding clans of Ingdanrad?"

"I know what a clan is. That's about it."

"Then you know more than most people. Ingdanrad was built by three rich, powerful clans. They don't control the city anymore — they share power with elected mages — but they're still rich as kings."

"Let me guess," I said, grabbing branches to pull myself up a steep section. "Neve's one of them."

"The prissy princess?" Tsiala snickered. "Yeah, she's from Clan Ríain. They pushed to let foreigners into the city. The bride is from Clan Níall, who won't tell the weather to anyone who's not Gallnach. That's why the wedding is so weird."

"Weird how?"

"Imagine an even prissier princess. That's Síona ó Fearghas, the younger daughter of Clan Níall's chief druid. Everyone expected her to marry a rich Gallnach merchant or whatever. Instead she's marrying a lowly Ferish soldier."

"Maybe they fell in love."

"Sure. And I follow Neve around 'cause I'm in love." Tsiala sounded like she was rolling her eyes. "Trust me, if you knew Clan Níall, you'd be suspicious."

"If you say so." I paused to find a foothold on the rotten, slippery needles. "Who's the groom?"

"Alesso Spariere. He used to serve in Eremur's military, then at seventeen, he defected to Ingdanrad."

"Oh," I said as things clicked into place. "So Neve thinks I can get close to him."

"Common ground," Tsiala said. "You're used to dealing with Ferish soldiers."

"You must be, too." I twisted to point at her curved daggers. "Those are Ferish blades."

"Yeah, but I'm no diplomat. I don't give a shit about itheran politics."

"Then why are you here?"

"To spy on naked girls in the hot springs."

I whirled so fast my foot slipped. Tsiala caught my arm, steadying me. A grin flickered across her face.

Burning with embarrassment, I crested the path and emerged onto a cliff. Icy wind rustled my skirts. White-capped waves rolled across the fjord's deep blue waters. I had the sudden memory of riding a kinaru with Akohin, clinging to him as the huge bird soared over the northern tip of Burren Inlet.

Tsiala appeared next to me, the wind stirring her wavy black hair. "Why are *you* here?"

"You know why. To track down Neve."

"That's not what I mean. Did the Parrs threaten you? Blackmail you? Or there's those rumours at the Mariners' Guild, but you don't *look* knocked up."

I knotted my fingers into my skirt to keep from slapping her. It seemed impossible to explain my reasons to someone who'd just admitted to not caring. Casting about for our own common ground, I remembered one of Temal's lessons.

"Imagine you're on a sinking ship out there." I pointed at the fjord. "The forest on this side is burning. The peninsula on the other side's fine. Which way do you swim?"

"That's a stupid question. Toward the peninsula."

"Then you're leaving a wildfire to spread. Soon you'll be trapped on that peninsula, watching flames roll in. If you swim *this* way, you can put out the fire before it burns up southern Eremur."

Tsiala pursed her raspberry-tinted lips. She looked annoyed. Like she wasn't used to losing arguments.

"Say yes," she said abruptly. "Spy for Neve."

"Why?"

"Because that's your wildfire." She pointed east. "This wedding could turn Ingdanrad on its head. If the Rúonbattai are trying to sway druids against the Ferish, you can be damned sure they'll take advantage of it."

*

In the grey chill of dawn, my family and I met Neve, Tsiala, and Júni at a ferry dock. Neve had a wagon-load of matching leather trunks banded with brass. A few sleepy itherans boarded along with us. The ferry sailed up the fjord, did a hard turn around the peninsula, and headed up Burren Inlet. Near twilight, we disembarked in Rutnaast, a Sverbian mining town. This was as far east as Eremur's ferries went.

As we unloaded our luggage, freezing rain began to fall. Neve started fretting about her furs and silks getting wet. Tsiala cast me an exasperated look. While she steered rain away from Neve and her trunks, I started melting ice on the pier. The wary looks from other passengers were better than someone slipping and tumbling into the ocean.

A familiar feeling prickled at me. Colourful specks danced across my vision. I grabbed a mooring post a second before the pier vanished, leaving me floating above murky blue water. *Okay*, I reassured myself. *Stay still and you'll be fine.*

Then I looked up.

A schooner had capsized, crushing the pier. Broken boards floated throughout the harbour. Trees, wagons, and rowboats had smashed into timber buildings, caving them in. A thick layer of undisturbed snow coated the wreckage. The entire place was a ghost town.

I blinked. Rutnaast returned whole and alive, bustling as people escaped the rain. I hadn't seen so much damage in the shoirdryge since the wasteland around Nettle Ginu. Thousands of people here had simply . . . vanished. Dead or escaped, I couldn't say, but the less time we spent here, the better.

We checked into a small, smoky inn. The rooms here were communal and segregated by gender. Another new bed, another strange place to lay my fir branch blanket. Neve changed into a lace-trimmed flannel gown. Júni, the other itheran lodgers, and I stripped down to our linen chemises. I was curious to see Tsiala out of her leather armour, but she hadn't removed it by the time I fell asleep.

Wildfire filled my dreams. The white-robed Rúonbattai cleric stood in the burning ruins of Rutnaast, wreathed by smoke and embers. She lifted a crossbow, loaded a burning bolt, and fixed her pale eyes on me.

I jerked awake, panting and sweating. Rikuja lay asleep in the next bed. The murmurs and shuffling of sleeping women filled the room.

"Psst," came a voice.

Tsiala sat against the wall in a sliver of moonlight. I draped my blanket over my shoulders and padded over to her. She wore a knit wool coat, cream-coloured and patterned with grey birds and geometric shapes. I wondered if it was Kowichelk-made. She handed me a flask. Recognizing the scent of mezcale, I took a swig. Neither of us seemed inclined to talk, so we just sat together in silence, her warm arm against mine.

14.

INGDANRAD

The closest thing to a ferry between Rutnaast and Ingdanrad was the postal ship, a two-masted ketch whose yellowing sails and peeling paint had seen better days. Thankfully, we were the only passengers, so while my family watched the passing scenery, I followed Neve into the warmth below deck. Tsiala's explanation of Gallnach culture had left me with plenty of questions.

"I know how Sverbian names work," I began. "I assume Lisehl comes from your mother. But I got lost with clan names and such."

"Oh, Gallnach names are simple," Neve said, picking at a canvas bag of exotic nuts. "My full name is Níamh ó Lónan ó Ríain."

"That's simple?"

"If you know the system." She held out her bag, offering me some. "Walnuts are marvellous, you know. They contaminate the soil so nothing else can grow around them."

Neve seemed perpetually distracted, so I'd given up fighting it. I tried a nut, surprised to find it soft and crumbly.

"Gallnach people have two surnames," she went on. "Patronym first, then clan name. My full name means Níamh, daughter of Lónan, daughter of Clan Ríain. These days we mainly just use patronyms. Most clans got scattered by the invasion of Gallun."

"Sounds familiar," I said. "It's easier to go by Kateiko Leniere than explain my history. Ferish people just assume my father was a carpenter."

"Oh yes, about that." She sprawled out on a bunk. "I didn't want to pry, but Tsiala mentioned you don't have a jouyen tattoo."

"It's complicated. I was born Rin, my parents became Tula, and I live on Iyo territory, but I'm not sworn to any of them."

"Hmm." Neve started tossing a walnut in the air and catching it. "How should I introduce you in Ingdanrad? A friend? Diplomat? Military liaison?"

"A friend, I guess. I'm not a formal liaison. And if there are Rúonbattai in the city, I'd rather not flaunt my work with the military."

"Then may I give you some advice, sweet pea? The best lies are closest to the truth. For example, I always say I grew up out east in Nyhemur. I *did* spend my childhood there at Sverbian boarding school. I just wasn't born there."

"Too bad that story won't work for me," I said dryly. "Otherwise we could say we're schoolmates."

"But saying we met naked in the hot springs is so much more fun." She grinned and tossed a walnut at me. "Don't worry. We'll start small with my family."

✳

As we sailed east, the long stretches of Burren Inlet all looked the same — rocky beaches, forested slopes, the occasional fishing ship. When I woke at dawn, I found the inlet transformed. Barren mountains soared so far overhead I had to lean back to see their peaks, backlit by the rising sun. Clouds of sparkling snow gusted into the sky.

"Look," Rikuja said with delight, pointing.

At the end of the inlet, terraces spiralled up a mountain like enormous stairs. At first the place looked uninhabited. Then, like a shoirdryge coming into focus, Ingdanrad revealed itself. The city had been carved *into* the mountain. What I'd thought were shadows were thousands of windows, doors, and archways. Snowy roads ran alongside the spiral of terraces, curving around natural rock pillars and flowing into bridges over narrow gorges.

"Yan taku," I breathed.

"You should see it in autumn," Neve said, appearing at my side. "Those terraces are golden with barley. Looks like the entire mountain's been gilded."

Ochre-sailed ships filled a harbour at the base of the mountain. Three flags gusted over the port. I recognized the Sverbian flag, a white raven on pale blue, and the Kae-jouyen crest, a moss-green heron on white. The third, a black crow on red, had the colours of Gallun. Neve explained that the crow was a war goddess whose caw foretold death. It was on Ingdanrad's flag as a guardian, watching over the city.

Neve pointed out landmarks. Midway up the mountain, a five-storey hospital had been dug into an immense cliff. Greenhouses and dormitory towers formed the visible tips of a sprawling underground university campus. The founding clans each had a walled villa high on the slopes. Higher yet was the Aerie, a stone-and-crystal pyramid where Ingdanrad's ruling mages met.

As we tied up at a pier, soldiers in red woolwraps swarmed toward us. On recognizing Neve, they bowed and drew back. Dockhands unloaded our luggage. All seven of us crammed into a horse-drawn sleigh. The horses were small but tough, protected by fluffy winter coats. Passersby watched curiously as we jolted up the mountain, following hairpin turns in the road.

At a walled terrace, we passed through tall gates into a courtyard. This was one of the few parts of the city with freestanding buildings. Icicles hung from gables above ivy-covered stone walls. Women dyed fabric in huge tubs, filling the air with a sour smell. Kids and dogs played in the snow, running and leaping and shrieking.

Neve had an odd expression. Relief, maybe, and a tinge of nervousness. Catching my eye, she smiled ruefully. "Remember I said we'd start small? I may have forgotten what it's like to be home."

❊

Inside Clan Ríain's great hall, we got swept into a torrent of Neve's family — aunts, uncles, cousins, second cousins, third cousins. Hardly any spoke Coast Trader, and I could hardly tell them apart. They were all small and pale, and almost everyone wore plum-coloured woolwraps. The only people who stood out were a few druids wearing burlap robes and red wool pendants looped into diamond-shaped knots. In the chaos, I didn't notice Tsiala and Júni had disappeared until Geniod quietly pointed it out.

Over a lunch of fish stew served at long tables, Neve explained that Ingdanrad had started as a surface city. As it grew and required more space for farmland, nearly everything had been moved underground. The villa's big windows and fresh air were a luxury here. Rikuja craned her neck to examine the vaulted ceiling, no doubt comparing the woodwork to the Iyo shrine. Dunehein and Geniod seemed more interested in the axes and swords hung on the smoke-stained stone walls.

Meals here were served in shifts, so as new people arrived, we had more introductions. Neve's brothers appeared with sweaty brows and flushed cheeks from working over hot forges. Both were fluent in Trader, though neither had their sister's Sverbian accent. We were still talking when servants laid the table for dinner. With it came more new people, including a woman with strawberry-blonde hair in burlap robes. To my shock, Neve introduced the woman as her mother, Laoise.

"Oh," I stammered. "I didn't know you were a druid."

Laoise turned an accusing eye on Neve. "You didn't tell them?"

"Tell who what?" A wiry man with round spectacles drifted over. His coppery hair was pulled back with a ribbon at the nape of his neck. Tiny burns flecked his tunic and woolwrap. "Oh. Welcome back, Níamh."

"Our daughter misplaced her family pride," Laoise said coolly. "She no longer finds it relevant to mention she's the child of druids."

Neve dropped her chin, looking guilty. "Papa, meet my new friend, Kateiko Leniere. This is her cousin and his wife, Dunehein and Rikuja Iyo, and her uncle, Geniod Tula. Darling guests, meet my father Lónan, chief druid of Clan Ríain."

I rounded on Neve, speechless. It took a special degree of flightiness to forget to mention *that*.

Geniod nudged me, then lifted a hand in greeting to Lónan. "Hanekei. It's an honour to meet you and your family."

Abashed, I repeated the greeting. The second Lónan and Laoise sat down at our table, a servant hurried over to pour water. Another swapped their wooden dishes with gold-rimmed porcelain. Yet another brought flagons of golden ale and red wine. It took me until well into dinner to work up the nerve to ask Lónan why he didn't wear druid robes.

He flashed me an understanding smile. "Clan Ríain specializes in metallurgy. We don't wear robes at work since it's a hazard around a hot forge." He unhooked one of Neve's gold earrings. Ignoring her protests, he laid it on his palm. The metal glowed white-hot and melted.

Dunehein leaned in to examine the molten gold. "Was that fire magic?"

"Not in the sense you think." Lónan rolled the gold into a ball and dropped it into his mug, making the water sizzle. "Heat is a key part of earth magic, from metallurgy to architecture to agriculture. Back in the old country, a few druids married Sverbian soldiers and shared their knowledge. Their descendants bastardized it into the crude weapon known as 'fire magic.'"

"It's not always crude." Feeling obligated to defend Tiernan, I rummaged in my purse for the gold coin he'd etched with a leafy nine-branched oak. "A Sverbian fire mage crafted this."

Lónan examined the coin, adjusting his spectacles. "You're sure the mage is Sverbian?"

I paused, taken aback. "Yes. You might've met him — Tiernan Heilind. He lived here about a decade ago."

"Heilind?" Lónan's brows creased. "It doesn't ring a bell. I meet too many mages to remember, though. It's an inherent part of being on the mage assembly."

"The what?"

"Ingdanrad's government. The chief druid of each founding clan has a seat, and the public elects four other mages — two Gallnach, one Sverbian, one Kae. Our ancestors here in Clan Ríain were the main proponents of the assembly."

"So you . . . have close ties to Sverbians?"

"*Some* Sverbians," Neve cut in. "Not the Rúonbattai. Speaking of which . . . Mama, Papa, there's something we should tell you."

She gestured for me to go ahead. Her family had heard about disguised sailors attacking Innisburren, so I skipped to our theory that the Rúonbattai's plan was to turn druids against the Ferish. Neve's parents looked strangely unfazed.

"Let them try," Laoise said breezily. "Ingdanrad has been neutral for more than a century."

Lónan nodded, adjusting his spectacles. "And the other two founding clans aren't fond of Sverbians. If the Rúonbattai try to recruit anyone, it'll be us."

"Maybe not," Neve countered. "Clan Níall are the agriculture experts. Just look at Mama."

Off our curious looks, Laoise explained, "My birth clan specializes in botany. I oversee the university gardens. If the Rúonbattai want a long treatise on the taxonomy of fungus, they know where to find me. Otherwise, I doubt they'll bother."

My family and I traded wary glances. We'd come all this way to warn the Gallnach, only for two of their most powerful druids to bury their heads in the sand. Preventing this alliance might be far harder than I'd expected.

*

Servants showed us to the guest chambers. My room was lavishly decorated — a four-poster bed with silk hangings, wrought-iron candelabras, a desk and chair carved from exotic wood. Someone had brought my carryframe and clothes trunk. I unpacked my embroidered fir branch blanket, pulled off my boots, and collapsed into bed.

After what felt like no time, a knock awoke me. Sunlight streamed through the curtains. Groggily, I opened the door. Neve held a breakfast tray, hanging her head like a scolded puppy. She set the tray on my desk and began pouring two mugs of dark liquid.

"Ever had coffee?" she asked. "I bought some beans in Port Alios."

I'd *heard* of it. Jonalin had handled shipments of it in Caladheå, but we could never afford it. Not wanting to admit that, I sniffed the liquid. It smelled like burnt earth. I took a sip and choked on the bitterness.

Neve perched on my chair, clutching her mug. "I meant to tell you about my family. I just . . ."

"You what?"

She huffed. "Look at them all. My older brother will be chief druid one day. The best earth magic I can pull off is flipping a pebble, so my parents shipped me away to boarding school, like they're *ashamed* of me. At least I could learn Sverbian and become a merchant or diplomat or something useful—"

Neve broke off, wiping her eyes. My irritation melted. I knew how it felt to get sent away from home, then to return as someone who no longer fit in, but at least my family was always supportive.

"My parents don't even listen to me," Neve went on. "They don't think it's suspicious that Síona ó Fearghas is marrying a Ferish soldier. 'It's just a young couple in love,' they say. They've spent so long shut up in this stone fortress, they've forgotten what the real world is like."

"So . . . it'll be a breeze convincing them of a Rúonbattai conspiracy to sway them against the Ferish?"

She gave a shaky laugh. "Maybe we need to trap a crow in the courtyard. An omen of death and chaos."

I sighed, thinking of my conversation with Tsiala. We were on the edge of a wildfire no one else could see. "Look, you and I can help each other, but we have to be honest. Equal. Not like dealing with Antoch Parr."

Neve nodded. "Agreed."

"In that case, I need a favour. I'm looking for one of Tiernan's contacts here, a Sverbian surgeon named Janekke Noorjehl. They were trading information about the Rúonbattai."

"Oh, that's easy," Neve said, brightening. "I'll have someone check the hospital. And speaking of Tiernan, I need to ask you something again. Full honesty this time."

"What is it?"

She took his dusty letter off the bedside table. "Is this man really just a friend, or is there something more?"

I grimaced. I'd set Tiernan and myself up for a lifetime of questions about our pretend affair. "He's really just a friend. Captain Valrose knows we're close, so it was the most believable story."

"Then in the name of honesty, I have to tell you something." Neve leaned in and whispered, "Tsiala thinks you're pretty."

✳

Even after Neve left so I could get dressed, her words rattled around in my head. Had Tsiala thought I was pretty before or after seeing me naked at the hot springs? Was it just a stray thought, or was she interested in me? Had she told me to spy for Neve so I'd be around more?

It didn't matter. Sure, Tsiala was lush, but looks didn't make up for her personality. She was rude, combative, judgmental, and perpetually bored. I would've transformed her into a stained-glass window if I could spend eternity looking at her and never hear another word out of her mouth.

I juddered around my room, wringing my hands. Every nerve in my body was alight. Sweat soaked my heavy wool dress. I needed air. I stumbled down the hall and out to the courtyard. Sunshine reflected off the snow, blinding me.

"Whoa." Tsiala got up from a bench. "Where's the fire?"

"What?" I squinted at her. "There's no — wait, are you stalking me?"

"Yeah. My first day off in weeks and I decided to stalk my employer's new friend."

I raised my hand to block the sunlight. She'd traded her armour for her patterned knit coat — the one she'd worn that night in Rutnaast, drinking mezcale in the dark, her arm pressed against mine. My breath caught.

"You okay?" Tsiala put her hand to my neck, checking my pulse, then leaned in and sniffed me. "Ah. Neve drugged you."

"What?"

"Coffee. She must've brewed it too strong. Not used to kitchen work, that girl."

"She — how do I cure it?"

"Eh. Burn off some energy." Tsiala drew a curved dagger and twirled it. "Feel like sparring?"

"On your day off? Sounds like *you're* desperate to impress *me*."

She blanched. I hadn't expected throwing her words back at her to work. A thrill of triumph shot through me. Thanks to Neve, I finally had an edge.

"Not with blades," I said, shaping fallen snow into a water whip. "With this."

Tsiala sheathed her dagger and unclasped her knit coat. As she tossed it aside, I stifled a gasp. Her sleeveless shirt exposed tattoos on every bit of her arms. Geometric ink patterns wrapped around her curving muscles. At her height, she could easily pick me up and —

I clamped down on that thought, but it was too late. Forget sparring. There were a hundred other ways I wanted to burn off energy with Tsi'alha Makōpa.

15.

WILDFIRE

Neve's first idea for reconnaissance was hosting a winter garden party for Ingdanrad's "eminent youths." I could meet Síona ó Fearghas and Alesso Spariere, and Neve could eavesdrop on Sverbian guests for any hint of Rúonbattai activity. Since we'd be outside, she suggested I wear my everyday wool dress and brighten it with my fox fur mantle. She and Júni delighted in painting my face with cosmetics and picking out my jewellery, settling on silver beads woven into my braid.

Servants arranged everything for the party. On a flagstone patio near Clan Ríain's frosty vineyards, we found wrought-iron furniture arranged around a bonfire. An icy breeze sent eddies of snow scurrying across the ground. Rune-engraved rocks kept tables of food and drink warm. The view was astonishing. We could see up to the mountain peak, down to the harbour, and out across the inlet, which sparkled under the sun.

Neve introduced me to each arriving guest. Several were from the founding clans, wearing plum woolwraps for Ríain, storm blue for Níall, or burgundy for Murragh. Others were the children of respected mages, scholars, artists, merchants, or militia officers. Two Kae in moss-green woolwraps were the teenage son and daughter of the Okoreni-Kae. Neve didn't mention anything about a brawny Sverbian other than his name, Ivar, but judging by the way she batted her eyelashes at him, I could guess why he'd been invited.

As I started wondering if Síona and Alesso had snubbed us, a sleigh whisked down the long mountain road. Out stepped a young man with dark features and the red woolwrap of Ingdanrad's militia. He reached back to help a pretty blonde girl climb down. While most druids dressed plainly, she'd belted her burlap robes with a gold chain and put her hair up in an intricate weave. She stood on her toes and kissed the young man's cheek. He steeled himself and led her hand in hand toward the party.

Neve swept forward and hugged the girl. They spoke in rapid Gallnach, all smiles and laughter, then switched to Coast Trader to make the introductions. Alesso kissed Neve's mittened hand, then mine. Síona gave me a warm smile and complimented my fox fur mantle. If she disliked foreigners as much as her clan supposedly did, she was good at hiding it.

Throughout the party, Síona seemed at ease, chatting with anyone and everyone. Alesso stood stiffly, hands behind his back, always late to laugh at a joke. I wondered what Síona saw in him. He was handsome enough — shiny black hair, a neat beard, a soldier's muscular build — but they seemed like complete opposites. She was a bright fuzzy bumblebee, bouncing from one conversation to another, while he was a mouse hiding in the shadows.

My attempts at talking to the couple went nowhere. Someone or another kept interrupting to discuss their wedding. When Síona got caught in a long conversation about her dress, Alesso backed away to gaze across the harbour. I poured two mugs of tea, still steaming thanks to the rune-heated rocks, and followed him. "You must be cold," I said in my best Ferish. "Try this. It's no Ferland black, but it's nice."

Alesso gaped at me. "You — where did you learn my language?"

"Caladheå. I apprenticed at an apothecary. When the Fourth Elken War broke out, I started serving as a war medic."

He chuckled incredulously. Accepting a mug, he said, "I used to serve in Eremur myself. It feels like a lifetime ago."

"What brought you to Ingdanrad?" I asked, trying to sound casual.

"I suppose it's not much of a secret here." Alesso turned to the bonfire and lifted his hand, pulling a ball of flames toward us. "Eremur's military couldn't teach me that. Ingdanrad's militia could."

"Ah." I smiled. "The power of the druids."

"In a fashion. Combat magic isn't the same as druidism." He released the flames, letting them wink out. "Síona's father has made that *very* clear."

"Ai, yeah — the chief druid. What's his name again? Fearghas ó Donnabhán?"

Alesso choked on his tea. He thumped his chest, coughing. "It's Fearghas *och* Donnabhán. You just called him a woman."

I winced. Neve had failed to mention that, too — though that might've been a genuine mistake. She'd been distracted like always while explaining Gallnach names, and she'd been introducing people by first name only so I didn't get overwhelmed.

"Don't worry," Alesso reassured me. "I made the same mistake after moving here."

"It's a lot, isn't it?" I gazed up at snowy terraces rising toward the mountain peak. "Hard enough to learn a new language, let alone marry into a new culture."

He shook his head. "You have no idea."

"Well . . ." I hadn't wanted to mention it, but I had him talking, confiding in me. "Actually, I was supposed to marry a Ferish lieutenant a few days ago."

"Really? Who?"

"Nerio Parr. Son of Captain Antoch Parr."

"Really." Alesso leaned in, his dark eyes sparkling. "I've never met the Parrs, but I've heard rumours. What's the captain like?"

I froze. "He's . . . effective. Very skilled."

"I should say so. His victories are impressive. But of course—" He cleared his throat. "I'm being rude. Dare I ask what happened with your engagement?"

"Nothing, really. It was an arranged marriage, and I . . . have someone else. A mercenary."

"Ahhh." Alesso's face softened. "The heart wants what it wants. I didn't truly understand that until Síona."

I pasted on a smile. "You must really love her."

"More than life." He cast a wistful gaze at the girl laughing with her friends. "I've been in Ingdanrad nine years and Síona's the only person who truly welcomed me. I know what people say — that I'm marrying her for money or power. But I'd still love her if she were a peasant with no postal box."

Every nerve in my body flinched. Technically *I* was a peasant with no postal box. It was a figure of speech, but still.

Alesso turned to me with a searching look. "Come to the wedding."

"What?"

"None of the guests speak Ferish. I just want to . . . merdo, to hear my own language on my wedding day, to swear about my father-in-law and have someone understand—"

"Sacro dios," I muttered, making him laugh. "Don't you have family coming? Friends?"

His face twisted. "My friends turned their backs on me when I left Eremur. As for family, I have none left alive."

"Oh," I said softly. No matter what I thought of Alesso, no one deserved to be alone at their wedding. "Tell you what. I can lend you my family. I've got a huge cousin who'll scare off anyone you dislike, his pregnant wife who'll sob with happiness, and an uncle who'll soothe your nerves with the best damned tea you can imagine."

✳

"You're marvellous," Neve proclaimed, spinning in circles as we walked back to the villa. "I knew you'd do well, but getting your whole family invited to the wedding?"

"Are you still suspicious about it?" I asked, tucking my hands under my arms. The sun had set, bringing a chill.

"Oh, more than ever." She fell back into step with me. "Síona's very coy about how they met. She just says it's a small town, but fifteen thousand people live here. What'd you make of Alesso?"

"I can't tell," I admitted. "He seems *too* determined to convince me they're in love. Plus he's clearly ambitious, if he defected from Eremur to learn fire magic — but he's only half the story. I mean, what does Síona get out of this marriage? Why agree to it unless she loves him?"

"Dunno. Maybe he's amazing in bed."

I elbowed her. She spun away, giggling.

Neither of us had heard anything about the Rúonbattai. I hadn't expected to, since no one here seemed concerned with a distant war they weren't part of, but a worse blow was coming. Tsiala awaited us at the villa gates with news. Janekke Noorjehl wasn't in Ingdanrad. She'd gone east to Nyhemur to treat rural patients, and she wasn't expected back for weeks.

I hadn't realized how much I'd been counting on Janekke's help until it got ripped away. Nerio had given me the name of another of Tiernan's contacts here, a druid named Iollan och Cormic, but he'd been emphatic that I should stay away from the druid unless absolutely necessary. "Not unless you or your family are *dying*, understand?" he'd said. "That man makes my father look like a paragon of virtue."

Still, we had plenty else to do. Tsiala went to the militia barracks and asked which bunk was Alesso's so she could leave a note about wedding plans. Scraping a quick look around, she found a bundle of letters under his bunk. It was odd for someone with no family or friends to have gotten so much mail. Odder yet that he'd hidden it.

Neve came up with a way to get a better look at the letters. Soon it'd be Ólmhain, the Gallnach's sacred day of winter. At dusk the Gallnach would go deep underground for their seasonal rites. So would Alesso for his formal conversion to druidism before marrying Síona. With only Sverbians to guard the city, the barracks would be left empty. The only problem was Tsiala couldn't read. I'd have to go with her.

Near sunset we walked down the mountain. Everything was eerily quiet, the road empty, the harbour market closed. The militia complex had been dug into the northwest mountainside. Dunehein and Rikuja lingered outside as lookouts, pretending to enjoy the view, while Geniod watched in his eagle body. Tsiala and I peered through a wall of windows, checking that the place was empty, then slipped through the lobby into the barracks.

They were a stark contrast from the villa. Twenty beds per room, all neatly made up with grey bedding. Twenty wooden chests for soldiers' belongings. Tsiala got onto her knees and fished under Alesso's bunk for his letters. I stopped her just in time from untying the string around the bundle. Thanks to Jonalin's obsession with sailors' knots, I knew we'd never be able to retie this one. Instead we slid the letters out from the loop of string. I skimmed a few, checking the signatures.

"Weird," I muttered. "They're all from Síona. Why bother writing letters when they live in the same city?"

Tsiala shrugged. "Maybe she's too high and mighty to come down the mountain in person."

I checked the dates. The letters were in chronological order, starting about three years ago. I could hardly make sense of the early ones. They were in Ferish but so full of spelling and grammar mistakes that it was like a child's writing. Over time they got more coherent, more like the thoughts of a sophisticated young woman.

"Ohhh," I said slowly. "I think Alesso was teaching her Ferish."

"Really?" Tsiala peered over my shoulder.

I tried not to think about how close she was. How the savoury scent of oiled leather armour filled my nose. Burning with awkwardness, I said, "My last lover taught me to read and write. We traded letters for practice."

"Sounds fascinating. Is that how you fell in love? Mooning at each other over the inkpot?"

I ignored her sarcasm. She'd made a good point. Síona's early letters were mundane, talking about the weather or her family. "Huh. It doesn't look like Alesso was trying to share his language with a lover — at least not at first. They did this for a year before the letters turned romantic."

Tsiala leaned against the bunk, twirling a dagger. "So the princess of Clan Níall learned Ferish for her own personal reasons. My, my."

"What's the point? Who else in Ingdanrad even speaks Ferish?"

"Nobody. Well, the linguists at the university, but they speak every language on this coast. Síona could have her pick. Which means ..." Tsiala arched an eyebrow. "Huh. *That* would be a scandal."

"What?"

"Síona's mother is a diplomat. She was an envoy to the Caladheå Council until Ingdanrad cut ties to Eremur. Maybe Síona wants to secretly reopen diplomacy."

Frowning, I kept flipping through the letters. "Wonder if she mentions — oh. *Oh.* I'm not reading that. Glad they have a healthy sex life, though."

Tsiala snickered. "Wow. Neve will be mad she missed this."

I skipped to the last letter. The handwriting changed from Síona's elegant loops to harsh strokes. I read aloud. "*My dear nephew. I deeply regret that I cannot attend your wedding, but I hope a gift of ten thousand sovereigns will help start your new life* ... Shit. Alesso said he doesn't have any living family. Lying bastard."

Tsiala whistled. "Goddamn, that's a lot of money. Who sent it?"

I flipped the letter over. "Armando Contere."

"Contere?"

I looked up. Tsiala had gone deathly pale.

"Fucking hell," she said. "Alesso Spariere isn't just some lowly soldier. His uncle's a warlord."

16.

WEDDING DAY

The Gallnach wouldn't come back above ground until tomorrow, and Clan Ríain's Sverbian servants had that time off, so we had the villa to ourselves. Tsiala and Júni joined my family in the shadowy, echoing great hall for a dinner of reheated mutton stew. I'd never known until now if Júni was Sverbian or excellent at faking the accent. It was difficult to notice her when Neve demanded so much attention — and when Tsiala had my attention without even trying.

Tsiala still looked unnerved by our discovery. Armando Contere lived in the southern colonies where she was from. The colonies were ever-changing, rupturing in and out of existence, the borders as slippery as the blood spilled to claim them. Contere had survived longer than most warlords in the region. Tsiala didn't explain why his mere name had rattled her, and I didn't ask.

It seemed Neve and I had *both* been right about the wedding. Alesso and Síona genuinely loved each other. They were also secretive, ambitious, and possibly forging a powerful alliance. What we didn't know was who they were allying against. It could be the other founding clans, Ingdanrad's mage assembly, Eremur, or the Rúonbattai.

On Neve's return to the surface, she kept switching between bewilderment, fury, and triumphant crowing that she knew there was something strange about this wedding. The only thing we felt sure of was we couldn't look away now. This wildfire was on the verge of erupting. So we decided to stick as close to Alesso as possible, following through on my promise to lend him a family.

Between my pretend engagement and Nicoletta's endless twittering about hers, I had a decent idea of what was traditional for Ferish weddings. Dunehein and Geniod took Alesso out for a night of drinking, his last chance as a "free man." In Gallnach marriages, only the bride got a ring, while in Ferish marriages, the groom did as well, so Neve's brothers crafted a gold ring for Alesso.

Early on the wedding day, he arrived at Clan Ríain's villa. Neve ushered him into a guest chamber we'd decorated with evergreen sprigs. Her brothers, Dunehein, and Geniod took over getting him dressed and ready. Geniod had made a special tea blend — fermented chokecherry leaves to imitate Ferish black tea, sweet fruit oils, and lavender to soothe the nerves. The scent wafted through the villa's halls.

Thankfully, we still had our fine clothes Captain Parr bought for my wedding. Neve lent me a silver filigree headband and an amethyst necklace, and she lent Rikuja thin gold cords to weave into her braid. It was traditional for Gallnach warriors to show off their finest weapons at weddings, so I sheathed my obsidian-handled knife on my hip. Neve went with ruby jewellery that made her strawberry-blonde hair look golden in comparison.

We met Alesso in the courtyard. He'd traded his red militia woolwrap for emerald green, the colour of the Ferish flag. A matching sash draped over one shoulder and a sword with an emerald set in the pommel hung at his waist. He looked on the verge of passing out. I felt a pang of sympathy. Just because his uncle was a warlord didn't mean Alesso was the same. Maybe he was like Nerio who tried to reconcile his hatred of Parr's methods with love for his last living relative.

I took Alesso's hands and spoke soothingly in Ferish. "You'll be fine. If you start to panic, just look for my face."

He gave a shaky laugh. "Thank you, Kateiko. I never thought . . ." He swallowed hard. "Let's just say meeting you was a welcome surprise."

❋

The ceremony site was the highest part of Ingdanrad, far above the treeline. Icy wind blew across a terrace encircled by jagged stone pillars. The only greenery was lichen growing on the rocks. Midwinter seemed like an odd time to get married here — then the pillars began to glow orange and radiate heat. The smell of burning lichen filled the air. Hundreds of guests crowded around, clutching their fur coats and holding their hats.

Alesso and Síona stood together on the terrace, her skirts gusting around their legs. She'd traded her burlap robes for a storm-blue woolwrap over a white silk dress. Her father, Fearghas och Donnabhán, performed the rites. His voice rolled out like thunder. Neve, at my side, quietly translated. The druid was calling on the mother of mountains to bless the couple with health, wisdom, prosperity, and children. In return they swore to care for the world she'd birthed. I half expected the goddess to smite my family for being in a sacred Gallnach site, but no earthquakes interrupted the wedding.

A few times, Alesso found my face in the crowd. Mostly his gaze stayed on Síona. Crystals decorated her blonde braid, sparkling in the winter sunshine. After the prayer, Alesso tied emerald-green cloth around her wrist, and she tied storm-blue around his. Alesso swept her into a deep kiss. Deafening cheers filled the mountainside as the new couple raised their joined hands, grinning.

The perpetual knot in my stomach tightened. Whatever this wedding meant, whatever alliance they'd been forging, it was done — and we'd helped. I glanced at my family and found Rikuja wiping her eyes. Despite everything, I laughed.

"I *knew* you'd cry," I said.

She elbowed me. "Hush, you."

Alesso and Síona left in a sleigh pulled by two white horses. Everyone else's sleighs followed in a convoy, bells jingling as we descended a winding road. Every time we neared a guard tower, soldiers inside rang huge brass bells in response. The clanging summoned people outside to watch. We passed the Aerie, the stone-and-crystal tower that housed the mage assembly, then the founding clans' villas, the university gardens and dorms, and hundreds of underground houses and workshops.

The only place big enough for the reception was the Hollow, a cavern low on the mountain's south side. I expected something dark and stuffy, maybe with dripping water. Instead a tunnel led into a vast bright hall. The sloping roof was glass, streaked with snow and ice, held up by wrought-iron columns. Flowering vines covered the stone walls. Neve looked delighted at my family's stunned expressions.

"It's one of the jewels of Ingdanrad," she said. "Clan Murragh designed it, Clan Ríain crafted the columns, and Clan Níall grew the vines. It's meant to show unity."

Long tables had been set with storm-blue linens, polished silverware, and vases of fresh flowers. Servants moved around the hall offering drinks. A harried man dashed past muttering about napkins. The newlyweds did the rounds, greeting guests, then took their seats on a raised dais. Alesso had insisted my family, Neve, and her brothers got places of honour near the dais, which earned us curious looks from other guests.

During the feast, Neve pointed out people from out of town — Sverbian diplomats from Nyhemur, the elderly Okorebai-Kae and her family, Gallnach who lived in Eremur or beyond. Geniod nudged me and pointed at a druid with curly red hair. Róisín ó Conn was talking with a Sverbian woman who looked unnerved by the druid's wandering gaze.

"That's a good sign," I whispered. "Róisín wouldn't have left Innisburren if they were still getting attacked by Rúonbattai."

"A bad sign if the Rúonbattai shifted their focus here," Geniod countered.

Preoccupied, I barely tasted the food. We'd been here two weeks with no sign of the Rúonbattai. No oak and lilac crests, no inter-ference in the wedding, no one trying to influence Neve's family. I wondered if she'd made it up to trick me into spying for her. It seemed strange for Tiernan's friend Janekke to leave Ingdanrad if she thought the Rúonbattai were a threat.

As the hall grew dark, servants lit candles in wrought-iron holders. After the feast, as the servants hauled away the tables, a commotion began on the dais. Síona's older sister Caoimhe, the future chief druid of Clan Níall, was leading a chant. Alesso, half laughing and half grimacing, got to his feet and raised his hands. Across the entire hall, the candles winked out.

Gasps rose around us, followed by oohs as everyone's eyes adjusted. Glowing runes spiralled up the iron pillars and across the glass ceiling, filling the hall with soft light. Caoimhe spread her arms and proclaimed, "Let the ball begin!"

Fiddlers, drummers, and other musicians began playing. A few men had leather bags with pipes that I recognized from the céilídh on Innisburren. I recognized the dances, too — the clapping and stomping and whirl of woolwraps. This time I wasn't injured, so I had no excuse when Neve dragged my family and me off to teach us the steps. Dunehein and Rikuja gave in laughingly. Geniod resisted until Róisín ó Conn showed up and pulled him in.

Eventually I collapsed on a bench, exhausted. Róisín followed with two cups of whisky. "Liquid bread," she said, handing me one.

I managed a smile. "The great uniter, right?"

Her gaze drifted across my head. "What's got you so wound up, lass?"

Without meaning to, I looked toward Alesso and Síona, tangled in the dancing. There was no point lying to Róisín, so quietly I said, "We think they're plotting something."

"Oh?" She fixed her pale green eyes on the couple. "They're plotting to make each other very happy tonight."

I sputtered. "That's—"

"Not our business? I agree." She sipped her whisky. "Anything else?"

"The Rúonbattai," I blurted. "They want to sway the druids here against the Ferish."

"So I've heard. The Parrs visited me on their way back to Caladheå." Róisín's gaze drifted toward the rune-lit glass ceiling. "I think we're safe for tonight, though. The Rúonbattai work in shadows. This isn't their time to strike."

"But . . ." I faltered.

"Look past the newlyweds, the guests, the servants. Who else is here?"

I looked. Around the hall's perimeter stood dozens of guards in red woolwraps. "The militia?"

"Exactly. They've protected Ingdanrad for more than two centuries before we got here." Róisín's eyes crinkled with a smile. "How about the same deal again? Promise to stay out of trouble, and I'll get you a few hours away from your uncle."

I pressed my fingers to my lips, thinking. Neve had given Tsiala the night off, and I didn't know anyone else here to dance with. I wondered if Tiernan had ever attended a wedding reception in this hall. If he were here now, would he ask me to dance?

That invasive weed burst into my mind again, wondering if he'd wanted to kiss me in Tjarnnaast. This pretend affair was messing with my head. Róisín must be getting a *wildly* wrong impression of things.

"Sure," I stammered. "I'll stay out of trouble."

Róisín winked, downed her whisky, and headed for Geniod. I couldn't hear their conversation, but I imagined her seducing him with the promise of some greenhouse restricted to druids, or an exotic herb that only grew underground. Geniod looked my way. I waved him off. Warily, he followed Róisín out of the Hollow.

The dances had switched from group ones to partnered ones. Neve twirled about the floor with a young man in a burgundy sash and woolwrap from Clan Murragh. Dunehein was easy to spot, towering over the crowd as he danced with Rikuja. I surreptitiously watched to see how people found partners. Mostly men invited women, but sometimes it went the other way.

Three dances in, no one had invited me. Neve had said my outfit was perfect, but now my collar seemed too high, my bell sleeves too wide, my black clothes too harsh among the jewel-toned wool-wraps. On noticing a Clan Níall boy eyeing me, I offered a smile. He returned it tentatively. *Okay*, I told myself. *Just talk to him. And hope he speaks Trader.*

I drifted over. "So, uh . . ." I waved at the vines on the walls. "I heard your clan grew those."

The boy nodded. "Aye. There's four types of vines, and they each bloom in different seasons."

"Really?" I tried to sound perky and interested. "Maybe you could tell me about them during a dance?"

He glanced me up and down. "Do you know how?"

"Not exactly, but I can learn."

"Yeah, good luck with that." He walked off.

Once, in Caladheå, I'd seen a man get kicked by a horse. That was roughly how I felt. Never had it been so clear that I didn't belong here.

"Yan taku," said a deep voice. "That was rude."

I turned, expecting a Kae boy. To my surprise, I looked up into the blue eyes of a young itheran man. His white-blond hair and beard were trimmed short, highlighting the angles of his face. A sword hung at his waist.

"Oh," I said, recognizing him. "We met at Neve's garden party. Ivar, was it?"

"You remembered." Ivar looked impressed. "I'd ask you to dance, but I don't know how myself."

"Right. You're Sverbian, I think Neve said?"

"By blood. My adopted mother's Kae."

"Oh!" I clapped a hand to my mouth. "I didn't mean to pry, sorry—"

"No worries." Ivar flashed a crooked smile. "Can I get you a drink instead?"

"Um—" I bit my lip. Neve had seemed interested in him, but I didn't see the harm in a drink. "Sure. Thanks."

He disappeared into the crowd. A few minutes later, he returned with two cups of amber liquid. "Hope whisky's all right. I couldn't find anything else."

"Whisky sounds great." I sipped it, breathing the sweet burnt-wood scent.

"That's a fine blade." Ivar nodded at my obsidian-handled knife. "Forged here in Ingdanrad?"

It seemed unwise to admit I stole it from a sacrificial altar in Brånnheå, the Rúonbattai's former base. *The best lies are closest to the truth*, Neve had said. "Nei. I found it on a military campaign."

"Eremur's military? You're a soldier?"

"War medic." I floundered for a way to get off the topic. "How about your sword? Was it forged here?"

"Sure was." Ivar patted his pommel. "Standard militia issue."

"You're—" I glanced at the red-woolwrapped guards stationed around the hall. "Not on duty?"

"Good guess." He winked. "Spariere invited me. We're not friends, exactly, but we're friendly — both of us being outsiders and all that."

"How sweet," came a familiar voice. "Here I thought you were twins."

Ivar jerked around, spilling his whisky. Tsiala had come up behind us. She wore a sleeveless gown of turquoise silk, tattooed arms on display, curved daggers at her hips. Her dark hair was pinned back on one side with a silver filigree leaf. Aeldu save me, she was lush.

She gave a dramatic bow, extending her hand. "May I have this dance, milady?"

I hesitated, not sure if this was more sarcasm. Considering how much it hurt when I got rejected, though, I couldn't do that to her.

I downed my whisky and took her hand, casting an apologetic look at Ivar.

Tsiala put her other hand on my waist. A shiver went down my spine. She pulled me into a dance. I followed without thinking, whirling across the dancefloor. It didn't match the sharp rise and fall of fiddles and pipes. It was a Ferish dance, one I'd done with young men at charity balls in Caladheå.

"I didn't know you were coming," I said.

"You think I don't like music?"

"Nei, I mean — I didn't know you were invited."

"Ah. So I'm not good enough to be here."

"I didn't say that," I snapped. "Can't you have a normal conversation?"

Tsiala scoffed. "Sure. How's the weather? Where was your knife forged? Wanna get drunk and see my other sword?"

"That's not — wait." I tried to pull away, but she kept her hand firm on my waist. "You were listening?"

"You weren't quiet."

"So you waltzed me off to — what? Stop me talking to a man?" I yanked free. "That's it, right? You're jealous."

She rolled her eyes. "Yeah. Everything revolves around you."

"Oh, fuck off." I turned on my heel.

I was tempted to kiss Ivar just to spite Tsiala, but he'd vanished. Instead I strode through the nearest doorway. My heart pulsed so hard it melded with the drumbeats. Mist gathered around my hands. Colourful spots flickered across my vision. I grasped at a stone wall as the world tipped.

Someone caught me. Silk brushed my cheek. I blinked, making a bronze blur solidify into Tsiala's face.

"Are you . . ." She touched my throat. "Did Ivar drug you or something?"

"Nei. I'm just allergic to bitchiness."

A startled laugh escaped her. She helped me sit against a wall. I rubbed my eyes, swallowing the nausea.

Tsiala hiked up her skirt and sat next to me. "Look, I . . ." She heaved a sigh. "I'm not good at this shit. Is it enough to say I'm fucked up and trying my best?"

I studied her dark eyes. She looked genuinely sorry. Shrugging, I said, "As long as you're okay with the same for me."

Her hand found mine. The warmth was a surprising comfort. "If you can walk . . . can I take you somewhere?"

Finally I noticed where we were. A dim corridor stretched off to either side, lit by runes on the stone ceiling. "We should get back to the wedding."

"We will in a way. You'll see."

Reluctantly, I let Tsiala help me up. She took me to the entry tunnel where guests had hung their outer clothes. I found my black fur cape and Tsiala put on an embroidered cloak with white fur trim. From there, she led me through a chain of corridors and up a dark spiral staircase. At the top, she fumbled with a latch and shoved a door. It groaned open. Icy air stung us.

I followed her into a snowy grove. The door had been built into a hillock. A crystal lantern post bathed the grove in soft light, sparkling on frosty trees hung with clumps of red berries. It was so quiet I could hear waves in the distance.

Ahead, set at an angle into a hillside like a sloping trap door, was an enormous window covered in glowing runes. I edged closer and realized it was the Hollow's glass roof. Far below me, dancers spun and whirled like a school of colourful fish. Síona stood out in her white gown, beaming as she danced with Alesso. Still dizzy from my bout with the shoirdryge, I stepped back.

"Aha." Tsiala emerged from the trees, brushing snow off a flask.

She pulled out the stopper and sniffed it. "Brånnvin. Neve always did prefer the Sverbian stuff."

"You've come here with her?"

"A few times. These are rowan trees. Supposedly they ward off evil spirits, so druids come here for 'quiet contemplation.' We come for . . ." She shook the flask, making it slosh.

I smirked. "That's why you brought me? To get drunk and show me your weapons?"

"Shut up." She pulled water from the air and flicked it at me.

I knotted my fingers into my muslin skirt. Every bit of me wanted to push her into the snow and kiss her, but my last drunken hookup at a wedding had been a disaster — and that was with a boy I'd known my whole life. I barely knew a thing about Tsiala. Which, I realized, she'd just created the solution to.

"Ai," I said. "You ever played clears?"

"Clear answer or clear drink, right?" Tsiala raised the flask. "Hit me."

"I'll start easy. How old are you?"

"Nineteen. You?"

"Eighteen." I began climbing the hillside, following the edge of the Hollow's sloping roof, holding my skirts above the snow. "Where'd you meet Neve?"

"A Gallnach settlement in the southern colonies." She drifted after me. "Neve insists you're not secretly in love with Tiernan Heilind. Is that true?"

"Yeah. There's nothing between him and me, I swear." I glanced back at her. "Where's your family? Still down south?"

Tsiala took a swig of brånnvin. As we passed a wrought-iron walkway that went horizontal across the Hollow's glass roof, she blurted, "Do you actually like girls? Or am I wasting my time?"

Heat flooded through my body. "You're not wasting it."

"That's not a clear answer."

"Fine, I like girls." *Just not necessarily you*, I thought. "What about you? Into boys, or . . . ?"

She shook her head. "Not interested."

"Good. Then Neve can have Ivar."

Tsiala snorted. We passed the peak of the Hollow's glass roof and kept climbing. A crow landed in a rowan tree, cawing. As we got farther from the glowing runes, we noticed more light ahead. A greenhouse pulsed with the golden-red flicker of candles.

I froze. Neve had told me about the crow on Ingdanrad's flag, a war goddess whose caw foretold death. This felt familiar — tunnels, a silent orchard, soldiers hiding in a shed. The Rúonbattai had ambushed us this way at Ivy House. The familiarness *itself* was unnerving. "Are there oaks or lilacs in this grove?" I whispered.

"Not that I know of. Why? You allergic to them, too?"

"Piss off. I'm serious. Something's strange about that greenhouse."

Tsiala passed me the flask. "I'll check. Stay here."

My temper flared. "I'm a warrior, too—"

"And you nearly passed out a few minutes ago. Don't be an idiot."

Tsiala crept forward, hiding behind trees. Near the greenhouse, she sidled up to a section of glass obscured by huge ferns. She peered inside and gasped. Clapping a hand to her mouth, she dashed back to me.

"Shit," she said between snickers. "Don't look."

"Why? Who's in there?"

"Your uncle and Róisín ó Conn. They're, uh, not so quietly contemplating each other's naked bodies."

My jaw dropped. "What?!"

Tsiala dragged me back down the slope. Near the Hollow's glass roof, she collapsed into the snow and dissolved into laughter.

"Bloody hell." I swigged brånnvin, trying to wash away the mental image. "Sneaky fucking druid. Acts like she's doing me a favour, and — yan kaid. Geniod went to her greenhouse on Innisburren, too!"

. "C'mon," Tsiala said, gasping with laughter. "It's normal. How do you think Rikuja got knocked up?"

I flung snow at her. "Stop talking — about my family — having sex!"

She grabbed my ankles and pulled me down. I shrieked. Tsiala's face appeared above me, backed by thousands of stars. Her body was hot against mine.

"Why?" she whispered, grinning. "You'd rather have it ourselves?"

My mind blanked. Nothing mattered except her mouth being so close to mine, her breath warming my face, her wavy black hair skimming my cheek.

The hillock door scraped. We both jerked up. "Hide," Tsiala hissed.

We scrambled away into the grove, crouching behind barren bushes. A man in burlap robes stepped through the door. He was solidly built, broad-shouldered, and thick around the middle. His long pale beard partly covered his wool pendant of a diamond-shaped druidic knot.

"Is that" — I peered through the bushes — "Síona's father?"

"Yeah." Tsiala shifted in the snow. "Merdo. We're not exactly allowed to be here."

But Fearghas och Donnabhán hadn't come after us. He climbed to the walkway across the Hollow's glass roof and waited, hands folded. A militia soldier in a red woolwrap came through the hillock door and shut it behind them. The man glanced around before crossing to Fearghas. Leaning in as if to whisper something, he drew a dagger and struck.

Fearghas collapsed. The soldier hauled him along the iron walkway, used his bloody dagger to smash through the glass roof, and threw the druid into the hall.

"Fuck," Tsiala said, a second before the screaming started.

17.

FOR WHOM THE BELL TOLLS

Tsiala hurled a chunk of ice at the assassin. It hit his chest, making him stumble. He threw a fireball back. I blocked it with a wall of snow, sending plumes of steam into the air. Another fireball grazed Tsiala. She swore and yanked off her burning cloak.

Panic seared through me. I coiled a water whip around the assassin's ankle and yanked. He toppled back onto the sloped glass and tumbled away. His startled shout faded as he vanished into the darkness.

"Are you—" I whirled toward Tsiala.

"I'm fine," she snapped. "Follow him. Hurry!"

I shifted into my wolf body and bounded down the snowy mountain. The scent of blood on his dagger led me through the dark. I veered around trees and crashed through bushes. Branches tore at my fur. The assassin couldn't have gotten far —

A fireball streaked past me, then another. I darted back and forth to dodge the assault. Trees burst into flames, lighting up the night. I'd never mastered water-calling in my attuned form. All I could do was distract him until Tsiala caught up.

"The road!" came her distant voice. "Don't let him escape!"

I bounded off the roof of the Hollow's entry tunnel. Empty sleighs filled the road ahead. Horses yanked at their hitching posts, spooked by the flames. On instinct, I ran at the horses, snapping and howling. They bucked and reared. One broke free and bolted.

CLANG. A watchman in a tower pulled the rope of a huge bell. Fireballs struck the tower, scorching the stone. The watchman stumbled back, but his job was done. Bells rang from the next tower, then the next, rising up the mountain.

Fire streaked past me. I ran for cover among the sleighs. One after another ignited, sending out waves of heat. I glimpsed someone's feet and darted under a sleigh in pursuit, only to find three men with drawn swords. To my wolf vision, their woolwraps all looked grey. I had no idea if they were militia soldiers.

More people ran past. Showers of sparks burst into the air. Among clanging bells and confused shouts and squealing horses, Tsiala called my name. I dashed toward her. She stood among the crackling flames, daggers drawn. She'd torn off her skirt at the knees so she could run.

"Where'd he go?" she panted.

I sniffed the air. Smoke drowned out the scent of blood. Memories of Tjarnnaast weighed down on me — a flaming village, scorched fields, the reek of burnt bodies. *Holy flames*, I thought with a wrench.

A bald eagle dropped from the sky and shifted. Geniod landed, sword in hand, dressed only in breeches and unlaced boots. "What in Aeldu-yan happened?" he asked.

"Assassin," Tsiala said. "He's disguised as a soldier. Brown hair, bloody dagger — and he's a fire mage."

"Yan taku." Geniod shifted back to an eagle and launched into the air. He circled, searching the fiery chaos, then took off southeast.

I streaked down the road after him, paws hitting the packed snow. Away from the firelight, everything looked like shadowy blurs, but I could make out a horse and rider galloping off. Geniod dove and tore at the rider with his talons. The man flung out a wave of fire, driving Geniod back.

In the distance, lanterns lit up iron gates across the road. The rider spurred his horse faster, kicking up snow. He shouted over the clanging bells. Archers in the gate-side towers nocked their bows. To my horror, they fired at Geniod. He soared straight up into the air. The gates creaked open. The horse and rider shot through the gap.

I skidded to a stop as the gates slammed shut. Geniod landed nearby, shifting back to human.

"It's no good," he said, panting. "The gates lead to a bridge over a canyon. There's no way around."

I shifted and rose on two legs. "You can go—"

Geniod shook his head. "I'm not leaving you. Not in all this."

"So we just let him go? He murdered Síona's father!"

Someone called out. We whirled. Four horses galloped past us and circled back around, slowing. The riders were Tsiala, two soldiers, and Róisín. She wore a simple brown dress with slits up the skirt. For reasons I didn't want to think about, she clearly hadn't had time to put on her druid robes.

"You lost him?" Tsiala asked, one hand on the reins, the other clutching a dagger.

"They let him through." I swept my hand toward the gate. "They must think he's a real soldier."

"Má sí," Róisín swore under her breath. She rode forward and shouted up at the towers. "Open the gate. I command you as a chief druid of Innisburren."

An archer called back in Gallnach. Róisín bristled, raising a hand.

"I'll open them myself if I have to," she called.

The gates glowed orange, making the snow around them sizzle. The soldiers recoiled. Róisín clenched her fist and the glow vanished. The gates opened.

Geniod and I shifted forms and took off. The others spurred their horses onward. Lanterns marked the end of the bridge, but everything beyond was dark. A soldier with us summoned a fire orb. His horse led the way, cantering along a steep road up the mountain. Hoofprints marked the snow ahead.

Out of nowhere, Róisín swore. "Stop!"

Everyone obeyed. She turned, scouring the darkness.

"Something's wrong," she said. "There's no other lights. Anyone would break their neck travelling this road at night."

"He's trying anyway." Tsiala pointed at the tracks.

"The horse is. That doesn't mean the rider went with it." Róisín turned back, examining the tracks. "Here—"

A fireball struck one of our soldiers. He fell from his horse, screaming. Tsiala flung water across him. The rest of us whirled, searching the shadowy boulders along the road.

I smelled blood, hot and metallic. Something moved among the boulders. I leapt. My claws found flesh. The man cried out and flung me away. I hit something hard and fell, dazed. Fire bloomed through the darkness —

A rock struck the man's head. He dropped. Stone tendrils sprang out of the earth and held him down. He writhed and spasmed, smearing blood on the snow.

Róisín slid off her horse and crouched at his side. "Sverb bastard," she spat. "You *are* militia."

He groaned. Spit foamed out of his mouth. A terrible feeling shot through me, like I'd been here before — but it wasn't from an oak crest. Jorumgard and Nerio had once gotten sick like this. I shifted to human and scrabbled across the snow. As I reached the assassin, he fell still. I checked his breath, his heartbeat. Nothing.

I exhaled, feeling deflated. "Poison. He didn't want to be captured."

Róisín pulled up his eyelids and stared into his glassy eyes. She cursed under her breath. "His spirit has passed to the otherworld. I can no longer see it."

Moaning from our burnt ally caught my attention. The promise Nicoletta had demanded came back to me. *If you come across someone in need, you won't turn your back on them.* I crawled toward the man. His skin was peeling, his uniform charred. The reek of scorched flesh made my stomach twist. Images of a blue-eyed man filled my head.

My pulse stuttered. The edges of my vision turned dark. I fumbled through my purse for my lavender oil. *Breathe in,* came Matéo's voice. I held the vial to the burnt man's nose, then mine. It was like trying to dam a river with a stone, but it was the only medicine I had.

In the gentlest voice I could manage, I reassured him while searching for somewhere to check his pulse. His right wrist had escaped the flames. I pressed my thumb to it, counting his heartbeats. Too many, too fast. He'd gone into shock. If he lost too much blood from his burns, he could be dead within the hour.

Sitting back on my heels, I said, "Right. Here's what I need."

✳

A short time later, we loaded the burnt soldier and dead assassin into a hay cart. The guards in the bridge towers had given us basic medical supplies — ointment, bandages, laudanum for the pain. I'd sealed the soldier's bandages with pine pitch. It was rough work, but he seemed stable enough for the trip to the hospital. The other soldier drove the cart while the rest of us followed with the remaining horses.

"Bet he's Rúonbattai," Tsiala said, nodding at the dead man. "A normal assassin wouldn't throw the body into the Hollow for everyone to see. He *wanted* people to panic."

"Why target Fearghas?" Geniod asked. He was shivering, bare-chested under a cloak borrowed from the bridge guards. "If the Rúonbattai need druids to repair farmland, it doesn't make sense to kill the chief of the clan specializing in agriculture."

"Fearghas was never quiet about his dislike of Sverbians," Róisín said. "They may think his successor will be easier to sway."

"You said the Rúonbattai wouldn't strike tonight," I countered.

"It seems I was wrong." Róisín sighed and passed a hand over her eyes. "Large gatherings are difficult for me. I see so much, it's like walking through soup."

Right, I thought bitterly. *Or the Rúonbattai swayed you to their side*. Deep down, though, I knew how unlikely that was. Neve had said Innisburren druids would never ally with the Rúonbattai.

Geniod pulled his borrowed cloak tighter. "We should split up. A few of us can hurry back with the news."

Róisín nodded. "Go ahead. I'll take the wounded man to the hospital. It'll be easier for me to explain why I'm transporting two bodies in militia uniform."

Tsiala and I returned on horseback while Geniod flew overhead. The chaos outside the Hollow had calmed. Soldiers with torches moved among the charred sleighs, cleaning up the wreckage and putting out the last fires. The bells had stopped clanging. As Tsiala and I slid off our horses, Rikuja dashed out from behind a sleigh.

"Thank the aeldu," she whispered. "Dune's out looking for you. Quick, quick — before you're seen—"

She dragged Tsiala and me into the dark trees along the road. Geniod landed nearby and shifted, looking as confused as I felt.

"Something's gone wrong," Rikuja said. "Síona's father—"

"I know," I said. "We saw him die."

"That's not the problem. I mean, it *is*, but Alesso's been arrested for the murder."

"*What?* Why?"

"Fearghas had a note in his pocket from Alesso. It told him to slip away from the wedding so they could meet above the Hollow. I don't know what motive Alesso could have, though. Maybe he's trying to seize control of Clan Níall."

"It'd be stupid to try on his wedding night," Tsiala said. "Besides, we caught the killer. He was a Sverbian militia soldier, probably Rúonbattai."

Rikuja looked taken aback. "Then you'd better go tell the militia captain. He thinks Alesso hired *you* to do the killing, Tsiala."

She blanched. "Why me?"

"They found part of your dress in the grove." Rikuja gestured at Tsiala's burnt, torn skirt. "You're the only woman here wearing turquoise silk who's strong enough to throw a heavyset man through a roof. Then the tower watchman saw you and a wolf chase a soldier down the mountain."

"That's bearshit," I protested. "We were chasing the assassin."

"It didn't look that way. Plus, some soldier claims to have seen Alesso paying Tsiala."

"Then they're lying," Geniod said. "Róisín will see—"

"No," Tsiala cut in. "That part's true."

I turned to her, speechless.

She looked away, rubbing her neck. "Alesso wanted to know if he could trust you, Kateiko. He paid me to spy on you. That's why he invited me to the wedding."

"You—" I drew back, horrified. "Is that why you took me to the grove?"

"Of course not. And I haven't told him anything. Well, not much—"

I slapped her. Tsiala reeled, stumbling in the snow. She put her hand to her cheek and brought it away bloody. My runed ring had left a gash.

"Fuck you," I snapped. "Saying those things tonight — playing clears so I'd get drunk and tell you everything—"

"That's not it!" She grabbed my wrist.

I shoved her. "Don't touch me. Don't ever fucking touch me again."

Rikuja and Geniod stared at her, their shocked expressions turning to disgust. It was the same way they looked at Captain Parr. Tsiala backed away and disappeared into the darkness.

Geniod touched my arm. "Whatever happened, I'm so sorry—"

"Ohhh, no." I rounded on him. "You're hardly doing better. Following me everywhere, never leaving me alone — then when you finally do, it's to fuck a druid?"

The blood drained from his face. "I—"

"Didn't expect me to find out? Because I trusted the man who offered to adopt me? Yeah. My mistake."

"Kako," Rikuja said soothingly. "Geniod didn't mean to upset you—"

"How would you know?" The answer hit me like a punch to the gut. "You *did* know. Dune, too, I bet. But not me — not the glass doll who'll shatter if you say the wrong thing. Right?"

Neither of them had an answer. I whirled, skirts swishing.

"Where are you going?" Rikuja called.

"To put out this damned wildfire."

Thoughts churned through my head. Nothing about Alesso pointed toward his innocence, but this was also the kind of situation the Rúonbattai thrived in. Fear and chaos. The only thing that could cut through that was the truth — and if it meant outing Tsiala as a spy instead of a murderer, so be it.

"Kateiko?" Ivar stepped out from the smoking wreckage, a torch in hand.

I started, jumping back into a sleigh. A shower of ash tumbled down.

"Sorry," he said, steadying me. "I was worried about you. That girl you danced with — people are saying Spariere hired her as an assassin."

I blinked up at Ivar. Sure, Neve liked him, but I no longer knew who to trust. A Sverbian soldier who was friendly with Alesso fell pretty low on my list of allies.

He lifted his torch, taking in my torn dress filthy with blood, dirt, and pine pitch. "Aeldu save you. Did that girl—"

"Nei. I'm fine." I bit my lip, caught by his mention of the aeldu. I'd forgotten about his adopted mother. "Are you really Kae? I mean . . ."

Ivar pulled up his sleeve, revealing a heron tattoo on his forearm. "My tema passed on all the Kae teachings. One is looking after other people."

Ever so slightly, my shoulders relaxed. "Sorry. It's been a long night. Look, I need to talk to the militia captain. Do you know where he is?"

"I think he's interrogating Spariere. I'll take you to him."

Ivar spoke in Sverbian to another soldier, who nodded. We wound through the smoking sleighs to the entry tunnel. Guards waved us through. A clamour of voices echoed from the main hall. The wedding guests must've been put on lockdown while the militia secured the Hollow. Ivar turned into a dark corridor. Halfway down it, he paused, swinging his torch around.

"What's wrong?" I asked.

"It's too dark. There's meant to be runelight on the ceiling." He drew his sword. "Be on your guard—"

His torch hissed out. Blackness folded around us.

"Kaid," Ivar swore. Dropping to a whisper, he said, "There must be a fire mage. Don't move. I'll put down the torch, then grab your hand. Okay?"

"Okay," I whispered.

Fabric rustled next to me, followed by the tap of the torch on the stone floor. Ivar's hand brushed against me and slid down my arm. I used my free hand to draw my knife.

"Please say you're an antayul," he whispered.

A soft laugh escaped me. "I'm an antayul."

"Good. Then—"

Footsteps echoed off the stone walls. A *thump* sounded close by. Ivar dropped, groaning. Something struck my head, and the world winked out.

✳

I woke groggily. My head was splitting from inside out. I lay still, testing my body. Fingers and toes moved. Nothing felt broken. When I opened my eyes, faint white lines shifted and blurred. I waited for the dizziness to pass, then eased myself into a sitting position.

The light came from an iron cuff around my wrist, etched with glowing runes. Darkness hung heavy around me. I pressed my palm to the ground and felt dusty stone. Fumbling further, I found a rough wall, then a door of cold steel bars. I lifted my wrist to see in the runelight. No latch, just the back of a thick lock. Worry crept into my throat. I pushed the door, pulled it, rattled it on the hinges. It didn't move.

"Ai!" I shouted. "Is anyone there?"

No answer. Bells clanged through my skull, sending out throbs of pain.

I collapsed. Where in Aeldu-yan was I? Images of a runelit glass roof floated through my mind. I plucked at my skirt. Layers of muslin, torn and filthy. I touched my head and gasped in pain. Dried blood flaked away from a gash. Next to it, I found something sharp in my hair. I tugged out the pins, letting the matted locks tumble over my shoulders, and untangled broken pieces of a filigree headband.

Neve, I thought distantly. She'd lent it to me. For . . . a wedding. Burning sleighs, a frantic chase up a mountain, a burnt man. Tsiala's bloody cheek. Why had I slapped her? Why did she fill me with hot fury?

He paid me to spy on you.

I rolled aside and threw up. The sour smell of vomit made me gag. I tried calling water to rinse my mouth, but nothing came. I pulled harder. My vision flickered. Pain burst through my head and the world went black. A scream wrenched out of me.

"Scream all you like," came a dull voice. "No one will come."

I froze. "Where—"

"Are we? Ingdanrad's dungeon."

"Where are *you*?"

"A few cells down, I think. I could not see where they left you."

The voice sounded painfully familiar. Quiet, deep, a thick Sverbian accent — but hoarse and flat. Like every drop of life had been squeezed out of it.

Hardly daring to breathe, I spoke into the shadows. "Tiernan?"

18.

A SEASON WITHOUT SUN

The clang of distant bells filled the darkness. Then Tiernan said, "Katja? Is that really . . ."

Something between a laugh and a sob burst from me. I pressed my face to the cell bars, peering down the dark corridor. White light reflected off a pool of murky water.

"How are you—" I stammered. "Were you at the wedding?"

"What wedding?"

I paused. "How long have you been down here?"

"Uh . . ." A faint tapping came from his cell. "Three months. I think."

"Three *months?*"

Tiernan chuckled dryly. "I guess you did not hear the news from Jorum."

"How could I? He's in prison, too!"

"*What?*" Metal clanged. "Here?"

"Nei. Caladheå. Fedos Valrose took over from Captain Parr, and — it's a long story. Valrose is cleaning house, getting rid of Parr's allies."

I wasn't sure what reaction I expected. Swearing, probably. The swelling heat of a fire mage's fury. Instead Tiernan laughed. It grew louder, warping into hysterics.

"Of course," he wheezed. "What are mortals but playthings for the gods?"

"What do you mean? Tiernan, what happened?"

No answer. I tried to stand, only for my knees to buckle. Dizziness, vomiting, ringing in my ears — I'd gotten a concussion. That explained my fragmented memories. I remembered talking to Ivar, then . . . blackness. Had he attacked me? Or had he been attacked, too?

"Who brought me here?" I asked. "Did you see them? Overhear anything?"

"Nothing noteworthy," Tiernan said. "I assume it was the prison guards."

"Guards?" I leaned against the barred door and shouted, "Ai! Why am I here?"

No response. I smacked the bars in frustration. My memory felt as shattered as my filigree headband. Tsiala was suspected of murder, so . . . was I, too? What about Neve and my family? I had no idea what was happening outside this dungeon. Between Alesso and the Rúonbattai, Ingdanrad could be in smoking ruins.

I put my arm through my barred door but couldn't reach the lock. Fighting off nausea, I felt my way around the rough stone walls. The cell was twice as long as I was tall. I knocked over a bucket, which rattled away, and touched a thin mattress that reeked of rotten hay. My knee landed in a puddle, making me yelp.

"What?" Tiernan asked.

"There's water here. But . . ." I pressed my hand into the cold puddle. "I can't *feel* it. As an antayul, I mean."

"Do you have an iron cuff?" Shuffling came from his cell. "Ah, yes. I see the light. Those are nullifying runes."

"What's that mean?"

"They strip away your magic. I have one, too. Otherwise I could simply melt these bars."

I stared at the runes in horror. There was a blank spot in my mind where my water-calling should be. The rest of my body felt numb. Through the ringing in my ears came a faint dripping I hadn't noticed until now.

Moving my wrist to use the light, I took stock of myself. Róisín's ring and Neve's amethyst necklace were gone. My fur cape was gone. My belt was gone, along with my obsidian-handled knife and purse. Panic swelled inside me. Had I been carrying my parents' makiri? Or had I left them at Clan Ríain's villa?

"Nei," I said. "Nei, nei, nei—"

"What now?"

The apathy in Tiernan's voice broke me. This wasn't the man who helped me rescue Hanaiko and Samulein from the Sarteres, who ended his friendship with Captain Parr for threatening my family, who held me after my parents' deaths. I reached for my lavender oil only to remember it was in my purse.

"Tell me you're real," I said breathlessly. "Tell me this isn't just the concussion—"

"I am real. Not that it matters."

"What are you talking about? Tiernan, what the hell happened?"

Silence.

"Goddamn it!" I smacked the floor. "Don't you remember? You gave me that coin in Tjarnnaast. You told me to find you at the Golden Oak. I've turned my life upside down to find you—"

My throat closed. I clutched at my neck, gasping.

"Katja?" Worry had crept into Tiernan's voice.

"I can't — breathe—"

"Amja, amja," he soothed. "Come. Can you see?"

I pressed my face to the barred door. Down the corridor, in the glow of runelight, a bony hand came through another set of bars.

"Imagine me holding your hand," he said. "Breathe in for five seconds, then out. Count with me. One . . . two . . ."

I breathed with him, clinging to his voice. My gasping eased. I slumped to the floor, weak and shaking as if I'd run up a mountain.

Quietly, Tiernan said, "I am sorry. I had forgotten the coin. I . . . hardly remember the sun."

My heart cracked. I thought of Jonalin, fresh out of prison, so miserable he wanted to die. He'd spent a year there without seeing the stars, then another year in a windowless cell at the parole house. Every time I saw him, I'd told him about the night sky.

"Okay," I said. "If you won't tell me your story, then I'll tell you mine. And I'll include everything I remember about the sun."

❋

I had no idea how long I talked for. I described blinding sunshine at Malana's wedding, golden beams falling through fog on the canoe trip south, a red haze over Caladheå from arson smoke. Sunsets on Innisburren had turned the snowy fields pinkish orange. Port Alios's windows had glittered like jewels. Sunrise had lit up the mountains as we sailed into Ingdanrad. When my voice turned hoarse, Tiernan tossed a half-full waterskin through his cell bars. I had to use my broken headband to pull it within reach. The water tasted warm and disgustingly stale.

Some parts I left out — fights with family and friends, my

romantic flailing, moments when I thought about tipping over the edge into Aeldu-yan. I also left out the vision my parents had shown me of the shoirdryge, where another me and another Tiernan lived together in a log cabin. He'd told me that dwelling on other worlds led people to madness.

When I fell silent, the only sound was dripping water. I wondered if he'd fallen asleep. Or died. Then he said, "You and *Nerio?* What a nightmare marriage."

I laughed. *That* sounded like Tiernan. "I, uh, need to apologize. Our excuse for breaking up was that you and I are secretly in love. Nerio read aloud in public from that letter you sent me. *Northern Nyhemur is stunning in winter. The snowy plains look infinite, as if one is floating among the clouds. Perhaps one day I can take you here.*"

"You . . ." His voice came out stilted. "Memorized it?"

"*That's* the part you find strange?"

"Well, the idea that we — obviously it would—" Tiernan blew out a breath. "When I wrote that, you had just lost your parents. I wanted to give you something to look forward to. My first few weeks here, I dreamed of making that trip with you. Somewhere along the way, I forgot that dream."

"Oh." My own voice sounded off. "Do you remember it now?"

"Some of it." The runelight shifted in his cell. "Everything there is so vast and open. The wind lifts veils of snow into the air like swirling, shifting dragonfly wings. The air is so clear you can see bison a day's journey away, and so cold your breath freezes like winter glass. Every windmill on the horizon feels like a distant friend. I wanted you to meet them."

Things always sounded so beautiful in his accent. Unbidden, my mind pictured riding together on his silver horse, Gwmniwyr, with my arms wrapped around him. Stargazing, campfires, snuggling under my fir branch blanket. The idea of touching him that way still felt like an invasive weed but no longer one I needed to uproot. *Would* it be so strange? Neve and Tsiala had both thought Tiernan and I might really be together.

"Then we'll go," I said. "We'll break out of here, find Gwmniwyr, and ride to Nyhemur. Two outlaws travelling the continent."

Tiernan chuckled. "Gods' sakes. How things change."

"What do you mean?"

"When we first met, you were a child half-dead in a stable. Now you are this fearless young woman. Plotting a prison break, negotiating with druids, defeating a shipload of Rúonbattai. You no longer need me."

"I do. Tiernan, of course I do." I paused before admitting, "I left out all the bad stuff."

He grunted. "My tale is only bad."

"I can handle it. I'm a grown woman now, right?"

Tiernan heaved a sigh. The rustling fabric sounded like he was settling in for a long story. "Jorum and I spent days searching Nyhemur. Following tracks in the snow, asking farmers if a cleric had passed by. There was . . . too much of a trail. Like we were being led into a trap. That was when I began to suspect the cleric, not Liet, was the temporal mage."

"You, too?" I straightened up, sending a throb through my skull. "I dreamed about her. She was Thymarai, using her bodyguard Liet as a decoy."

"An apt analogy. By that point, we were a fair ways south, so I wondered if she was fleeing home to Ingdanrad. We stopped at one of their garrisons on the Nyhemur border. By chance, I knew a few men there. I served with them part-time in the militia while doing magical research here. Jorum and I stayed up drinking with them. Stupid, I know, given that we were following a temporal mage who could predict our every move — but we had been on campaign for weeks, sleeping in the snow and reeling from the Battle of Tjarnnaast. I was finally home. Safe among old friends. Once we started to nod off . . . they tried to slit our throats."

I sucked in a breath. "Oh, no."

"I have no idea why. Maybe the cleric told them we were stalking her. Maybe they resented me for defecting to Eremur. Either way, Jorum killed three men on his own. I fought off a fire mage, setting the garrison alight. We insisted it was self-defence, but . . . there was no proof. It looked like we returned their hospitality by committing mass murder and burning the place down."

"So they arrested you?"

"They arrested *me*. I took the fall for Jorum."

"What? Why?"

"Because . . ." Tiernan sighed. "I could get off lightly. Due to my past service with the militia, and Ingdanrad's protections for mages, I got life in prison. There are no such protections for Jorum. He would have been hanged."

"Oh," I said with faint horror.

"I could not sentence my closest friend to death. Especially not when he has a chance at a family. I told him to make amends with Yotolein, get married, become a father to Hanaiko and Samulein. He belongs with you all. You told him as much in Tjarnnaast."

The perpetual knot in my stomach turned inside out. "That's not — you belong with us, too!"

Tiernan gave a bleak laugh. "There *was* a slight hope of that. Jorum swore to find Captain Parr and figure out a way to free me, maybe a prisoner swap between Ingdanrad and Eremur. Instead, Valrose replaced Parr and arrested Jorum."

"Yan kaid." I slumped against the wall. "But then . . . why hasn't Jorum taken Valrose's deal? If he'll go free, why not admit you're here?"

"I can only guess, but probably because Valrose would paint the news on every signboard in Eremur. If the entire province thinks I am some dangerous, out-of-control mage, I can never return. Jorum knows what that will cost me." Fabric rustled, then footsteps echoed. He seemed to be pacing. "Remember in Tjarnnaast, I mentioned losing the woman I wanted to marry? That woman is Marijka Riekkanehl."

Every coherent thought fell out of my mind. I'd assumed Tiernan's lover was dead, not his friend who supplied medicinal herbs to Agata's apothecary. Sweet, gentle, patient Marijka. Very much alive Marijka. Had he been dreaming of her while locked up here? If he married her and moved to her cabin in the woods, would I ever see him again?

"What happened with her?" I scraped out.

"I made a stupid mistake and drove her away. It was ten years ago, but Jorum still believes I can make it right, that Maika and I can start our own family."

"Aeldu save us. So you and Jorum are in different prisons protecting each other for the same bloody reason."

Tiernan laughed bitterly. "Like I said. We are playthings of merciless gods."

We both fell silent. The *drip drip drip* went on. I'd built up months' worth of things to discuss with him, but I couldn't remember them. I felt exhausted inside and out. I wished I had Neve's over-brewed coffee. Instead I swigged stale water and closed my eyes. Perhaps a brief nap . . .

✳

I dreamed of Neve dancing, ruby jewels glinting, plum woolwrap swirling. The crowd shifted into a school of rainbow fish, the glass-roofed Hollow into a turquoise pool. I swam to the surface and broke through. Tsiala stared at me. She shifted into the white-robed cleric, lifted a crossbow, and fired.

I snapped awake, gasping. Sweat drenched my back. I lifted my hand to dry myself and saw the glowing runed cuff around my wrist. Everything came rushing back — including a question I'd asked Neve in the hot springs. She hadn't answered.

"Tiernan?" I ventured. "How'd you get into Ingdanrad the first time? Did you swear neutrality?"

Silence.

"Come on. We just told each other everything."

"Not true. You left out the bad stuff."

I rolled my eyes. Remembering Neve's offer to trade secrets, I said, "If I tell you something bad, will you answer the question?"

Tiernan paused. "I suppose."

"Right then." I lay on the floor, bunching my hair into a pillow, and propped my feet against the wall. "Remember in Brånnheå, you killed a Rúonbattai soldier so I didn't have to? You said taking a life marks a person."

"I remember."

"I've still never killed anyone in battle. Wounded them, yeah, but never landed the final blow. But after the Battle of Tjarnnaast . . . I think I killed someone."

"Who?"

"An Eremur soldier." His blue eyes flickered through my mind. "He'd been stabbed. Coughing blood, begging for help. He was desperate to get home before his wife gave birth. That's the last thing I remember him saying. It was like I . . . vanished from the world. When I came back, he was dead in my arms. Blank blue eyes staring at the smoky sky."

"He was badly wounded," Tiernan said gently. "There was nothing you could do."

"Maybe, but I wasn't with him in his final moments. Not really. He must've looked up at me, thinking he wouldn't die alone, and . . . I should've quit then. I should've left it to the other medics. But there were so many bodies — some *were* the other medics—"

"Amja, amja. I know. I saw." He was quiet awhile, then said, "If I may ask . . . is it that soldier you feel guilty about? Or is it your parents?"

My breath hitched. I'd pushed aside the memories of my parents' deaths. Tema had died in my arms, a bolt lodged in her chest. Temal had died in a muddy field, fending off soldiers so I could escape the massacre of our camp. I hadn't been with him in his final moments, either. Now I'd lost their makiri, the last fragments of their spirits—

I curled up on the stone floor, knees to my chest, sobbing so hard I couldn't breathe. Tiernan spoke soothingly from his cell, which made me cry harder. I couldn't hold his hand, couldn't touch his hair to link our spirits. I was sinking into the cold ocean again. The only light in the darkness was the runed cuff around my wrist.

Nei, I thought distantly. *Tiernan has that light, too. I'm not alone.*

Once again, he talked me back to breathing normally, counting the seconds. When my gasping had slowed, he said, "Is that why you quit being a medic?"

"Yeah." I wiped my eyes on my filthy sleeve. "I couldn't do it anymore. I'd either panic or blank out. Nica made me promise to try anyway if someone needed help, so I did tonight, and . . . I got so on edge that I slapped Tsiala, ran away from my family, and wound up in prison."

"Quite the adventure." A faint tapping came from Tiernan's cell. "Look at it this way. If you stabbed me and left the knife there, would you expect it to heal?"

"Huh? Of course not."

"Trauma is the same. You are still at war, scared and grieving and exhausted. The knife is still in you. Maybe one day, when you have healed, you can return to medicine."

I shrugged. "Maybe."

"In the meantime, it is my turn to tell you a secret." Tiernan sighed. "Only foreigners have to swear neutrality in Ingdanrad. Gallnach people are granted refuge automatically. I was allowed in because, well . . . I am half Gallnach."

"*What?*" I jerked up. My hair snagged on the stone floor, making me yelp. "Seriously?"

"In a way. My ancestors were druids who married Sverbian soldiers."

"Ohhh." My shoulders dropped. "Neve's father said people like that adapted druidism to fire magic. And . . . yan taku. I mentioned the coin you made, and he asked if you're really Sverbian."

He chuckled. "Of course a metallurgist would notice. Most people never do. I look passably Sverbian, Jorum and Maika helped refine my accent, and I go by Heilind instead of och Heile. My first name is sort of a . . . secret signal to other Gallnach."

"Tiernan?" I rolled it across my tongue. "Like Lónan or Róisín."

"Exactly. Only people that have heard Gallnach names recognize it."

"Wait — so Neve and her family knew?"

"Undoubtedly. It is a grave offence to out another Gallnach person, though."

I lay back down, thinking it over. "Why didn't you ever tell me?"

"Mm." He made a noise as if he was stretching. "People can have unpleasant reactions. Not that I expected you to, but if you mentioned it to family or friends, not fully understanding the history of Gallun or why we hide . . ."

"That's fair," I admitted, thinking of Kirbana forbidding Narun to mention his Gallnach crewmates.

We lapsed into silence. The incessant dripping prickled at me. I was nodding off again when firelight appeared down the corridor. Footsteps, splashing water, cursing in Ferish. I sat up, squinting. A tall figure carrying a torch peered into my cell.

"My, my," Tsiala said. "What did you *do*?"

19.

COUP

I got up, swaying from the concussion. Tsiala was dressed in her black leather armour. She set her torch in a bracket, examined the lock on my cell, and began trying a ring of keys.

"Seriously," she said. "I thought you were with your family. How'd you get locked up in the hangman's ward?"

"The what?"

"This floor is for the worst offenders. War criminals, rapists, people who like fermented cabbage. That's why the place is so empty. Most people are just held here before they get hanged."

The knot in my stomach twisted. "I didn't do anything. I have no idea why — Wait. If you weren't looking for me, why are you here?"

"I'm looking for Alesso." Tsiala jammed a key in the lock, muttered, and tried another. "The militia captain was found strangled to death. A note pinned to his clothes said, 'Free Alesso Spariere or more bodies will come.'"

I sucked in a breath. "Kaid."

"Yeah. It's chaos up there. The deputy captain's missing, and nobody can agree on who should take over command. At this rate, we're gonna see how many deaths a ten thousand-sov wedding gift can buy."

"Are you actually planning to free Alesso?"

"Depends what he says." The lock clanked and she swung open the cell door. "You, however, may go."

I grabbed the key ring and crossed to Tiernan's cell. He slumped in the shadows with his arms folded over his knees, his sleeve veiling the runelight. I tried the same key that had opened mine. Relief washed over me as his lock clicked.

"Come on." I yanked open his door. "We'd better hurry."

"What?" he asked.

"Murders. Problems. Let's go." I snapped my fingers.

A hoarse laugh came from the darkness of his cell. "You want the help of another murderer?"

"You don't belong in here any more than I do. And if you've forgotten, my family's up there."

"All right, all right." He got to his feet, groaning. "Though I am not sure how much help I will be."

Tiernan stepped forward into the torchlight, squinting. He looked like a ghost. Pale and gaunt, skin stretched over his bones, dark half moons under his eyes. His ragged beard blended into a mat of long hair. Dirt flaked off his loose brown shirt and trousers.

On impulse, I hugged him. He inhaled sharply, then folded his arms around me. His ribs felt like the ridges of a seashell, and he reeked of stale sweat, but he was *here*. Alive. He twined his fingers into my tangled hair, sending a shock up my spine.

When we pulled apart, Tsiala was staring. "Who's this?" she asked.

"Tiernan Heilind," I said. "Tiernan, meet Tsi'alha Makōpa."

She eyed him like he was grime scraped off the prison floor. "*You're* Antoch Parr's infamous fire mage? The man Kateiko's supposedly having an affair with?"

"In the flesh," he said dryly. "You must be Alesso Spariere's infamous spy. Any chance of unlocking this?" He raised his runed cuff.

I sorted through the key ring. Taking a guess, I tried a small silver one. The cuff fell open, making the runelight wink out. Tiernan's eyes went wide. He caught the wall for balance, glancing around like Róisín, seeing things we couldn't.

"Gods help me," he breathed, reaching for the torch. A flicker of flame broke free and drifted toward him. "I had forgotten how it feels."

I unlocked my own cuff. A cloud lifted from my mind, taking some of the headache with it. I could finally sense the water dripping into puddles.

"So we're going together?" Tsiala asked. "Had enough of slapping me?"

I scowled. "Depends what you say."

"Right, then." She took the torch from its bracket and thumped Tiernan's back. "Better keep up, old man."

Tiernan took one step and staggered. I caught him and draped his arm over my shoulders for support. Tsiala's mouth twisted, and she stalked off.

We climbed a spiral staircase to a larger floor of cells. The only sound other than our footsteps were the snores and rustles of sleeping prisoners. Tsiala whispered that she'd already checked here and hadn't found Alesso. A second staircase led to a torchlit corridor where two men in red woolwraps lay dead. Blood smeared the floor as if they'd been dragged there.

"Is that your work?" I asked Tsiala, swallowing my nausea.

"No," she said. "They were dead when I got here."

Tiernan rolled them over, peering at their faces. "Någvakt bøkkhem," he swore. "The prison guards."

The corridor led to the guard post, a warm room with timber furniture and a guttering hearth fire. The scent of smoke and whisky filled the air. A flaxen-haired man slumped against the wall in a pool of blood. Shattered glass and the splinters of a stool covered the floor.

"*That's* my work," Tsiala said. "I barely got a word out before he attacked me."

Tiernan checked that body, too. "Not a guard I recognize. And by this point, I know them all."

"Really?" Tsiala asked. "That's who I stole the keys from."

Tiernan got up, frowning. "So a chief druid and the militia captain are murdered, the deputy captain goes missing, and the prison guards are replaced by imposters. Sounds like a coup."

Dread pierced me. "A ten-thousand-sov coup?"

"Maybe. Most soldiers here are too loyal to be bought, but . . ." He eyed Tsiala. "We should be cautious. And since we are all apparently criminals, we need disguises."

✳

I kept watch while Tiernan cleaned up. He scrubbed his face, cut his beard short, and hacked his hair off to his chin. The prison was part of the militia complex, so Tsiala slipped off to the barracks and returned with a stack of clothing — tunic and trousers for Tiernan, shirt and leggings for me taken from the women's wing. She gave me worn leather boots to replace my heeled ones, along with two bronze pins to fix my hair into a bun. Their sharp points made me think they were more than just decorative.

She also brought woolwraps for us all. Tiernan helped me wrap the red cloth around my body like a cocoon and belt it. The top half draped over the belt and hung to my knees. As he pulled back from having his arms around me, I saw jealousy flicker across Tsiala's face. *Good*, I thought scathingly. Let her be jealous.

Tiernan put on his own woolwrap with practised ease. It looked strangely right on him. Something in the way he moved, shifting it aside as he knelt to take the imposter guard's sword and sheath. I pictured him as a young, healthy soldier in a woolwrap. There was a whole side of his life, from his ancestry to his Gallnach name, that I was only now learning.

"Stop staring," Tsiala whispered into my ear. "You're embarrassing yourself."

She thrust a dagger into my hand and grabbed a torch. We padded down another corridor and into the complex's dim lobby. The air felt fresher here. Marble statues of druids lined the long chamber and arched doorways led off in every direction. Tiernan looked longingly at the wall of windows overlooking the harbour. I knew we should stay out of sight, but I tugged him toward the windows anyway.

"By the gods," he murmured, pressing his palm to the pane. "I thought I would never see outside again."

Starlight shone on his gaunt face. Down along the harbour were strings of lantern posts, topped with glowing crystals instead of glass-encased fire. Snow fell through the pools of light and settled on the piers. The dark outlines of ships rocked with the tide.

"We'll make it to Nyhemur," I said. "I promise."

Tiernan's mouth twitched with a smile. "I promise to keep you warm."

His words flooded through me like summer sunlight, sprouting a thousand weeds in my mind. Maybe he *had* wanted to kiss me in Tjarnnaast. He cupped my jaw, his gaze flickering over my lips.

Tsiala cleared her throat. Faint voices sounded from deep within the complex. Tiernan waved his hand, extinguishing our torch. The voices grew louder. It sounded like three men speaking Sverbian.

"Stay back," Tiernan whispered. "I will try talking to them. If it goes wrong, I will signal with a spark. Try to disarm only."

Out of a doorway emerged three figures. They saw us in the starlight and jerked, reaching for their swords. Tiernan lifted his hands in peace. He drew forward and fell into rapid conversation. They gestured toward the prison, voices rising in question, then turning sharp. Tiernan folded his hands behind his back. A spark appeared in his fist.

I lashed out a water whip, tripping one man. Tsiala lunged. Her curved dagger slashed a man's arm. She whirled, slicing another's throat. Blood sprayed through the air. He fell, clutching his neck.

"You call that disarming?!" I cried.

The other men bore down on Tsiala. I yanked open the outer doors. With a sweep of my arm, snow billowed into the lobby. I swirled it around the soldiers, surrounding them with an icy maelstrom. Steaming fireballs erupted through the snow. Tiernan flung up his hands and deflected them. One hit a hanging banner, which burst into flame.

Tsiala leapt into the blizzard. A man's voice cried out. The fireballs ceased, and I let the snow drop. One man lay dead. Another gurgled, grasping his slit throat. Tiernan put his sword through the man's heart, ending his pain.

"Damn," Tsiala said, prowling among the marble statues. "The third fled. Probably to report escaped prisoners."

"People will know soon, anyway," Tiernan said, wiping his blade on a soldier's woolwrap. "These men were coming to get the 'viirelei bitch.' Someone named Jarlind wants to question you, Katja. Either of you know that name?"

"He's a Sverbian lieutenant," Tsiala said. "Not sure which side of this coup he'd be on."

"Then we had better keep moving." Tiernan pulled the flames from the burning banner and shaped them into an orb to light our way. "I suggest we head to the Hollow. If Neve is still there, perhaps she can help us."

Neither Tsiala nor I had a better idea. The Hollow was on the other side of the mountain, and we'd be too exposed outside, so underground it was. Tiernan led us through an arched doorway into the combat training hall. Racks of javelins and arrows lined the walls. In the centre of the room was a square pit spattered with blood. A spiral staircase led down to a winding tunnel, thick with stale air. I felt like a rabbit in a warren.

The tunnel seemed endless. Tiernan kept having to stop and catch his breath. At a crossroads, he deliberated, then beckoned to the right. We continued down another tunnel, emerging into a cavern. Carts and wagons stood among stacks of crates. Pulleys had been built to move goods through the ceiling. Their timbers creaked, making my hair stand on end.

"This is the warehouse district," Tiernan explained. "Right under the harbour market. It should be quiet this time of night."

We crept past huge shelves of casks stamped with the contents and place of origin. Brännvin from Nordmur, cider from northern Eremur, wine from southern Eremur. Farther along, a pile of grain sacks had been torn open, spilling golden wheat. The kernels crunched under our boots. I peered around for signs of battle. Behind a stack of crates, something moved.

"Tiernan," I hissed. "Someone's here."

He jerked, making his fire orb flicker. "Show yourself," he called. "We do not wish you harm."

"Who are you?" called a man. This one had a thick Gallnach accent.

"Militia," Tiernan said. "The loyal side."

The man's relieved laugh echoed through the cavern. He stepped out from behind the crates. Thin and beardless with a smattering of freckles, he didn't look much older than me. A red woolwrap hung from his waist.

"The name's Séamus och Bréac," he said, lifting a hand in greeting. "No offence, but I don't recognize you two."

"Two?" Tiernan sounded confused.

I turned. Tsiala had vanished. Which meant—

A black and red blur appeared out of the shadows. I lunged in front of Séamus. Tsiala's dagger nicked my arm as she swerved.

"What's wrong with you?" I shrieked.

"With *me*?" she snapped. "You think he's lurking here for fun?"

"Whoa." Séamus stumbled back, hands raised. "I didn't mean to cause trouble."

"Yeah?" Tsiala levelled a dagger at him. "Then what *are* you doing?"

He swallowed hard. "Standing guard. Alesso Spariere's being held in the lower levels instead of the prison. You know, in case someone gets ideas about freeing him."

Tiernan and I exchanged a glance. We'd have to choose between going down or continuing to the Hollow. He stayed silent, letting me decide. I hated turning away from my family, but I didn't even know where they were. I could save them faster by finding Alesso and ending this.

"Look," I said. "Séamus — can I call you that? We need to see Spariere. Maybe we can talk him down."

"Why you?"

"Because . . ." I dug my nails into my palms, trying to think. *The best lies are closest to the truth.* "We both served with Eremur's military. Spariere trusts me."

Séamus looked skeptical. "I'll have to take you there myself. They won't let you in otherwise."

Tsiala grabbed my wrist. "No way. That's a trap if I've ever heard one."

I wrenched free from her grip. "It's not your problem. You're not coming."

"What? Why not?"

"This!" I shook my wrist in her face. "You can't even respect the part about 'don't touch me again.' How can I trust you not to kill everyone?"

Tsiala rolled her eyes. "So I'm the villain now? Fine. Run off with your precious fire mage, get married, have babies — *if* he lives that long. The pathetic old man can barely stand."

I punched her.

"Go fuck yourself," I snapped. "Because *I* sure won't do it for you."

For a moment, Tsiala just stared. She spat blood on the stone floor, then strode past me, knocking into my shoulder. As she vanished into the shadows, her voice trailed after her. "Your loss."

✳

Séamus led the way in silence, carrying a torch. Tiernan kept sneaking odd looks at me. I was too furious to care what he thought. I couldn't believe that a few hours ago, I'd been tangled up with Tsiala in the snow, thinking about kissing her. This had been one of the longest nights of my life.

As we passed through yet another dark tunnel, Séamus cleared his throat. "So, uh, I didn't catch your names."

"Tiernan och Heile," he said without hesitation. "My companion here is Katja of the Kae nation."

"Och Heile?" Séamus frowned. "I heard a mention of that name. Something about . . . the Nyhemur border?"

"We were stationed there." Tiernan sounded out of breath, struggling to keep up. "Came back to provide extra security for the wedding, and thank the mother of mountains we did. What on earth happened?"

"Your guess is as good as mine. I just follow orders."

"Lieutenant Jarlind's orders?"

Séamus spun, making the torch gutter. "I'm no traitor, I promise you that."

"Are you saying Jarlind is?" I asked.

"Can't be sure, but" — Séamus turned forward to keep walking — "he's always been too big for his britches. Same with Spariere. I wouldn't put it past 'em to strike a deal."

The tunnel ended in an iron-barred door. Tiernan balked with recognition. "You're taking us to the catacombs?"

"Aye." Séamus passed me the torch and fumbled with a key ring. "We're hoping it'll put the fear of the dead into Spariere. Nothing like being held prisoner among thousands of Gallnach spirits bent on revenge."

Tiernan cast me a questioning look. Aikoto tradition said I wasn't supposed to enter other nations' sacred sites. So far, though, I'd survived a Rúonbattai stavehall and the Ferish sancte where my cousins had been held in the orphanage. A Gallnach burial ground couldn't be any worse. Hopefully.

Séamus shouldered the door open, knocking loose a shower of dust that made him sneeze. The echo was startlingly loud. Beyond the door was the longest spiral staircase I'd ever descended. Cobwebs brushed my skin, and the flickering torchlight made me dizzy. Tiernan had to lean against the wall for balance.

At the bottom, I stepped through another door and gasped. Pathways of glowing runes marked a grid across an enormous cavern. Between the paths were thousands of headstones of every shape and size. Stalactites hung from the ceiling. I followed Séamus in awestruck silence, hoping the Gallnach spirits buried here knew I didn't mean any harm.

The cavern led into another, then another, each filled with graves. Three soldiers stood guard outside a warren of towering stalagmites. Séamus spoke to them in rapid Gallnach. All I caught was the names we'd given, Tiernan och Heile and Katja Kae. The soldiers looked us over, then waved us into the warren.

Shadows fell heavy across us. Deep within the warren, tied to a stalagmite, was Alesso. He slumped somewhere between standing and kneeling. His face was mottled with bruises, one eye swollen, his clothes torn. A runed iron cuff hung around his wrist.

"Is he . . ." I faltered.

"Alive," Séamus reassured me. "He didn't take well to being arrested."

I hurried to Alesso's side. He groaned as I touched his neck. His pulse was weak. "Alesso," I said, cupping his jaw. "It's Kateiko. Can you hear me?"

His unswollen eye fluttered. "K'ko . . ."

"Yes! It's me. Listen, you have to stop this — call off your men—"

"Not . . ." Alesso's breath stuttered. "Not mine."

"Jarlind's, then," I said impatiently. "You can't really want this. Not on your wedding day—"

"Not me. Jarlind. Roo . . . Rúon . . ."

I froze.

"Go," he breathed. "Run."

I whirled. Tiernan saw the terror in my eyes. He drew his sword at the same time Séamus drew his.

Their blades clashed. Fire burst from Tiernan's hand, lighting up the cavern. The reek of charred skin filled the air. Wincing, Séamus struck again and again. Tiernan dodged and parried, but he was tiring fast. I flung ice under Séamus's feet. The young man slipped. His head cracked against a stalagmite. As he lay dazed, soldiers swarmed into the warren.

I coiled a water whip around a soldier's ankle. He went down hard. I drew my dagger and lunged. He swung his fist, connecting with my head. Stars blinked across my vision. We rolled across the uneven floor, grappling. He wrested the dagger from my hand—

"Not the girl!" someone snapped.

The soldier sliced open my thigh. I shrieked. He jerked back — and a sword bloomed through his chest. Tiernan yanked out his blade and kicked the man aside.

I sat up, pressing my torn woolwrap to my gushing wound. Pain wreathed my mind. Tiernan panted as he faced off against Séamus and two other soldiers.

"Back down," Tiernan said. "We can still—"

"No, no," a deep voice interrupted. "It's too late for that."

A tall figure stepped forth from the shadows. Golden hair, broad shoulders, a braided beard — for a second I thought Liet had risen from the dead. This man had no tattoos, though. Just a sickening smile and a lieutenant's silver trim on his woolwrap. A band of runelight fell through the stalagmites, glinting on his sword hilt.

"The infamous Tiernan Heilind," he said. "I was content to let you rot in prison. Instead you walk right into my hands *and* bring the girl we locked up? That dungeon must've addled your brains."

"Lieutenant Jarlind, I suppose." Tiernan's voice was thick with fury.

"Indeed." Jarlind glanced at my leg. "She needs stitches. If you want her to live, I suggest surrendering."

"Neil!" I cried. "Tiernan, he's Rúonbattai—"

Jarlind backhanded me across the face. I collapsed. When my vision cleared, Séamus was behind Tiernan, holding a dagger to Tiernan's throat.

"Better." Jarlind fixed his attention on me. "As for *you*, girl. Who are you?"

"No one," I gasped. "I'm no one—"

He stomped on my hand. I screamed.

Jarlind crouched near me. "You had a place of honour at Spariere's wedding. You also showed up with *this*." He drew the obsidian-handled knife from his boot. "How does a teenage girl come across a sacred blade lost in Brånnheå years ago?"

My thoughts felt like shattered glass. Jarlind was bound to kill us, yet Tiernan had still surrendered to protect me. He'd always protected me. It was time to start fighting my own battles.

"I stole the knife." I eased upright, swaying. "And it wasn't all I stole."

"What?" Jarlind snapped. "What else?"

"This." I used my good hand to pull a bronze pin from my hair. The locks tumbled down my back.

He edged closer to see, frowning. The second he got within reach, I lunged, driving the hairpin through his eye and into his brain. Nausea crashed over me.

Tiernan moved almost too fast to track. He seized the dagger at his throat, reached back over his shoulder, and yanked Séamus's head forward, stabbing the dagger into the younger man's ear. Séamus howled with pain.

Flames erupted. Blinded, I threw an arm over my eyes. Heat rolled over me. The warren became a maelstrom of fire and clashing metal. When the light dimmed, Tiernan stood panting, surrounded by an orange glow. Scorched bodies lay around us. Alesso, still tied to a stalagmite, wasn't moving. His head lolled onto his chest.

"Katja." Tiernan's voice sounded far away. His sword clattered to the stone floor, then he collapsed.

I scrambled toward him. His tunic was torn and bloody over his stomach. I peeled it off his skin, exposing a horrid wound. I could see *inside* his body.

"Nei," I said. "Nei, nei — hold on—" I pressed my hands to the gash, trying to staunch the bleeding.

Tiernan's lashes twitched over his grey eyes. "For . . ."

"What? For what?"

He coughed. Blood frothed on his lips. "Forgive . . . yourself." His lashes fell shut.

I felt myself scream but heard nothing. There was only raw pain in my throat. Only his closed eyes. Only the dimming of orange light.

With the darkness came a strange calm. There was, truly, nothing I could do. Bandages wouldn't be enough. I had no medicine. No help. I'd never make it back up that spiral staircase. It was just a matter of time until my leg bled out.

At long last, we could rest. This was a good place for Tiernan to die, surrounded by his Gallnach kin in their graves. I lay next to him. Trailed my fingers through the pool of our mixed blood. Draped my hair over his body. Knotted my wet fingers into his hair, joining our spirits.

"Okay," I whispered. "If you have to go . . . take me with you."

20.

WIND & RAIN

Voices floated around us, nebulous and gossamer-thin like an algae bloom in water. The accents sounded foreign. They hovered above Tiernan and me, calling our names. *Our* names. How did Gallnach spirits know me? I struggled to listen, to sort sound into meaning. Some voices sounded Aikoto. My aeldu were here, too.

Tema and Temal, I thought. *You found me.*

Something warm and solid touched my arm. Was this part of dying? Did the dead become as real as the living? I summoned all my strength, trying to reach for them. The voices grew sharp. I felt pressure on my thigh — then pain seared my body. A scream tore from my mouth. It felt like my spirit getting ripped from my flesh and bones.

Hands slid underneath me. The ground fell away, letting my limbs hang loose. I was floating. If I had the strength to open my eyes, I felt sure I'd look down and see my body next to Tiernan's. If I looked across, maybe I'd see his spirit floating, too.

I'll find you, I thought. *We'll go together.*

✳

Sheets of rain gusted across me. Wind howled into my skull, wild and raw. I fumbled through darkness, soaked and shivering. Hands numb. Feet numb. Hair swirling across my face, blinding me.

"Tiernan?" I called, getting a mouthful of water. "Tiernan!"

No answer. No anything. No ground or sky, no up or down, only an endless torrent of wind and rain. I screamed. Water flooded down my throat into my lungs. I grasped at my neck, choking.

Help, I begged. *Please, help me!*

Silky fur brushed my skin. Warmth coiled around me. The purr of a mountain cat vibrated my bones. *We're here, little fireweed*, Temal soothed. *But you can't stay.*

I tried to protest. All that came out of my mouth was water.

The outline of a swan appeared in the gusting rain. It wrapped soft feathery wings around us. *My child*, Tema whispered. *It's not your time yet. When it is, we'll be here.*

✳

I woke gasping. A blurry face appeared, silhouetted against white light. Dark hair, a long nose, an angular jaw. *Temal*, I thought — but the man's hair was cropped short. Geniod.

"Kako," he breathed. "I thought — oh, thank the aeldu."

He brushed my hair off my face. I tried to speak and only managed a faint rasp. He propped me upright and held a mug to my mouth. I retched, spilling water onto a blanket draped over me.

"Wala, wala," Geniod soothed. "It's okay. You're safe now."

Safe. My parents had sent me back. I'd touched them, heard their voices, only to lose them again. A crushing weight settled on my chest. I'd lost someone else, too, if only I could remember . . . Who had I been searching for? How did I get there?

My right hand was a mess of purple bruises. I pulled back my wet blanket and found myself in unfamiliar, bloodstained clothes. One side of my leggings had been cut away from a bandaged wound on my thigh. Images flickered through my mind. Swirling fire, the obsidian-handled knife, a hairpin in a man's eye. I lifted a fistful of my hair, matted with blood. Not all of it was mine.

"Tiernan," I rasped. "He . . ."

"He's alive," Geniod said. "We found you in time."

"Alive?"

Geniod pointed. Tiernan lay in the next cot, his eyes closed within their gaunt sockets. His tunic had been cut open. Bloody bandages covered his stomach. He looked beyond the veil of death — until I noticed the uneven rise and fall of his chest.

"The healers sedated him," Geniod said. "I don't know how long he'll be out."

As my eyes focused, I took in our surroundings. A wide hall of grey stone. Rows of cots. Dozens of wounded bodies. Healers in white woolwraps bustled about, working with a forced calm I knew too well. Glowing crystals hung from the high ceiling, bathing the place in stark light. The familiar scent of bleach made my stomach turn.

"You're in the hospital's military wing," Geniod explained. "Dunehein and Rikuja are outside. The healers are only allowing one visitor per patient. Although technically . . . you have three." He patted a small table by the wall. Next to a pitcher of water were a carved swan and mountain cat.

I gasped. Geniod handed me the makiri. I kissed the polished wood and cradled them to my chest, ignoring my bruised hand. They were *here*. Everything valuable I'd been carrying had been stolen by Jarlind and his men, but I still had these fragments of my parents' spirits.

"Where were they?" I scraped out.

"In your room at Clan Ríain's villa. Remember? You thought it'd be too risky to carry them in your purse."

Yan taku, I thought. If I'd brought them to the wedding ... Exhaustion rolled over me. Geniod refilled my water mug and coaxed me to drink. He eased me back onto the cot, traded my wet blanket for a dry one, checked my pulse and temperature. I let him fuss. I had a vague memory of being mad at him but couldn't remember why.

"Get some rest," he said gently. "We'll still be here in the morning. I promise."

✳

When I woke again, the hall had turned deep blue with shadow. A thin wash of daylight showed through arched windows along one wall. Geniod was asleep on the floor, using a folded towel as a pillow. A stranger dozed in the cot to my right. His red woolwrap draped over the side, peeking out from his blanket. The cot to my left held nothing but bloody linens.

Tiernan was gone.

I flung off my blanket and whirled toward the nearest healer. "Where is he?" I demanded.

The pale-haired woman dashed over. She spoke, but the words were foreign. I gestured wildly at the empty cot.

"Where *is* he?" I cried. "Where'd you take him?"

I swung my legs off the cot, sending pain shooting through my thigh. The healer pushed me back down. I shrieked, flailing. She let go with a wince. Geniod scrambled up, looking bewildered. He gripped my shoulders to hold me still.

"Kako, what's wrong?" he asked. "What happened?"

"Tiernan's gone! You said he'd be here! You promised!"

Geniod looked over at the empty cot. He went pale.

I screamed. I'd lost Tiernan in that endless dark rainstorm. I'd left his spirit there and returned to the living world alone. I struck out at Geniod, the pale-haired woman, the other healers who came running.

"You let him die!" My shouting echoed off the stone walls. "*You let him die!*"

Colourful spots flooded my vision. They'd never showed up so fast, so strong. *Not now*, I thought — a second before the world went dark.

✳

Someone shook me awake. A woman's face came into focus above me — curly red hair, pale green eyes, even paler skin. Róisín ó Conn. The hall around us was bright and full of noise.

"Keep calm," Róisín said. "Tiernan och Heile is alive."

I jerked upright. Behind her, the cot was still empty. The bloody linens had been stripped away. Geniod stood nearby, hands clasped in front of his mouth. He looked unsettled. With a wrench, I remembered why I was mad at him. The greenhouse.

Róisín leaned in close to whisper. "Och Heile was moved to a guarded room along with Alesso Spariere. They're both under investigation."

"Alesso's alive, too?"

"Shh. Not here. Too many ears." She cast a pointed look at the soldier dozing in the next cot. "Can you walk?"

I pushed off my blanket. My feet were bare. With effort, I could wiggle my toes, but everything felt numb. The healers must've given me needlemint tincture, which meant the best I could do was fall out of bed. Geniod picked me up instead. He carried me down a corridor and into a small room, where he settled me on another cot. Róisín shut the door and settled into a chair, adjusting her burlap robes.

"The militia wants to question you," she said. "Given that we're cleaning up an attempted coup, talking to them is risky. I want to help you, Kateiko, but I need to know everything you did last night."

Hesitant, I looked to Geniod. He knelt by my cot and held my hand. My anger felt muted. Sure, he'd lied to me about Róisín, but he wouldn't have slept with her unless he trusted her. He wouldn't have brought me here unless he believed she could help.

Sifting through my shattered memories, I recounted the story as best I could. Róisín's gaze drifted over me. Every time I hedged at the truth, she looked me in the eye, cowing me into honesty. She was stripping me apart from the inside, pulling on my tendons to see how I worked.

Her brows furrowed as I relayed Tiernan's story about getting attacked at the Nyhemur border. Geniod voiced what we were all thinking. If the guards responsible were linked to the Rúonbattai, and we could prove Tiernan had fought back in self-defence, then he could walk free. Róisín cautioned me that an attack three months ago probably wasn't related to this coup, but she promised to look into it.

With a spark of hope, I continued my story, describing our escape from prison. At the part about killing Jarlind, my throat started to close. I breathed like Tiernan had taught me. Five seconds in, five seconds out. Róisín's face crinkled with a sympathetic smile.

Once I'd recovered, she said, "We owe you our thanks. And I owe you an apology."

"What for?" I asked.

She looked toward Geniod, but to me she said, "I told you to trust the militia. I can make excuses — I think the traitors knew who I am and avoided me — but they're just excuses. I should've seen this coming."

I shrugged. I could hardly blame her when I'd ignored Tsiala's warning about a trap.

"Sounds like I've got work to do," Róisín said, getting to her feet. "If you need anything, ask for Pádraig och Aindrias. You can trust him."

"Who's he?"

"My nephew. He's a medic here." She glanced out the window and sighed. "Don't speak to anyone else. If people ask questions, say you don't remember. We still don't know who's on our side."

❊

Back in the main hall, a Kae girl in a moss-green woolwrap made the rounds with a lunch trolley. She gave us a shy smile and ladled me a bowl of broth. The savoury scent made my stomach growl, but my bruised right hand was too stiff and sore to use, and I was clumsy with my left. I spilled my first spoonful across my lap. Geniod drew up a stool and fed me. I put up with it, determined not to be like the many stubborn patients I'd treated over the years.

"I, ah . . ." He couldn't meet my eyes. "I owe you an apology, too."

I grimaced. "Apology accepted. No need to discuss it."

"Kako," he said, gentle but firm. "I mean it. Róisín and I talked before waking you. I ended things with her."

I spluttered on the broth. "Why?"

"Because you come first. I should've been there for you."

My protest faltered. I hadn't had time to contemplate Geniod being with Róisín. I didn't even know if it was a whisky-soaked hookup or serious. She was sworn to her people on Innisburren. Would he move there for her? Leave our family in Nettle Ginu behind? Take back his offer of adopting me? The thought hurt more than I'd expected.

"Why her?" I asked abruptly. "She's so . . . *weird.*"

A startled laugh burst out of him. "You really want to know?"

"Yeah. I'm sick of people lying to me."

"Fair enough." Geniod set aside the broth. "Imagine being with someone who can see your spirit. They see the best of you, the worst, and everything in between — and they still want to spend time with you. They know what will cheer you up, so they do it. They know what upsets you, so they're careful. And they don't only do it for you. They do it for everyone you care about. Through that kindness, you see *their* spirit."

"That sounds terrifying."

He smiled wryly. "Romance is always terrifying."

"Then . . ." I picked at my blanket. "If Róisín's really that special, you should be with her."

His eyebrows shot up. "I thought—"

"It wasn't about her. Not really. I was mad at Tsiala, and freaked out about treating another dying soldier, and I took it out on you. Sorry. You've done so much for me already, and you deserve to be happy."

"I appreciate that." He kissed my hair. "To be honest, there's a few things we'd have to work out. Róisín has responsibilities of her own. I'll talk to her, though."

"Just promise one thing. Never, ever tell me about her greenhouse."

Geniod chuckled. "Deal. And speaking of romance, there's something you should know about Tsiala." He fished through his breeches pocket and produced an iron spider. On its stomach was an engraved rune. Bits of red fluff were tangled in its sharp wire legs.

"What's that?"

"A tracking rune. Tsiala was trying to find Alesso so she could stick it on him. Then even if he escaped, we could find him. When you separated in the warehouse district, she knocked into you and stuck it on your woolwrap instead."

I scoffed. "So she could keep spying on me?"

"So she could rescue you." Geniod smiled softly. "The moment you left with Séamus, Tsiala took off running to find us. She felt sure you were in danger, so Róisín brought her nephew Pádraig, the healer. The tracking rune led us straight to the catacombs. If it weren't for Tsiala, we wouldn't have found you in time."

✳

The golden light of afternoon was falling through the windows when a healer wheeled a trolley of medical supplies to my cot. The young man, Pádraig, was small and stocky with a smile as warm and comforting as freshly baked bread. Dark circles marked his eyes, and his mess of brown curls needed a combing. Although he wore a stained white woolwrap instead of burlap robes, the knotted wool pendant around his neck probably meant he was a druid like his aunt Róisín.

"Glad to catch you awake," Pádraig said as he measured my pulse. "I've been checking in but always had to hurry off to another patient. My apologies—"

"It's fine," I interrupted. "I'm used to triage. I'm a war medic myself."

Relief crossed his face. Satisfied my heart was working, he examined my thigh. The bandages came off with surprising ease. Underneath, a long gash had already started fusing shut. Unless I'd slept for days, there was only one explanation.

"Healing magic?" I asked.

"Aye." Pádraig used a damp cloth to wipe away dried blood. "There was no time to stitch your wound and cauterizing it could've sent you into shock. Sealing it magically saved your life, but it can have complications."

"Like what?"

"Essentially, it sped up your natural healing. The process puts incredible strain on the body. It's like sprinting up a mountain. Soon after your uncle here carried you in . . . your heart stopped."

Ice went down my spine. "I *died*?"

Geniod's pained look answered my question. He knelt at my side and kissed my hair. "I flew straight to Clan Ríain's villa to get your parents' makiri. I thought at least they could guide you to Aeldu-yan."

Tears pricked my eyes. I wiped them away with my good hand. "They didn't. They sent me back."

His face flickered through a dozen emotions. I wondered what would've happened if he hadn't taught me to read makiri. Maybe I never would've met my parents in that storm. Maybe I'd still be lost there — or maybe the storm would've vanished, leaving nothing but darkness.

Pádraig gave me a weary smile. *He* must've had a strange day — saving me, accidentally killing me, then finding me alive. He rebandaged my thigh, then examined my bruised fingers. Suspecting bone fractures, he bound them together, sending sparks of pain up my arm. The needlemint must've been wearing off.

Next he examined my head, peering at the gash I'd woken up with in prison. I was caught off guard when he asked permission to touch my hair. Most itherans didn't know our taboos. He worked carefully, washing the wound, then swabbing it with vodka to disinfect it. The sharp burn made my eyes water.

"This will all have to heal naturally," he said. "We can't risk putting your body under more stress. For the next few days, it's bed rest, water, bland food. You know the drill."

"What about . . ." I glanced at Tiernan's empty cot.

Pádraig fixed me with a sharp look. His pale green eyes had an echo of Róisín's. "Medic to medic, I won't sugar-coat it. Your friend's too fragile to use more magic on. It'll be weeks before it's safe to take him off sedatives. And . . ."

"What?" I pressed.

The young druid rubbed his jaw. In his eyes I saw the same guilt and grief I knew from Tjarnnaast. "There's a chance he won't ever wake."

✳

Numb from another dose of needlemint, I lay in bed counting the crystals hanging from the ceiling. Thirty-two, thirty-three . . . I kept losing track, picturing Tiernan lying on a cot somewhere, unconscious and alone. Even if I had the strength to move, he wasn't allowed visitors.

What did the place between life and death look like for him? Maybe I'd been caught in a rainstorm because I remembered drowning. I didn't know if he'd ever gotten so close to death. Or if I wound up in a storm because I was an antayul, then . . . was he trapped among flames? Screaming for someone to put out the fire? To guide him away to safety?

Sverbian legend said upon death, people's spirits took a boat across an ocean to Thaerijmur, a land of abundance. Tiernan had named his sword Hafelús after the torch on that boat. I'd always assumed he would make that journey one day, but I hadn't known he was half Gallnach. Maybe their crow goddess would lead his spirit back to the catacombs. Maybe he'd never find his way out of that in-between place. I pulled my blanket over my head so Geniod wouldn't see me cry.

Forgive yourself. Those were Tiernan's last words. For what, though? Killing Jarlind, or leading us into a trap and getting us killed?

No, I told myself fiercely. I'd survived. Tiernan would, too. I'd make sure of it.

21.

COLLATERAL DAMAGE

Raised voices drew everyone's attention. Two men in red wool-wraps were arguing with a healer. They pushed past her and scoured the hall, their gazes landing on me. Geniod got up from his stool, looking wary. The soldiers' boots slapped the stone floor as they drew near. The taller one, blond and bearded, was carrying my tattered muslin dress.

"Kateiko Leniere?" he asked. He sounded distinctly Sverbian.

I nodded.

He tossed the dress across my cot and set the broken shards of my filigree headband on the bedside table. "Are these yours?"

"Uh—" Róisín had told me to say I didn't remember anything, but there was no point denying this. Hundreds of people had seen me at the wedding reception. "Yes."

"We found those in the prison," said the other soldier, who sounded Gallnach. "Anything to say for yourself?"

"Can't this wait?" Geniod asked. "My niece needs rest—"

"Your niece," the Sverbian interrupted, "is under investigation for murder."

I stared at them, baffled. "In the prison?"

"And elsewhere." He settled onto a stool. "Seems like you and Tsiala Makōpa had quite the night. Sneaking into a sacred rowan grove, 'witnessing' the assassination of Fearghas och Donnabhán, freeing a mass murderer from prison, and stealing militia uniforms to impersonate soldiers. Your trail throughout the city is littered with bodies."

My shattered mind couldn't think up a defence. Technically that was all true. If I said I only killed Jarlind, I'd be throwing both Tiernan and Tsiala under the cart for the other deaths.

"This is ridiculous," Geniod said. "Róisín ó Conn has already questioned Kateiko—"

"We didn't ask you." The Gallnach man unhooked a coil of rope from his belt. "Kateiko Leniere, you're under arrest."

Panic surged through me. I had no idea if these men were loyalists or Rúonbattai. If they took me away—

"Stop!" Pádraig shouted from across the hall. He stormed through the rows of cots, a bloody scalpel in hand. "Mother of mountains. How dare you harass my patient?"

"Your patient's a murderer," snapped the Gallnach soldier.

"Oh? You put her on trial already?" Pádraig glowered up at the soldiers. "This girl is on her deathbed. She leaves this hospital when I say she can."

"She's dangerous. We have to put a nullifying cuff on her, at least—"

"You'll do no such thing." Pádraig brandished his scalpel. "Do you know how much pain those cause? I'll have to give her so much needlemint her heart will stop. *Again.*"

The Sverbian soldier rose from his stool. "Fine. If you won't hand over the girl, we'll take her uncle as collateral."

"What?" I cried.

Geniod looked stunned. He drew a measured breath, then turned and put his hands behind his back. The Gallnach man uncoiled his rope and bound my uncle's wrists.

"We'll release him when the medics release you," the soldier told me. "Behave yourself and no harm will come to him."

"It'll be fine," Geniod reassured me. "Kianta kolo."

Temal's mantra. *The sap will flow.* Even after a long winter, spring always came.

❋

The Sverbian soldier stayed to watch me. When the Kae girl returned with her trolley, she looked surprised to see him instead of Geniod. She edged close enough to pass me a bowl of mutton stew and hurried on. I fumbled to eat with my left hand, burning with humiliation under the soldier's gaze.

As daylight slipped away, Pádraig appeared. "Time to get you cleaned up," he said. "A female healer will you help you bathe."

He helped me onto a wheeled cot and rolled me away. My guard followed us down a corridor, but with a pointed look from Pádraig, the man let us go in alone. Instead of a healer, I found Rikuja, who burst into tears, and Dunehein, who wrapped me in a bear hug. I hadn't fully believed they were alive. Rikuja let me feel her baby bump, assuring me they were fine.

"Thank you," I told Pádraig, clasping his hand.

He winked. As he left, he said, "You've got half an hour."

The room had a basin set into the stone floor, built with steps and handles so injured people could get in and out. Dunehein stayed behind a canvas screen while Rikuja helped me undress and bathe. They said Tsiala had been arrested. Neve and Róisín were raising hell, storming into the militia complex and insisting the soldiers had it all wrong. Róisín's instructions for me were clear — stay put, keep quiet, don't do anything stupid. She was determined to prove Jarlind and the Rúonbattai were behind all this.

Rikuja braided my wet hair and helped me into a grey hospital-issue dress. She promised to burn my stolen militia uniform. Some of the blood on it was Jarlind's. I didn't owe his spirit the peace of reaching Thaerijmur, but I didn't want it hanging around here.

All too soon, Pádraig returned me to the main hall. Someone had put clean bedding on my cot. I placed my parents' makiri on the bedside table to watch over me. The glowing crystals on the ceiling were dimmer at night to let us patients sleep, but I was afraid to close my eyes. Afraid to fall back into that rainstorm.

More and more, I was coming to understand Jonalin. Waking after his overdose must've felt like rising from the dead. How did you move forward from that? All the grief and guilt and hopelessness that made me want to die were still here, with more piling on top, but now I knew the terror of dying. The dark, the cold, the aching loneliness. I retched, feeling water in my lungs. My guard barely looked over.

For a year, I'd given Jonalin the stars. For a night, I'd given Tiernan the sun. As for me, I missed open air. Breathing freely. Maybe visiting the plains of Nyhemur with Tiernan was exactly what I needed. Dragonfly-wing veils of snow, the impossible vastness of the sky, and befriending distant windmills. Somehow, we would make it there. That dream was worth living for.

✳

I woke to voices. Neve was speaking Gallnach with a skinny young soldier. He must've replaced my guard overnight. She held a leather-bound book to her chest, twirling her strawberry-blonde hair and making doe eyes up at him. Sighing, he waved her past.

"Morning," she chirped, dropping the book on my bedside table with a *whump*. "I brought you something to read."

"What?" I sat up groggily.

"Literature. It's a human right, even for prisoners."

She left before I could ask what she meant. I pulled the book onto my lap. The gilt lettering on the cover was in the angular symbols of Gallnach. It was just like Neve to forget I couldn't read her language. Annoyed at being woken for nothing, I slid it back onto the table.

By midday, though, it was clear the militia wasn't allowing me visitors. Bored and desperate for a distraction, I flipped through the book, looking at illustrations of crystal formations. Tucked into the pages was a letter. I snuck a glance at my guard. He was cleaning his nails with a dagger, equally bored. I unfolded the letter and laid it flat against the pages. The curvy, looping handwriting had to be Neve's.

Good news, sweet pea. A Sverbian soldier confessed and
named Lieutenant Jarlind as the ringleader of this coup.
The RB framed Alesso to cast suspicion on all Ferish people
by extension. Jarlind planned to kill everyone in his way,
then emerge with Alesso's dead body, setting himself up as
the saviour of Ingdanrad. Instead, once word got out that
Jarlind was dead (a hairpin through the eye, impressive!),
the coup fell apart. It's clear who our real saviour is.

Our darling Tsiala got caught up in all this by accident.
Apparently, just because my loyal bodyguard has a Ferish
accent and accepted a few gold sovs from Alesso, she must

be his hired assassin? Rubbish. (By the way, I had no idea he paid Tsiala to spy on you. You must be furious, sweet pea, but I hope you can forgive her. I'm sure she had her reasons.)

Anyway, she and Geniod are being treated fine in prison, and Tiernan is stable. A former militia captain has come out of retirement to replace the murdered one. He's asked Róisín ó Conn to help him interrogate every soldier and weed out the traitors. The process may take weeks, but I'll keep slipping you news, and I'll write to Lieutenant Parr and your family in Caladheå to explain everything.

xoxo — the strawberry visiting the hospital

P.S. Destroy this letter.

✳

Neve returned the next morning with another book. My guard this time was a burly man with a goatee who seemed immune to her charms. As their conversation shifted into an argument, Neve's face darkened. She shook out her white skirts like a goose angling for a brawl, then unleashed a torrent of what had to be insults, threats, or both. The man blanched and let her give me the book. This letter had been hastily scrawled.

Morning, sweet pea. Alesso's letters vanished from under his bunk, so I dropped a hint to the militia to go looking. Once Síona heard their private correspondence might be exposed, she broke down and admitted everything. It's *quite* a story. Three years ago, she heard about a battle in Brånnheå that provoked a fire spirit into erupting a volcano.

(Sound familiar?) Realizing the RB were active again, Síona hired Alesso to teach her Ferish so she could secretly reopen diplomacy with Eremur and form an alliance against the RB.

Instead, she found an ally in Alesso. When he was younger and serving in Eremur's military, the RB razed his village, killing his parents and four sisters. Grief-stricken, he defected to Ingdanrad, vowing to learn fire magic to turn the RB's power against them. Síona, bless her heart, swooned over the tragic soldier trying to avenge his dead family.

She persuaded Alesso to reconnect with his estranged uncle, the warlord Armando Contere. (I met him once. Handsy fellow, ugh.) Anyway, the trio struck a deal. Contere sent ten thousand sovs as a wedding gift, which Alesso would donate to our militia to buy weapons and armour. In exchange, the newlyweds would move south to Contere's territory and teach combat magic to his soldiers. Together they'd build an alliance that could defeat the RB.

Naturally, the mage assembly is in an uproar. We have strict laws against teaching magic to outsiders. My father speaks of hanging Síona and Alesso for treason. Other members say we've been neutral too long and it's about time someone took action. The one thing the assembly agrees upon is holding an inquiry into Clan Níall. If the rest of the clan knew about the planned alliance, they might all be accused of treason.

No news of Tiernan, Tsiala, or your uncle. Stay strong.

xoxo — the strawberry raiding my clan's library

P.S. Yesterday, leaving the hospital, I noticed Ivar on a cot across the hall. He's unconscious with a head wound. No one knows what happened. I dearly hope he didn't join the RB, the handsome fool.

The next time Pádraig came by, I persuaded him to let me try walking. He fetched me sheepskin slippers and wooden crutches. My guard followed us like a burr stuck to my skirt. The world tilted and colourful specks flitted across my vision, but I pushed on to see Ivar.

He looked strangely tranquil, motionless except for the rise and fall of his chest. Bandages circled his head. I figured he was sedated like Tiernan, but Pádraig said they hadn't given him anything. Ivar's mind was simply elsewhere. I pulled down his blanket and touched his calloused fingers, seeking out memories. He had a simple gold ring on his right hand, a braided leather bracelet on his left.

I remembered him taking my hand in the dark. It must've been my right hand, since I'd fumbled to draw my knife with my left. Then . . . a thump. His groan. His body falling. Jarlind or his men must've attacked Ivar to get to me. One more person suffering because they tried to help me. One more person I couldn't help in return.

✳

The light moved in an endless cycle — blue dawn, golden day, rosy dusk, and soft white at night. The same faces came and went. Pádraig changed my bandages and gave me needlemint tincture. The Kae girl brought barley porridge for breakfast, broth for lunch, and soup or stew for dinner. Neve visited each morning with a new book. For days, her slipped notes were brief reassurances that everyone was okay. Then, tucked into an illustrated botany tome, came a longer letter.

Hello, sweet pea. Róisín's interrogation of the militia has uncovered worrying news. Séamus och Bréac wasn't the only Gallnach soldier who sided with the RB. Some were bribed, some genuinely believe all Ferish people are dangerous. A few already wanted to assassinate Fearghas och Donnabhán. We founding clans opened our city to strangers, yet they repay us in blood, ranting and raving that we haven't done enough. Ungrateful scum.

Everything's such a mess that the militia doesn't know what to make of you and Tsiala. As soon as you can leave the hospital, you two will stand trial. Don't worry. The charges won't stick. Tsiala's sworn as my bodyguard to protect both me and my companions. You just have to say everything you did was self-defence.

Be careful, though. Don't mention your uncle's tryst with Róisín, or it'll seem like that's the only reason she's defending you. Don't mention we were investigating Síona, Alesso, or the RB. If the militia thinks you're a spy for Eremur, you'll never leave this city alive. Say I brought you as a friend and you got caught in this by accident.

xoxo — your friend, the strawberry

P.S. No change with Tiernan.

Wonderful. So Geniod and Tsiala were stuck in prison waiting for me. After Pádraig got formal word of the impending trial, he examined me to estimate when I'd be well enough. My leg didn't matter much, since I could sit during the trial, but he was worried what hours of interrogation would do to my heart.

"Perhaps if I come along," he mused as he changed my bandages. "They won't need me here much longer."

"You don't normally work here?" I asked.

"Not in the military wing, no. I only help out during emergencies. Usually I work in neurology."

"Near-what?"

"The study of the brain. It's one of the most important and fragile parts of the body. Take your friend Ivar, for example." Pádraig nodded across the hall. "The external wound isn't bad, but if there's internal bleeding . . . well."

I thought of Malana, struck in the head during the Ivy House battle, bleeding out her ear. She'd gone deaf on that side and still had balance problems. I wondered if Pádraig could do anything for her. In a better time, I could've spent hours asking about his work.

He finished with my bandages and straightened up. "I want to run some stress tests on you tomorrow. Physical exertion, emotional strain, the like. If you clear them without trouble — and that's a big if — I'll look at releasing you. Deal?"

I nodded. "Deal."

22.

THE AERIE

Neve didn't come the next morning.

It's no big deal, I told myself. She was probably busy or didn't have news. Still, I'd come to rely on her daily reassurances. Even my guard, the burly goateed man that she'd bullied into letting her pass, kept looking around for her.

In early afternoon, two men in red woolwraps entered the military wing. They gave a scroll to the healer in charge, an elderly matron. Her lips pursed as she read. She thrust the scroll back at them, fetched a cloak and comb from a cabinet, and strode over to me.

"Up you get, lass." She pulled off my blanket. "You're summoned to trial."

"Now?" I gaped at her. "Pádraig hasn't cleared me—"

"I'm aware. Seems the muttonheads in the Aerie aren't fussed about patient safety."

"The Aerie? My trial's with the mage assembly?"

She thrust the comb at me in answer. With my good hand, I undid my rumpled braid and ran the comb through my hair. The matron licked her thumb and washed a smudge off my cheek, plucked at my grey linen dress, and shrugged in resignation. I tucked my parents' makiri into my pocket and slid my feet into my sheepskin slippers. The matron clasped the cloak at my throat and beckoned to the two soldiers.

The smaller man snapped a runed cuff around my wrist, numbing my water-calling, and bound my hands behind my back. I couldn't use crutches that way, so he supported me as I limped across the hall. Outside, I lifted my face to the sun and sucked in cool mountain air. The hospital looked immense from here, built into the base of a cliff with rows of windows stretching up and away to each side. The terrace ahead had greenhouses and snowy gardens where healers probably grew medicinal herbs.

Slush soaked my slippers as we crossed to a waiting sleigh. I couldn't climb up, so the larger soldier lifted me. The driver clicked his tongue and the small woolly horses jerked forward. The air grew cold and thin as we rose. Crows circled overhead, their caws echoing off the mountains. I shuddered, hoping they weren't another omen of death.

The Aerie stood atop a rocky slope, one of the few freestanding structures in Ingdanrad. It looked like a colossal geode — a steep pyramid of rough stone, fronted by a wall of translucent white crystal. The reflecting sunshine burned my eyes. Since I couldn't shield them with my hands bound, I had to keep my head down as we approached. Guards in steel armour heaved open the tall doors.

Blinking away the glare, I stepped into a vast, airy atrium. A turquoise pool occupied the centre of the room. Within it stood an immense wrought-iron tree, rising through a gap in the upper floors to a glass ceiling four storeys up. Ferns and curtains of witch's hair hung from the branches, creating the illusion of a real tree. Agriculture, metallurgy, and architecture — the specialties of Ingdanrad's founding clans.

My escorts led me along a bridge over the pool, then to a staircase that spiralled up the tree trunk. It felt like climbing into a forest. Narrow walkways radiated out like wheel spokes to each floor. I kept having to pause, panting and dizzy. Pain streaked out from my thigh wound. At the top, my escorts let me collapse on a bench. A clerk standing outside a pair of carved doors said I'd be called soon.

I'd never been so uncomfortable in so many ways. My wet slippers had given me blisters, the nullifying runes filled my head with cottonwood fluff, the ropes around my wrists chafed, and my spine itched in a spot I couldn't reach. At least the wait gave me time to look around. Three bronze birds roosted in the branches — the Gallnach crow, Sverbian raven, and Kae heron.

The carved doors swung open, making me jump. Tsiala emerged, hands behind her back, each elbow held by a soldier. Clad in a brown prisoner's dress that fit snug over her muscular shoulders, she looked like a warrior queen going to her execution — chin up, eyes forward, standing taller than her escorts.

"What happened?" I burst out. "Did they sentence you?"

"Not yet." Tsiala smiled bleakly as she was led away. "Guess it depends on you."

My escorts took me through the doors into a large chamber. Six figures sat behind a long table atop a dais, silhouetted by sunlight coming through the slanted crystal wall. Four wore burlap robes — Neve's father Lónan, Clan Murragh's chief druid, and two elected druids. Another woman wore a silk robe in the pale blue of the Sverbian flag. A man with a greying braid wore a sleeveless shirt that showed off his numerous tattoos, including interlocking lines around his upper arm and a heron on his forearm. He must've been Hanlin, the Okoreni-Kae.

Amidst the mage assembly was an empty seventh seat. Neve had mentioned in her letters that Síona's sister, Caoimhe, had become the new chief druid of Clan Níall. Since the entire clan was under investigation for treason, though, they'd temporarily lost the right to sit on the assembly.

I was shown to a wooden chair in the centre of the room. Along the right wall sat Dunehein and Rikuja, Neve, her mother and brothers, her handmaiden Júni, and dozens of unfamiliar people. Along the left wall sat Róisín and several soldiers. One, an older man with gold trim on his woolwrap, was probably the militia captain.

The Clan Murragh druid rose to her feet. Looking down from the dais, she said, "Kateiko Leniere. Please state your age, occupation, and nation for the assembly."

"Uh . . ." I shifted in my chair. "Eighteen. A war medic for Eremur. I was born Rin, but my family left to form the Tula-jouyen. I was never initiated into either."

A quill scratched to my left. Next to the seated soldiers, a young woman was taking notes.

The Murragh druid cleared her throat. "Miss Leniere, you have been charged with murder, theft of a militia uniform, impersonating a soldier, and freeing a criminal from prison. Do you contest these charges?"

My mind blanked. "Nei — I mean, I did those things, but—"

A clamour went up across the room.

"It's not how it sounds!" I protested. "People were trying to kill us!"

The Murragh druid raised a hand for silence. "You claim these actions were in self-defence?"

I took a deep breath, remembering Neve's advice. "Yes. I got caught in this by accident."

The woman nodded and took her seat. Lónan rose next. The light from the crystal wall dimmed as if humbling itself in his presence.

"Miss Leniere," he began in a steady voice. "You came to Ingdanrad as a guest of my daughter, Níamh ó Lónan ó Ríain. Where did you meet?"

"The hot springs in Port Alios."

"And when were you visiting there?"

"Last month."

"It was more than visiting," Róisín cut in.

My pulse skipped. *Sneaky fucking druid*, I thought, not for the first time. She'd promised to help, only to turn on me.

Lónan adjusted his round spectacles and peered at Róisín. "You see dishonesty in the girl?"

"No. I see heartache." Róisín got to her feet, fingering her knotted wool pendant. "Nerio Parr, a lieutenant in Eremur's military, told me the story. They were in Port Alios to get married."

"Married? To a Parr?" The Sverbian woman in the assembly leaned forward, examining me.

"The wedding didn't happen." Róisín's gaze drifted over my heart. "They had a terrible fight and Kateiko fled here. With Ferish fanatics and Rúonbattai waging a holy war against each other, it's dangerous to be in Eremur. Especially since she lost the protection she'd hoped to gain from the Parrs."

The Murragh druid gave Róisín a sharp look. "Are you claiming the girl's a refugee?"

"Merely relaying the facts. It's not my job to interpret them."

It felt like I'd fallen through the Aerie's atrium and landed on my feet. Róisín had turned that around so fast I felt dizzy.

Lónan went on questioning me, walking through every step of Alesso and Síona's wedding night. I floundered to respond, trying to avoid any indication of being a spy. Lónan kept glancing at Róisín, who confirmed I was being honest. Occasionally she broke in to add something, like that I'd saved a militia soldier's life by treating his burns. A seed of hope bloomed within me. With her help, maybe I could get through this.

"You have no recollection of getting taken to prison?" Lónan asked.

"Nei," I said. "I had a concussion. I don't remember any of it."

"Why do you think Lieutenant Jarlind sent you there?"

Admitting I stole a sacred knife from Brånnheå was still a terrible idea, especially in front of a Sverbian mage. "I don't know. Maybe he saw me with Alesso Spariere and thought I'd be a problem. Maybe he knew I was engaged to Nerio Parr and wanted to ransom me."

Lónan peered down through his spectacles. "And when you left the prison, why did you free a mass murderer?"

The hall fell silent. Outside, a crow cawed, sending ice down my spine. Why *had* I freed Tiernan?

Because I needed him, I thought. I hadn't considered what would happen if we got caught. Once he woke from the sedatives, he'd go on trial, too. He could be hanged. He must've known that, yet he came anyway because I asked. I'd repaid years of kindness by destroying his life.

My throat closed. Colourful specks flitted across my vision, turning the crystal wall into a vast glittering opal. *Not now*, I thought. *Shit, not now not now not now*—

✳

"I told you!" Neve shrieked. "I *told* you she wasn't ready!"

I opened my eyes. Dunehein and Rikuja crouched over me, their worried faces backed by the glass ceiling. They helped me sit up.

Hanlin, the Okoreni-Kae, had left his seat with the mage assembly. He called water into his cupped hands and held it to my mouth, checked my pulse, then beckoned the militia captain over.

"Remove her bonds," Hanlin said. "She clearly doesn't have the strength to be a threat."

The captain untied my wrists and unlocked the runed cuff. A cloud lifted from my mind. I rolled my shoulders and shook out my arms, making my joints crack and pop.

"Hang in there," Rikuja soothed. "You're doing great."

Dunehein looked over my wounds, using his bulk to shield me from view. Leaning in, he whispered, "Trust Lónan. Follow his lead."

He helped me back to my chair, which had toppled over. Rikuja kissed my hair, then they were escorted back to their seats. I squinted up at Lónan. It was hard to see against the bright crystal wall, but I could've sworn he winked.

"Do you remember the question?" he asked me.

I nodded. Hanlin's gesture had given me the answer.

"The first time I met Tiernan Heilind," I said, "I was half-dead in a stable. He offered me water, food, and help. Kindness is his first instinct. Ask anyone who's met him. I don't know exactly what happened at the border garrison, but Tiernan says he fought in self-defence, and I believe it. Of all the militia soldiers I've met here, past or present, he was the only one I was sure I could trust. That's why I freed him."

"And you admit to stealing militia uniforms to disguise yourselves?" Lónan asked.

"Yes. It seemed like the safest way out of the prison."

Lónan paced the dais, hands folded among his draping sleeves. "Tsiala Makōpa confessed to killing three soldiers in the militia complex. She claims one was an imposter prison guard who attacked her, and the other two were after you. Do you agree with her version of events?"

"Yes. The two in the lobby worked for Jarlind. They called me the 'viirelei bitch.'"

Hanlin made a disgusted sound. The Sverbian mage leaned over to whisper to the Murragh druid.

"Do you think Makōpa's use of lethal force was justified?" Lónan asked.

In truth, I wasn't sure. I hardly knew Tsiala and hadn't been allowed to speak with her. I didn't know if she understood Tiernan's conversation with the soldiers or had some inkling Jarlind was a traitor. I didn't know if she was fully in control or running on fear and nerves. All I knew was I owed her my life. I wasn't going to destroy hers as well as Tiernan's.

"Yes," I said. "It was justified. She was doing her job as a body-guard, and her instincts were right."

"Then why did you separate from her in the warehouse district?"

"Because . . ." I rubbed my knuckles, remembering the feel of punching her. "We thought Séamus och Bréac might lead us into a trap. So Tiernan and I went with him, and Tsiala went to get help. She's the reason we're alive."

The rest of the questioning went smoother. From the moment Tiernan and I entered the catacombs, everything we'd done had genuinely been self-defence. I described a soldier cutting my leg, Tiernan surrendering, and Jarlind stomping on my hand. My bruised, bandaged fingers were proof. As I described trying to save Tiernan, my breath started to hitch.

"That'll do," Lónan said. "We don't need you passing out again."

Soldiers led me to a seat along the left wall. The mage assembly called people up to testify about my character. Róisín explained how I helped defend her village against the Rúonbattai. Neve described the public attention my engagement to Nerio had gotten, with gossip and rumours running rampant in Port Alios, and said it would be no surprise if Jarlind had targeted me to get to the Parrs. Júni said I'd always been open and friendly, and as a Sverbian she'd never felt unsafe around me.

The assembly adjourned, departing through a side door to make their decision. The militia let Dunehein and Rikuja wait with me. They insisted it had gone well, but the perpetual knot in my stomach was now made of snakes. I couldn't even remember what I'd said. The light from the crystal wall turned golden as we waited. Still the assembly didn't return. A clerk emerged from the side door to fetch Róisín.

I was faint with hunger when the main doors opened. Tsiala stepped in, chin held high, escorted by a soldier on each side. Róisín and the assembly filed back in and took their seats. The only one who remained standing was Lónan.

"These are unusual circumstances," he said. "We have seven mages on the assembly to prevent deadlocks, but Clan Níall's absence complicates things. The vote to convict Kateiko Leniere and Tsiala Makōpa of murder is three for, three against."

Tsiala and I traded glances across the hall. She looked as stunned as I felt.

"The assembly unanimously finds you both guilty of theft, impersonating soldiers, and freeing a murderer from prison. We don't look lightly on outsiders interfering in our politics. However, we acknowledge your services to Ingdanrad, and furthermore, we acknowledge the Aikoto Confederacy's sovereignty in sentencing their own members."

Hanlin rose. "Prison has never been our people's first resort. We believe in rehabilitation over punishment. I offer a choice to Kateiko Leniere, as well as to Tsiala Makōpa in solidarity with our

Kowichelk Confederacy neighbours. Two months in prison, or the equivalent time — eight hours a day for six months — in unpaid labour. You'll have free rein within the city the rest of the time."

"What kind of labour?" Tsiala asked.

"For you, cleaning and maintenance in the militia complex. While there, you'll train alongside new recruits in *non*-lethal combat."

A wry smile crossed Tsiala's face. "I'll take the six months."

Hanlin nodded. "For Miss Leniere, it'll be working in the hospital. Damage must be mended, not repaid with more damage."

I stared up at him in astonishment. I wasn't ready to return to medicine. Every time I thought about treating someone's wounds, I panicked. Surely Róisín would've told the assembly that—

Oh, I thought. They were offering a chance to mend *my* damage. I'd work with people like Pádraig and the elderly matron, safe in a hospital, not alone and terrified on a battlefield. And even if I couldn't visit Tiernan, I'd be near him. That was better than wasting away in prison.

"Fine," I said. "I'll take the six months."

23.

CLOSER

Róisín offered to accompany me back to the hospital. She, Dunehein, Rikuja, and I piled into a horse-drawn sleigh driven by an acolyte who'd accompanied her from Innisburren. Rikuja kept fussing over me, draping a wool blanket over my lap and making sure my injured leg had enough room. Nothing seemed real. I was still inside a colossal geode, the twilit sky forming another crystal wall trapping me in the mountain range.

"I'm sorry for throwing you off by bringing up your engagement," Róisín said as we descended the steep road. The sinking sun made our shadows stretch long across the terraces. "The militia captain already knew. Alesso Spariere mentioned it when we interrogated him. I figured it was better to spin it in a way that made you look sympathetic."

I managed a smile. "I'm sorry for doubting you."

She fixed her pale green eyes on me. "There's another problem I *can't* solve. I looked into that fight at the border garrison. The soldiers there say Tiernan och Heile was acting strange. Paranoid, jittery, constantly reaching for his sword. The men he and Jorumgard Tømasind killed had no apparent connection to the Rúonbattai. No one out there had seen a silver-haired cleric or heard any mention of her. All evidence shows you freed a murderer from prison."

A horrifying thought crept into my head. Captain Parr had turned into a barefoot, rambling drunk after the cleric slipped through our grasp in Tjarnnaast. Sure, he hadn't launched the holy war, but I definitely believed he could've. Maybe Tiernan had lost control, too. Maybe I really had loosed a violent criminal on Ingdanrad.

Bearshit, I told myself. This was how the Rúonbattai thrived, tearing people apart through fear and suspicion. My parents wouldn't have sent me to find Tiernan if he'd turned dangerous. I slipped my hand into my pocket to touch their makiri. Ever since I died, the wood had felt warm like it had on Yanben. Their spirits felt closer now.

Róisín leaned forward in the sleigh, resting her elbows on her knees. "Och Heile narrowly avoided the noose before. If you want to save him, you need evidence he's innocent. Otherwise, he'll wake to a death sentence."

"How . . ." I lifted a hand helplessly. "If you couldn't find anything, how can I?"

"Start with this." From a deep pocket within her robes, she drew the obsidian-handled knife. "If there's any Rúonbattai hiding under the rocks, this should lure them out."

*

The matron in charge of the hospital was astonished that I'd left as a prisoner and returned as an employee. She said help was always welcome, but she had no intention of putting me to work until I recovered. For now, she lent me a medical apprenticeship textbook in Coast Trader, a hefty tome with a crumbling spine and stained pages. Since I wasn't formally an apprentice, I wasn't allowed to learn healing magic, but I *was* allowed to learn procedures for sterilizing surgical tools and changing bedpans.

No longer under guard, I was granted privacy from the male patients — a corner cot tucked behind canvas hangings. Dunehein scrounged us dinner from the hospital kitchen. While we were eating, Geniod arrived, free from prison. Dirt coated his skin and clothes, but he looked in better shape than me. "Told you it'd be fine," he said with a smile.

Neve brought my clothes and fir branch blanket from her villa. She said my family was welcome to keep living there if they wanted to stay the six months, which of course they did — although they insisted they'd earn their keep. Neve suggested places they could help out. Geniod agreed to work in their greenhouses, Dunehein in the lumberyard. Rikuja leapt at the chance to help Clan Ríain's carpenters restore the historic woodwork in their older buildings.

Only after they bid me goodnight did I work out the timing of my sentence. Rikuja's baby was due in midsummer. She wanted to have it at home in Toel Ginu, surrounded by her family, but I couldn't leave Ingdanrad until late summer. When the time came, I'd have to convince her and Dunehein to go home, which meant I'd have to prove I was okay without them.

Pádraig appeared in the morning, apologizing for his absence yesterday. He'd been elbow-deep in surgery when soldiers came to get me. The upside, he said wryly, was if I could survive a murder trial, I could survive a bit of magical healing. He let me choose between my hand, head, and leg. I chose my hand. He gave me a strong dose of needlemint, tied my arm to a wooden board, and fused my fractured finger bones back together. When he finished, only a few greenish bruises remained.

While visiting the hospital, Geniod told me that Róisín had finished weeding traitors out of the militia. There'd be a mass hanging in the harbour market. The mage assembly had asked her to help with the inquiry into Clan Níall next. Given that they had hundreds of members, she'd be here a while longer. She and Geniod had agreed to enjoy this time together without expectations for the future.

One evening, my family brought a bundle of letters. The earliest, dated a month ago, was from Nerio. He'd reached Jorumgard in prison, learned about Tiernan's imprisonment here, and wrote to ask if Tiernan was willing to reveal his location to Captain Valrose in exchange for Jorumgard's freedom. The letter must've gotten delayed in transit. Another letter, dated last week, was in response to Neve's message about the coup. *This changes everything*, Nerio had scrawled hastily. *Keep in touch*.

The third letter was from Jorumgard. *Hang in there, little pint*, he'd written. *Tell Dune and Rija congrats on their baby. It'll be one of the greatest honours of my life to be the tiny pint's uncle.* To no one's surprise, Rikuja burst into tears when I read it aloud.

Kirbana had written the fourth letter, reassuring me that she, Narun, and Yotolein were doing fine in Caladheå. The fifth was from Hanaiko, who was still taking refuge in Toel Ginu with the other kids. She said they loved living with Rikuja's parents, since it was like having grandparents, but they missed us terribly. Writing back to explain we couldn't come home was one of the toughest letters I'd ever written.

✳

Just when I started to think Tsiala had forgotten about me, she showed up at the hospital, dressed in her knit wool coat. She'd brought a pair of aluminum crutches. "From the Clan Ríain forges," she explained. "I thought you might want fresh air."

I wasn't wholly sure I wanted to talk to her. Then again, she *had* saved my life. At least I'd gotten enough practice with the hospital's heavy wooden crutches that I made it outside without faceplanting. We settled on a bench overlooking the snowy hospital gardens. Puffy clouds filled the sky, looking like pools of molten gold in the sunset.

Fumbling for somewhere to start, I said, "How have you been?"

Tsiala shrugged. "Okay. Neve's keeping me on as a bodyguard, even though I can only work evenings."

"That's good." Silence. "Uh . . . how are your 'non-lethal' combat lessons?"

She shrugged again. "They're fine."

I looked her over. No visible bruises, black eyes, or split lips, not even scraped knuckles. "A week of training with grown men and you're fine. Are you even going?"

"Yes! I—" Tsiala blew out a breath, stirring a lock of hair. "They're not grown men. I got stuck with the children."

"*Children?* After you confessed to murder?"

"Well, they're teenagers, but—" She waved a hand impatiently. "Itherans are so small! They keep punching me in the crotch!"

A laugh bubbled out of me. It felt insolent after all the misery we'd endured, but the more I tried to hold it in, the more it grew. Tsiala's lips twitched at the corners, and soon she was cracking up, too.

Once we could breathe again, she said, "Look. I wish I could just say sorry, thanks, glad you're alive. But you deserve to know who I am, and . . . that's a long story."

I gestured at my crutches. "I'm not going anywhere."

"Yet." She rested her elbows on the bench back. "You've heard about the plagues down south, right?"

I nodded. "Influenza two decades ago, pox before that, consumption before that. An Iyo healer told me itherans brought the diseases from overseas."

"Yeah. They killed most of the Kowichelk Confederacy. Entire nations wiped off the earth. Empty villages, abandoned shrines in the rainforest, hundreds of thousands of bodies in mass graves. Some survivors moved into itheran colonies. Others wound up at refugee camps. Nineteen years ago, my mother stumbled into a camp, sick with influenza and going into labour. She lived just long enough to name me."

I winced. "That's awful. I'm so sorry."

She shrugged. "It could've been worse. The midwife who helped with the birth adopted me. I grew up calling her Yonna, the Kowichelk word for *grandmother*. She taught me to fish and hunt and call water. When I was seven, she told me the truth — or what she knew of it. My mother hadn't said which nation she came from or who my father was, and she didn't have any tattoos, so there was no hint on her dead body.

"I think Yonna told me then 'cause she didn't have long left. The spirits had started singing her name, and she died of fever a few months later. This is all I've got left of her." Tsiala plucked at her cream-coloured wool coat, patterned with grey birds and geometric shapes. "Hummingbirds are her nation's crest. When her coat started to unravel, I made a new one."

"You can knit?" I asked, surprised.

"No. I willed it into existence with my mind."

I stared at her. Sometimes talking to her was like hearing myself.

"Anyway, after Yonna passed, Ferish priests took me to an orphanage. It was . . ." Tsiala clicked her tongue. "Rough. I had to keep both hands on my food or some other kid would swipe it. I split so many lips the priests sent me to another orphanage, where the same thing happened again. When I was thirteen, they got rid of me for good. They cut off my hair, dressed me in trousers, and stuck me in a line of boys to see a military recruiter."

"And the recruiter took you?"

"Yeah. I was taller than the boys and I'd stomped most of them. The recruiter figured it out soon enough, but he didn't care as long as I could fight. I spent a year in training, then went straight into the ranks of Armando Contere."

"Alesso's uncle? The warlord?"

"The same." Tsiala smiled bleakly. "I was in awe the first time I saw him. Thousands of men at his command, saluting and taking orders. *That's power*, I thought. If I could be like that, I'd never be scared again. But soon enough . . . I heard the rumours. He'd take a liking to some woman in the military camp, a servant or medic or who-ever, and start inviting her to his tent. Sooner or later, she'd vanish.

"Nobody knew where these women went. I heard every guess under the sun. Strangled, drowned, escaped, sold into slavery, knocked up and sent away to a sancte. I started asking around for their names. Most people had forgotten, but someone mentioned a Kowichelk woman from way back. She had my mother's name, and she disappeared about six months before I was born."

"Oh," I said in faint horror.

"I don't even know if . . ." Tsiala shook her head, stirring her chin-length hair. "Did she *want* to be with Contere? Did he banish her or did she flee? What about those other women? How many half siblings do I have that I'll never meet?"

My heart cracked open. Words weren't enough, so I pulled off my glove and laid my hand over her bare one. She tensed but didn't pull away.

"I vowed to kill him so he'd never do it again," she said. "I knew I'd have to strike in battle, make it look like an enemy got him, but I was a lowly foot soldier. Never got near the commander. I waited a whole goddamned year for the chance, and . . . I failed. Couldn't go through with it. Instead I ran and never looked back."

I twisted on the bench to face her. "You didn't fail. Taking *anyone's* life is hard enough."

Tsiala turned away. "Yeah. I'm not a monster, just the bastard daughter of one."

"You're not." I grabbed her chin and pulled it toward me. "He was never a father to you. You know who your real family is? Your mother, who found somewhere safe for you, and your yonna, who raised you."

She looked somewhere over my shoulder. Tears pooled in her dark eyes, but her mouth twisted with the refusal to cry. Our breath clouded in the cool air, mixing together.

"Those men in the militia complex . . ." Her voice wavered. "I don't trust anyone who calls a girl 'the viirelei bitch.' You think I'm this heartless murderer, but I was *not* gonna hand you over — not in a million years—"

I hugged her. She went rigid.

"Does this mean I can touch you now?" she asked.

"Yes, you idiot."

Tsiala slid her arms around my waist. Her fingers dug into my back like she needed to know I was real. A floral scent lingered around her. I pictured Neve dousing her in perfume, then an annoyed Tsiala calling water to scrub herself clean as she walked to the hospital.

A window had opened into her spirit. Six years defending herself in orphanages, then everything with Contere — of course she turned out rude and combative. And it probably wasn't simple jealousy that made her dislike Tiernan and pull me away from Ivar at the wedding. She'd learned not to trust male soldiers. Which included . . .

"Wait," I said, pulling back from the hug. "Alesso's your *cousin*?"

Tsiala laughed. "Apparently. That's why I agreed to spy on you — to get closer to him. Other than my father, he's the first of my blood family I've met."

"Did you tell Alesso?"

"God, no. And I didn't actually spy on you, either. I just told him you're disgustingly nice and wanted his wedding to go well."

"High praise." I glanced toward the arched windows of the hospital. "And now he's under guard and you can't talk to him."

"Yeah." She sighed, lifting her face to the last rays of sunlight. "He'll probably be hanged for treason."

I squeezed her hand. "Whatever happens, I'll be here."

"Same for you." She wove her fingers into mine. "Sorry for being bitchy about Tiernan. You two were all over each other, and I didn't know what to think. But you've said there's nothing going on, so I should trust you. Whatever happens . . . I'll be here, too."

✳

Late the next afternoon, studying my medical textbook in the hospital gardens, a blackbird alighted on a frosty stake and croaked. I flinched. After dying once, Neve's story about a crow goddess foretelling death had me on edge. Looking closer, though, the bird had the curved beak and larger stature of a raven. I went back to reading about chemical burns.

Croak.

I stared at the raven. It tilted its head, staring back. "Akohin?" I ventured.

The raven bobbed its head. I broke into a grin. He and Ainu-Seru lived several hours north at Se Ji Ainu, their mountain domain, and often drifted over the rest of the Turquoise Mountain range. It was no surprise they'd spot me here eventually.

As Akohin continued staring, I realized the problem. He no longer bothered wearing clothes and we were in full view of a five-storey hospital. I tucked my textbook into a satchel, picked up my crutches, and hobbled into a greenhouse. Akohin followed. Flowerpots hung from the ceiling and lush green foliage adorned the garden beds. A damp earthy scent filled my nose.

The raven shifted into a lean seventeen-year-old boy. Someone had left behind a grubby wool cloak, which Akohin draped over his shoulders. His shaved white hair was stark against his tanned skin. Unsure what to say, I hugged him. He started slightly, but returned the hug, avoiding my long braid. He'd grown taller than me since I'd last seen his human form.

I settled on a pile of burlap sacks filled with potting soil. "This is a nice surprise. Is Ainu-Seru with you?"

"Not physically." Akohin didn't explain what that meant, and I knew not to pry. He perched next to me. "What are you doing in Ingdanrad?"

Since I was supposed to be studying, I gave him the short version of my journey here. As I talked, I realized he might know something that would prove Tiernan's innocence. He and Ainu-Seru saw and heard things that people thought were secret.

In answer, Akohin shook his head. "Sorry. We haven't seen Tiernan or Jorumgard since the Battle of Tjarnnaast. I have no idea what happened at the Nyhemur garrison."

My rickety scaffolding of hope collapsed, burying me in splintered wood. "Did you see the Rúonbattai cleric? She was out east in Nyhemur for days, maybe weeks. Ainu-Seru would recognize her, right?"

"He would, but we weren't watching the land then. We were with you."

"What?"

Akohin picked at his fingernails, long and sharp like talons. "We followed you from Tjarnnaast to Nettle Ginu. I was only six when my tema died, but I remember the grief. I was . . . worried about you."

I paused, taken aback. So not only had Geniod been watching me the entire journey, but Akohin and an ancient tel-saidu had, too. *Everyone* was spying on me.

"You're upset." Akohin's face clouded over. "Sorry. I—"

"Nei. It's fine." I grabbed his hand, scared he might flee. "Just — how much did you see?"

"Not much. We were always outside, and we left after your cousin's wedding."

"Malana's? You stayed that long?"

The blood rose in his cheeks. "I like weddings."

"Really? But you . . ."

"I know, I know. *I* don't want to get married. But I like seeing people happy, and . . . Ainu-Seru and I wanted to help." Akohin blushed deeper. "Did you notice how warm it was for winter? We did that."

I gaped at him. I remembered wondering if a saidu was messing with the weather, or if the dusty wasteland I kept seeing in the shoirdryge was bleeding into this world. I'd thought I was losing my mind. I could hardly be angry, though. A tel-saidu's presence seemed like the most sacred blessing Malana could get for her wedding.

"Anyway," Akohin said, "we haven't seen any sign of the Rúonbattai all winter. No Sverbians skulking about the mountains, no soldiers bearing their sigil, no oak and lilac crests."

I frowned. "I suppose that's some comfort."

He looked at me sideways, tilting his head like a bird. "For what it's worth, *I* believe Tiernan's innocent. He was always kind when

I worked at the Golden Oak. I once spilled hot mead on a drunk patron, and just as the man was about to hit me, Tiernan dragged him outside."

"That sounds like Tiernan," I said with a wry smile.

Akohin glanced out the glass walls at the darkening sky and sighed. "It's getting late. I should go."

I felt a twinge of disappointment. It had been nice seeing an old friend, a tiny spot of familiarity in this strange city. As he got up, I burst out, "Will you visit me again?"

"Here?" Akohin's pale brows furrowed. It looked like every fibre of him wanted to refuse, but he said, "We'll be close by. If you need me, just speak to the wind."

24.

THE FOURTH FLOOR

A few days after Akohin's visit, Pádraig finished healing my thigh wound and released me from the hospital. I packed my things and returned to my room in Clan Ríain's villa. Everything was exactly how I'd left it — curtains open, trunk shut, Temal's sword and my carryframe leaning against the wall. I spread my fir branch blanket across the four-poster bed. After months of travel, it felt strange to lay it somewhere semi-permanent.

Other than the obsidian-handled knife, the things Jarlind's men took from me seemed lost for good. Neve told me not to worry about repaying her for the amethyst necklace. She offered to have her family forge another runed ring like the one Róisín had given me, but I figured I'd better not risk it. The runes drew on my strength to amplify my water-calling, which could easily kill me again.

The biggest loss was my purse, which had held my Eremur identification card, Tiernan's gold oak coin, and the lavender oil from Matéo. My last ties to Caladheå were falling away. I felt root-less. I'd landed in a surprisingly good place — a beautiful villa to live in, a decent job, family and friends — but this wasn't a home. I was an outsider at best and a prisoner at worst.

At least my letters were still here. I knew Tiernan's at a glance, its dusty envelope stamped with elk sigils. Its creases had worn smooth and the postscript was so familiar I could hear it in his voice. *Northern Nyhemur is stunning in winter. The snowy plains look infinite, as if one is floating among the clouds.*

"We'll make it there." I kissed the paper. When I looked in the mirror, charcoal covered my lips.

Tucked in with my letters was a scrap of paper where Nerio had written Tiernan's Ingdanrad contacts. I'd forgotten about them. Janekke Noorjehl was still away treating patients in rural Nyhemur, but a spark of hope ignited in me. Maybe she'd heard something about the garrison fight, or maybe she knew something about when Tiernan initially got arrested.

Below Janekke's name, Nerio had written *Iollan och Cormic. Druid at the university. Incredibly dangerous! Only contact in a crisis!* Surely this counted as a crisis, but it was also surely wiser to try Janekke first. I lifted my parents' makiri off the windowsill, feeling their gentle warmth. I already knew what their advice would be. They'd raised me to be cautious.

At night, I slipped outside and spoke to the wind. A warm breeze rustled my skirt. Within minutes, a raven swooped down from the sky. I handed Akohin some second-hand clothes I'd scrounged up. I'd also brought pastries, sheep cheese, and barley loaf from the kitchens. Food was usually the best bribe for teenage boys.

It was a big ask, but I wanted Akohin and Ainu-Seru to track down Janekke. Clan Ríain's healers had given me a map of the circuit that Ingdanrad medics did through Nyhemur. The difficult part was Akohin wouldn't recognize Janekke, so he'd have to ask around, lying about who he was. He looked petrified but said if it could save Tiernan, he'd do it.

On my first hospital shift, the matron got me to write the first-year apprentice exam. She wanted an idea of my skills so she knew which ward I'd be most useful in. I'd been an apothecary apprentice for two years, so I figured it wouldn't be too hard. I set up in the medics' break room, which smelled like an unsettling mix of bleach and pickled herring, and turned over an hourglass.

The exam went wrong in every possible way. It was in Coast Trader littered with Gallnach terms, so reading it was like wading through mud. The bleach in the air made my eyes water and head throb. Thinking about Tjarnnaast made my hands shake so much I splattered ink over one answer I'd done well. I breathed five seconds in, five seconds out like Tiernan taught me, only to get distracted about how in Aeldu-yan to save him.

I returned my ink-blotched papers to the matron's office, wishing I could hide under a cot and never come out. Her lips pursed as she read. I wondered if she'd revoke my labour sentence and send me to prison instead. At least I'd be out in time to go home with Rikuja, although she probably wouldn't want me around for the birth, considering how useless I was. Colourful specks flickered across my vision. *Shit*, I thought, *not again* —

The matron looked up from her desk. "It's ironic you didn't reach the question about combat neurosis. You might've done well there, lass."

I blinked away the specks. "What?"

"Nightmares, flashbacks, mood swings, tremors. Trouble sleeping, breathing, and concentrating. Intense reactions to certain smells or other sensations. Sound familiar?"

My answer caught in my throat. It was so accurate it hurt.

The elderly woman's eyes crinkled as she smiled. "This was a test of your health, not your skills. I'm sure you're a competent medic, but you're not fit for duty yet." She dipped a quill into an inkpot, scrawled a note, and set it on top of my exam. "Take these papers upstairs to Pádraig. The fourth floor needs a good chore girl, and you need a good neurologist."

❋

I didn't understand the scope of Ingdanrad's hospital until I read the directory at the foot of a stone staircase. Underground was the kitchen, laundry, records hall, and morgue. First floor was the military wing, surgery, and apothecary. Second was the visitors' quarters, dining hall, and prayer rooms. Third was midwifery. Fourth was internal health. Fifth was external health — dentistry, optometry, burns, and dermatology. Off in separate buildings were the mental asylum and plague sanatorium.

On the fourth floor, a pair of open doors revealed a hall with a dozen wrought-iron beds. Dust motes floated in sunbeams from the arched windows. The place was eerily quiet and had the musty smell of camphor. I continued down a corridor, reading engraved metal signs on doors. Lung disease, tumours, cardiology, neurology. I knocked on the last door and heard Pádraig's voice call, "Come in."

I stepped into a bright hall ringed by bookshelves and potted trees. Thick rugs covered the stone floor. Whatever I'd expected, it wasn't this. Pádraig and a Sverbian woman sat on squashy torn-up couches by a crackling hearth fire. The woman was saying she'd been dizzy for days. She kept dropping things and stumbling into walls. Her husband thought she'd gotten into his vodka, but she insisted she never touched the stuff.

Pádraig checked the woman's skull for wounds and shone a glowing runestone into her eyes, then had her kneel on a rug. He guided her through a series of poses, putting her head down like she was about to somersault, then twisting it side to side. When she stood up, she said with surprise the dizziness was slightly better. Pádraig sent her off with instructions to repeat the motions every few hours until it cleared up.

"That's amazing," I said after she left. "How does it work?"

Pádraig chuckled. "Honestly, I don't know. A medic first observed it in children, who spend a lot more time upside down than adults." He glanced at the papers in my hand. "How'd the exam go?"

I handed them over sheepishly. He sat behind a cluttered desk and put on a set of square spectacles. It was a wonder he could find them among the mess of scrolls, books, empty vials, and tea-stained mugs. He hummed as he flipped through my exam.

"About what I expected," he said. "We'll talk about this properly in a few days. Right now, I'm getting this ward back on its feet after my stint in the military wing. Thank the mother of mountains you're here to help."

I glanced around the hall. "You run your own ward? At your age?"

Pádraig removed his spectacles and peered at me. "How old do you think I am?"

Inwardly, I kicked myself. With his small stature and messy brown curls, he looked about fifteen. "Uh . . . twenty?"

"I'm twenty-seven." He pursed his lips like the elderly matron, then broke into a teasing smile. "Don't worry. Everyone thinks I'm a teenager. Can't grow a beard, no matter how hard I try."

My shoulders eased. As embarrassing as it was to be a chore girl again, at least I'd be working for someone with a sense of humour.

"Anyway," he said, "as you probably noticed, the fourth floor is a ghost town. We only had a few in-patients before the coup, so we brought them to the military wing with us and shut this floor down. We're just starting to reopen. You'll meet the other medics soon enough — oh, and Og the Destroyer."

"Who?"

"I'll introduce you. I think he's around." Pádraig rummaged through his desk clutter, found a leather bag, and shook out a few scraps of dried jerky. He handed them to me, then rang a brass bell.

Scrolls exploded off a bookshelf. A black-and-white ball streaked across the hall and leapt onto the desk. I burst into laughter. The fluffiest cat I'd ever seen did laps around the desk, sniffing the air. I held out the jerky scraps. The cat inhaled them, then licked my palm clean.

Pádraig grinned. "Og the Destroyer is our therapy cat. Snuggling a warm, purring cat is the best medicine around."

"Why is he called that?" I asked, scratching Og's chin.

"Because he destroys the heart of everyone he meets. That, and he claws up the furniture." Pádraig nodded at the torn-up couches.

Og bonked his head against my hand, searching for more jerky. Realizing I had none, he stalked off, tail in the air, and curled up in front of the fire. Even his rejection was oddly reassuring. At least this time, it wasn't because I was an outsider.

✳

I spent the next few days dusting, sweeping, mopping, scrubbing, bleaching, and hauling firewood for each internal care ward, a lavatory, and a small kitchen. All the fresh food in the pantry had gone mouldy. Pádraig's potted trees were dying after three weeks of neglect, so I watered them and pruned off the dead leaves. Across the fourth floor, I kept finding decomposing mice, courtesy of Og.

The Kae girl who'd passed out meals in the military wing brought up baskets of produce and paper-wrapped packages of meat. Her hair was cut into blunt bangs over her eyebrows, which along with her moss-green woolwrap made me think she must be part Gallnach. She introduced herself as Círa. As we unpacked the food, she explained that she ran the fourth-floor kitchen, preparing nutrient-rich meals for the patients here. When the floor closed, she'd gone to help in the military wing.

"Somebody sure missed me," she said, tossing a chicken heart to Og the Destroyer. "I'm not supposed to waste food on a cat, but I can't resist spoiling him." She flashed me a grin I couldn't help returning.

Last, I prepped the in-patient hall, which was shared by the internal care wards and the burn ward upstairs. I stripped off the bed linens, put on fresh ones, and set up canvas privacy screens. The windows had frozen shut, so I had to melt the ice in order to air out the musty camphor smell. Geniod gave me flowers from Clan Ríain's greenhouses to put on the bedside tables.

Finally we began moving patients up from the military wing, putting them on wheeled cots and rolling them into an elevator powered by earth magic embedded in the stone. We had ten patients total — four civilians who'd been here before the coup, five soldiers seriously burned during it, and Ivar, still comatose, blank and pale and wasting away. Pádraig had examined Ivar repeatedly and couldn't tell what was wrong. He hadn't found any sign of bleeding in the brain.

I soon learned Círa was also an antayul. Fascinated, I watched her prop Ivar upright and call broth from a bowl into his open mouth. Even unconscious, he had the reflex to swallow, but Círa had to monitor him closely in case he choked. In Eremur, we'd fed honey and mushed fruit to coma patients. It wasn't enough to survive on, but they'd either woken or died of their injuries long before dehydration or starvation became a problem.

That also meant I'd never seen how much work went into caring for a coma patient long-term. Medics turned Ivar every two hours to keep him from developing pressure sores. They bathed him with a damp cloth, changed his bedpan, rubbed salve into his skin, and moved his limbs to slow the atrophy of his muscles. I desperately hoped the medics downstairs were taking as much care with Tiernan.

Once our patients were settled, Pádraig sat me down on his squashy couches to talk. His first question was about the detailed description of laudanum I'd given on my exam. He seemed impressed that I'd treated Jonalin's overdose when I was fifteen. My other exam answers had been far more scattered — stopping in the middle of sentences, shifting between Coast Trader and Ferish, going off on tangents I didn't remember writing.

Pádraig's immediate concern was that I kept passing out, which was likely to result in further injury if I hit something hard or sharp. He asked if I had a history of it. I explained that I occasionally fainted while having strange visions, but I could usually control it. Only since the coup had I started blacking out from stress, which I chalked up to the concussion.

"Maybe," Pádraig said, rubbing his jaw. "If you're willing, I'd like to try inducing a blackout so I can observe it myself."

"Induce it how?" I asked warily.

"For starters . . ." He opened a cabinet with hundreds of glass vials. "Scent can be an intense trigger. Any of these stress you out?"

I looked over the labels with awe. Perfumes of rose, lilac, violet. Essences of juniper, garlic, ginger. Tinctures of willowcloak, pennyroyal, needlemint. Wine, whisky, brånnvin, mezcale. Enough oils, vinegars, syrups, and herbal infusions to stock a pantry. Some

I wasn't sure how they could be bottled, like woodsmoke or leather or rainfall. I was curious to smell them, but I chose the camphor.

Pádraig smiled sympathetically. "Must be tough in a hospital."

He arranged pillows around me on the couch, had me take off my boots, and asked if I'd be okay with him examining me while I was unconscious. He offered to fetch a female medic, but I waved that off. As I opened the camphor vial, memories surfaced of a blue-eyed man spitting blood. A man who died alone in my arms because my spirit had left the world.

Pádraig sat next to me on the couch. "I also have good and bad news. I may as well use this opportunity to tell you."

I bit my lip. "What's the news?"

"The good part is Tiernan och Heile is recovering. He's stable enough that we can use healing magic on his wound, and if all goes well, we'll take him off sedatives later today. It'll probably take a day for him to wake. The bad part is once he awakens . . . he'll go to trial and most likely be hanged."

I blanched. I'd known this was coming, but *today*? I wasn't any closer to proving his innocence. Akohin hadn't returned with Janekke yet. Did I finally have to track down Iollan och Cormic? Just how dangerous was he? How could talking to a druid be worse than seeing Tiernan hanging limp from a noose, his face twisted in agony —

Colourful specks flitted across my vision. *Well*, I thought in resignation, *here we go again*.

❋

The pungent smell of ammonia prickled my lungs. I retched, opening my eyes to a vial under my nose. Salt of hartshorn, used to rouse people after fainting.

"Má sí," Pádraig muttered, replacing the vial's stopper. "That certainly worked. Need anything? Water? Painkillers?"

I sat up blearily on the squashy couch. "Nei. I'm fine."

He pressed his hands to my head, frowning. "Are you familiar with the mechanics of fainting?"

"Uh . . . sort of?"

"It happens when there's not enough blood in your brain. If your heart rate drops, the blood falls out of your head and down through your body. It winds up here." He touched my sock-clad feet.

I looked at them, bemused. "How do you know?"

"Earth magic. We druids can sense the iron in blood." Settling back on the couch, Pádraig said, "Most people faint due to a specific trigger, such as gore or intense pain. For you, it's evidently the thought of Tiernan dying."

I squirmed internally, wondering if he shared some of his aunt Róisín's magic. He was seeing straight into my spirit.

"There's . . . an interesting factor to that." Pádraig drummed his fingers on the couch arm. "In your culture, someone's blood meeting the ground is a euphemism for death, aye?"

"Yeah. Why?"

"It seems like your body's emulating your conception of dying. Now, this is a sensitive topic, but I'm not here to judge. Just to help." He leaned forward, resting his elbows on the white woolwrap draped over his knees. "Do you *want* to die? Is suicide something you've thought about?"

My answer stuck in my throat. I'd been ready to die alongside Tiernan in the catacombs, but when I wound up alone in that rainstorm . . . As if summoned, Og the Destroyer jumped in my lap. I wrapped my arms around the fluffy cat. He bonked his head against me, purring.

"It's a common feeling for people who have been through war," Pádraig said gently. "Especially people who lost loved ones there. It's nothing to be ashamed of. It means your brain is sick, just as if your heart or lungs were sick."

"Then . . ." I blinked back tears. "How do I cure it?"

"Time and effort. There's no magic fix for this. But if you're willing, we've got six months to work on it."

I buried my face in Og's fur. "There's not much hope if I have to see Tiernan hanged."

"Oh, there's hope for you both." Pádraig crossed to his desk. Rummaging through the clutter, he produced a folder. "I found Tiernan's medical records from when he first arrived in Ingdanrad thirteen years ago. He had combat neurosis just like you. My predecessor treated him."

"Really?" I asked in astonishment.

"Seems his family got caught in a terrible war in some remote part of Sverba. He lost everyone and everything, so he fled here as a refugee."

"Yan taku," I muttered. Tiernan had told me about losing his family, but he hadn't explained how.

Pádraig set the folder aside. "Given Tiernan's history and the border soldiers' description of his paranoia, there's evidence he wasn't in his right mind. I *might* be able to convince the mage assembly to send him to the mental asylum. It's not a pleasant place, but it'll buy you time to figure out something else."

Time. That might be enough. I squeezed Og in a hug, making him meow indignantly. Instead of dying with Tiernan, we might both get a chance at living.

❉

I did my chores in a cloud of nerves, waiting for news. At first everything went well. The medics healed Tiernan's stomach wound without trouble. A day after he went off the sedatives, though, he hadn't woken. Two days after, he still hadn't. On the third day, Pádraig sat me down in the neurology ward and explained that Tiernan was comatose.

The words floated through my head, refusing to take root. It wasn't possible. Tiernan was just resting. A long, well-deserved rest. In a few hours, he'd wake up. Then ... what? A trial? The noose? No. It wasn't possible. I'd figure something out.

The military wing transferred him upstairs to the in-patient hall. For the first time in a month, I got to see him. Dark hollows framed his eyes. His hair and beard were growing long again, and his skin looked translucent. I touched his neck, searching for a heartbeat. It was fainter than the brush of a moth's wings, but it was there.

Okay, I thought. *He's asleep. How do I wake him?*

An iron cuff etched with nullifying runes circled his thin wrist. Maybe that mental cloud was weighing him down. "Can't we take this off?" I asked. "He's not going to leap out of bed and burn the place down."

"Militia captain's orders," said his guard, an older Gallnach man with a pointed silver beard. "All mage prisoners wear a cuff."

I cast about for other ideas. The canvas screens around Tiernan's bed blocked the late afternoon sunlight. *I hardly remember the sun*, he'd told me in the dungeon. Judging by his pale skin, he'd been kept in a windowless room. Maybe sunlight would wake him. I started pulling the screens aside.

"Oi!" The guard grabbed my elbow. "What are you doing?"

I yanked out of his grip. "Just fixing them—"

The guard scoffed. "You *want* everyone to look on the face of a murderer?"

"He's a human being!" I snapped. "He deserves to see the damned sun! He—" Colours flitted across my eyes. I swayed.

"Whoa, whoa." Pádraig hurried over and caught me. "Let's go have a cup of tea."

"I don't need tea. I need to wake him!"

"Listen, Kateiko. He's in a coma. You need to accept that he might never wake up."

I stared over Pádraig's shoulder at Tiernan's motionless form. It felt like the Sverbian trickster god was playing a cruel joke. I'd wanted more time and I got it. He was stuck between death and life, and I didn't know if he was at peace or screaming for someone to guide him out of the flames.

Here, I thought. *I'm here. Come find me.*

Ice crackled across my body. Pádraig stumbled away, cursing. Frost spilled across the stone floor. It shot up canvas screens like ivy, wreathed iron beds, bloomed up walls and windows. Everything turned white and glittering.

The snowy plains look infinite, as if one is floating among the clouds.

Tiernan's guard tackled me. We went down hard, knocking the breath from my lungs. I scrabbled across the frosty floor toward Tiernan. Someone grabbed my legs. I kicked out. We rolled, striking, toppling over canvas screens, knocking into beds. White bedsheets and woolwraps blurred into white frost.

Strong hands pinned me down. Cold metal clamped onto my wrist. A cloud rolled through my skull and crushed my watercalling. The frost melted, soaking the hall.

I screamed. No words, just raw sound. I needed that frost to guide Tiernan. I had to save him from the flames. Colourful stars bloomed across my vision — then everything went dark.

✳

Geniod nudged me awake. I found myself on a cot in the candlelit neurology ward. The nullifying cuff was gone. Pádraig explained that he'd sedated me for several hours while the healers mended the frostbite I'd given everyone. I expected Geniod to lecture me, but instead he handed me a letter.

It was from Jorumgard. He'd told Captain Valrose that Tiernan had been undercover, investigating Rúonbattai soldiers in Ingdanrad's militia, and kept it secret in case there were traitors in Eremur's military as well. Now that we'd killed Jarlind and stopped the coup, we could reveal the "truth." Valrose had begrudgingly kept his word and released Jorumgard from prison.

He's free, I thought in disbelief. He was also no longer a mercenary for Eremur, since Valrose had no interest in keeping him on. Jorumgard was an ordinary civilian now, free to be a husband and father. He'd gone straight to Yotolein's flat and made up with him. They were finally going to make their relationship public, starting with visiting Toel Ginu to tell Hanaiko and Samulein.

I'd been drowning again and they'd thrown me a lifeline. Jorumgard was joining our big, messy, tangled family. I could visit them once my sentence ended in late summer. And somehow, somehow, I would wake Tiernan. In winter we'd travel to Nyhemur to befriend windmills and float among the clouds. That dream could pull me above water while my loved ones here held me up. I just had to remember how to swim.

I scooped up Og the Destroyer, drawing on the cat's warmth for courage. "I want to do it," I blurted.

Geniod looked up. Pádraig, reading at his desk, took off his spectacles and said, "Do what?"

"Get better. I want to be a medic again, save Tiernan, go home. I—" My throat tightened. "I want to live."

25.

HONEYBEE

The first thing Pádraig said about my recovery was that looking after Tiernan wasn't my job. "Your priority is *your* health," he emphasized. I couldn't handle feeling useless, though, so we compromised that I'd keep studying my medical textbook. If I could pass the first-year apprentice exam, he'd consider putting me back on medical work.

Pádraig also said after months of instability, a routine could take some stress out of my life. With his guidance, I set a schedule. Half an hour of study over my lunch break. Two nights of makiri-reading lessons each week with Geniod. Two nights of physical therapy with Dunehein. One night of mental therapy with Pádraig. One night of water-calling practice with Tsiala, who'd gotten permission from Neve to take that time off. The last night was free for whatever I wanted.

Everything felt surreal. I'd burned through my emotions, turning into a charred husk. My body felt foreign and weak from so long in a hospital bed. Rikuja had to remind me that I should reply to

Jorumgard's letter and explain that Tiernan was comatose. Recalling how incomprehensible my apprentice's exam had been, I asked Neve to help me with the letter.

After the inquiry into Clan Níall finished, Róisín came by to tell us about it. The conclusion was Síona and Alesso acted alone, and the rest of the clan was innocent. Síona's sister, Caoimhe, their new chief druid, had taken up her seat on the mage assembly. She'd declared that although the couple's plans were misguided, their loyalty to Ingdanrad was clear, and if they were hanged, Clan Níall would abandon the city in retaliation. "Good luck feeding fifteen thousand people without our farms," she'd said sardonically.

The assembly had dissolved into a shouting match, but Caoimhe's threat worked. Síona and Alesso were sentenced to ten years of work at the university, teaching Ferish to linguistics students and raising a generation who could read any secret correspondence they tried to have. They'd be confined to Ingdanrad and they'd have to return the ten thousand sovs to Armando Contere. Tsiala grumbled that they got off easy, but she looked relieved that her only known cousin wouldn't be hanged.

With the inquiry over, Róisín was returning home to Innisburren, making this her last night with Geniod. "Have fun in the greenhouse," Dunehein teased, making Róisín laugh and Geniod elbow him in the ribs. Thankfully I had plans to distract me from that image. Since it was my first free night, Neve had invited me to play cards and drink whisky with Tsiala, Júni, her brothers, and a few cousins our age. It sounded reasonably low stress — but just before we parted ways, Róisín took me aside.

"I need to warn you," she said quietly, fiddling with her woollen knot pendant. "Be careful with Níamh ó Lónan."

"Neve?" I asked in surprise. "How come?"

"I can't tell. That's the problem. Looking into her spirit is like throwing a net into the ocean and hauling up a beehive — bees, honey, and all."

"She *is* easily distracted. I asked for help writing a letter and she went on about paper-making."

Róisín shook her head, making her curls bounce. "I can see through distraction. People have an essence that doesn't easily change. This feels . . . deliberate. There's something inside Níamh that she doesn't want me to see."

✳

In my next makiri-reading lesson, Geniod suggested asking my parents about Neve. Now that I could sense their spirits in the carvings, he was teaching me to focus the connection. I wrapped my hand around Tema's makiri, closed my eyes, and imagined looking out the window of a plank house. A ghostly swan landed on the windowsill. Its feathers brushed at the edge of my mind. I stepped back, inviting it through the window. The swan stayed put. I could never manage to coax it inside.

"Give it time," Geniod reassured me. "This takes years of practice, remember."

He took the swan carving to speak with Tema. After several moments, he opened his eyes. She'd shown him memories of flying above Ivy House through wind, rain, and sun. We'd spent a month scouting the place before attacking. Like usual, her advice seemed to be a cautious approach, waiting and watching Neve.

Strange events began vying for my attention, though. On a blustery day, I headed into the in-patient hall to batten down the shutters. An Aikoto woman with a lined face, long braid, and tattered deerskin cloak sat next to Ivar, holding his hand. Wondering if she was his adopted mother, I looked around for someone to ask. Círa was walking about with her lunch trolley, passing out bowls of broth.

"Oh, yeah, that's Olina Kae," Círa told me quietly. "She visited Ivar once after the coup and hasn't been back until now."

"She left her son alone here for a *month*?" I asked.

Círa shrugged. "She's a hermit. Lives on the edge of town. I only see her a few times a year when she comes to the Kae district to trade."

I approached the woman, planning to explain how Ivar had gotten hurt defending me. The moment I got close, she swung her head up. Her eyes flitted across me. She jerked to her feet, knocking over her stool, and strode out. Moments later, I looked out the window and saw her hurrying away through the sleet.

The guilt of spooking Olina away from her son plagued me. Yet when I arrived at work the next morning, I found Ivar awake, sitting upright against a pile of pillows. It was like seeing the dead rise. He caught sight of the obsidian-handled knife on my belt and flinched.

"It's okay," I said, lifting my hands. "I won't hurt you."

Ivar's face crinkled as if he was trying to identify me. A medic shooed me off. In the neurology ward, Pádraig explained that Ivar had to remember how to speak. Recovering from a coma was a long road. The healers planned to reintroduce him to things slowly so his brain could catch up on the time he'd missed.

"Olina must've done something," I mused as I swept. "Maybe she called on the aeldu to send him back."

"Maybe," Pádraig said at his desk, sifting through Ivar's medical records. "Or *she* brought him back. Some coma patients remember hearing their loved ones' voices while they were out."

"Really?" I straightened up, clutching the broom. "So Tiernan might be able to hear me?"

The druid took off his spectacles and fixed his pale green eyes on me. "It's possible. I don't want you to get hung up on the idea of coaxing him awake, though. He has to make this journey at his own pace, and you need to—"

"Focus on myself, I know. But talking can't hurt, right?"

"You've clearly never met my sister-in-law." Pádraig pinched the bridge of his nose. "All right, then. We'll add it to your routine. Ten minutes a day of talking to him."

❋

I couldn't tell Tiernan much with his guard listening in. I gave him a sanitized version of everything since the coup, told him about Jorumgard and Yotolein getting back together, and read my mail aloud. Captain Valrose and Eremur's navy had spent the winter holding a siege against Gåmelheå, the last Nordmur town under Rúonbattai occupation. Nerio had sent a copy of the *Sol vi Caladheå* announcing the navy's recent capture of the town.

The Rúonbattai had gone quiet everywhere. They'd lost their base in Tjarnnaast, the sanctuary they were building in Nordmur, and any chance of Lieutenant Jarlind swaying Ingdanrad's druids to their side. With no more fuel for the Ferish holy war, it was dying out. Caladheå was calming and starting to rebuild. Kirbana had written a letter saying she, Narun, Yotolein, and Jorumgard would visit Toel Ginu on the spring equinox to retrieve their kids.

Each day I told Tiernan how the sun looked. One afternoon, as I described how the sunlight sparkled on the frosty windows, someone pushed aside a canvas privacy screen. A pale woman in bloody white robes stepped through. I started in surprise, knocking a vase off the bedside table. *The cleric*, I thought wildly. *She came for her knife.*

"Amja, amja." The woman lifted her hands in peace. "Sorry, miss. Didn't mean to spook you."

I took a deep breath, holding my chest. It wasn't the silver-haired cleric from my nightmares. This woman had a warm smile, sharp blue eyes, and hair as golden as autumn wheat. She glanced down at her bloody apron and clicked her tongue in understanding.

"Forgot about that." She untied the strings and hung the apron on a canvas screen. Underneath she wore a white medic's woolwrap along with typical Sverbian attire, a cream-coloured bodice over a white dress. "I've been out of town for weeks and just got back. I came to see Tiernan and got roped into doing surgery."

"You're a surgeon?" I asked. "Are you Janekke Noorjehl?"

"Indeed I am. Who are you?"

I sagged with relief. "Kateiko Leniere. I sent Akohin to find you."

Janekke looked from Tiernan to his silver-bearded guard. Without missing a beat, she told me, "Come. I want to discuss his treatment with you and Pádraig."

Instead of going to the neurology ward, she turned the corner toward the kitchen. Círa agreed to give us a few minutes alone as long as we kept an eye on the stewpot simmering in the hearth. The moment she left, Janekke seized a paring knife and thrust it at me.

"Prove it," she said. "Show me your tattoos."

I drew back, startled. "I don't have any—"

"Then prove *that*." Janekke flicked her knife toward my clothes.

I pushed up my sleeves, showing her my arms, then unbuttoned my dress below my collarbones. Janekke relaxed and set down the paring knife.

"Sorry again," she said. "Tiernan told me not to talk to anyone until I verified their identity. I thought he was paranoid, but it was useful when your cousin showed up."

"Who, Akohin? We're not cousins."

"Not him. A girl named Tessa or something. Chin-length black hair, Ferish accent, built like a warrior. She came about six weeks ago. Said you sent her."

I stared at her blankly. "I didn't send anyone then. And none of my cousins have Ferish accents."

Janekke's brows crinkled. "She knew everything about you. Tattoos, family, where you worked in Caladheå, how you met Tiernan."

The perpetual knot in my stomach twisted. "What'd she want?"

"She said the Rúonbattai found out I was helping Tiernan, so they were coming for me. I packed up that night and went to treat patients in rural Nyhemur. I thought I'd be safer on the move."

"I definitely didn't send that message. I came here hoping to *find* you—" The knot in my stomach turned to ice. "Oh. Fuck. I know who it was."

❊

The second my shift ended, I changed into my wolf body and bounded up the mountain to Clan Ríain's villa. Tsiala came walking up the snowy road from the militia complex, clad in her black leather armour, twin daggers on her belt. I bounded in front of her and snarled. The flash of terror on her face filled me with hot, spiteful pleasure.

"What the hell?" she spluttered as I shifted back to human.

"You sent Janekke away?" I snapped. "You know I need her help!"

The blood drained out of Tsiala's face. She backed up, raising her hands. "Neve made me do it."

"You're blaming Neve? *Really?*"

"I—" Tsiala turned at the swish of an oncoming sleigh. She pulled me off the road and into piled-up snow. The fur-dressed couple in the sleigh passed without sparing us a glance. "I didn't have a choice. Neve's like that couple, ready to plow through anyone in their way. Me, I'm just trying to stay alive."

"And I'm not?"

"Dunno." Her voice came out barbed. "Are you?"

It felt like she'd slapped me. Regret spilled across her face, but I was too livid to care. I pushed past her and headed for the villa. Neve wasn't in the great hall, so I went to her room and flung open the door. She was in lambskin slippers and a linen chemise, perched in front of a gilt mirror as Júni brushed her wet hair. The air was thick with the scent of rosewater soap.

"Hello, sweet pea," she said, seeing me in the mirror. "Are—"

"Is it true?" I interrupted. "You made Tsiala send Janekke away?"

Neve's dark-eyed reflection blinked at me. "Did Tsiala tell you that?"

"Kateiko found out," Tsiala said, following me in. "And I'm not gonna lie to her anymore."

Neve drummed her fingers on her dressing table, covered with cosmetic tins, perfume bottles, and loose ribbons. Flickers of a dozen expressions crossed her face. She waved off Júni, who put down the hairbrush and stepped away.

"It had to be done," Neve said, turning on her stool to face me. "Between Alesso, Síona, and the Rúonbattai, we had enough to deal with. Tiernan's clearly special to you. If Janekke told you he was in prison, you would've put all your focus on freeing him."

"You *knew* about him? You had no right to keep that from me!"

"Oh, darling." She cast me a sympathetic smile. "I didn't want to hurt you. This is my home, though. I've devoted my whole life to protecting it."

"Protecting it how?"

"This, for starters." Neve lifted a hand. A gold hairpin flew off her dressing table and landed on her palm. "I'm a druid, like the rest of my family."

I backed up, remembering the hairpin I'd driven into Jarlind's eye. "You lied about that, too?"

"My entire life is a lie." She twirled the pin. "I was four when those Ingdanrad mages got murdered in Caladheå. We cut off formal diplomacy, but my parents refused to leave Eremur unchecked. They pretended I'm hopelessly awful at magic and sent me to boarding school so I'd learn to pass as a wealthy Sverbian. A Clan Ríain druid came as my handmaiden and taught me magic in secret. Now I'm, let's say, an *in*formal diplomat."

Tsiala scoffed. "Call it what it is. You're a spy."

"Burn wine, brånnvin," Neve said dismissively. "It's all the same work. Everything politicians and military captains say in public is a sham. The things they say after a few drinks, or what their wives gossip about in the tea room . . . They don't realize what they're giving away. Imagine my delight when Antoch Parr delivered you, Kateiko. You were exactly what I needed to investigate Alesso Spariere."

"*Delivered* me? I thought Parr was blackmailing you!"

She gave a derisive laugh. "He thinks so, too. I *let* him find out I'm Gallnach. He needs me too much to spill my secret."

I shook my head in disbelief. "If your parents raised you as a spy, why didn't they believe you about anything? Síona and Alesso conspiring, or the Rúonbattai trying to sway them?"

"Oh, they believed me." Neve coiled her wet hair and stuck the gold pin through it. "We made our own arrangements. I just didn't tell you."

I understood now what Róisín meant about throwing a net into the ocean and hauling up a beehive. Neve pretended to be a honeybee, flitting from blossom to blossom, but the teasing and flightiness were all an act. She was a wasp ready to sting. I reached for my obsidian-handled knife, wondering if I'd make it out of this room alive.

Neve clicked her tongue. "I'm not your enemy, sweet pea. And if I were, it'd be three against one. We're all mages here."

Júni smiled apologetically and lifted her hand. Flames bloomed above her palm. I couldn't bring myself to look at Tsiala, afraid what I'd find written on her face, afraid she'd attack me if she was commanded to.

Neve draped a silk robe over her shoulders, padded across a woven rug, and pressed her palm to an oak armoire. The metal lock sizzled and melted, letting the doors swing open. Standing on her toes, she took a bundle of papers from the top shelf, then dropped them on her writing desk.

"A peace offering," she said. "Before she left, Janekke gave Tsiala her research on the Rúonbattai cleric. I've been going through it, adding what I know, looking into people. We can work on it together, or you can take it back to Janekke."

"Together?" I fought the urge to smack her with the bundle. "Like when you lied about your family being druids, then promised we'd work together?"

Neve waved that away. "We'd only known each other a week. Things have changed."

"Yeah. Dying sure puts things in perspective. I'm not wasting any more of my life with shitty people." I grabbed the papers and turned to leave.

"Wait," she said. For a second, I thought she wanted to apologize. Instead she said, "If you breathe a word of this to anyone, you *will* regret it."

I looked back at her. "One day you'll wake up and realize everyone hates you. One day your crow goddess will come for you, and as you die, you'll realize just how alone you are."

26.

UNMOORED

I was in a frosty orchard before I realized I'd left the villa. My family would worry when I didn't show up for dinner, but I couldn't go back there. Couldn't eat in the great hall surrounded by Neve's family or sleep in the room they'd offered me. I half wished Tsiala would come after me, but I wouldn't know what to say if she did.

The farther I walked, the more I realized how much Neve had manipulated me. Insisting I meet her alone in Port Alios, claiming Parr made her paranoid, making me feel guilty about stalking her. Claiming her parents were ashamed of her so I'd pity her. She'd made a big deal about keeping our investigations secret in case the militia thought I was a spy, but *she* was worried about getting caught. Nerio's letter about Tiernan had gotten mysteriously delayed and only turned up after I found out about his imprisonment myself.

I wondered if anything with Tsiala had been real. Neve could've planned the whole thing — instructing her to flirt with me, saying

Tsiala thought I was pretty, finding excuses for us to be together. Maybe it was to distract me, maybe to keep me around. Furious as I was at Neve, I was furious at myself, too. I should've known better after Captain Parr's manipulations. How was I so goddamned naïve?

In a daze, I headed for the hospital. I climbed the stairs to the fourth floor and stood in the doorway of the in-patient hall, looking across the beds at Tiernan's motionless form. His night-shift guard, a middle-aged man with a red moustache, sat picking his teeth. I couldn't even talk to Tiernan in private. I might not ever again. I backed into the corridor and went to the neurology ward. The door was unlocked, the candles lit, but no one was there.

I set Janekke's papers on a table and drifted through the room, trailing my fingers over bookshelves, potted trees, torn-up couches. I opened a medicine cabinet and took out a vial of reddish-brown laudanum. If I downed it, would I end up in that rainstorm again? Could I find Tiernan's spirit there? Or would my parents send me back again even though their makiri weren't here with me?

The door swung open. I jerked, dropping the vial. It shattered on the stone floor. Pádraig blinked like a spooked owl. He had an open book in one hand, a mug in the other, and a chunk of bread clamped between his teeth.

Pádraig set his things on his desk. "Isn't tonight your physical therapy? Did I get the wrong . . ." He removed his spectacles and looked at the spilled laudanum. "Má sí. Have a seat."

I collapsed onto a couch. Pádraig sat on the other, steepling his hands.

"Did something happen?" he asked.

I shrugged. If I told him about Neve, aeldu knew what she'd do to me.

Pádraig twisted his lips back and forth, thinking. "All right. How are you feeling?"

"Lost at sea. Back in that freezing fog around Algard Island, not knowing what's real, and . . ." I slumped over, resting my head on the couch arm. I didn't know if I should be talking to Pádraig. Sure, Róisín said I could trust him, but maybe that was a lie, too.

Gently, he said, "It's okay if you don't want to talk. Let's try this." He rummaged through his desk and produced paper, charcoal, and a writing board. "Write down everything you're questioning, everything you're not sure is real. When you're done, see if there's anything you want to discuss."

I rolled the charcoal stick between my fingertips, turning them black. Even here, it felt like Neve was watching over my shoulder. *Go ahead, then,* I wrote. *Read this. I'll drag you down to the ocean floor with me. You have the earth, but I have water, and I've felt its depths. I've drowned more times than I can count, and I keep rising to the surface. I'm remembering how to swim.*

From those lines came a flood of words. Og the Destroyer jumped on the couch and curled against me, purring. Distantly, I was aware of Pádraig walking to the door and speaking into the corridor. Círa brought me a mug of lavender tea and left. Only when my hand cramped did I stop writing, feeling like I'd woken from a dream.

"So?" Pádraig prompted. "Anything you want to talk about?"

I read through the pages. Some had smudged beyond legibility. As for the rest, the only people I wanted to share it with were my parents, and the only way I could was through their makiri, which I'd left at the villa. If Neve really wanted to torture me . . .

"I left something in my room," I said. "But I can't go back there, I *can't*—"

"We'll get it," Pádraig reassured me. "Your family's outside in the corridor."

"What? Really?"

"Tsiala Makōpa tracked them down and said you had an argument. They showed up here looking for you."

I didn't want to face them. Once again, I'd selfishly vanished without telling anyone. Yet other than Tiernan, they were the only people in this city I trusted wholeheartedly, the only ones I trusted to retrieve my parents' makiri. I got up, wondering what to do with my papers. The thought of Tiernan answered that.

"Can I burn these?" I asked. "I mean — it won't mess with my head?"

Pádraig chuckled and gestured toward the hearth fire. "Burn away."

✳

While Geniod fetched the makiri, Círa took Dunehein, Rikuja, and me to the Kae-jouyen district. One terrace held plank houses, workshops, and stables. Others had snowy gardens, frosty berry patches, and rows of leafless fruit and nut trees. One had a grove of rioden so tall and thick they must've been older than Ingdanrad. Círa led us into the grove along a flagstone path, passing through tangled nettles and dead ferns. In a clearing, a stone bridge arched across a frozen pond to the Kae gathering place.

Inside, the building felt achingly familiar — rich with the scents of smoke and fish oil, furnished with bark mats on the floor, lit by painted vellum lanterns. Hanlin, the Okoreni-Kae, welcomed us without question. He and the other elders there explained Ingdanrad was a refuge for Aikoto people as well as Gallnach. Hanlin said he would've mentioned it after my trial, but Neve had assured him we'd be fine staying with Clan Ríain.

Geniod returned with the makiri, Tema's fir branch blanket, and Temal's sword. Once the Kae went home, I told my family what had happened. Neve could try and silence me, but I refused to give her power over me anymore. Geniod's fury was quiet, locked in the grip of his hands. Dunehein's swearing filled the gathering place. Rikuja walked out and returned a few minutes later with bloody, splintered knuckles. She was becoming more of a mother bear every day.

We slept on grass-stuffed mattresses in a side room. I dreamed of an octopus wrapping its legs around me, dragging me down through the water. I bit and writhed and dug in my nails. Every time I tore off a leg, another one wrapped around me. I woke screaming and thrashing under my blanket. It was a small mercy that here in the gathering place, sheltered by the rioden grove, only my family could hear me.

Dawn brought the overwhelming prospect of disentangling ourselves from Neve. My family had all been working at Clan Ríain's villa, so as well as retrieving the rest of our belongings, they had to find new jobs. It was another small mercy that Ivar was still recovering his speech, so at the hospital, I only had to tell him hello and goodbye. For all I knew, he and Neve were closer than they let on. Maybe he'd approached me at the wedding reception to spy on me.

Pádraig suggested keeping up my routine as much as possible. Unfortunately, today was meant to be my water-calling practice with Tsiala. Cutting myself free of her and Neve left me unmoored. I had no home in Ingdanrad, no friends, no lover. Círa invited me to help test new recipes in the fourth-floor kitchen, but I was too worried she had some secret motive.

Instead my family and I went to see Janekke. She lived in a two-storey home dug into a rock face, part of a long row of identical homes. The place smelled stale and musty. Bats had gotten in and coated her sitting room in guano while she was away, so we crowded into her dim, candlelit kitchen. Cobwebs hung off the shelves.

"Let's see," Janekke said, rummaging through her cupboards. "I haven't had time to replenish my supplies. I've got brännvin and . . . perhaps herbal tea?"

"Tea's good for me." Rikuja patted her baby bump.

"No offence, Janekke," I said, "but if Tiernan insisted you check people's identities, we should check yours, too."

"No offence taken. Although I don't suppose you'd know anything about me, so . . ." She hummed as she filled the kettle from a water pail. "You know Marijka Riekkanehl, right?"

"Yeah. She supplies medicinal herbs to the apothecary I worked at."

"And she saved my life." Dunehein pulled up his shirt to reveal a long scar across his stomach. "I got stabbed during the Ivy House mission."

Janekke bent over to inspect it. "I could've fixed that *without* the scar." She winked and set the kettle on her iron stove. "Marijka and I trained as medics together. Did she ever bring you some of her spiced apple cake, Kateiko? With smashed chestnuts on top?"

I smiled at the memory. "Every year at harvest time."

"We invented that recipe. Whenever school got too stressful, we'd smash chestnuts with a hammer and bake something. The secret ingredient is repressed rage."

She told us other stories about their friendship, from their early years at school to the year Tiernan moved to Ingdanrad and began courting Marijka. It was strange to hear about the couple gallivanting around, young and reckless, kissing each other in the university library and getting caught by a scandalized librarian. The thought prickled in a way I couldn't name.

Janekke had heard a general account of the coup, so we told her a more thorough version, followed by the recent incident with Neve. She promised to keep it secret and apologized for trusting

Tsiala. She'd handed over her research on the Rúonbattai cleric with the expectation that it would go to me and Nerio. We spread the papers across her kitchen table, looking through the notes Neve had added.

"This research was driving me batty," Janekke said. "Maybe that's why my new nocturnal roommates felt at home. See, when Tiernan first asked me about the Rúonbattai's temporal mage, he thought it was Liet. I pretended to be looking for a former patient so I could access official records — hospital, stavehall, militia, university, and so on — and I wrote down every Sverbian man in the right age group.

"There were hundreds of names. It took months to go through the list, narrowing it down to fire mages who lived here in the decade before the Third Elken War, had a soldier brother with the initial *M*, and were still alive. I got it down to eight possibilities. Then Tiernan and Jorumgard turned up, fresh from the Battle of Tjarnnaast, claiming the temporal mage is a *woman*. So I had to start all over."

"How far did you get this time around?" Geniod asked.

"About a hundred possibilities. We don't know if she was formally ordained as a cleric — in fact, I expect not, given her radical views on magic and the gods — so we can't use that in the criteria. Thankfully, Neve ruled out most of them." Janekke pointed at red lines struck through several names. "She colour-coded her work. Very thoughtful."

"*If* we can believe her," I countered. "Maybe she's throwing us off the trail."

"That's possible." Janekke leaned back in her chair and sipped her brånnvin. "Give me a few days to go through it all. I expect you've got enough to deal with."

*

In all the upheaval, I'd forgotten about the spring equinox until the Kae began decorating their gathering place for the festival. At work, Círa asked if I wanted to join her family for the pre-festival feast. Flustered, I said I'd be busy with Pádraig, not wanting to explain I had therapy.

Half an hour later, in the neurology ward, Pádraig returned from the kitchen with a mug of smoky-scented tea and gave me a pointed look. "You know, the point of setting a routine is to take stress out of your life. It's not supposed to take *over* your life."

"But—" I began.

"Tomorrow's your free night, aye? We'll do your therapy then." He sipped his tea and added, "If it helps, Círa is the sweetest person on this good earth. You could do worse for a friend."

So after work, my family and I went to Círa's plank house. That, too, was achingly familiar — not just the food and laughter and kids running everywhere but also the unspoken knowledge that becoming friends meant befriending each other's families as well. Neve had made a point of taking me places alone. I'd told Pádraig a bit about it, and he'd explained that abusive people often cut off their victims' social connections. It made it harder for the victim to get help and for anyone else to notice what was happening.

Most of Círa's family here were distant relatives. She'd grown up in a fishing village in southern Eremur with a Kae mother and Gallnach father. The village didn't have a school, so when she was thirteen and her brother was ten, they moved here to live with a great-aunt. Círa had done a five-year medical apprenticeship, then another two years specializing in nutrition, and then started running the fourth-floor kitchen last year. Her brother had recently started at the university.

"He lives in the dormitories now so he doesn't have to go up and down the mountain every day," Círa explained. "You might meet him later tonight, although he tends to show up at festivals for an hour and then take off with some girl."

When Rikuja mentioned this would her last festival before becoming a mother, Círa declared we had to make it special. She and her girl cousins swarmed in, dusting Rikuja's face with sparkling mica powder, painting patterns on her hands, finding a ribbon to twine into her braid. Next they came for me, persuading me to swap my dirty work dress for a borrowed shirt and leggings, richly embroidered with flowers and leaves.

The festival itself blended Aikoto and Gallnach culture. Kegs held cranberry wine, ale, and whisky. Drummers played alongside pipers and fiddlers. Most people wore moss-green woolwraps, but a few wore the copper red of the Yula fox crest or the grey-trimmed white of the Dona seagull. As they danced, whirling and stomping, it looked like blossoms swirling through the rainforest. Círa kept coaxing me to join, but I preferred lurking by the wall with a mug of whisky.

My mind drifted to the rest of my family. Yotolein was taking Jorumgard to Toel Ginu to spend the Iyo festival with Hanaiko and Samulein. In Nettle Ginu, Malana and Aoreli would be celebrating their first spring equinox as wives. Emehein had his wife, Kirbana had Narun . . . I was the only one left alone.

Almost only, I corrected myself. Geniod stood across the gathering place, nursing his own whisky. He raised his mug in wry salute. And of course Tiernan was alone in the hospital, trapped in his own mind. Here I was without him, pretending everything was normal when I'd been turned inside out, my guts bared for everyone to see.

One of Círa's cousins tapped my arm. Leaning in to be heard over the music, she said, "Some girl's looking for you. She's waiting outside."

It felt like I'd been punched. "Who?" I scraped out. "An itheran?"

Círa's cousin shook her head. "Looks Aikoto. Tall, wavy hair, two daggers on her belt."

I downed my whisky and headed out into the chilly night. Strings of glowing crystals hung from the trees, reflected on the frozen pond. A handful of people sat on log benches around firepits, drinking and roasting nuts in the coals. Tsiala hovered nearby, hands in the pockets of her knit wool coat.

"What do *you* want?" I said.

"To apologize," she said. "And talk."

"It's a little late—"

"Give me five minutes. Then if you want me to go, I will."

I grit my teeth, remembering my parents' advice for talking to Parr. No fear, no anger, no bearshit.

We settled by an unlit firepit near the edge of the grove. Icy wind blew over us, making me shiver. Tsiala unclasped her coat and held it out. I didn't want to accept, but my teeth were starting to chatter. Odd considering how mild the winter had been. I draped her coat over my shoulders, soaking in her body heat, forcing myself not to look at her muscular, tattooed arms.

Tsiala picked up a charred stick and began picking off flakes of ash. "I'm sorry. Really. I wanted to tell you about Neve — what she's like, how she was controlling you. Thing is, she does it to me, too."

"What do you mean?"

"Remember how I vowed to kill my father? When I couldn't do it, I fled to a Gallnach colony. I was fifteen, broke, and starving. Neve was nineteen, rich, and powerful. She took me in. I told her everything — my mother's death, Yonna's death, the orphanage, my father's military camps. Now, if I question or criticize her, she says I'm 'welcome to go back home.' As if I've got a goddamned home to return to."

I sucked in a breath. It hurt to hear, yet it also felt like the stories Neve spun, manipulating me into sympathy. "Why should I believe that?"

"Dunno." Tsiala threw the charred stick into the woods. "But you and me, we made a promise. We said whatever happens with Alesso and Tiernan, we'll be there for each other. Neve can't take that from us."

"Is that the only reason you're here?"

"No. I ..." She flicked ash off her fingers onto the snow. "I wanna start over. I want a chance with you without Neve interfering. If we'd met in the fish market of Port Alios, or that smoky inn where we drank mezcale together in Rutnaast, or this festival tonight — everything would be different."

If we'd met in another world, I thought. I'd cut myself loose from Neve and swum to the surface only to find it frozen over. The life I wanted was out there, but I hadn't been able to reach it. I'd been pounding my fists against the ice, forgetting I could melt my way through. Kianta kolo. Even after a tough winter, spring always came.

A hot breeze washed over us. Tsiala glanced around, frowning. A smile tugged at my lips as I realized why the weather was being so strange. If Akohin liked weddings because he got to see people happy, he probably liked festivals, too. Overhead, the dark silhouette of a raven circled in the starry sky.

"Spying on me?" I said under my breath. "What are you, my uncle?"

Akohin cawed back. I'd never known a raven could sound insulted. His presence gave me an idea, though. After I'd hurt him by being a poor friend, he'd only let me back into his life if I went his way — stripping off all my disguises, my defences, and walking naked through the icy mountains to prove my loyalty. Only then had Ainu-Seru protected me with his warm wind.

"It's not enough to cut Neve out," I said. "If we'd met in the fish market or that inn, I wouldn't have been alone. And I'm not ready to be alone with you. Being with me means being with my family and friends, too."

Tsiala nodded. "I can do that."

"Don't be so sure." I smiled wryly. "Do you have to go back to Clan Ríain's villa tonight?"

"No. Neve gave me the night off. It's the least she owes me."

"Then we're going inside to dance. Dune will tease us, Rija will worry, and Geniod will watch our every move. You'll meet Círa, and you'll hate how bubbly she is, and you won't say a single rude or sarcastic thing. If you survive the night . . . then we'll see."

27.

GHOST NATION

I woke to birdsong. The night had been so warm that we'd left a window cracked in the side room. Geniod and Dunehein were asleep, stretched out on their mattresses. Rikuja's was empty. So was the one we'd set out for Tsiala. My spirits plummeted. Last night had gone well, I'd thought. Now Tsiala had left without saying goodbye?

Then I heard voices among the birdsong. I pushed off my embroidered blanket and padded barefoot toward the main room, stopping in the doorway. Mugs littered the place and canvas tarps covered the large Kae drums. Rikuja and Tsiala knelt on bark mats by a flagstone hearth, their backs to me. Tsiala was kneading dough on a varnished board.

"You've *never* baked with duck potato flour?" Rikuja was saying.

Tsiala shook her head. "We always used brassroot down south. And we call it frybread, not flatbread."

I watched in silence, remembering what Róisín said about bread being the great uniter. Rikuja scrutinized Tsiala's handiwork, telling her to add more water, showing her how to handle the dough. I'd never seen Tsiala like this, soft and quiet, the hint of a smile in her voice. Her hair fell in rumpled waves, exposing her neck. The muscles in her arms and shoulders flexed as she kneaded the dough.

In another world, she could've been a baker or blacksmith or sailor. I thought of Samulein, always getting in fights at school, and how we'd been teaching him other ways to live. Tsiala had lost her yonna, her only teacher, when she was seven. Everyone else — the orphanage priests, her father, and Neve — saw her as only a soldier. *If* everything she'd told me was true.

"Ai," Rikuja said with a laugh. "I forgot to bring cooking oil from the storage shed. Baby brain."

"I'll get it." Tsiala set the board aside and got up, unfolding her long legs. As she crossed the room, she pulled water from the air to wash dough off her hands.

I drew back into the side room, pulled on my boots, and slipped out the door. Ainu-Seru's warm wind had brought spring overnight. The pond had cracked open, melting icicles dripped honeycomb patterns into the snow, and patches of rotten evergreen needles showed through the whiteness. I followed Tsiala to the storage shed. At the sound of my footsteps, she whirled.

"Merdo," she muttered, letting her hands fall from her dagger hilts. "It's just you."

"How do I know this is real?" I blurted. "How do I know Neve didn't send you to spy on me?"

Tsiala shrugged. "Ask Róisín."

"What?" I glanced around, half expecting the druid to appear.

"She spent hours looking into my spirit during our trial. If she thought I was a threat, she would've warned you, right?"

She had a point. Róisín had only warned me about Neve.

Tsiala drew forward. She stopped close enough for our breath to mix. "Ask yourself, too," she said quietly. "Does this *feel* real?"

I looked up into her dark eyes, framed by thick lashes. It had felt real in the moments I glimpsed her spirit — silently drinking mezcale together in the dark, her hair skimming my cheek as we lay in the snow above the Hollow, talking on a bench outside the hospital. Her nails had dug into my back as we'd embraced. Like she, too, had been asking if this was real.

We'd both suffered enough. I was tired of drowning, fighting, pounding my fists against the ice and trying to break through. We deserved to breathe. We deserved our spring.

I kissed her. Tsiala drew a sharp breath. She slid her hands up my neck and cupped my jaw, holding me close. Her lips were soft and full — everything I'd imagined and more. The scent of dough under her nails mixed with the crispness of morning sunlight. It smelled like new life, fresh and full of possibility. It smelled like hope.

✳

Flustered, Tsiala and I returned to the gathering place trying to pretend nothing had happened. Rikuja wasn't fooled. She gave us a look and pointed out Tsiala had forgotten the fish oil. The others woke while we were frying the bread. Dunehein's grin said an onslaught of teasing would come later. After Tsiala left, though, the first comment came from Geniod.

"Look," he began, "if you're happy, so are we. We just want you to be careful."

"Don't worry," I said dryly. "I don't need bloodweed with another girl."

Rikuja spat out a mouthful of water. Laughing, she said, "Aeldu save me. I won't lie, that's a weight off my mind."

I couldn't wholly say I was happy, what with paranoia flowing through me like poison, but it was a step closer. At the hospital, mopping the corridors, I caught myself whistling. Or rather a medic caught me, leaning out of the lung sickness ward and asking me to keep it down. It was just as well Pádraig had moved my therapy to today, since I had a *lot* to discuss.

He asked if writing my thoughts down had helped. I supposed it had in that I'd survived the discovery of Neve's betrayal. Pádraig gave me a charcoal pencil and a leatherbound journal, small enough to fit in my dress pocket, and suggested I keep recording my thoughts. "Think of it as a vault," he said. "Whenever something comes up that you don't have time or energy to deal with, or you're not sure is real, put it in the vault. Later, you can walk through it with people you trust."

I was astonished by how much poured out of me. Water-calling practice with Tsiala brought new worries, new daydreams, new things to analyze. Ivar recovered his speech enough for me to tell him about the Rúonbattai coup and thank him for protecting me. Digging through my memories of that night turned into pages of thoughts.

Talking to Tiernan's unconscious form kept me in a see-saw of confusing emotions. I traced the blue veins under his pale skin like rivers on a map. Where would that map lead me? To Nyhemur's snowy plains and windmills? The dream was melting away with the warm weather. Terrified of forgetting the way he had in prison, I filled my journal with daydreams of it. I'd be his memory for everything slipping away, his witness for everything he was missing.

Janekke told me she'd looked into a few names Neve had crossed off the list of potential Rúonbattai clerics. They all checked out. One was dead, one hadn't left Ingdanrad in decades, and the others didn't have brothers. Unfortunately, working from Neve's version of the list, Janekke had narrowed it to nothing. No one in Ingdanrad's recorded history matched our description of the cleric. The woman was a ghost.

My family's next step in disentangling from Neve was finding somewhere to live long-term. We wanted a space of our own instead of staying in the Kae gathering place, but that didn't leave many options. None of us wanted to live in a dark, stuffy underground home like Janekke's. An above-ground place would cost most of the sovereigns Nerio had given me in Port Alios, which we agreed to save for an emergency.

Hanlin put forward another option. A Dona couple had been living in a log cabin among the fruit and nut groves, then left Ingdanrad after the coup. We could stay there if my family helped with the Kae-jouyen's seasonal work. The first job was the smelt spawn, which was just starting as ice cracked on a nearby river. It was unusually early for this far inland. Unlike the warm weather, that wasn't Ainu-Seru's doing. Waterways were the domain of anta-saidu alone.

We had a look at the cabin to see what work it needed. A good clean, for starters, and some rearranging. When I returned from the hospital the next evening, everything was done. My family wanted to surprise me. They'd moved the makiri shelf from over the door, the Dona way, to over the kitchen stove. Wooden screens divided the bedroom, one side for Dunehein and Rikuja, the other for Geniod, while I had the loft. Finally, I hoped, I could lay my fir branch blanket somewhere for more than a few weeks.

❋

Spring rose like a gangly fawn figuring out its new legs. My family's next job was helping the Kae plow and plant their garden terraces. The snowmelt had been light, though, and the rain was no more than an occasional sprinkle. Antayul walked the gardens every day watering the crops with the little moisture they could pull out of the air.

Ivar, too, was a fawn tottering around the fourth floor, rebuilding the muscles that had atrophied while he was comatose. Pádraig discharged him as an in-patient and scheduled him for weekly therapy. As Ivar packed up his few possessions, he said maybe he'd see me around the Kae district. I smiled back hesitantly, still not sure how close he was to Neve. Círa, passing with her lunch trolley, cast a dark look at Ivar's back. Later in the kitchen, I pried the reason out of her.

"He's . . ." She sighed, brushing her bangs out of her eyes. "He acts Kae, but he isn't. Not really."

I frowned. "Because he's adopted? That's a bit harsh."

"No! I mean Olina never had him initiated into our jouyen. Isn't that weird, to adopt a son and not give him your family crest?"

"He has a heron tattoo. He showed it to me during the coup—"

"It's not a true Kae tattoo. I don't know who gave it to him. Besides, he doesn't try to be part of the jouyen. He never comes to ceremonies, or asks the elders for guidance, or helps with fishing or gardening. If he *does* visit our district, I'd want to know why."

Uneasiness crept into me. Despite feeling self-conscious about my lack of tattoos, I'd never dreamed of getting them outside a formal initiation. Maybe Ivar didn't feel welcome among the Kae, or like he deserved to be initiated, or . . . My thoughts spiralled. I wrote them down in my journal with a reminder to tell my family.

Secretly I was glad Ivar wouldn't be around the hospital as much. Seeing him awake, talking, and walking made me sick with resentment. It wasn't fair for him to recover while Tiernan lay comatose. Out of reach. Tiernan's motionless, withering body seemed to be trapped in winter while everything else grew and shifted around us.

Elbow deep in dishwater, a thought struck. This wasn't the first time Tiernan had been trapped. Maybe the militia was keeping him comatose, though I didn't know how. Sleeping medicine, perhaps, but I'd seen Círa prepare his broth and feed him countless times. When I next visited Tiernan, I subtly examined him. His silver-bearded guard ignored me, busy darning a sock. The only unnatural thing on Tiernan's body was the iron cuff to nullify his magic. Or at least that's what I'd been *told* the glowing runes did.

I copied the designs into my journal and showed Pádraig. Gently, he told me they were standard nullifying runes. He showed me the entry in a dusty reference tome. I hadn't realized how high my hopes had gotten until they crashed into the stone floor. Sure, I hated the thought of the militia keeping Tiernan comatose, but at least there would've been a way to wake him.

"Listen," Pádraig said, rubbing his temples. "I agreed that you could talk to Tiernan for ten minutes a day. Using that time for wild conspiracy theories won't help either of you. If being around him makes you more paranoid—"

"It doesn't," I cut in. "I'll stop thinking about it. I promise."

✳

"We've been together two weeks and you've already forgotten about me?" Tsiala's voice drifted through the barren chestnut trees near my cabin.

Startled, I looked up from my journal. Tsiala plunked down next to me on the garden bench. She had two herb-and-cheese scones that smelled freshly baked. Right — she'd asked Neve for the night off. We'd planned to meet at the harbour market after work. The sun was already sinking behind the inlet. Crickets chirped among the trees.

"Shit," I said. "Sorry. I lost track of time—"

"You can make it up to me with a kiss." She winked and leaned in.

I still wasn't used to that. Every time we kissed, I discovered the softness of her lips all over again, the warmth of her breath, the roughness of her calloused hands. It always left me dizzy, wanting more. My nightmares had been replaced by dreams I'd never speak aloud. Yet for all that my body craved her touch, my spirit wasn't ready.

"What are you writing?" she asked, nodding at my journal.

Admitting I'd been writing about Tiernan was a terrible idea on par with eating raw Ferish pepper. Instead I repeated what Círa said about Ivar not being truly Kae. Tsiala half listened, picking bits of browned cheese off her scone. The bored look she always used to wear crept back onto her face.

"You're obviously busy," she interrupted.

"What? I said sorry—"

"Yeah, well." She started to walk off.

"Stop!"

My volume surprised us both. I hadn't meant to yell, but it felt too much like when Jonalin used to shut down. I closed my journal and set it aside on the bench.

"You're the one who wanted another chance," I said. "So sit down and tell me why you're upset."

Tsiala blew out a breath, stirring her hair. She sat back down. "I'm not upset. I'm jealous."

"Of . . . *who*? Círa? Ivar?"

"Not that kind of jealous. I mean . . . you have all these traditions. Family crests, festivals, a certain way of frying flatbread. I don't even remember how to speak my language."

I gaped at her. "Really?"

"Well, I remember one word." She picked at her nails. "Makōpa means *Ghost Nation*. It's all the Kowichelk people who got wrenched out of our homes by itherans. Adopted, sent to the orphanage, sold into labour, whatever. There's thousands of us. Itherans forced their cultures onto us and made us forget ours. Most of us don't even know our real nation."

"I didn't know," I said quietly. "I thought since you'd gotten tattooed . . ."

"They're not traditional." Tsiala slid off her knit coat, exposing the geometric patterns wreathing her arms. "Me and the other Makōpa kids in my father's army gave them to each other. We wanted a way to recognize each other if we died in battle."

My throat tightened. I twined my fingers into hers. "I'm sorry. We promised to be there for each other, and instead I'm yelling at you and making you miserable."

"You can make that up to me, too." She lifted my hand and kissed my fingertips. "I was thinking about ways to see each other more, and . . . I could take over your physical therapy. We can ease into combat training. Sparring, sword-fighting, whatever you want. It'll help you feel safe again."

Safe wasn't the word I'd use for rolling around with Tsiala, feeling her muscles flex, tangling together . . . Warmth flooded through me. "Won't you be exhausted? You've already got combat lessons at the militia complex."

She grinned. Leaning in, she whispered into my ear. "Don't worry. I've got stamina."

28.

RUNES & RECORDS

Late one evening, leaving the neurology ward after therapy, I passed through the dark in-patient hall to say goodnight to Tiernan. His guard's chair was empty. Strange. Maybe Og the Destroyer was roaming about and the guard had gone to investigate. I took the rare chance to sit with Tiernan alone, holding his bony hand.

That's when I discovered glowing runes *inside* his iron cuff. Their light wasn't noticeable during the daytime. I lifted his arm, craning my neck to see between his thin wrist and the cuff. The inner and outer runes were different. My pulse skipped. I copied the inner ones into my journal, then hurried off before his guard returned.

My problem now was identifying them. Dunehein, Rikuja, and Geniod knew nothing about runes. My medical textbook made no mention of these, and Pádraig's dusty reference tome was in Gallnach. If I asked him for help again, and he thought I was becoming obsessed, he might ban me from seeing Tiernan.

On my next lunch break, while I frowned at my journal instead of studying, Círa asked what I was staring at. I made her swear not to tell Pádraig, then I showed her the runes. She turned my journal this way and that, examining them with bemusement.

"Never seen them," she said. "But my brother Finín studies runes at university. I can take you to meet him after work."

Tsiala and I had agreed to visit the harbour market to make up for me forgetting last week, but I was impatient to know about the runes, so we picked her up on the way. The sprawling university campus was like its own village with countless buildings dug into cliff faces. Signs pointed down ramps and stairways to underground lecture halls, laboratories, and workshops. The botany department's greenhouses, ponds, and gardens took up most of the outdoor space.

A terrace high up the campus had a courtyard full of people enjoying the warm spring evening. Círa stopped at a food stall and bought a mutton pasty to bribe Finín into helping us. The highest terrace housed the dormitories, a half-dozen identical towers of grey stone. In the northeast tower's candlelit atrium, students chatted and studied at circular tables. Five storeys of balconies rose up to a glass roof, beyond which the first stars had appeared in the darkening sky.

Círa went straight to a group of teenage boys. Books, papers, quills, and inkpots covered their table. They all looked like itherans except one, who glanced up at us and groaned. He was every bit Círa's brother, with the same straight black hair, triangular jaw, and a smile floating across his lips.

"I smell food," Finín said. "That means you need a favour."

"This one's not for me," Círa said, handing him the paper-wrapped pasty. "Meet Kateiko and Tsiala."

"Má sí," said another boy. "Finín, your sister's friends are lush."

"We're taken," Tsiala said coolly, slipping her arm around my waist.

315

Finín laughed. "Ignore these bludgeheads. They'll wind up married to their books."

He inhaled his pasty, packed papers into a leather satchel, and pushed back from the table. Until now, I hadn't noticed his chair. It was wicker with a high back, padded seat, and two large aluminum wheels. His booted feet rested on a thick stirrup. He cocked an eyebrow as if daring Tsiala and me to say something. We didn't.

"Come on, then," he said. "Let's talk in my dorm."

Finín turned his chair and rolled away, clattering on the stone floor. The wheels had attached rims for him to grab and push himself along. I'd seen hospital patients in similar chairs, but those had to be pushed by an attendant. Finín seemed fine on his own, though I recalled Círa saying he lived here so he didn't need to go between campus and the Kae district every day.

Next to the stairs was an elevator like in the hospital, powered by earth magic in the stone. Finín touched a panel of glowing runes in the wall, making the elevator rumble to life. We emerged high in the atrium. Finín continued down a corridor and unlocked a door. Inside the dark room, he tapped the wall, making crystals on the ceiling bloom with light.

His room was modest, furnished in pine and brass. The bottom of a bookshelf was packed with leatherbound tomes. The upper shelves — out of his reach, I supposed — held limestone carvings and model sailing ships. A window looked across the dark campus and to the inlet beyond. Since there were no chairs, we girls perched on his bed, covered with a patchwork blanket in green and brown earth tones.

I handed over my journal, open to the page with the runes. "Do you know what these do?"

Finín studied them, frowning. "No idea. Where'd you find them?"

"On the nullifying cuff of a hospital patient. He's a prisoner, and ... I think the militia's keeping him comatose so he can't stand trial."

Finín's eyebrows shot into his hair. "That'd be wildly unethical. Not to mention illegal and probably impossible."

"Probably? Not definitely?"

"Well, in theory — but testing it — I mean, even nullifying runes are a huge political issue. Bodily autonomy and all that."

"Can you look into it, anyway?" Círa asked. "If the militia's messing with our patients, I want to know, too."

"Sure. Is this all of them?" Finín began flipping through my journal.

A squeak burst out of me. "Don't — that's private—"

Tsiala snickered. "What are you hiding?" She plucked the journal from Finín's hands and pretended to read aloud. "Last night, my lover and I kissed under the stars. It was the most magical moment of my life—"

"Stop that!" I grabbed at the journal, but she held it out of reach. "I didn't even see you last night!"

"Your loss." Tsiala tossed the journal back at Finín, who caught it deftly. "There you go, scholar boy. Copy those runes and nothing else. Otherwise, you answer to me."

✳

It took another week for Tsiala and me to finally reach the harbour market. Strings of glowing crystals hung over cobblestone laneways. A salty breeze rustled the canvas roofs of ramshackle shops that leaned at odd angles, held up by rope and driftwood stakes. People swarmed past, talking, drinking from paper cups, browsing the wares.

Every corner had performers — drummers and pipers, dancers in vibrant woolwraps, fire mages twirling blazing rods and hoops. Clan Níall druids made seeds bloom into flowers. Clan Ríain druids spun molten gold into wire. A young man cracked a pair of whips so fast and well timed it sounded like music. As I dropped a few pann into his upturned hat, Tsiala swore behind me.

I spun. Neve stood arm in arm with Ivar. He was back in his red militia woolwrap, sword on his hip, while she was in Clan Ríain's plum. Gold beads sparkled in her strawberry-blonde hair. They looked like a mythical couple from folk tales — a tall, dashing soldier and a small, beautiful maiden.

"Hello, sweet pea." Neve cast me a glowing smile. "It's been a while."

Fury crackled through me. I wanted to slap that smile off her face, but I was already serving a criminal sentence. Assaulting the daughter of a chief druid would not be wise.

Neve stood on her toes and kissed Ivar's cheek. "Would you give us a moment, darling?"

"Of course." He tapped two fingers to his forehead in salute to Tsiala and me. "Enjoy the market."

The moment he left, Neve swept over to us. Her floral perfume washed over me as she leaned in to whisper. "It's not what you think. I'm keeping an eye on Ivar."

"Why?" I asked, narrowing my eyes.

"I know he's not really Kae. So where does his loyalty lie? How *did* he get injured during the coup?"

"Are you saying he's Rúonbattai? Róisín ó Conn cleared out all the traitors—"

"Not all. She can't interrogate coma patients. A few days after she left town, Ivar mysteriously woke up."

It felt like someone had dropped ice down my dress. Neve was right. Maybe my theory of runes keeping people comatose wasn't so wild, after all.

"Don't listen to her," Tsiala told me. "She's messing with your head."

Neve clicked her tongue. "I would never—"

"Oh, shut up," Tsiala snapped. "Know what? I'm done. Your family might own half this city, but you don't own me. Find a new goddamned bodyguard."

For once, Neve seemed speechless. She fiddled with a gold bracelet, then said abruptly, "Check the records."

"*What* records?"

"All of them. Hospital, militia, stavehall. There's something strange about Ivar. You'll see."

✳

Tsiala dodged my attempts to ask her about quitting. All she said was she could live in the militia barracks, and she had enough money saved to get by until her criminal sentence was done. After that, she could get a paying job. I wanted to help but didn't know how, so I just kissed her and said, "I'm proud of you."

At work, I asked Círa about the possibility of runes keeping Ivar comatose. He'd been wearing a gold ring that could've had hidden runes like Tiernan's cuff. According to Círa, Olina had claimed it was a family heirloom and the medics weren't to remove it under any circumstances. The day after Olina visited Ivar again, he'd woken from his coma. I hated taking instructions from Neve, but I reluctantly asked Círa to pull Ivar's medical records.

Everything looked normal. His surname was listed as Kae and the birthdate meant he'd just turned twenty-four. There were notes on an exam for militia eligibility, a few combat injuries in his teens, and pox two years ago. The attending medic had noted that Ivar's case was mild since he'd already had it as a toddler. I flipped back to the start, wondering how I'd missed that. The first fourteen years of his life were missing. No record of his birth, the pox, or any cuts and broken bones that active young boys often got.

"Was Ivar born here?" I asked.

"I think so," Círa said. "My cousins here grew up with him. Olina's a herbalist, though, so she probably treated him as a child. Ivar only would've started coming here because the militia mandates it."

That made sense. Still, after my shift, I hurried downstairs to the surgery to catch Janekke. She agreed to look into other official records. A few days later, she came up to the fourth floor with unexpected results. First, Ivar had enlisted in the militia as an earth mage. He'd never shown any sign of knowing magic. Second, the Sverbian stavehall had no record of his birth.

Hanlin had explanations for both those things. Ivar's birth mother had gotten pregnant out of wedlock, so she gave birth in secret with Olina's help. Olina and her husband, a Gallnach druid, adopted the baby. The druid taught Ivar earth magic before dying of illness, after which Olina raised Ivar alone.

Something felt off, though. As I reread Tiernan's letter before bed like usual, I found it. The tunnel between Tjarnnaast and Nyhemur had been dug with earth magic. Tiernan had been surprised because as far as we knew, the Rúonbattai had no surviving earth mages.

That didn't prove Ivar was Rúonbattai, and I didn't know where else to look for information. Tsiala suggested we could check his library records. I thought she was joking until I arrived at the militia complex for our combat lesson. She strode outside, carrying a canvas satchel that held something suspiciously book-shaped.

"C'mon," she whispered. "Act natural."

"You stole a book?" I said, aghast.

"Ivar's on night shift. He won't notice it missing until dawn."

"What if it's warded? A tracking rune or something?"

"I worked for a spy, remember? The book's bound with string, so I untied it and took out the page with the tracking rune. I'll put it back when we're done."

Away from the militia complex, she showed me the book, covered with fawn-coloured suede. Under the title was a gilt design of a lilac. I was torn between kissing her and smacking her for being reckless. Then again, Tiernan had once stolen an oak and lilac tapestry from a stavehall, potentially triggering the Fourth Elken War, and I'd forgiven him. The book was written in the angular symbols of Sverbian, so we hurried to Janekke's home.

She took one glance at the cover and started laughing. "*The Lilac Queen: A Tragic Tale of Love and Loss*. Looks like a romance novel."

"*What?*" I rounded on Tsiala.

She scowled. "How would I know?"

"Well, we've got it now," Janekke said. "Might as well take a peek."

She settled into her sitting room to read. Tsiala and I occupied ourselves by playing cards in the kitchen. She'd beaten me eighteen to one by the time Janekke drifted in, stretching.

"Honestly, I don't know what to make of it," she said. "It *is* about the Rúonbattai. Might be a true story, might be someone's wild imaginings. The author is anonymous. They wouldn't be the first person to romanticize a pretty awful part of history."

"What's the story?" I asked.

Janekke pulled up a stool and began flipping through the book. "The heroine is a Sverbian fisherman's daughter named Maud. Poor and plain, but sweet as honey. She comes of age soon after the

Second Elken War. One day, working in Caladheå's fish market, she meets a naval soldier named Bødar."

Tsiala snickered. "What kind of name is Bødar?"

"Hush." Janekke swatted Tsiala's arm. "Bødar's poor and plain, too, though he cuts a fine figure in uniform. He asks Maud for the smallest fish she has. When she asks why, he shows her a tiny kitten in his pocket, a mouser for his ship. Maud falls head over boot. She'd gladly marry him the next day, but he wants to set his life up first. He'd fought the Ferish in the war, and with immigrants pouring in from Ferland, he wants to make a safe home for Maud. A tall fence, the toughest locks, servants to protect her.

"So Bødar saves up, leaves the navy, and buys a merchant schooner. Rich Ferish immigrants want all the exotic luxuries they had back home — silks, spices, coffee. Bødar makes good money bringing hothouse blooms from the southern colonies. Maud jokingly calls him the Lilac King. He buys a beautiful home in Caladheå, and on the doorstep, he asks her to become his Lilac Queen.

"Married life is far from what Maud expects, though. Bødar forbids her from visiting their Ferish neighbours, shopping at Ferish markets, even talking to Ferish people in the street. She starts to get antsy. When she falls pregnant, she doesn't want to tell him until she knows what's going on, so she starts eavesdropping. One night, she overhears him plotting to murder a Ferish merchant. Maud can't believe her ears, but over time, she discovers her husband isn't just a murderer. He's a Rúonbattai captain, a founding member. His merchant business is a cover for war crimes — slaughtering Ferish immigrants, sinking their ships, razing their settlements.

"Maud panics. She flees to Ingdanrad and gives birth to twins. Terrified that Bødar will find out and come to claim their children, she insists there be no record of the births. Soon after, she falls for a Sverbian fire mage named Athall. It's like she's been holding her breath for years and can finally let go. She has her marriage dissolved in the eyes of the gods and weds Athall. He adopts her twins, and the book ends with them living happily ever after."

Tsiala snorted. "Of course they do."

"Hold on," I said. "A pregnant woman shows up without a husband, gives birth, and doesn't record it? That sounds like Ivar's mother."

"Exactly what I thought, but . . ." Janekke flipped toward the book's end. "The timelines don't match. Maud gave birth fifty-two years ago."

"Fifty-two? That'd be around when the cleric was born — oh. Yan taku." I rubbed my temples. "The cleric's brother, M. What if that's her *twin*?"

Janekke's brows crinkled. "Did her letters ever mention a twin?"

"Not specifically, but" — I paced the kitchen, ducking onion strings dangling from the ceiling — "it would fit. Their birth father's a Rúonbattai captain, the Lilac King. The Rúonbattai gifted lilac seeds to the Iyo-jouyen fifty years ago. I bet Bødar forged the alliance with the Iyo."

"What a life for Maud," Tsiala said, shuffling the deck of cards. "Escapes an abusive war criminal, then their kids follow his footsteps into leading the Rúonbattai? That's hardly a happy ending."

"If it's true, this book might be the only record of their birth." Janekke opened a glossy wooden cabinet and took out her research on potential clerics. "Let's see if anyone on this list has the matronym Maudehl."

We spread the papers across her table. Her original list and Neve's added notes were in Sverbian, so all I could do was wait. The candles were guttering when Janekke looked up and sighed.

"No luck," she said. "Maybe the author changed the names to protect the real people. Maybe it's all made up."

Tsiala prodded the book as if she expected it to bite. "The question remains, why the hell does Ivar have it?"

"Who knows?" I said. "Maybe he likes romance stories. Maybe Neve gave it to him."

Our eyes met. That sounded like something Neve would do. Tell us to look into Ivar, then frame him by planting a suspicious book in the barracks where Tsiala was now living. If Tsiala got caught stealing again while serving a criminal sentence, I dreaded to think what would happen.

Tsiala reached across the table and took my hand. "She doesn't own us. Remember that."

❋

Outside Janekke's home, Tsiala kissed me goodnight and headed north to the militia complex to return the book. I went south to the Kae district and padded through moonlit chestnut groves. I was supposed to be doing combat training tonight, so Geniod, Dunehein, and Rikuja had gone to visit the Kae gathering place. Our cabin's windows were dark. The door was ajar, creaking in the wind.

I drew my obsidian-handled knife. Heart thudding, I crept toward the cabin and peered through a window. Nothing moved in the shadows. I listened by the door, then nudged it fully open, letting moonlight spill in.

The place had been trashed. Broken glass crunched under my boots as I edged into the kitchen. I fumbled around for the tinderbox and lit a candle. Spilled flour, shattered jars, kindling, and papers littered the floor. An inkpot had spilled on my writing desk, staining it black. My parents' makiri were still on their shelf over the stove. I clutched them to my chest, faint with relief.

In the bedroom, the wooden dividing screen had been knocked over. Clothes, pillow down, and dry grass from the mattresses lay everywhere. It was the same in the loft, where Tema's fir branch blanket had been pulled off my bed. Temal's sword lay outside its sheath. Tiernan's letter had been ripped in half, right through *snowy plains*.

I felt sick. Like a stranger had grabbed my hair, violating something sacred. I crawled under my blanket and pressed the torn letter to my lips. His gold oak coin had already been taken from me in prison. This letter was my only scrap of him left. Our past, with the last words he wrote me, and our future, with the dream of visiting Nyhemur.

Neve, I kept thinking. She wanted revenge because Tsiala chose me over her. I needed proof, though. My parents would've seen who did this. I tried meditating, seeking their spirits, but couldn't hold the connection. My hands shook and my breath stuttered. I was still there when my family returned. Numb, I passed the makiri to Geniod.

Usually, he stayed silent until he finished talking to them. This time he spoke aloud. "It's not someone they've met. Otherwise they'd show me a memory. I mean, they saw the person tonight, but the dead don't see the way we do. They saw . . . a bird? Long neck, long legs, pale feathers . . . a heron."

"A Kae person?" Dunehein asked.

"No, wait — it's changing. Still pale, but it looks like . . . a raven?"

A white raven. The sacred bird on the Sverbian and Rúonbattai flags. A raven disguised as a heron wasn't Neve. It was Ivar.

29.

REFUGE

Working by candlelight, my family and I sorted through the mess. Nothing was missing. The purse of gold sovs from Nerio was still in a secret compartment Rikuja had built into the log walls. Ivar must've been searching for the book, though I wasn't sure how he knew it was missing, why it mattered enough to abandon his post, or why he thought it was in our home. If it had a tracking rune that Tsiala missed, he could've followed it straight to us.

Unnerved, we headed out into the city. Dunehein and Rikuja checked on Janekke while Geniod and I hurried across the mountain to find Tsiala. She was at the militia complex, safe and sound. She'd returned the book to Ivar's bunk with no trouble. Janekke, too, was safe at home.

We didn't dare admit to the theft publicly, so my family agreed to only tell Hanlin. The man seemed disgusted by Ivar's actions but not surprised. He revealed that Olina *had* asked to initiate Ivar into the

Kae-jouyen. Their okorebai had refused because she didn't believe Ivar was truly committed. Still, it didn't prove he was Rúonbattai. Maybe he was interested in their history, or had terrible taste in fiction, and wanted to retrieve the book before anyone realized how suspicious it looked.

I couldn't sleep that night, and at work, I was a nervous wreck. Every noise made me jump, every motion in my peripheral vision made me whirl. I mopped the neurology ward three times before Pádraig asked if I was okay.

"What am I supposed to do?" I burst out. "Ingdanrad's meant to be a refuge. Instead I've been betrayed, thrown in prison, *murdered* — and now my home gets broken into?"

Pádraig took off his square reading spectacles. "Yet you're still here. That shows incredible strength."

I scoffed, leaning the mop against the wall. "That's your solution? Keep existing?"

"Existing can be an act of defiance. If people are determined to lock you away, or hurt you, or threaten you into silence . . ." He gave me a pointed look. "It means they're afraid. Of your power, your voice, your convictions. Your mere existence is a reminder they haven't won."

"What would you know?" I grumbled. "No one's coming after *you*."

Pádraig rested his elbows on his desk, steepling his fingers. His pale green eyes looked so much like Róisín's. He closed a folder of medical records and beckoned me to the squashy couches. Og the Destroyer jumped up next to us, shedding a cloud of black-and-white fur.

"My parents raised me as a girl," Pádraig said. "When I was thirteen, I told them I was a boy. My aunt Róisín already knew, of course. She'd looked into my spirit and seen a boy, no question. The rest of my family came around in time. Other people on Innisburren, though . . ."

"Oh," I said softly. I saw it now — his small stature and beardless face, the curves under his loose tunic and woolwrap. "People didn't take it well?"

"Most people are . . . confused at best." Pádraig's mouth quirked with a smile. "You don't seem to be."

I shrugged. "It's normal to me. When my cousin Malana was four or five, she told her parents she's a girl. They changed her name, let her grow her hair long, and that was that."

"Hm. Círa said it's more accepted in Aikoto culture, but I thought she was just being nice." He pulled Og into his lap and stroked the cat. "Anyway, I wanted to build a new life where people only knew me as a man, so I moved here to Ingdanrad. It was fine for years. Until the book burning."

"Book burning?"

Pádraig deposited Og back onto the couch and crossed to his bookshelves. He pulled off a singed tome and handed it to me. The gilt lettering was in Gallnach. I gingerly leafed through the crumbling pages, which had anatomical diagrams of people, animals, and plants set among the text.

"A medical treatise," he explained. "Research on variations in male and female physiology. I wrote it along with mages at the university. A couple years ago, Gallnach religious extremists broke into the campus library, stole books they considered dangerous, and threw them in a bonfire."

"They had a problem with *research*?"

"You'd be surprised." Pádraig settled back on the couch, crossing his legs. "Kae water-callers extinguished the fire, but the real damage was already done. Those extremists saw my name on the cover and started spreading rumours — some true, some not. People accosted me in the street, demanded my resignation from the hospital, hung a noose outside my home."

I clapped a hand to my mouth. I'd noticed a few people react strangely to Pádraig, refusing to make eye contact and avoiding him in the corridors, but I'd never given it much thought, figuring they were afraid he could see their spirits like Róisín could. "That's horrible."

"Yet I'm still here." He swept his arm toward the bookshelves, potted trees, and thick rugs. "Sometimes we have to make our own refuge. Surround ourselves with people who'll protect us, people who make us stronger."

A bitter taste surfaced in my mouth. "What if those people turn on you?"

"Then you push them out and close ranks. Refuge isn't a fixed thing. And if you run out of people to fall back on, well . . ." Pádraig scratched Og's chin. "There's always cats."

※

Pádraig's advice was a compass setting me on track. I'd already laid the foundations for my refuge — a house, a community with the Kae, a circle of friends. Now I needed to build those foundations into a fortress. I had three months to convince Dunehein and Rikuja I'd be safe so they'd go home to Toel Ginu to have their baby. The first step was recruiting Pádraig and Janekke to put protective runes on our cabin, hindering further break-ins.

A respite from my constant stress came via the upcoming Gallnach sowing festival, Abhain. Pádraig and several other medics would be away from the hospital to perform druidic rituals, so with no patient sessions scheduled for the fourth floor, there wasn't much for me to do. The hospital matron gave me the choice to work anyway or take the day off and add it to the end of my six-month sentence. I chose the day off.

Círa was taking it off, too. A Sverbian medic from the main kitchen downstairs would cover her work. Since Círa was the only one trained to call broth down the throats of coma patients, Tiernan's meals would be honey and mushed fruit. She assured me he'd be fine for a day, though I knew it wasn't enough to survive on long-term. The realization that his fate was linked to Círa's made my breath catch and my vision go dark. It had been weeks since I'd been so close to fainting.

"What exactly happens on Abhain?" I asked, trying to distract myself as I scrubbed dishes.

"Lots of things," Círa said, cutting up a chicken carcass for bone broth. "It's the sacred day of water, so mainly it's about praying for rain. Goodness knows we need it this year. Some professions have their own traditions, too. Shepherds bless their flocks and drive them out to pasture for the season. Fishermen throw part of their catch back into the ocean to bribe the Folk into staying there."

"The Folk?"

"Spirits from the otherworld. In Gallun, they live in underground forts among the hills. When Gallnach refugees sailed across the ocean, some Folk followed, swimming in the ships' wakes. Now they live in the waters around our villages. Whenever the barrier between worlds grows thin, like on Abhain, they sneak onto land and cause trouble — kidnapping people, seducing them, dragging them into the ocean and drowning them."

"And you . . . believe that?"

Círa shrugged. "I've never seen Folk myself, but I'm not taking chances by going swimming on Abhain, you know? Anyway, you should come to the festival. There's music, food, dancing. It's one of my favourite holidays. And it's considered good luck if antayul attend the rain ritual."

Some spirit must've blessed *me* with good luck. The Gallnach were so desperate for antayul to attend the rituals that the militia captain gave Tsiala the same deal as me, to take the day off and add it to the end of her sentence. As a warm breeze blew over Ingdanrad, rustling the new leaves, an idea brewed in my head. There was another antayul I could invite. Someone who really, really liked festivals.

✳

Leaving the hospital after work, I spoke to the wind. It had been weeks since Akohin visited at the spring equinox, so I wasn't sure if he was still around. I'd reached the crabapple trees in the Kae district when a raven descended from the sky and shifted forms. I hugged Akohin, grateful he still had the clothes I'd given him.

Easing into my plans, I asked if he wanted to have dinner with my family. We roasted trout in a firepit, cooked flatbread in the coals, and drizzled it all with smelt oil. At twilight, Akohin and I walked across the garden terraces. The crops were sprouting, although they were pale and sickly from lack of rain.

"I was thinking," I began, "maybe you'd like to attend a festival with my friends and me, not just watching from the sky. Círa's brother Finín is coming, so you won't be the only boy."

Akohin frowned, picking at his talon-like nails. "Watching is easier. I don't belong here."

"You belong more than me. There's other Dona in Ingdanrad. There aren't any . . . whatever I am."

"It's not that. Ainu-Seru and I are more than just companions. We're . . . each other. Two spirits entwined together." He ran a hand over his shaved white hair. "That's his presence in my body."

I couldn't hide a shudder. "That's what you meant in Dúnravn Pass? That you're never lonely?"

"Yeah. It's . . . incredible. Sacred. What I think, he hears. What I feel, he feels. I never need to work up the courage to say I'm sad or angry or scared."

"But you *are* lonely. Right?" I folded my hand over his larger one. "I know how hard it is to admit."

Akohin looked away, toward the strip of red sky over the inlet. "How could I be? I'm never alone."

"It's normal to have more than one person in your life. I mean, Tsiala can't be everything to me. I've got Dune, Rija, and Geniod, family who will always have my back. I've got Círa and Nica for girl stuff, and for teaching me about their cultures. And Tiernan for . . ." My voice caught. *For befriending windmills and floating among the clouds.*

Tiernan had done so much for me over the years. Huge things, like helping rescue my cousins, negotiating with Captain Parr to get my family and me residency in Eremur, and recommending me for the apothecary job. Smaller things like teaching me to ride horses and carving the coal newt figurine that lived on our makiri shelf in Shawnaast. He'd shaped so much of my life. Trying to build a new one without him was like navigating without the sun.

I shook my head and went on. "You used to have so many people. Your uncle, his ship crew, kids at the orphanage. The entire Dona-jouyen. Nhys and your stablehand roommate at the Golden Oak. You don't miss any of that?"

Akohin shrugged. "I was different then. Meeting people now . . . What if they find out what I am? Half human, half saidu? The Rin rejected my great-great-grandfather for that very reason."

"If people don't accept you, push them out of your life and fall back on the ones who do. A wise druid told me that recently."

He hesitated, rubbing his white hair. I'd already thought up a solution for that. Tsiala had knit him a grey wool cap that fit snug over his head. He tried it on, peering at his reflection in a garden reservoir.

"It suits you," I said, smiling at his reflection.

"Tsiala's never met me. Why'd she make it?"

"Because I asked her to. And I'd like you to meet her. You're both important to me."

Akohin pulled the cap off. "All right. If it matters that much."

30.

ABHAIN

Near dawn, with a glimmer of light coming through the loft window, Akohin poked me awake. I threw my pillow at him, regretting my promise to wake early for the Abhain rituals. We scrounged up leftover flatbread in the dark, trying not to wake my family in the bedroom, and stumbled outside into cool air. The sky was deep purple behind the snowy mountain peaks.

Akohin seemed jittery, repeatedly tugging his cap down. He'd trimmed his nails so they no longer looked like talons. We met up with the Kae near their plank houses, where I introduced him to Círa and her brother. Finín had traded his wheelchair for a four-wheeled cart pulled by one of Ingdanrad's small woolly horses. He gestured for me to lean over so he could whisper in my ear.

"No luck with those runes on your patient," he said. "I've checked all my textbooks. Now I'm *really* interested."

"So you're still looking?"

"I've got a few ideas. Break down their structure, analyze the parts—"

Finín was interrupted by a toddler petting his horse. Her parents scolded her, but Finín grinned and said it was fine. More kids swarmed around, cutting off my chance to speak with him further.

"Here," said Círa, handing me a glass vial. "Collect some dew. It's got magical properties on Abhain. Maidens dab it on their faces to glow with life and become irresistibly beautiful. There's an old saying about it. 'One drop for a fling, two drops for a ring, three drops for a king.'"

I cocked an eyebrow. "How many drops are *you* using today?"

A blush crossed her face. "That," she said primly, "is none of your business."

Our group followed a road north around the mountain. Gallnach people trickled out of their underground homes and joined us, some on foot, some in wagons or carriages. Their bright woolwraps mirrored the blues, golds, and reds of the sunrise and the pale green of barley growing across the terraces. Near the edge of town, our convoy turned down a steep road, zigzagging through dense forest.

The first ritual took place at a mossy spring deep in the woods, bathed in yellow-green light filtering through sickly leaf buds. Algae rings around the pool showed the water level was lower than usual. Tsiala had agreed to meet us here, but I didn't see her yet among the gathered crowd. Druids hauled up buckets and handed them to people. It took me a second to recognize Pádraig, dressed in a burlap robe instead of his usual white woolwrap.

"Wash your hands and face to purify yourselves," he instructed, passing me a bucket. "Supposedly this spring contains healing magic. Between us, I'd rather rely on medicine, but at least it's refreshing."

Akohin, Finín, Círa, and I took turns scooping water onto our faces. The cold made us gasp. Finín was joking about whether he needed to purify his horse when a smiling woman approached with a bucket. She spoke Gallnach to Finín. His face darkened. Círa tried to intervene, but the woman kept talking. She dipped her hand in the water and reached for Finín's legs. He slapped her away. The woman huffed, looking indignant.

"Excuse me," Pádraig interrupted, "I'll kindly ask you to leave this young man alone."

The woman turned. In a thick accent, she said, "What's it to you, lad? You even old enough to wear those robes?"

Pádraig gave a tight smile that didn't reach his eyes. "Two years older than the last time we met."

The woman blanched. She scurried off, dropping her bucket and spilling water across the dirt.

"Wow," Akohin said under his breath. "What a horrid old bat."

Finín snorted with laughter. "C'mon. Let's go to the next ritual before she tries that again."

While the others went ahead, I whispered to Pádraig. "Who was that woman? One of the religious extremists that burned your book?"

He nodded. "They've spent the last two years in prison. If they're getting released . . . well, it's bad news for us all."

The second ritual was with a gnarled old rowan growing by the pool. Hundreds of colourful ribbons hung from its branches. Círa gave us each a moss-green ribbon — "I've only got Kae ones," she said apologetically — to give in offering to the nature spirit who lived inside it. I edged toward the rowan. Aikoto and Sverbian sacred trees gave me visions of the shoirdryge, so a Gallnach one might, too.

Akohin drifted after me, looking up into the branches. "Huh. There *is* a spirit here. An edim-saidu. It's dormant, though."

Curiosity overwhelmed me. I sank into meditation, sorting the water around me into a mental picture. White lines ran through the dark grey of the rowan and into its leaf buds. When the lines faded, I opened my eyes.

The rowan had withered. Frost clung to its barren limbs. Dead branches and curls of bark littered the snow under it. Distraught people moved around me, hanging ribbons that looked jarringly colourful against the wintery whiteness. High in the rowan perched a crow, the Gallnach war goddess who foretold death. I stumbled back, horrified.

Someone caught me. "Whoa there," came Tsiala's voice. "You okay?"

I turned, blinking away the vision. She was here. Alive. My hand skimmed her hair. I cupped the back of her neck and pulled her down into a kiss, breathing the familiar scent of her oiled leather armour.

"Yeah," I said. "I am now."

✳

The rain-summoning ritual took place in a meadow of dry yellowing grass. Pádraig and the other druids gathered in a circle, swayed, sang, and spun ivy-wound branches in an intricate dance. Steely pipe music and pounding drums carried across the meadow. I wondered if the ritual would work while the anta-saidu in this region were dormant. It sure felt like they'd abandoned us to a drought.

As the music faded, though, Círa gasped and pointed. Dark clouds were gathering over the western mountains. A hum of energy filled the crowd. Akohin couldn't quite hide a smile. When I raised my eyebrows at him, he put a finger to his lips.

With the rituals done, the festival began. Food sellers set up covered wagons around the meadow. Finín had brought a picnic blanket in his cart, so we claimed a spot and let his horse loose to graze. Círa suggested we pool our money and she'd organize a springtime feast. I paid Akohin's share, brushing off his protests with a reminder that he used to slip me free food at the Golden Oak.

The crops were struggling so much that the food sellers had turned to seafood and forage. Círa bought a bit of everything — fresh oysters, crackers with herring roe, sorrel and nettle salad, wild mushrooms, and fiddleheads. She also bought a barley flatbread called bannock. The Gallnach made a special type for each of their four sacred days in the year. Abhain bannock had the rune for water cut into the crust.

As we ate, I caught Círa fiddling with a vial and staring at Pádraig, who was talking to another druid and gesturing at the clouds. So that's who she wanted to attract with the dew. I nudged her and whispered, "Have you tried, you know, asking Pádraig out?"

Círa turned pink and shoved the vial under the picnic blanket. "Of course. I offered to make him dinner and he thought I was offering leftovers from the in-patient ward. He's as lush as a rain-forest and just as dense."

I snorted. "Maybe you need to see him away from the hospital." I got up and waved my arms. "Ai, Pádraig! Want to join us?"

He glanced around as if expecting another Pádraig to step forward. Looking bemused, he said goodbye to the other druid and came over. Círa squeaked and smoothed out her bangs. Finín turned a laugh into a hacking cough.

"Don't you two see enough of me at work?" Pádraig asked.

"No," Círa said. "I mean — of course but—"

"By god," Tsiala said. "Sit down before you give the poor girl an aneurysm."

Pádraig sat. Círa looked ready to faint. Well, at least she'd be in good hands.

"You people are hopeless." Finín rummaged through his cart and produced a bottle of whisky. "How about a drinking game? Something to break the ice?"

Tsiala snapped her fingers. "I've got one. Anyone heard of Never Ever?"

"I have," Akohin said. "I used to work in a pub. I've seen every drinking game under the sun."

She nodded approvingly. "We played it in the military camps down south. It works like this. I've never ever eaten sheep stomach. If you have, drink."

"That's all us Gallnach." Finín pulled the cork out with his teeth and sipped the whisky.

Círa drank next. Pádraig's gaze flickered to her lips on the bottle. As she passed it to him, their hands brushed. Redness bloomed in his cheeks. Maybe there *was* something about that dew.

Tsiala grinned at me. "We'll go in a circle. You're next."

I thought for a moment. "I've never ever been tattooed."

Groans came from the circle. Tsiala, Akohin, Círa, and Finín all drank.

Akohin's turn was next. He chewed a herring cracker, thinking, then said, "I've never ever met my father."

Surprise flickered across Tsiala's face. I couldn't tell what that meant — if she was relieved someone else came from a splintered family, or if she was debating whether to admit she knew her father. Either way, she drank along with the rest of us.

When her turn came again, she was ready. "Right. I've never ever kissed a boy."

Círa and I both drank. Grinning sheepishly, Finín reached out for the bottle.

"What?!" Círa cried. "You never told me about that!"

"And I never will." He swigged whisky and wiped his mouth.

We kept going around the circle. A few rounds in, Akohin took a deep breath and said, "I've never ever kissed anyone. And I probably never will."

Tsiala smacked the grass. "Merdo. He's got us all."

Everyone laughed and drank. No one commented on Akohin's statement, no one questioned it. Catching my eye, he mouthed, *Thank you.*

In time, the game shifted to talking and drinking whisky. We all felt strangely warm, shedding our coats and cloaks, though we weren't sure if it was the alcohol or the weather. A mass of velvety purple clouds drifted overhead, casting a dark shroud over the meadow. Círa flopped onto her back, pointing out shapes in the swirling clouds.

Akohin lay next to her, folding his hands under his head. "You know, if you blow into the sky *really* hard, you can move the clouds."

Círa scowled. "I'm not drunk enough to believe that."

"I'm serious. Watch." He puffed out his cheeks and blew. The clouds parted, letting through a band of sunlight.

She gasped. "It worked! Pádraig, look! It worked!"

Pádraig chuckled. "Go on, then. Show us."

Círa blew into the sky. The clouds separated like the wake behind a ship. Pádraig, Finín, and Tsiala all swore in shock. Akohin winked at me. I clamped a hand to my mouth, doubling over in silent laughter. Across the meadow, people craned their necks, pointing at the pair of sunlit rifts in the clouds.

A cold breeze gusted over us. Shivering, I pulled my cloak back on. Círa wrapped the picnic blanket around her shoulders. A moment later, the breeze turned hot. Wind swirled through the dry grass one way, then another. Dust billowed across the meadow. People everywhere looked around in confusion. Food sellers began battening down the covers on their wagons.

Shit, I thought. *I got the wind drunk.*

Akohin wrung his hands, thrumming with energy. He and Ainu-Seru were a diving osprey, hurtling through the sky toward a lake. Maybe they'd snatch a fish in their talons and rise triumphant. Maybe they'd smash into the water and break every bone in their body. Either way, it was too late to turn back.

Droplets fell from the clouds and splattered on the hard dirt. We leapt to our feet. In seconds, the droplets became a deluge, wiping the dust clouds from the air. Warm rain soaked us, running down our faces, sticking our clothes to our skin.

Shouts of joy went up from the crowd. People laughed and sang and wept with relief. Akohin beamed. This wasn't what I'd meant by opening himself up to people, but I hugged him anyway, brimming with pride. He returned the hug, grazing my wet braid, connecting our spirits.

"Blessed rain!" Círa spun, arms wide, skirts whirling out. "Mother of mountains, the ritual worked!"

She slipped in the mud. Pádraig caught her. By accident or not, their lips met. He blinked in shock, then pulled her closer and kissed her again. Finín whooped and clapped, making everyone laugh and join in.

This was nothing like the cold rainstorm I'd died in, alone and screaming for help. This was life itself washing over us. I'd never wanted so much to live, to clutch this joy to my chest and carry it forever. I wished Tiernan could see it. I pictured him here grinning at me, his wet hair stuck to his cheeks, rain steaming off his skin.

Tsiala pulled me into her arms and pressed her lips to mine. Guilt twinged inside me. The most beautiful girl in the world was right here, kissing me with a familiar hunger, and I was distracted by an unconscious man somewhere else. I looped my arms around her neck and kissed her back, shoving all thoughts of fire mages from my head.

We couldn't stay here long, though. The meadow was becoming a cesspit of mud, and Finín had to leave before his horse and cart got stuck. Sheltering his eyes, he asked if Akohin wanted to come back to the Kae district to dry off. Akohin cast me a nervous look before agreeing. I felt uneasy about leaving him, but that was the safest place for him to sober up.

Tsiala leaned over to whisper in my ear. Nodding at Círa and Pádraig, who were holding hands and blushing, she said, "Why don't we give those two lovebirds some space? I know somewhere private we can go."

I frowned up at her. "Last time you took me somewhere alone, we got caught in a coup."

"This place is special. No one else knows about it, not even Neve."

That *was* tempting. If this would be our one day off during our six-month sentences, I wanted to make the most of it, and it was comforting that Tsiala knew what I was worried about and was trying to fix it. We followed a steep path through the woods, grabbing branches to keep our balance. Sheets of rain tumbled through the canopy. At a mossy cairn, Tsiala turned north and pushed through the soaked underbrush. We had to hold back an overflowing creek so we could cross. On the other side, she pulled aside a tangle of shrubs.

I stepped through the gap onto a stone ledge. Blurred by the rain, a narrow waterfall plunged down a cliff into a chasm, sending up clouds of mist. Tall thin pines rose around it. High above us, a timber bridge joined two rocky outcrops in front of the falls. It felt like being back home in the northern rainforest.

"It's beautiful," I said faintly.

"So are you." Tsiala came up behind me and slipped her arm around my waist. "You must've used the dew this morning."

Warmth rushed through me. "Nei. I didn't."

"Ah. So you're just naturally irresistible." A trace of laughter floated in her voice. She pulled my wet braid aside and kissed my neck.

Prickles shot down my spine. She'd been pushing further over the weeks — grazing her fingers against my body, pinning me down during combat lessons — but I'd held her at bay. My body was at war with my mind and spirit. They dripped poison, whispering that she was still on Neve's side and this was all some fucked-up mind game.

"Wait," I said breathlessly.

Tsiala pulled back. She bit her lip as if it took all her strength to keep still. I felt the same, like the rain was coursing through my veins, filling me with life and lust. It wasn't enough, though. I needed to see her as she was — no deceit, no defences. I needed her to be as vulnerable as I always felt.

"Take off your weapons," I said. "And your armour."

Tsiala set her daggers on the ground. With practised ease, she undid the ties and buckles of her armour — bracers on the arms, greaves on the legs, spaulders on the shoulders, and finally the cuirass around her torso. The rain had gotten through the gaps and soaked her tunic and leggings, making them cling to her curves. I beckoned for her to keep going.

She raised her eyebrows. "Is this revenge for spying on you in the hot springs?"

"It's only fair."

Tsiala shrugged. "I've got nothing to hide." She unlaced her boots and yanked them off, then peeled off her wet clothes, baring her bronze skin.

"Yan taku," I said under my breath.

I'd always thought she was lush, but *this* . . . Rain streamed over her broad shoulders, off her breasts, down her ridged stomach and muscular thighs. Tattoos wrapped around her legs in the same geometric patterns as her arms. I drew close and kissed her, making her inhale sharply.

"Can I touch you now?" she asked huskily.

"I suppose." A smile played across my lips. "Know how to take off a corset?"

She grinned back. "Don't need to."

"What do you—"

Tsiala scooped me up, making me shriek. She deposited me on a mossy bed under cover of a sprawling pine. It was welcome relief from the driving rain. Hiking up my skirt and petticoats past my knees, she said, "Bet you five pann I can leave these on and still make you scream."

✳

Some time later, we collapsed panting on the moss. I owed her five pann for the first round. My clothes had come off on the second. By the third, we'd accidentally turned the rain into steam, turning this patch of forest into a sauna. The poor plants had gone from drought-struck to boiled.

"Aeldu save me," I said. "This must be why the Aikoto Confederacy doesn't let antayul marry each other."

Tsiala laughed. "So you're a lawbreaker now?"

We both already were, but I didn't mention that, distracted by the thought that we were almost halfway into our six-month sentences and hadn't discussed what we'd do afterward. I had no desire to stay in Ingdanrad, but it was the closest Tsiala had to a home these days. I pushed that thought aside for later, wanting to savour today.

"Where's that bridge go, anyway?" I asked, pointing at the one high in front of the falls.

"Dunno." Tsiala propped herself up on one elbow and traced circles on my bare stomach. "I've never seen anyone on it, and I can't find a way to reach it."

"You spend a lot of time here?"

"Mm. I needed a place to escape from Neve. Now it's your place, too."

I pulled her down into a kiss. We only separated when sunshine fell onto our skin. The clouds had parted and the rain had stopped, leaving the scents of damp soil and clean mountain air. Water dripped off the foliage around us. Birds chirped nearby.

I got up, squinting in the brightness. "Oh," I breathed.

Sunlight caught the waterfall, turning it into a river of molten gold. Tsiala moved behind me, pressing her naked body to mine, wrapping her arms around my waist. We stood together in blissful silence. Whatever happened, at least we had this refuge.

31.

COTTAGE IN THE WOODS

Akohin answered my questions about the bridge. It was an ancient Aikoto shrine to the tel-saidu, just like the sky bridge between Tula and Iyo territory, but this one had long been forgotten. The paths there had been reclaimed by forest. It seemed like a sore topic, a reminder that our people no longer revered Ainu-Seru, so I dropped the subject. It was just as well, since I didn't want him to ask why Tsiala and I had been there.

Returning to work was depressing. That daydream of Tiernan in the rainstorm, soaked and grinning at me, kept surfacing. At his bedside, I fingered the glass vial Círa had given me. Instead of collecting Abhain dew, I'd collected water from the purifying spring. Pádraig didn't believe it had healing powers, but he didn't know everything.

What would I say if Tiernan woke? The thought of telling him about Tsiala made me squirm. During the coup, he'd seen me punch her and tell her to go fuck herself, and now I was . . . well, doing it for her. *It's none of Tiernan's business who I sleep with*, I reminded myself. I uncorked the vial and dabbed water on his forehead.

Nothing happened. No flutter of an eyelid or twitch of a finger. Just the slow, steady rise and fall of his chest.

Frustration billowed through me like a rising flood. I flung myself against the window, looking past the hospital terraces toward the inlet, holding in a scream. We were both trapped in this city. Nyhemur had never felt so far away.

I couldn't look at Tiernan anymore. I retreated into the corridor, slid down the stone wall, and flipped through my journal. Several pages back, beside my entry about Ivar breaking into our cabin to retrieve the *Lilac Queen* novel, was a scribbled note. *How could Maud afford to get here?*

It took a moment to remember writing the note. I'd been looking at Nerio's purse of gold sovs in our secret wall compartment, recalling the long journey here. Canoes to Innisburren, a naval cutter to Port Alios, a ferry to Rutnaast, the postal ship to Ingdanrad. Ship fare for the entire journey would be expensive. While talking about Neve in therapy, Pádraig had told me ways that abusive men controlled their wives, like withholding money so the women couldn't flee. Bødar, the Lilac King, sounded like that kind of man.

Check the records, Neve had said. *All of them.* We'd checked everything except the harbour records that might say how the Lilac Queen got here. None of us could access them, but Neve was a registered merchant with enough influence to cajole some port clerk into giving her access. After work, I grudgingly hiked up to Clan Ríain's villa to ask for her help.

She showed up a few days later with her findings. In the same month Maud from the novel arrived in Ingdanrad, a woman named Mårit Audehl arrived with a shipment of lilacs. The crates were stamped with the sigil of Bryngard Ødarind, registered at the Mariners' Guild as a floral merchant. B. Ødar and M. Aud, the Lilac King and Queen. Mårit had stolen from her husband to fund a better life for their twins.

Mårit Audehl's name was the key we needed. The stavehall had recorded her divorce from Bryngard and remarriage to a Sverbian fire mage, Ainar Thallind, called Athall in the novel. Janekke, incredulous, said they'd been her neighbours. By the time Janekke moved in, the couple were empty nesters, but an elderly neighbour remembered the couple's twins — a girl named Astra Måritehl and a boy named Magnús Ainarind.

I wrote the names in my journal beside sketches of oaks and lilacs. Astra, the cleric who haunted my dreams. Magnús, the cleric's elusive brother M. The only record of either was Mágnus enlisting in the militia at eighteen, then quitting at twenty-six, which matched Astra's account in her letters of M joining the Rúonbattai shortly before the Third Elken War. Janekke's neighbour recalled that Astra had started clerical studies as a teenager, though the stavehall had no record of her being ordained as a cleric.

We scoured places linked to the family, searching for oak and lilac crests. Mårit and Ainar had passed away several years ago, leaving their home unoccupied, so Dunehein and Rikuja pretended to look for somewhere to raise their baby and got the landlord to give them a tour. Geniod searched the university gardens where Mårit had worked, and I searched the smithy where Ainar had worked. Tsiala took the militia complex and Janekke took the stavehall.

The research felt like hiking an unfamiliar trapline, checking at every step for bear clamps, pits, and snares. Asking the wrong questions to the wrong people could be dangerous. Róisín had only interrogated the militia, leaving thousands of civilians who were potentially traitors. Yet for all our efforts, we found nothing. No oak crests. No Rúonbattai.

At Tiernan's bedside, I kept thinking, *I wish you were here to help*. We'd started this research by reading Astra's letters to Councillor Halvarind, draped over the couches in Parr Manor's library in sweltering heat, drinking apple cider pilfered from Ivy House's cellars. I missed how he scratched his beard while thinking, lit up when we had a breakthrough, and talked so fast in his excitement that his accent blurred.

One warm, breezy evening, Neve turned up with more news. Her mother, Laoise, had worked with Mårit at the university gardens and remembered a strange event from long ago. Mårit had brought a baby to work. A young woman showed up in a fury and took the baby away. Laoise had comforted a weeping Mårit, who said the young woman was her estranged daughter, Astra, and the baby was her grandchild. Astra had forbidden her parents from any contact with the baby.

In three decades of letters, Astra had never mentioned having a child. She didn't even seem interested in men, writing instead of affection for her female friend, O. The baby could've been Magnús's, but Astra had never mentioned a niece or nephew, either. I couldn't shake the feeling Neve was lying again, yet everything else she'd said about the family checked out. Somewhere in the world, there might be a third generation of Rúonbattai.

✳

As spring passed, Akohin visited occasionally, staying overnight at my cabin or in Finín's dorm. He'd taken an interest in Finín's rune studies. Over three centuries of Gallnach settlement here, Ainu-Seru had seen all manner of runes, yet he didn't recognize the ones inside Tiernan's nullifying cuff. Finín was diving deep in his attempt to identify them, pulling dusty tomes from the library's restricted section.

I edged through spring in an uneasy rhythm. Mostly I kept up my schedule, although more often than I cared to admit, Tsiala persuaded me to ditch lessons and sneak off to our waterfall refuge to tangle together naked among the bushes. "We're still water-calling," she said with a wink, waving at the clouds of steam. "And it's physical therapy of a sort."

We still hadn't discussed what would happen when our criminal sentences ended. She never brought it up, and I didn't know what to say. I'd been telling myself I didn't use the dew on Abhain because I didn't believe in it, but honestly I didn't know what I wanted — a six-month fling or something longer.

I tried to imagine a life with Tsiala. Maybe we'd settle in Nettle Ginu, reclaim my trapline, fish and swim in the rivers. Maybe we'd go to Caladheå. I could return to the apothecary and she could start something new, no longer bound to being a soldier. Would she ever be happy here, though? What if she wanted to move back south to Kowichelk territory to reconnect with her own people?

Every time I talked to Tiernan, guilt tinged my words. I was no longer sure about my promise of visiting Nyhemur together. There'd be no good way to tell Tsiala that I wanted to take off east with a man, travelling alone together for weeks. She tolerated my endless worrying about Tiernan, but everyone had limits.

As I studied on my lunch break, Círa slid me a mug of raspberry iced tea. "You okay?" she asked. "You've been reading that entry on ulcers for ten minutes."

Sighing, I shut my textbook. I told her about the Nyhemur trip, and not having a home to return to, and feeling constantly unmoored. "It's hard for Tsiala, too. She's never been able to choose where she lives or what she does, and soon she will. It's unfair to ask her to commit to anything if . . . well, if I'm not ready to commit."

"Hmm." Círa plucked a bean from a bowl and popped it into her mouth. "I'm no expert — this thing with Pádraig is still pretty new — but there's a Gallnach saying that your first thought in the morning is always of your true love."

"So you're in love with food?"

She threw another bean at me. "Very funny."

I opened my journal. My first entry each morning was usually about my dreams. Sometimes they were about Tsiala, though I was too embarrassed to record the ones where we were naked. Sometimes they were nightmares of Astra, furious and ghostly, firing a crossbow at me. Apparently, I was in love with both women. Wonderful.

✳

That evening after combat practice, Tsiala and I lay exhausted among the chestnut grove, the sun warming our sweat-soaked bodies. Her leather armour lay scattered across the grass. I propped myself up on my elbows to look at her. "What's the first thing you think of in the morning?"

Tsiala smirked. "You need to ask?" She edged closer and flicked her tongue against my ear.

My nerves crackled. Part of me wanted to drag her off to the privacy of the cabin loft, but I pulled away. "Don't you ever daydream about anything else?"

"Sure. Cottage in the woods, four kids, a dog. Although medicine hasn't figured out a way for me to knock you up, so we'll have to steal the kids."

I gave her a sour look. "That's not something to joke about."

She rolled her eyes. "Sacro dios. Don't be so sensitive."

"Sensitive? My cousins were stolen by itherans—"

"So was I. You don't see me harping on about it."

I caught myself before saying something I'd regret. Jonalin and I used to get into spats like this, me being sarcastic, him getting offended. *Shit*, I thought. *So this is how I made him feel.* Before I could think of a way to turn the conversation back around, cold wind gusted over us. I shivered.

Pale purple specks floated through the sky. A sweet scent filled the air. As the specks drifted down through the trees, I got up and caught one. A petal, small and silky. Lilacs.

A raven swooped down and shifted into Akohin, flushed and panting. "I didn't know what to do — I just thought you should see—"

"Slow down," I cut in. "Where'd they come from?"

"Up the mountain. A garden. I've flown over it dozens of times, but the lilacs weren't in bloom — I never paid any attention — and there's an oak, Kateiko, a *crest*."

I dropped the petal in horror. "A *Rúonbattai* crest?"

"Yeah." He paced between the trees, wringing his hands. "The magic's faint. I couldn't feel it 'til I got close, but it's like the one in Tjarnnaast. I'm sure of it."

Stunned, I sank onto the grass. The petals felt like thousands of eyes drifting through the sky. My throat closed. I clutched my neck, gasping.

"Whoa." Tsiala dropped to her knees. "You all right?"

I breathed like Tiernan had taught me. Five seconds in, five seconds out. Picking up a petal, I focused on it and sensed nothing. It must've lost its magic after falling off its bush. All Astra would've seen through the crest was a raven and some wind, not the petals coming here.

Of course if I decided to destroy the crest, she would have a vision of me trying before I even got there. My best chance was to go now, before she could counteract. I'd have no time to prepare, no time to get my family. Rikuja was getting a maternity checkup in the hospital along with Dunehein, and Geniod had gone to the harbour market.

"Okay." I clapped my hands together. "Ako. What's the garden like? Is anyone there?"

"Not at the moment," he said. "It's by a cottage in the woods. The—"

Tsiala scoffed. "*Seriously?* Were you eavesdropping?"

"The whole place is quiet," Akohin went on. "Someone's living there, though. There's fresh woodchips by the lumber pile, and the garden's been pruned and weeded."

"Right. If we hurry, we can destroy the crest before they return." I got to my feet and sheathed my sword. "Tsiala, you up for wrecking a garden?"

"Uh . . ." She rubbed her neck. "I'll slow you down."

"Really? We have one spat and you leave me to the face the Rúonbattai alone?"

"No! That's not—" Tsiala blew out a breath. "I don't have an attuned form that can keep up."

"Oh," I said in surprise. I thought back to the coup when she'd sent me ahead to chase the assassin. Once she got ahold of a horse, she'd kept up fine. The closest horses were in the Kae stables. "Okay, then. Get your armour on. I'm going to steal you a horse."

✳

As the sun dipped lower, we raced along zigzagging roads up the mountain. The horse's thundering hooves drowned out my wolf claws clicking on the flagstones. Akohin flew overhead, guiding us. Where the road forked north, toward the university campus, we turned southeast onto a dirt track. Our footfalls tossed up clouds of dust behind us.

The track wound up through the forest. As it narrowed, we shifted to single file. Akohin cawed to signal we were close. Tsiala pulled back on the reins, slowing her horse to a trot. I shifted back to human and instantly snagged my skirt on a clump of nettles.

"We should continue on foot," I said. "If someone turns up, we don't want them to hear us."

Tsiala led her horse off the track and tied its reins to a branch. On Akohin's directions, we circled through the woods to avoid the cottage, then crept through the underbrush to the edge of a clearing. In the centre of a large fenced garden stood a sprawling nine-branched oak. One branch had a reddish tinge. Lilac bushes grew around the oak's trunk. Petals floated through the air and landed among neat rows of herbs, root vegetables, and vine-wrapped trellises.

"That's it?" Tsiala whispered. "Astra Måritehl's deep, dark magic is a veggie garden?"

"A cursed garden," I whispered back. "Can you feel that?"

Like Akohin said, it was faint but definitely present — the strange sense that we'd been here before and would be again. Tsiala shuddered.

"It's probably got protective runes." She stepped back and started feeling the air.

I wondered if the shoirdryge had signs of any runes. Knowing Akohin would warn us if anyone came, I closed my eyes and sank into meditation. Ainu-Seru had been bringing rain clouds when he could, but the vegetation was still struggling. The garden was various shades of dark grey. When I'd done this in Nettle Ginu, my vision turned black, marking the shift to the wasteland. This time, the patches of grey shifted and brightened. I opened my eyes.

A lush green garden sprawled ahead, sparkling with recent rain. Boot prints crossed the mud. All the plants seemed weeks behind — the beans small, the tomatoes green, the lilacs not yet in bloom. It must've been a late spring, but it was the first Rúonbattai crest we'd found that wasn't dying or forgotten in the shoirdryge. This garden looked . . . *nice*. Like the kind of place Tsiala had joked about raising a family in — if it had been a joke.

Cawing jerked me back to my world. Panic surged through me. Tsiala spun, hands on her daggers, searching the woods.

Akohin dropped from the trees and shifted to human. "Someone's coming," he whispered. "A woman. She's got a heron tattoo."

"A Kae woman?" I said. "What's she look like?"

"Older, maybe in her fifties. Long braid, patched deerskin cloak, a wicker basket of mushrooms. Guess she's been foraging."

"So she lives here? Why would a Kae woman have a Rúonbattai oak in . . ." I trailed off. "Oh. Kaid. It's Olina."

"Ivar's mother?" Tsiala hissed. "Fucking hell. Neve was right."

I drew my sword. Footsteps rustled through the underbrush. Wind circled around us, stirring the leaves. Olina emerged from a tangle of alder saplings. She blanched. The basket slid from her arm, scattering mushrooms across the forest floor.

"Go," she breathed.

I held my sword ready, my other hand raised to call water. "I know who you are. I know what that oak is—"

"Did it see you?" Olina's eyes looked wild. "You can't be seen here! He'll kill you!"

"Who, Ivar? I'm not afraid of him—"

A strangled laugh tore from her throat. "You should be. He already got you killed once. Run, child, while you still can. Run and don't ever come back."

Halfway back to the Kae district, it clicked. Astra had only entrusted her oaks to her closest allies. In her letters to Councillor Halvarind, she'd mentioned a woman called O. I'd just stumbled upon the cleric's oldest friend, and for some reason, she'd spared my life.

I veered into the city. Tsiala and Akohin followed without question. At Janekke's home, I banged on the door. A clatter and a yelp came from inside, then the door swung open. Janekke brandished a cleaver, her bodice and dress splattered with red. I shrieked.

Tsiala swung off her horse. "You doing surgery at home?"

"Beetroot tea," Janekke explained, lowering the cleaver. "I've been on edge ever since *someone* claimed the Rúonbattai were coming for me."

"Well," I said grimly, "they might be now."

Janekke paled. "Come in. Pour yourselves some tea. I'll get changed and be back in a flash."

While she scrubbed her stained clothes in the candlelit kitchen, I tried to remember everything Astra had written about O. She'd confessed to missing her deeply while O was away caring for a sick relative. It had seemed like they might be more than friends, especially since O begged Astra not to join the Third Elken War, but Astra had chosen war over O.

"I don't remember anything about O having a son, though," I said. "Guess Astra kept both their children secret."

"Isn't it obvious?" Tsiala draped her elbows over her chair back. "It's the same kid."

"What? How?"

"Hanlin told us. An unwed Sverbian woman got knocked up, gave birth in secret, and Olina adopted the baby. Remember what

Neve's mother said? Astra forbid her parents from seeing the baby, probably because she wasn't keeping it."

I leaned back in my chair, stunned. "Sacro dios."

For half a year, Astra had haunted my dreams, and I hadn't realized her son was right here. *He'd* noticed *me*, asking about the obsidian-handled knife I'd stolen from his mother's altar. Ivar thought I'd stolen the *The Lilac Queen*, too. He'd trashed my home looking for it, terrified that I would discover his grandfather and mother were both Rúonbattai captains. All this — my death, my parents' deaths, Tiernan falling comatose — was because of Ivar and his family.

"I'll kill him," I said, gripping my sword hilt. "I'll fucking kill him—"

Akohin touched my shoulder. "I'm no warrior, but if there's one thing I've learned" — he tilted his head at the window, which rattled from a gust — "violence won't make you feel better."

"It makes *me* feel better," Tsiala said.

Janekke chuckled as she hung her wet clothes by the fire. "I'm not above violence, but let's not be hasty. Ivar's had plenty of time to attack you again and hasn't, Kateiko. Waking from a coma to find his allies hanged must've spooked him into caution."

"Sure," I said, "but our trip to Olina's house might spook him into action. Even if she doesn't tell him, Astra will. She'll have foreseen us destroying her oak crest."

"Would she?" Janekke frowned thoughtfully. "Her visions are of the most likely future, right? It sounds like that's exactly what happened. You paused to check for traps, then Olina turned up, so you confronted her instead of destroying the oak. If you could do it again, you'd probably do it the same way."

I mulled that over. If it was true, Astra wouldn't have seen any sign of us. "Maybe," I conceded. "But my vote's still for killing Ivar."

"The words of a warrior, not a surgeon." Janekke wagged a finger at me. "These people are like warts. You can't just cut off the surface. You have to dig deep and cut out the root."

Akohin's mouth twisted like he was going to be sick. "I hope there's a point to that analogy."

"Killing Ivar won't get us closer to his birth mother. We know who she is, but not where she is. Until then, Ivar might be useful alive."

32.

CLOSING RANKS

"You did *what*?!" Dunehein bellowed in our cabin.

"I did what Tiernan would've," I snapped. "He's too comatose to do it himself."

Dunehein winced. Rikuja touched his arm, coaxing him to sit. He managed to stay quiet as I explained everything. The harder part was what came next. On the way here, I'd made up my mind to ask them to go home to Toel Ginu. Rikuja's baby wasn't due for two months, but it was too dangerous for them to stay.

Not surprisingly, they protested. Surprisingly, Geniod took my side. I'd expected him to say something about the importance of family and sticking together. We debated late into the night, burning the candles to stumps. They finally relented when I said even if Ivar didn't come for us, I couldn't deal with the stress of worrying about them.

"Okay," Rikuja said, rubbing her baby bulge. "Suppose we leave. What about this cabin? The Kae let us stay if we help with their work, and suddenly they'd have one set of hands instead of three."

"Akohin's offered to take your place," I said. "He said he can handle living here for a few months, and Ainu-Seru will protect him."

Dunehein chuckled. "I'd like to see Ivar attack the wind."

Everything happened astonishingly fast. Dunehein and Rikuja arranged passage on the postal ship to Rutnaast. From there, they could get a ferry to Caladheå, then canoe to Toel Ginu. The night before they left, Tsiala brought a baby blanket she'd knitted with blue Iyo dolphins, which made Rikuja burst into tears and hug her. Somehow, I vowed, I'd get Tiernan and me out of here alive to meet their baby.

❋

When I next saw Hanlin, I asked what he knew about Olina and Astra's friendship. It wasn't much. He and Olina had grown up together, but the woman had always been quiet and kept to herself. Her druid husband had built their cottage in the woods so Olina had space to grow medicinal herbs, and after moving there, she'd pulled away from the other Kae.

Now that I knew Ivar's ties to the Rúonbattai, I felt sure he'd deliberately gone comatose after the coup. If Róisín had looked into his waking spirit, she would've seen everything. So he put on a gold ring etched with coma-inducing runes, then when it was safe to wake, Olina visited him in the hospital and removed the ring. And if they knew how to make the runes, maybe *they* were keeping Tiernan comatose.

Without the ring, though, I had no proof. My only hope was Finín identifying the runes on Tiernan's cuff, and he had to take a break from researching it. His university exams were soon and he needed to study. I felt more useless than ever, juddering about the hospital with mops and brooms, trapped in the stone walls while Tiernan was trapped in his mind.

I couldn't tell him any of this with his guard listening in, so during my daily ten minutes at his bedside, I sat in silent thought, picking at my fingernails until they bled. Ivar wasn't likely to betray his birth mother, but maybe there was a crack in Olina's armour. She hadn't wanted her friend to go to war, hadn't believed the Sverbian gods tasked the woman with a holy mission. *What would you do?* I thought, tracing the veins on Tiernan's bony hand.

As I walked home from work, taking a shortcut across a terrace of barley, a garter snake slithered across my path and vanished into the green stalks. An idea surfaced. Tiernan had suggested using a metaphorical snake, the Ferish symbol of evil, to scare the Sarteres into giving back Hanaiko and Samulein. We could kidnap Ivar and use him as leverage to scare Olina into talking.

"But what will that trigger?" I mused after combat practice with Tsiala, slumped in the cool shade of a chestnut tree. "If Astra expects to see Ivar through the oak, and he doesn't show up, she'll know he's about to go missing even before we reach him."

Tsiala took a swig from a waterskin. "Not if we destroy the oak."

"Same problem. That'll tip her off that we're onto her son and her friend." I lay back on the grass, gazing into the chestnut tree's foliage. "There's got to be a better way. Something else that would scare Olina into talking."

Tsiala lay next to me. She laced her fingers with mine, rubbing her thumb over my palm. "What about that volcanic eruption a few years back? That convinced Síona to build an alliance against the Rúonbattai."

I laughed dryly. "That's not something I want to bring up. My friends and I caused it."

"What? How?"

"We killed some Rúonbattai, oosoo came to eat the corpses, and Nerio killed an oosoo. A jinra-saidu woke up in a rage. Boom, volcano."

Tsiala's thumb stilled on my palm. "Nerio Parr did that? And you forgave him?"

"He made a mistake. It—"

"A *mistake*?" She sat up, an odd look on her face. "He murdered a sacred animal. My *ancestor*."

It felt like I'd missed a step going downstairs. I'd forgotten that Kowichelk legend said their confederacy had been born from oosoo. "We were in battle," I said, pushing myself upright. "Nerio was protecting us—"

Tsiala scoffed. "God, you sound like an itheran."

"What does *that* mean?"

"You've seen what they do. Sweep into our lands and destroy everything, claiming they're helping us. Do you have any idea what they took from me?" She tore up a handful of grass and curled her fingers into it. "I never attuned. The most sacred part of my life, and it never fucking happened."

"Oh," I said, taken aback. "I'm so sorry—"

"Bearshit. If you were sorry, you wouldn't defend a murderer."

"So I shouldn't have defended *you* in our trial?"

Tsiala rolled her eyes. "Yeah. Butchering a sacred animal is so much better than killing some shitty men who wanted to rape and murder you."

"You didn't know what they'd do," I snapped. "You could've disarmed them like Tiernan said—"

"Oh, here we go. Sorry the sun doesn't shine out my ass like your precious old man."

My nerves prickled. "What's your problem with him?"

"My problem?" Tsiala laughed, throwing away her handful of torn-up grass. "He got locked up for mass murder, you can't prove he's innocent, and you still talk like he's the sun and the moon."

"What are you *talking* about?"

"I've had to fight for everything. Your time, attention, forgiveness. I'm too violent for you, too dishonest, too messed up — but I'm a mercenary, just like your beloved fire mage. You act like you're above it all, this selfless war medic saving the world, but you're just as fucked up and vengeful and hypocritical as anyone else."

I stared at her, aghast.

"Yeah. *Now* you've got nothing to say." She got up and sheathed her daggers.

"Wait." I scrambled up and grabbed her wrist. "Where did this — can't we talk about this?"

"Why?" Tsiala turned to look me in the eye. "Do you honestly think this is ever gonna get better?"

My voice faltered. I pressed my fingertips into her skin, feeling her pulse, her warmth. Some desperate, lonely part of my spirit whispered to say yes. *Yes, we can work this out. Yes, we can make a future together.* Instead I said, "I don't know."

She pulled free of my grip. "Then let's quit wasting our time."

*

Near dusk, as cricket chirping filled the grove, Akohin showed up. He took one look at my expression and settled next to me under a chestnut tree. "You okay?"

"I . . ." Words floated around me, slipping out of my grip like eels. "I think Tsiala broke up with me."

"Oh." Akohin pulled off the wool cap she'd knit for him. Twisting it, he said, "I'm not an expert here. Do you, uh, want a hug?"

I curled into him, resting my cheek against his rough cottonspun shirt. I'd been going over the fight again and again, trying to figure out how things went wrong. It had all happened so fast, and now my relationship was just . . . over. Two and a half months thrown out a porthole into the sea.

Akohin listened in silence as I described the fight. When I finished, he said, "I remember this Sverbian couple staying at the Golden Oak. The wife was furious that her husband ate breakfast without her. I thought it was ridiculous, but Nhys said half the time couples are fighting about something different than what they say."

"Then how in Aeldu-yan do I know what this was about?"

"Dunno. Have you fought about anything else recently?"

I looked back through my journal. We'd been bickering about our imaginary cottage in the woods when Akohin showed up with Olina's lilacs. I'd been glad to drop the subject, but maybe Tsiala was still upset. About what, I didn't know, since she veiled everything in sarcasm.

The further back I went in my journal, the more I realized how often she'd irritated me. Rude comments, mocking me for caring about things, pushing me to skip lessons so we could sneak off to have sex. And the jealousy — aeldu save me, the *jealousy*. Not just about men, but about my whole life. Family, friends, job, home, connections to my culture.

Her last question rang in my head. *Do you honestly think this is ever gonna get better?* I'd been trying to imagine a future together, but I wasn't sure I wanted one with her. I was tired of fighting, staying silent to *avoid* fights, doubting everything, prying answers from her. Pádraig had told me to surround myself with people who made me stronger, but Tsiala made me feel weaker.

I took my pencil from my pocket and started writing. Pages and pages later, I looked up as if waking from a dream. After breaking up with Jonalin, I'd been in shock for weeks, struggling to comprehend the hole torn in my chest. Tonight I felt . . . relieved. I could push Tsiala out of my refuge and close ranks.

"You know," Akohin said, tossing his cap into the air and catching it, "it's getting too warm for this, anyway. Would you feel better if we burned it?"

I snorted. "Maybe. But what about your hair?"

"Eh." He ran a hand through his white locks. "I've been thinking about dyeing it back to black."

I eyed him, trying to remember how he looked with dark hair. We could raid the gardens and make herbal dye tonight. Dyeing *my* hair sounded good, too. I needed to change it, to reclaim it as my own, as something Tsiala had never touched.

✳

I woke to the bright scent of crabapples. Geniod had been making new tea blends, experimenting with Gallnach ingredients, but today he'd brewed an old favourite, the sunrise-coloured tea he always made after a bad night. My life suddenly felt small. Him and Akohin at home, Círa and Pádraig at the hospital. It was a tiny comfort that Tiernan wasn't awake to see my mood swings.

I felt as if I was standing at the junction of a dozen rivers, buffeted by their currents. Hurt that Tsiala had given up so easily, guilty that I hadn't tried harder, angry that she'd pushed for this relationship and then walked away, confused that she hated Tiernan so much, worried that I was as hypocritical as she'd described, afraid that I'd be alone forever, paranoid that she and Neve were playing mind games with me . . .

I didn't have room in my mind to strategize about approaching Olina. I couldn't think straight, let alone outwit a cleric who could see the future. Tiernan and I had always worked so well together, bouncing ideas off each other, piecing together knowledge from our cultures and religions. I was terrified of missing something, making the wrong move, and ruining our chances of ever catching Astra.

"How are you feeling?" Pádraig asked at my next therapy session.

"Exhausted." I slumped over on a torn-up couch with Og the Destroyer in my arms. "Too exhausted to give a shit about Tsiala. I'm . . . exhaustipated."

Pádraig choked on his tea. After recovering, he said, "I'm sure the apothecary can give you something for that."

His advice was to focus on what I could control. Forcing Olina to betray an old friend wasn't one of them. Protecting myself was, which included patching the holes Tsiala had left in my schedule. Geniod took over my combat lessons, and Akohin offered to join me for water-calling practice. If Ivar was going to come for me, I needed to be ready.

Akohin had another suggestion. If we couldn't persuade Olina to talk, then Ainu-Seru could spy on Ivar instead. I protested that it would leave Akohin unguarded, but he pointed out that Ivar *was* the biggest threat. "Besides," he said wryly, "I'm excellent at running away."

Reluctantly, I agreed to the plan. I had enough to deal with. The medical apprentice exams were soon, and the hospital matron agreed to let me try writing them again. If I passed the first-year exam, I could start basic medical work, which would mean being assigned to another ward. If I passed the second-year exam, I could stay on the fourth floor and help care for Tiernan.

After losing Dunehein, Rikuja, and Tsiala, I dreaded moving to another ward where I didn't know anyone. On my free nights, I joined the second-year apprentices for a study group. It was embarrassing to be with a bunch of fifteen-year-olds, but they were fascinated by what I'd done at that age — bandaging my wounds with wild bogmoss, saving Nerio and Jorumgard from coal newt poisoning, treating Jonalin's laudanum overdose.

The exams were held on the university campus in a cavernous lecture hall. Even with early summer sun falling across the rows of desks, the stone walls kept the room cool. At first, the rustle of papers and scratching of quills distracted me, but I sank into meditation and started flying through the questions. Months of therapy with Pádraig let me push aside the overwhelming memories of treating burnt soldiers in Tjarnnaast.

I passed the first exam at the top of the class — not much of an accomplishment considering I had far more experience, but it proved I wasn't as hopeless as I'd convinced myself. The second exam went well, so I was confused when the hospital matron sat me down to talk. She wanted me to take the third-year exam. If I passed, I could take over Tiernan's daily care. I'd gotten better at preventing blackouts, so Pádraig wanted to see how I fared with more exposure to Tiernan.

The matron gave me the next day off to study. I hunkered down in the fourth-floor kitchen with my textbook and a list of exam topics, crossing off the ones I knew, circling the ones I needed to focus on. Círa answered my questions and kept me supplied with food and iced tea. I'd never been so set on learning anything, determined that Tiernan wouldn't suffer from lack of care.

Before the exam, Finín surprised me outside the lecture hall to lend me his lucky charm, a rowan leaf pressed in amber. He promised that no matter if my results were good or bad, he'd buy me a drink. He'd already passed his exams. "With distinctions," he added, grinning.

The day after the exam, as I came up from the hospital's underground laundry, Círa grabbed my hands and spun me around. "You did it!" she sang. "You scraped a pass!"

I gasped. "Really?"

She beamed. "You must be the first person to finish three years of an apprenticeship in a week. Pull out your finest clothes, girl, because we are going *out* tonight!"

✳

One hangover later, I dressed for my first day back as a medic, pinning up my dyed black hair and belting a white woolwrap over my work dress. It seemed fitting that today was the summer solstice. The Aikoto name, Jinben, referred to meeting the sun. Here I was, about to start looking after a jinrayul — my own personal sun. *Maybe Tsiala was right about how I talk about Tiernan*, I thought, then squashed that thought. It wasn't my fault she got jealous over everything.

Pádraig met me in the in-patient hall to go over procedures. After months of watching medics care for Tiernan, I'd memorized the steps — changing his bedpan, turning him to avoid pressure sores, moving his limbs to work the muscles. Círa taught me the meticulous work of calling broth down Tiernan's throat. I'd be sharing responsibility with the night-shift medics, but Pádraig stressed that if I noticed any change, good or bad, I should immediately report to him and only him.

Twice a week, I pulled the canvas privacy screens shut and took off Tiernan's grey linen robe to bathe him. *This is weird*, I kept thinking, wiping a damp cloth across his bare skin. Thankfully, since he'd already given me permission to touch his hair, washing it didn't feel like violating his privacy. I considered shaving his beard to keep him cool but decided to draw the line at changing his appearance. Instead I trimmed it short like he usually did in summer.

On a hot, dusty evening, I was walking home from work when Akohin dropped from the sky and fell into step beside me. "Ainu-Seru just saw something," he said breathlessly. "You know that waterfall where Tsiala took you? And the bridge with no paths?"

"Yeah," I said.

"Ivar went into a hidden tunnel and came out at the bridge. Then a storm petrel flew down and shifted into the Okoreni-Rin."

"The *okoreni*? Fendul was here?" My pulse jumped. I hadn't seen my childhood friend since last autumn, when I convinced his family to stand aside and let us pass through Rin land to Tjarnnaast.

"He and Ivar got into an argument," Akohin said. "The Rúonbattai had promised not to kill a sacred animal, that they'd find another way to wake the saidu, but nothing else has worked. So they're going to do it. Murder an animal and destroy southern Eremur."

"Yan kaid." The blood drained from my face. "But they don't have the druids' support. The coup failed."

"Ivar's an earth mage. Maybe he plans to rebuild Eremur alone. But listen — that's not the worst part. Fendul kept saying, 'You have to convince Liet not to.'"

I stopped in the middle of the road. "Liet's dead. I watched his body burn."

Akohin shrugged.

"Shit." I stumbled off the roadside and collapsed onto a boulder. I'd never wanted Tiernan's help so desperately. Taking a deep breath, I said, "Okay. We can't wait any longer. We need to talk to Olina."

33.

THE DIVINE TWINS

Geniod and I crept through the bushes surrounding Olina's home, a stone cottage lined with flowerbeds. This was as close as we could get without being seen by the oak. Akohin landed on the thatched roof and did a decent impression of a crow's caw. Like we expected from someone who'd married a druid and knew their superstitions, Olina opened the door and peered out. Akohin took off in a rush of black feathers, cawing.

Olina came outside wielding a knife. She followed Akohin down a flagstone path toward us. The moment she stepped into the bushes, Geniod swung out from behind a tree and caught her. I wrenched the knife from Olina's hand and held it to her throat.

"You," she gasped, writhing in Geniod's grip. "Foolish girl. I told you to never return—"

"How?" I cut in. "How can you stomach it?"

"What? Stomach what?"

"Murdering a sacred animal. Making the saidu kill hundreds of thousands of innocent people. That's *your* jouyen's land. *Your* family who'll suffer."

"No." She shook her head, her neck twisting against the knife. "They promised not to—"

"Like they promised the Rin-jouyen? Because your son just told the Okoreni-Rin he's breaking that promise."

"You're lying. Ivar would never—"

It is true. I heard him.

Olina blanched. A breeze stirred stray hair around her face. She looked up into the forest canopy, her jaw falling open. A shaft of greenish-gold sunlight fell through the trees onto her face. "Who . . ." she breathed.

Akohin dropped from a tree and shifted to human. Standing tall, shoulders thrown back, he said, "Us."

"But that voice—"

"We're connected." Akohin tilted his head, looking eerily bird-like. "We used to be like you. Living alone, avoiding the world. You know what scared us most? That one day we'd return to the world and find it burned to the ground. That everyone we loved would be gone, and we'd have to live with the guilt of having done nothing."

Olina's eyes fell shut. Tears slid down her cheeks. "Let me go and I'll help you."

"Why would we—" I began.

"Astra can see this side of the cottage. I have to go back inside like nothing happened. Come around through the drying shed, away from her oak."

Geniod and I exchanged a look. We released Olina and I gave her knife back, my other hand ready at my sword. She pinched the air, making it shimmer.

"Protective runes," she explained. "You would've been dead before you reached my door."

Olina crossed the flagstone path to her home. Geniod, Akohin, and I crept through the bushes around the back of the cottage. Bracing ourselves, we stepped into the open and entered a timber shed. It was warm and bright with south-facing windows. Gauze-covered racks held all manner of medicinal herbs, filling the air with a riot of scents.

Geniod opened the far door, which led into a shadowy kitchen. Olina had closed the shutters and lit a vellum lantern painted with herons. The place reminded me of Yotolein's flat in how it mixed cultures — wooden makiri on the mantelpiece, a druidic knot of red wool hung on the wall, flasks of fish oil next to tins of foreign spices on the cluttered shelves.

We'd caught Olina in the midst of making dinner. A kettle whistled in the hearth and a scaly trout lay on a cutting board. She picked up a fish knife, then put it down and wrapped a rag around her hand, moving toward the kettle with a flustered look. Geniod cut her off, making her flinch.

"Let me handle it," he said gently. "You'll hurt yourself."

"Whose fault is that?" she said, but passed him the rag.

Olina settled in a chair at the long wooden table. She reminded me of the Rin elders I'd grown up around — tanned skin, laugh lines around her eyes and mouth, dirt under her stubby nails. I felt as if I'd threatened one of my aunts.

She nodded at the obsidian-handled knife on my belt. "You're tempting fate by wearing that. Ivar already stole it back once."

My hand went to its hilt. "When?"

"During the coup. He lured you into a trap, pretended to get hurt defending you, then took the knife. Ai, he was livid when he woke in the hospital and saw you wearing it."

"Then he can come for it again. I'll be ready."

A bitter smile crossed Olina's face. "What do you want from me, child?"

I sat across from her, folding my hands on the table. "Everything you know about Ivar and Astra. But first, tell us how Liet's still alive."

Olina laughed softly. "Liet is two people. The cleric Astra Måritehl and her twin brother, Magnús Ainarind."

"*Magnús?* M is the golden-haired, tattooed fire mage?"

"Indeed. They commanded the Rúonbattai together, using Astra's visions of the future and Magnús's military expertise." Olina traced a scorch mark on the table. "You read their mother's novel, didn't you? *The Lilac Queen?*"

"Yeah. You mean Mårit wrote it?"

"About a decade ago, yes. Her health was failing, she'd become estranged from her children, and she wanted to record her history before she passed. To tell Astra and Magnús why she loved their father and why she left him. As for everything else I know about that family . . . it's a long story. I'll tell you on one condition. Listen and don't interrupt."

I nodded. So did Akohin, lingering by the wall.

Olina took a steadying breath. "Astra, Magnús, and I were six, maybe seven, when we first met. I was foraging in these woods and found two kids flinging sparks at each other. We became instant friends. I was too quiet to fit in with Kae kids, and they were too wild to fit in at school. Somehow we balanced out. These woods became our secret refuge. The twins saw me attune here for the first time, I had my first kiss with Magnús, I held Astra as she cried over her first heartbreak.

"When they were eighteen, a sailor said they were the spitting image of a couple he once knew, Bryngard Ødarind and Mårit Audehl. The twins demanded answers from their mother. Her confession tore a chasm in their family. Magnús wanted to change his second name to Bryngardind, but Astra and I talked him out of it. It'd be dangerous to take the name of a murderer. So Magnús left instead. He'd just started serving in the militia, and he asked to be deployed to the Nyhemur border.

"Astra went to Caladheå to look for their father. To her horror, he'd been killed a year before, stabbed in an alley. He'd left everything to the twins, including a pressed lilac for Astra and an oak leaf preserved in resin for Magnús. He'd known about them for years but didn't come for them because they were safer in Ingdanrad, a place where Ferish soldiers had no foothold. He'd planned to come after they turned eighteen.

"My best friend returned home broken by grief, furious at her mother for keeping the secret until it was too late. She, too, rejected her second name, Måritehl. The twins began signing their letters to each other with an oak and lilac, inspired by the crest I inherited from my temal. While Magnús forged a new life at the border, Astra began studying to become a cleric, seeking answers from their gods. It was then she discovered her . . . unusual skill.

"She'd always been extraordinarily perceptive — finishing our sentences, predicting the weather, thrashing Magnús and me at cards. In the austerity of a stavehall, her talent bloomed. She started *seeing* the future. The clerics said it was a gift from the gods. With practice, Astra began seeing the past, too. She realized if she retraced her father's steps, she could witness his life. She could finally know him.

"During those years, she'd started exchanging letters with a young man she'd met in Caladheå, Gúnnar Halvarind. He was from a wealthy, well-connected family, so he offered to help with Astra's research. She spent months travelling the coast, watching her father grow up, go to war, fall in love, build his fortune as a merchant. She saw him lead Rúonbattai soldiers in terrible crimes against Ferish immigrants.

"Yet she also saw the Ferish commit atrocities in her present time, supposedly a time of peace. They dammed rivers, flooding the land and destroying Sverbian, Gallnach, and Aikoto villages. They deliberately infected us with pox. They tore up our sacred ground and built statues of war criminals. When we complained, they murdered us. When a Sverbian newspaper reported their crimes, they burned down the paper's office.

"And Astra, with her magic, saw crimes people thought were secret. Priests abusing children. Boys shoved into illegal fighting rings. Girls kidnapped, shipped to mines and lumber camps, and forced into prostitution for Ferish workers. Astra reported it all, but most judges and military captains were Ferish, and they ignored their own people's crimes. Sometimes they threatened her for interfering.

"Astra came home changed. She'd seen why her father wanted to drive the Ferish out of Eremur. She'd also seen him forge alliances with the Rin and Iyo. To Astra and Magnús, it felt like fate. They saw us three as a similar alliance, a rebirth of their father's work. I wanted no part of it. Putting more blood in the ground wouldn't heal the damage. My first love and my best friend had turned into people I didn't recognize.

"So I cut ties. I married a druid and moved to this cottage. When Magnús left the militia and Astra quit her clerical studies, I guessed why. They'd joined the Rúonbattai, following in their father's footsteps. I thought I'd lost them forever. Then in our late twenties, Astra showed up here begging for help. She'd gotten pregnant by Gúnnar Halvarind."

"Wait," I cut in. "*Councillor* Halvarind? That's Ivar's father?"

Olina glared at me. "What did I say about interrupting?"

"I've read Astra's letters to Halvarind! She never mentioned having his child!"

"Of course not." Olina sipped the chokecherry tea Geniod had made. "Gúnnar was married with children, and his wife suspected he was having an affair. Astra didn't dare put the evidence in writing."

"Did she ever tell Halvarind? Or Ivar?"

"Hush, girl. I'm getting to that. Astra had seen visions. She would give birth to twins, a healthy boy and a stillborn girl. There's no pain like knowing your child will die. She wanted to give birth here in secret — away from the mother she'd rejected, the woman whose husband she was sleeping with, and anyone who knew her ties to the Rúonbattai. She was determined to protect her son.

"Deep in grief over her lost daughter, Astra started asking me about Aikoto religion — aeldu, makiri, the sacred parts of the body. I figured she felt betrayed by her gods and was looking for solace elsewhere. Instead, she started experimenting with magic. She infused oak and lilac saplings with her blood. They became an extension of herself, her ability to see through time. A living, growing, bastardized makiri.

"Astra wanted to plant them in my garden. We had an awful fight. She'd stolen sacred parts of my culture and twisted them into something profane. Yet once she explained why, I gave in. She'd seen terrible visions — an influenza epidemic, another war — and wanted my husband and me to adopt Ivar and raise him here in safety. The oak crest would let her watch over Ivar. Watch him grow up.

"Just like she predicted, Ferish rebels tried to overthrow Caladheå, sparking the Third Elken War. Astra left to join Magnús and the Rúonbattai at the front. He was a skilled captain, and with her predicting the future, they were unstoppable. I suspect they got their commander killed on purpose. Either way, they were the natural choice to take over, the divine twins of a founding captain. They took the shared name Liet — partly to hide their identities, partly so they'd always be equal.

"Their first step was to back out of the war and go into hiding. They wanted to rebuild the Rúonbattai their way. Once the dust settled, Astra asked me to bring Ivar to Caladheå to meet Gúnnar. She vowed that unlike her and Magnús, Ivar would grow up knowing his father. For a few weeks, we had peace, forgiveness, each other. Then in an instant, it all fell apart.

"Eremur's military raided a stavehall looking for Rúonbattai. Astra saw it just in time to get my husband, Ivar, and me out. She and Magnús got arrested along with several mages they'd recruited from Ingdanrad. In prison, she made another oak crest to watch over Magnús. With it she saw the mages plotting to betray the twins in exchange for their own freedom. So she and Magnús slit their throats. Every single one. Gúnnar swept in to clean up, using his Council influence to clear the twins' names.

"Astra didn't tell me that of course, but I knew her. I drew the line there. She murdered her own people and shattered ties between Eremur and Ingdanrad, all in the name of her divine mission. I took Ivar and said if she wanted to see him, she'd have to come to us in Ingdanrad. Astra let us go. She and Magnús retreated to Brånnheå and lived there for the next decade.

"Ivar grew up only seeing his birth parents once a year. Every spring on his birthday, Astra came to visit us secretly in the woods. Every summer, we visited Gúnnar in Caladheå. Beyond that, my husband and I raised Ivar as our son. We taught him to use magic to nurture and heal, not as a weapon the way Astra and Magnús did. I was reluctant to let him train for the militia, but by then my husband's blood had met the ground, and I knew Ivar might have to defend himself one day.

"When he was fifteen, the Rúonbattai went silent. We thought Astra and Magnús had died, and I felt . . . relieved. Raising Ivar to love his mother had been the hardest thing in the world. Then as he turned eighteen, about to start serving in the militia, Astra came for him — just as her father had meant to come for her and Magnús at that age. She wanted Ivar to join the Rúonbattai.

"I pleaded with him to refuse. Astra insisted she just needed an earth mage to do some construction. Ivar said he wanted to spend time with his mother and uncle. How could I argue? So every now and again, he took leave from the militia to work for the Rúonbattai, digging tunnels and whatnot. I wanted to believe that was all. I wanted to believe I'd raised him to be better than his mother. That coup, though . . . The moment I heard, I knew. Ivar planned it and set Lieutenant Jarlind up as the figurehead."

I shook my head in disgust. "And you didn't tell anyone?"

"He's my son," Olina said with an edge. "You should be thankful I'm talking to you at all."

"Why are you?"

"Because I know who you are, child." Her gaze flickered toward the obsidian-handled knife. "You got Gúnnar executed for treason. Killed Magnús in Tjarnnaast. But like Astra, I know both sides of the war. She shot your tema. Her mercenaries killed your temal. Ivar had you thrown into prison, then the men under his command killed you.

"Our families keep tearing each other apart. I don't know if you truly want that. But I know you're working in the hospital, using your skills to nurture and heal like I tried to teach Ivar. You're here with this boy" — Olina nodded at Akohin — "whose spirit is entwined with a tel-saidu. Meanwhile, my son's plotting to use the saidu for genocide. It seems your parents did a better job than I did."

My throat tightened. Geniod came over from cleaning up the kitchen. Moving behind Akohin and me, he laid a hand on each of our shoulders.

"I got lucky with these two," he said. "You've had to fight Astra's influence every step of the way, Olina. I can't imagine how hard that's been."

She looked away, into the dying fire. "I can only hope that when she dies, Ivar will come back to the light."

"You can help us with that." I leaned over the table. "Do you know where she is now?"

"No. I haven't heard from her in months. If Ivar has, he won't tell me."

"What about her oak crests? She has two more, right? Nine total to match the sacred oak's branches?"

Olina shrugged. "I'm not sure. The only others I know about were in the Caladheå prison and Gúnnar's home, and you already destroyed those."

I rubbed my eyes, frustrated and exhausted. We'd learned so much, yet I didn't know how to use any of it. I needed to write all this down in my journal so I could process it. I needed to write a long letter to Nerio and Jorumgard. Most of all, I needed to talk with Tiernan — yet he remained ever out of reach. I pushed my chair back, then paused.

"Ivar's coma," I said. "It was deliberate, right? You visited him in the hospital, then the next day, he woke up."

Olina couldn't meet my eyes. Without seeming to realize, she rubbed her ring finger. "I have no idea what you're talking about."

34.

FIRST THOUGHTS

I sprinted into the neurology ward, tripping over Og the Destroyer in my haste. "The runes," I gasped. "I was right."

Pádraig looked up from his cluttered desk. "What on earth—"

"Inside Tiernan's cuff. Runes keeping him comatose. I've been looking for proof, and—"

"Má sí." Pádraig took off his square reading spectacles. "Close the door and have a seat."

I paced the room instead, wringing my hands. Mist trailed after me. "It must be the Rúonbattai. Ivar did it to himself. His mother practically admitted it—"

"They didn't do it. Not to Tiernan."

"How do you know?"

"Because *I* did it."

My mist crackled into frozen fog. I turned slowly to face Pádraig.

"Hear me out." He lifted his hands in peace. "I found runes inside Ivar's ring and couldn't identify them, so I wrote to my aunt Róisín. She wrote back saying it's old dark magic. Very obscure. Very illegal. By then, Olina had removed the ring and Ivar had awoken. That's what gave me the idea for Tiernan. Remember I tried to get him transferred to the mental asylum? The militia refused. They were set on hanging him."

"So you trapped him in a coma?!"

"You wanted to clear his name. I was buying you time—"

A shrill laugh tore out of me. "You're holding him prisoner! And this whole time — aeldu save me, you told me to forget about the runes. Everyone in this city is a fucking liar!"

Pádraig winced. "You're right. I should've told you the truth. For that, I'm sorry. But I'm not sorry for keeping both of you alive."

"*Both* of us?"

He sighed and ran a hand through his messy curls. "You were blacking out from the thought of Tiernan dying. You admitted to thinking about suicide. I was afraid if he died, you'd follow him."

My insides twisted. I wanted to shout that he was wrong, but in truth, I didn't know. Waking from death without Tiernan had felt like getting my spirit ripped out. I knotted my fingers into my white medic's woolwrap and bit back a frustrated scream.

Pádraig got up from his desk. "I didn't tell you at first because I was breaking the law and we hardly knew each other. Then you were betrayed by Neve, Ivar, Tsiala . . . I was terrified of making things worse. I wanted you to believe I was on your side, because I *am*. Truly."

"Yeah, that's easy to believe now."

"Aye, well." He smiled wryly. "If you want to wake Tiernan and let him stand trial, we'll talk about it. But my professional advice is to process your feelings first. I expect you have a lot of them."

That was an understatement. After Pádraig left to give me some space, I switched between laughing with hysterical relief and sobbing into Og's fur. I wanted to break everything in sight, but smashing up the neurology ward might get *me* sent to the asylum. If I was going to have a breakdown, it needed to be in private.

The long summer evening had faded, but I went to Janekke's home, anyway. She lit up when I asked about her and Marijka's recipe for spiced apple cake, the one where they smashed chestnuts to vent their stress about medical school.

"Oh, we're going to have such fun," Janekke said, clapping her hands. "You know what I like best about living inside a mountain? Soundproof cellars."

*

I was still picking chestnut out of my clothes by the time I got home. Geniod and Akohin were stunned by the news. I'd burned through my emotions and wanted to be alone, so I clamped a slice of apple cake between my teeth and climbed up to the loft. By candlelight, I leafed through my journal, putting my memories in this new context.

Pádraig was right, much as I hated to admit it. If Tiernan had woken, he'd almost certainly be dead by now. The only thing he could say in his defence was to blame Jorumgard for torching the border garrison, which he'd never do. Still, if by some tiny chance I'd found a way to clear his name, he could've been awake this whole time, at my side. The thought itched somewhere deep that I couldn't reach.

I dreamed of Olina's cottage in the woods. Tsiala drifted through the garden as lilac petals floated around her. She glanced behind me, then walked off into the forest. I turned to see what she'd seen. Tiernan stood in the cottage doorway — only it was no longer

Olina's home but the log cabin where the other Tiernan and I had lived together in the shoirdryge.

Sparrow song woke me. Groggily, I fumbled through the dim loft for my journal. I'd just finished writing down the dream when I remembered Círa's words. *Your first thought in the morning is always of your true love.*

I flipped back through the pages. Ever since Tsiala had broken up with me, I'd stopped recording my dreams about her. From then on, my first thoughts had been about Tiernan. Relief he couldn't see what a mess I was, wishing he was awake to help me with Olina, determination to pass my exams so I could look after him, daydreams of lying next to him amidst the snowy plains of Nyhemur.

"Fuck," I said under my breath.

I felt it out as gingerly as poking a bruise. I'd been thinking of Tiernan as a good friend, but it was so much more. I wanted that life in the log cabin, waking up together, laughing as we made tea. I wanted to kiss him — *oh*, that thought made me shiver — and weave my fingers into his dark hair and fold my body into his so I'd never lose him again.

Tsiala must've figured it out long ago. She'd asked if things could ever get better between us, and I hadn't been able to say yes. I couldn't give her my heart because it was trapped in a hospital bed, nestled in the crook of a comatose man's skeletal arm. Tsiala must've felt like a ghost in our relationship, fighting with another ghost for my love.

This wasn't supposed to happen, I thought with rising panic. Tiernan belonged with Marijka Riekkanehl. That was the whole reason Jorumgard had hid Tiernan's prison sentence — so Tiernan could return to Eremur a free man, an innocent man, and rekindle his relationship. He had talked about marrying Marijka. Starting a family. Who was I to get in the way?

Even if things didn't work out with Marijka, it was stupid to hope he'd want me. I was eighteen, wrecked with grief, figuring out how to cope without my parents. It had been painful enough worrying that Jonalin still saw me as a child, and he was only a few years older than me. Tiernan had just turned thirty-three. As if he'd wait for me to get my life together.

And yet . . . and yet. I'd touched his tangled hair in Tjarnnaast and felt the same grief. Down in the dungeons, I'd given him the sun and he'd given me air, talking me back to breathing. He wanted to take me to Nyhemur to befriend windmills and float among the clouds. *I promise to keep you warm*, he'd said and cupped my jaw as if he wanted to kiss me. The memory sent dizzying heat through my body.

We made each other better. Stronger. I couldn't wake him to face his death at the noose, nor could I leave him trapped in a coma. I'd break him out of Ingdanrad if I had to. As a sparrow whisked past the loft window, an idea struck.

✳

"Ako," I whispered, shaking him awake. "We need to talk."

He sat up, bleary-eyed and bare-chested, his wool blanket falling off. Geniod was still snoring behind the wooden screen. Akohin pulled on his shirt and boots. In the kitchen, I handed him a mug of huckleberry tea and beckoned him outside. Sparkling dew clung to the grass.

"Did you mean what you told Olina?" I asked, settling on a log bench by the firepit. "Feeling guilty about doing nothing while the world burned?"

Akohin nodded. "Every word of it."

"But in Dúnravn Pass, you said Ainu-Seru doesn't want to fight anymore. You said it upsets him."

"Things change." He sipped his tea, steam wafting around his face. "We were . . . different then."

"Different how?"

"You know how trees can petrify? They fill up with mineral-rich water, and gradually the wood decays, leaving just the minerals. They still *look* like trees, but they're not. Being connected to Ainu-Seru was like that. His spirit was taking over mine."

I shuddered. "That sounds terrifying."

"I welcomed it. Better than feeling my own pain, I thought. But then you showed up, and . . . I remembered the good parts of being human. Caring about people. *Being* cared about." Akohin gazed up at the brightening sky. "Ainu-Seru never got to share that with my great-great-grandfather. By the time Imarein went back to the Rin, he was too far gone, more saidu than human. They rejected him. You saved me just in time."

"Oh," I said, stunned.

"And now Ainu-Seru's felt all this." He gestured across the garden terraces. "Befriending Finín and Círa. Dancing with strangers in the rain on Abhain. Your uncle saying he 'lucked out' like we're his kids, which I guess makes you my sister."

"*Oh.*" I hugged him, spilling his tea. He was right. Sometimes he felt like a younger brother tagging along behind me, sometimes like an older brother watching over me. With our dyed black hair, we even looked the same. We were the divine twins of the Aikoto Confederacy, an undead girl and a half-saidu boy. "In that case . . . I need a favour. A big one."

✳

I caught Pádraig on his way up the hospital's stone stairs. "Let's do it," I said, falling into step. "Let's wake Tiernan. I've got a plan to get him out."

Pádraig blinked, never fully awake until he'd had his tea. "First things first. It's Tiernan's choice whether he stands trial or not."

"Like it was his choice to be comatose?"

"Ouch, but fair point." The druid fell silent as we passed the second floor, bustling with visitors heading to the dining hall for breakfast. Out of earshot, he said, "You should have reasonable expectations, too. It'll be weeks before he's well enough to leave the hospital."

"I know. That's fine. I'm stuck here for another month myself."

"And the mage assembly may call him to trial before then. If they expect to hang him anyway, they won't care if their interrogation gives him a heart attack."

"I know. I won't let him get to the Aerie."

Pádraig sighed. As we passed the third floor, the screams of newborns and women in labour echoed off the walls. Once the noise faded, he said, "All right. Let's get started."

The first step was removing the runes from inside Tiernan's iron cuff. While I distracted his guard with a made-up story of someone skulking around, Pádraig pressed his fingers to the iron. With a flicker of light, the runes vanished. The next step was making sure Tiernan didn't wake *too* soon after our distraction, which would make it obvious we'd done something. I added laudanum to his broth at each meal, which would keep him out overnight.

Geniod let me off my makiri-reading lesson that evening. I couldn't concentrate, couldn't eat, couldn't sleep. Worries crowded my brain like a flock of migrating geese. What if Tiernan didn't wake? Or didn't remember me? Or remembered everything and blamed me for leading him into the trap that landed him here? What if, after all this, he wouldn't even speak to me?

In the morning, Geniod had to physically hold me back from going to the hospital early. I couldn't give any hint that I expected Tiernan to wake. Once I reached the fourth floor, I couldn't bring myself to enter the in-patient hall. I lingered in the hallway, my hand on the door, terrified of finding bad news. I was about to look for Pádraig when someone shouted inside.

I shoved open the door. Tiernan was seizing in his bed, coughing and turning blue. A medic was trying desperately to open his mouth. Shards of a clay mug lay in water on the floor.

"Move," I snapped. I dropped to my knees at Tiernan's side and closed my eyes, forcing myself into meditation. His lungs were full of water. "Hold him down!"

The medic pinned down his shoulders. The guard took his legs. I extended my mind deep into Tiernan's body and pulled. Water flew out of his mouth and spattered across his linen robe. His body fell limp.

"Nei," I said. "Nei, nei, nei — come on, Tiernan—"

"He's too weak—" the medic began.

"Shut up!" I grabbed Tiernan's bony hand. The hall faded. There was just us floating together. "Come back to me. Goddamn it, I can't lose you now—"

My throat closed. Colourful spots flickered across my vision. We were back in the catacombs, bleeding out together. But I wasn't helpless this time. I hadn't died and come back to life and passed three medical exams just to give up.

"Come on," I gasped. "Breathe with me. Five seconds in, five out. One, two, three, four—"

Tiernan's chest convulsed. His grey eyes flew open. They darted toward the vaulted ceiling, figures rushing throughout the hall, windows overlooking the mountain. Terror racked his face.

"It's okay — you're okay—" Something between a laugh and a

sob tore out of me. I cupped his bearded jaw, clinging to the feel of bristles against my skin. "Look at me, Tiernan. I'm here. I've got you."

His gaze settled on me. The terror eased. Ever so slightly, his lips moved. I leaned in close to hear. His breath was warm on my cheek as he whispered a single word, the nickname he'd given me so long ago. "Katja."

35.

SAND & SNOW

The rest of Tiernan's speech was slow to return. All he could manage were single words in Sverbian or Gallnach. I understood things like *water* or *pain*, but beyond that, his guard had to translate. Pádraig said remembering how to speak was like fumbling in the dark. Sometimes people found a word in their mind and lit it up, making it easy to find again. Sometimes hearing or reading words lit them up. The more I spoke to Tiernan in Coast Trader, the more he would remember.

So I narrated my tasks aloud — feeding him, bathing him, easing him into physical therapy. His wry smile softened the awkwardness like we were sharing a joke. When I felt sure he could understand me, I explained he'd been comatose for five months and would soon stand trial. All I could say in front of his guard was that I would defend him. Tiernan stared at the ceiling, seemingly lost in his own world, but when I got up to give him space, his fingers twitched, reaching for me.

"Okay," I soothed, taking his hand. "I'll stay."

From then on, I lived at his side, skipping my lessons and sleeping on a cot. Yet despite my efforts to help him relearn Trader, Tiernan kept speaking in a jumble of Sverbian and Gallnach, insisting he *was* speaking the trade language. He seemed confused that I didn't understand, then annoyed. I couldn't imagine how hard it was for him, but it was a slap in the face when he gave up and turned away with a scowl.

A linguist from the university spent an afternoon talking to Tiernan and copying down what he said. The man took his notes home to analyze. He came back the next day looking baffled. Tiernan's grammar was rooted in both Sverbian and Gallnach, yet he spoke in the patterns of a single language. His vocabulary was a mixture of six-century-old dialects and non-existent words.

I'd expected Tiernan might not want to speak to me. I hadn't expected *this*. The man I loved had awoken as a different person, and I was powerless to change him back. I wondered if his combat neurosis from long ago had returned, but even Pádraig was bewildered, admitting he'd never seen anything like this.

Janekke seemed oddly unruffled. She quizzed Tiernan about Sverbian history — famous battles, kings and queens, the changing names of conquered cities. He knew everything prior to six centuries ago. Beyond that, his answers were completely different to recorded history.

In private, Janekke told me, "It's not a medical problem. Well, not wholly. He told you about his ancestors, right?"

"The druids who married Sverbian soldiers?" I asked.

"Right. Over generations, their two cultures merged into one — a unique language, a unique view of history. I reckon Tiernan's confused, thinking he's back home in Sverba. Like how we wake up each morning expecting our own bed."

I blinked at her. "So he really *is* speaking a trade language?"

"Indeed, just not the one he thinks he is." Janekke patted my arm. "Give me an hour and I'll sort him out."

Her methods usually involved sharp objects and lots of blood, but I had no better choice. I left them alone and did chores around their fourth floor. When I returned, Janekke was beaming and Tiernan gave me a sheepish smile.

"Hello, Katja," he said.

I sank to my knees at his bedside, stunned. "Hello to you, too."

✳

Day by day, Tiernan remembered bits of Coast Trader. I brought tattered books up from the second-floor visitors' quarters so he could practise reading. Once we could talk without a translator, I asked him what being comatose had been like.

"Like sleeping," he said. "Sometimes there was nothing. Sometimes I was trapped in . . . a sand ocean."

"A desert?"

"Yes. A desert at night, dark and empty. I feared I would die alone . . . then I heard your voice."

My breath hitched. "You *could* hear me?"

"Aye. And on the horizon, snow began falling. I felt I was meant to meet you there, yet I could never reach it. Time and time again, I thought about giving up, but . . ." Tiernan smiled faintly. "Well. Here you are."

"Nyhemur." I scraped out a laugh. "You remembered."

I'd had the same kind of vision when I died, searching for him in a rainstorm, but had found no sign of him. Our spirits had wound up in different worlds. Yet by some magic, some force of will, I'd broken into his world. We'd found each other again. I leaned over and kissed his hair. It was the most I dared to show him of my feelings.

At first, it didn't seem like he'd actually *understood* anything I said during his coma. It was fun surprising him with news. He whooped with joy at Jorumgard and Yotolein getting back together. I thought I could get away with not mentioning Tsiala — then out of nowhere Tiernan asked, "What about that warrior girl? Are you still together?"

I stared at him in both awe and horror. There was no good way to explain she broke up with me because I was secretly in love with him. "Nei," I stammered. "It didn't work out."

"Ah. Sorry," was all he said, though as he scratched his beard, it looked like he was covering a smile.

We desperately needed to talk alone, but we had no chance to slip away from his day or night guard. Remembering how Neve passed me information during my hospital stay, I tucked letters into Tiernan's books, relaying everything we'd learned about the Rúonbattai. One letter had my plan to break Tiernan out. He responded with a sharp shake of his head.

Setting my last trace of caution on fire, I took a vial of pukeweed essence from the neurology ward and spiked the day guard's water flask. Within minutes of drinking it, the man rushed off to be violently ill. Tiernan cast me a disapproving look. I closed the canvas screens around his bed, blocking out the afternoon sunlight and the rest of the in-patient hall.

"Why not?" I hissed. "I didn't go through all this to watch you hang—"

"And I will not let you throw your life away," Tiernan snapped, heaving himself upright. "You already freed me from prison once. The militia will never stop chasing you."

"There's no other way. You're not strong enough to break out alone—"

"I could be."

"What? How?"

Tiernan sighed and rubbed his jaw. "An old contact. Iollan och Cormic."

I paused, taken aback. Nerio had said the druid was "incredibly dangerous" and I should only contact him in a crisis. Pádraig putting Tiernan in a coma had bought me time for another option. Now we had no time and no other options. "What can he do?" I asked.

He looked toward the ceiling. "I cannot explain. Talk to Janekke. She will take you to Iollan."

✳

Outside the hospital, I spoke into the wind. A raven and an eagle arrived and shifted into Akohin and Geniod. As we climbed a dusty road toward the university campus, Janekke explained that Iollan was one of Ingdanrad's leading theological researchers. His main subject, rift magic, was about finding rips in the fabric of worlds. He'd written a book theorizing that people could pass from one shoirdryge to another through these supposed rifts.

"So he's a scholar?" I asked. "What's so dangerous about that?"

"Everything," Janekke said dryly. "He's cut from the same cloth as Astra Måritehl. Think of what she's done, crossbreeding Sverbian temporal magic with Aikoto blood magic. Then imagine what someone like that could do messing around with shoirdrygen."

Geniod frowned. "And *how* does Tiernan know this man?"

"He spent a year as och Cormic's acolyte, helping with research while serving in the militia. I don't know the details, but . . . their experiments were borderline illegal. Tiernan backed out and left Ingdanrad. They've barely spoken in a decade. He must be desperate to want och Cormic's help now."

Janekke showed us to the theology department's terrace. In the centre of a courtyard grew a rowan, oak, and rioden — the sacred trees of Gallnach, Sverbians, and Aikoto. Iollan's workshop, one of many built into the cliffs, had frosted windows that obscured the inside. Smoke puffed from a row of chimneys. Janekke knocked on the door. When nothing happened, she knocked again.

"Not home," shouted a man with a faint Gallnach accent.

Janekke leaned close to a window and called, "We're here about Tiernan Heilind."

Footsteps sounded inside, then a pale man in burlap robes flung open the door. His knotted wool pendant was studded with volcanic glass. At first glance, Iollan och Cormic looked plain as bannock — medium height, medium build, short brown hair, stubble on his jaw. As he studied us, though, I glimpsed the same coldness in his eyes that I'd seen in Astra's. A shudder went down my spine.

The temperature swelled as we entered his smoky workshop. Iollan's current acolyte, a young man in a red militia woolwrap, was tending kilns built into the stone wall. Golden liquid burbled through a network of glass orbs and copper pipes. Racks and shelves held a huge array of tools — hammers and tongs, surgical knives, compasses, sextants, brass scales, glass lenses of all sizes, inkpots and quills.

"Liquid fire, eh?" Janekke asked, trailing her fingers across a stack of limestone blocks. "Is this for the militia?"

"We all have our side jobs," Iollan said dismissively. "Now be quick. What do a Sverbian surgeon and three viirelei want with me?"

As fast as possible, I explained Tiernan's situation and my plan to break him out. Iollan listened in silence, spinning a globe on a bronze stand. When I finished, he pressed his finger to the globe, stopping its spin.

"No," he said.

"*No?*" I echoed.

"You're asking me to break the law to help a criminal. A man who walked out on me, stealing incredibly sensitive research. Frankly, if Tiernan och Heile dies, it's one fewer problem for me."

I stared at him, aghast. No wonder Tiernan had feared dying alone in a dark desert if this was the kind of person he'd worked with. Geniod drew forward, hand on his sword hilt. Janekke flung out her arm, blocking him before he stepped onto a rune painted on the stone floor.

"There must be some way to make it worth your while," she said to Iollan.

"Bribery? Really?" His lips quirked with a smile. "None of you have anything I could want."

"I do," Akohin said.

Iollan rounded on Akohin. "What's that, boy?"

"You study theology, right? Spirits and the fabric of worlds? I have three thousand years of knowledge about that." Akohin lifted his hand. A gust rattled the windows.

The druid's eyes widened. "You — how—"

"I'm bonded with an air spirit. If you help us, we'll grant you an hour of our time. You can ask anything you want — though we don't promise to answer."

Iollan's lips pulled back in a smile, baring his teeth. It was the look of a wolf eyeing prey. "You have yourself a deal."

✳

As it turned out, Iollan wasn't just studying rifts between shoird-rygen. He was trying to *make* them. The fabric of the world was woven from earth, heat, water, and air, so he believed a sufficiently strong druid, fire mage, or water-caller — or air-caller, if one existed — could tear a rift in our world. One way to become that strong was with amplification runes, like the bronze ring Róisín had given me months ago. Tiernan had backed out of the project, but Iollan had spent years inventing better amp runes.

Amplifying Tiernan's fire magic now was pointless. Even if we removed his nullifying cuff, he was too weak to use magic. However, Iollan had a different idea. A medical researcher at the university had written a treatise about using healing magic to stimulate muscle growth. It was a slow, laborious process, but if we amplified the magic with Iollan's runes, we could speed up Tiernan's recovery. In weeks, he'd have a fighting chance of escaping the militia alone.

Back at the hospital, I talked it over with Janekke and Pádraig. It'd be painful and risky, but as long as Tiernan consented and the runes could be easily removed, we were legally allowed to try it as an experimental therapy, and we could claim it was to get him to trial sooner. Pádraig admitted it would be immensely valuable research. Círa agreed to put together a protein-rich meal plan to pair with the therapy.

"Are you *sure*?" I asked Tiernan for the hundredth time, sitting by his bedside.

He squeezed my hand. "You led me out of the desert. I trust you to lead me through this."

Janekke and Pádraig spent a few evenings in Iollan's workshop, lending their medical expertise. His acolyte brought the finished rune designs to the hospital. I muttered a quiet prayer to my aeldu before painting the runes on Tiernan's chest, back, and limbs with my black hair dye. It would last several days, but I could scrub it away if something went wrong.

At first Tiernan felt nothing. Once we began physical therapy, stretching and working his muscles, he started to grimace. He described it as the full-body aches that followed days of horse-back riding. I gave him willowcloak to numb the pain. Following Pádraig's suggested schedule, we alternated each hour between therapy and rest. Whenever Tiernan started to waver, I coaxed him to do just a little more — another minute, another stretch.

I forgot what day it was until Pádraig reminded me. He and the other Gallnach medics would be gone all night at Cághain, their summer festival atop the mountain. Janekke agreed to sleep in the second-floor visitors' quarters in case I needed help. Instead of the red-moustached guard who usually watched Tiernan overnight, a skinny young Sverbian soldier turned up at dusk.

Tiernan shook me awake in the dark. The glowing white runes on his iron cuff washed out his gaunt face. I jerked upright, terrified he was dying — then it dawned on me. He'd gotten out of bed on his own. Putting a finger to his lips, he nodded at his guard, slumped over asleep in his chair. The boy clearly wasn't used to night shift.

"We can finally talk in private," Tiernan whispered. "The night medic is gone, too. She slipped off with a man."

The woman had been eyeing the cardiology medic for months. Looking around the shadowy hall, I got an idea. The only other patient was a woman recovering from tumour surgery and dosed up on laudanum. She wouldn't wake for hell or high water. I slipped my arm around Tiernan and helped him stumble to the hall's far end, where he settled on a window-side bed. I pulled the canvas screens close, shutting us in.

"What did you want to talk about?" I whispered.

Tiernan gazed through the arched windows at the moonlit hospital gardens. "I need to tell you something. Janekke says you are sick of secrets, yet . . ." He pressed his fingers to his temples. "Words still escape me."

Hope welled up inside me. Maybe he shared my feelings. What he'd said about searching for me in the desert, as if we were meant to be together . . . I perched next to him and twined my fingers into his. "Then can I tell you something?"

"Go ahead."

"I . . ." My throat started to close. "Had a vision. Last autumn. My parents' spirits led me through the shoirdryge to a log cabin in the woods. I saw the other me living with the other you."

Tiernan didn't reply. I stole a glance at him. He was looking at me with furrowed brows.

"And . . ." He sounded strangled. "How do you . . . feel about that?"

Suddenly my words were gone, too. My heart skipped like a pebble across a pond. I cupped his jaw, rubbing my thumb through his beard. His breath hitched. I reached deep inside myself, scraping up every shred of courage, and kissed him.

The dark hall faded. There was nothing except his soft lips exploring mine, the prickle of his beard, our breath mixing together. His fingers tangled into my loose, sleep-tousled hair. My nerves crackled with fire—

"Wait," Tiernan gasped, pulling away.

It felt like I'd fallen out the fourth-floor window and smacked into the ground. "Sorry. I'm an idiot—"

"Katja." He grabbed my hands. "Wait, please. I—"

He looked about to faint. I checked his pulse, breathing, temperature, the dilation of his pupils. I *was* a fucking idiot for springing this on him.

"Någvakt bøkkhem," he swore under his breath. "I thought I would have more time."

"Time for what?"

"To figure this out." Tiernan pinched the bridge of his nose. "Last year in Tjarnnaast, you were a traumatized teenage girl. Now I have woken to find a skilled, confident, beautiful young woman. I am still catching up. Learning who you are now, trying to understand these new feelings for you."

My breath caught. "You *do* have feelings for me?"

"More than I can explain." He rested his forehead against mine. "And that is the issue. I need time. I need . . ."

I kissed his cheek. Every part of me longed to pull him down onto the bed and tangle into him, but I'd have to wait. I wanted to prove I was patient and confident and everything else he saw in me. I wanted to be someone he could fall in love with. Someone he trusted to lead him out of the desert, time and time again.

36.

FREEDOM

After that night, I threw myself into my work — mostly for Tiernan's sake but also to distract myself. I monitored his vital signs, tracked his side effects, and kept a tight schedule of therapy and rest. Now that he could get out of bed, I scrounged up an old tunic and trousers to swap for his linen robe. I took detailed notes on his progress, from how many steps he could take to how many books he could lift.

I hated seeing him in constant pain, but willowcloak was the strongest medicine I felt comfortable giving him. Tulanta hallucinations would confuse him more, needlemint would turn his limbs into wet noodles, and laudanum could stop his heart. He bore it all with gritted teeth, never snapping at me, never complaining — though he became more distant than ever, no longer holding my hand or touching my hair.

It felt like a race. The sooner Tiernan recovered, the sooner the mage assembly would call him to trial. As I supported him on a walk around the in-patient hall, the only time we had an excuse to step away from his guard, he leaned in close. "I have a favour to ask," he whispered. "The militia took my horse, Gwmniwyr, and my sword. If you can recover them . . ."

I wasn't sure how. The only militia soldier I knew besides Ivar was Alesso Spariere, whom I hadn't spoken to since the coup — and he wasn't a soldier anymore, since he'd been kicked out for treason. He *did* owe me for saving him from Lieutenant Jarlind, though. Geniod tracked him down at Clan Níall's villa, and Alesso promised to look into it.

He sent word two days later. Gwmniwyr, always exceptionally calm for a warhorse, was at the militia's training stables. Tiernan's sword, made of a rare alloy with unusual forging techniques, had been sold to a collector. Alesso felt confident he could discreetly buy them back, but Clan Níall was watching his and Síona's money to ensure they didn't forge any more secret alliances. Thankfully, I'd saved the gold sovs Nerio had given me in Port Alios. Soon after the deals were settled, a naval courier brought a letter from Nerio.

Dear Katja,
The information you have uncovered is incredible. I looked up the arrest records from the stavehall raid in Caladheå. There is no mention of any mages being released, so I suspect Gúnnar Halvarind got Astra's and Magnús's records wiped. That made me wonder what else Halvarind covered up, so I went back through the paperwork we seized from Ivy House. In his will, Halvarind left two farmhouses to "Ivar Astrind." Sverbian men can legally use their matronym instead of patronym, but we had dismissed the property deeds as forged. There was no evidence an Ivar Astrind existed.

Now that we know otherwise, we are looking into the farmhouses. One is in Nyhemur. Your uncle Yotolein recruited Tula scouts, who found the house boarded up and abandoned. Farmers in the area insist the place is cursed and avoid it. I can guess why. Built into an outer wall is a stone mosaic of an oak and lilac, evoking that strange sense that one has been there before and will be again. However, we have found no sign of any active Rúonbattai there.

The other property is up the coast on Algard Island and suspicious for several reasons. First, it is not a farm-house at all but a muddy field. Second, do you recall canoeing through frozen fog in that region last winter? The fog is still there despite everywhere else having an unusually hot, dry summer. Viirelei traders believe a dormant water spirit has lost control. So many ships have wrecked in the area that the navy is avoiding it.

We suspect Astra Måritehl is hiding there in the fog. Tula scouts found another oak crest, her ninth and possibly last, in a stavehall's stained-glass window two leagues from the muddy field. The Tula are searching for tunnels between the two places. Ivar may have done "construction" there. I know your sentence is done soon, so let me know where to reach you next. Best of luck with Tiernan.

Sincerely, Lieutenant Nerio Parr,
1st Royal Eremur Special Forces

P.S. Rikuja gave birth last week to a healthy baby boy. She and Dunehein named him Noluhein.

I slipped the letter to Tiernan along with a note asking if he'd be okay escaping to Nettle Ginu. He nodded. The Tula settlement was remote enough he could recover safely, yet still hear news about the war. My family would look after him until I caught up — although with each sunset, ticking away the days until my sentence was over, it started to seem like we might become free at the same time.

How wrong I was.

⁂

Distant voices woke me at sunrise. I sat up groggily on my cot. Tiernan was already out of bed, dressed but barefoot. He and the red-moustached night guard were watching the door. Six soldiers poured into the dim in-patient hall, swords drawn. I backed away and shoved open a window.

"Ako," I hissed into the sky. "Now! Hurry!"

The soldiers circled Tiernan. Their lieutenant, a man with a silver-trimmed woolwrap, spoke in Gallnach. Tiernan lifted his hands, stammering out a response.

I shoved through the circle. "What's going on?" I demanded. "I'm his medic. He's not cleared to leave!"

The lieutenant glanced me up and down. "*You're* in charge? Where's Pádraig och Aindrias?"

"He's not here yet! It's still dawn!"

"Then tell him your patient's gone to trial." The man unhooked a coil of rope from his belt.

I reached for my obsidian-handled knife. If Tiernan went to the Aerie, his next stop would be the gallows. This couldn't all be for nothing—

An enormous black-and-white whirlwind smashed through the windows. Glass rained across us. The kinaru crashed into an empty bed, mangling the wrought-iron frame. Its webbed feet slapped the stone floor as it heaved itself upright.

Fire bloomed from a soldier's hand. Gusts swept through the shattered windows, swirling the fire aside. A mattress burst into flames.

"Don't!" I cried. "Don't hurt it! Kinaru are sacred!"

The lieutenant shouted an order. His soldiers drew back. The kinaru swung its head on its long neck, peering down at us with red eyes. It spread its sail-like wings as if daring anyone to attack.

Tiernan grabbed me. I yelped. He pinned me against his chest, yanked my knife from its sheath, and held the blade to my throat. "Trust me," he whispered.

"Now see here—" the lieutenant began.

"He won't harm her," the night guard interrupted. "They're in love. It's plain as plaid."

Tiernan scoffed. "The bitch is nothing to me. I just hoped to have my way with her. Shame there was no time."

I sucked in my breath. I'd never heard him sound so callous. The lieutenant hesitated, weighing my shock. I sank into it, wearing my fear and despair and exhaustion for all to see. Tears slid down my cheeks. Even the night guard looked like he doubted his own words.

Tiernan dragged me toward the kinaru, using me as a shield. He'd have to let me go to climb onto the bird. Across the hall, Círa appeared in the doorway, wide-eyed with shock. An idea struck.

"Cut me," I whispered.

"What?" Tiernan hissed back.

"Distract them. Círa can heal me."

He swore under his breath. The knife slipped down and bit my collarbone. Tiernan shoved me away and dropped the knife with a ringing of metal. I collapsed, clutching the cut, smearing blood up my throat to make it look worse. Soldiers cried out and ran toward me.

Huge wings rustled behind us. When I turned, Tiernan was astride the kinaru. It launched out the broken windows. The bird dipped, sinking toward the stone terrace, then flapped hard and caught Ainu-Seru's wind. The last I saw of Tiernan was him looking back toward me.

❋

Once Círa had healed me, the lieutenant hauled me down to the militia complex. He put me in a cold stone room with no windows, only a dusty skylight, and questioned me over and over. Using Neve's advice that the best lies were closest to the truth, I admitted I'd fallen in love with Tiernan and thought he felt the same. I insisted the rune therapy was to prepare him for trial, which I'd promised to defend him in. Hours must've passed when Hanlin arrived. The lieutenant saluted the Okoreni-Kae and gave us the room.

Hanlin settled across the table from me, his greying braid draped over one shoulder. "Quite the day," he said. "I've never seen a kinaru in Ingdanrad. I'm sure one rescuing your lover has nothing to do with your friend, the Dona boy with a kinaru tattoo instead of a seagull."

I looked down at my nails, still crusted with my blood. "You knew?"

"We Kae have scholars devoted to studying saidu. Which is why the militia came to me today — luckily for you. I told them kinaru only answer to tel-saidu, and that there's no way you could've been responsible for this breakout."

I gaped at him. "You defended me?"

Hanlin glanced through the dusty skylight at the vivid blue beyond. "Ainu-Seru's kept us alive, bringing us rain throughout a hard summer. I'd rather have him as an ally than an enemy. Two chief druids, Lónan och Cathal och Ríain and Caoimhe ó Fearghas ó Níall, seem to agree. We talked the rest of the mage assembly down from another trial. Once your current sentence ends in a week, you're free."

"Thank you," I said fervently. "We won't forget this."

A soldier escorted me through the complex. I emerged blinking into the lobby lined with marble statues of druids. Geniod swept me into a hug, muttering thanks to the aeldu. Akohin whispered that Ainu-Seru had gone with Tiernan, seeing him safely to Nettle Ginu. It had worked. After all this time, Tiernan was free.

Since my patient was gone, and Círa had insisted I needed to recover, I'd been given the rest of the day off work. Sweat beaded on my brow as we walked to the Kae district. What with working in the hospital all day, every day, it had been ages since I'd felt afternoon sunshine. Far northwest, on the other side of the Turquoise Mountains, Tiernan was probably basking in the same sun.

In our cabin, I glimpsed myself in the tarnished mirror and started with surprise. Three weeks of living in the hospital with Tiernan had taken its toll. My face was pale and drawn, dress wrinkled and sweat-stained, hair limp and greasy. The black dye had turned to dark brown. While he'd been growing stronger, I'd been fading.

His words lingered on my skin, stinging like itchbine. *The bitch is nothing to me.* I crawled into a bath and tried to scrub them away. Of course he'd lied to protect me, of *course*, and yet . . . He'd pulled away when I kissed him. Maybe now that we were apart, his feelings would fade. Maybe he'd go back to seeing me as that traumatized teenage girl.

Clean and dressed, I drifted outside. Geniod was whittling a bowl by the firepit. He probably needed to occupy his hands, since there was no point making dishes a week before we left.

"Where's Ako?" I asked, perching on a log bench.

"At the Kae gathering place," Geniod said. "I need to talk to you alone."

Something in his voice threw me. He sounded guilty.

"People are saying you're in love with Tiernan." Geniod set his whittling on the dirt. "I understand, but this isn't what you think it is. That vision of the log cabin, the other you and Tiernan living together . . . Your parents didn't show you that. The swan and mountain cat were her parents. The other Kateiko's."

Ice crept over my skin. "How do you know?"

"Your parents told me. Remember at Malana's wedding, a swan and mountain cat attacked you in the shrine? I asked your parents why, and they said it wasn't them. Neither was the log cabin."

"Then how . . ."

"You used the rioden saplings in the shrine to conjure the visions. Sacred trees are a conduit to other worlds. You saw into the shoirdryge's Aeldu-yan, not ours."

"Yan kaid." I folded my hands over my mouth, feeling as if I'd been turned inside out. In my worst moments, desperate for my parents' help, I'd been communicating with strangers. "And you're telling me *now*?"

Geniod winced. "I was worried about telling you back then. You were suicidal, and . . . searching for Tiernan and Jorumgard gave you purpose."

"You—" I leapt up from the bench. "You had no right to keep that from me. It's my life!"

"I know. I'm so sorry—"

"Bearshit," I snapped. "You did the same thing with Róisín, lying to protect me. I told you how sick I am of lies!"

"I know. And" — Geniod ran a hand down his face — "you *died*, Kateiko. Aeldu save me, do you know how much that hurt? How scared I was of losing you again? The more people betrayed you, the worse you got. But after today, you literally bleeding out to save Tiernan — I can't sit by and watch anymore."

"So you decided to ruin it? The one good thing I have?"

"You deserve the truth, not some fantasy you've built up. This isn't what your parents wanted for you."

It felt like he'd slapped me. How *dare* he? Lie for so long, then blame me for falling for Tiernan? Breathing hard, I said, "I'm not running away again. This time, I want *you* to go."

※

Akohin found me in a heap under a chestnut tree, sobbing so hard my breath came in starts and gasps. He stroked my hair while I cried myself to exhaustion. A cool breeze rustled the leaves overhead, dappling us with light and shadow.

Nothing felt fair. For so many years, other people had been controlling my life, from the Rin-jouyen sending me away to my six-month sentence in Ingdanrad. The one thing that felt like mine — my love for Tiernan, my desire to be with him — had been tainted. If strangers hadn't shown me that vision of the log cabin, would I have gone looking for him? Freed him from prison? Cared for him in the hospital? Dreamed of travelling to Nyhemur with him?

Footsteps crunched on the dry grass. Akohin nudged me. I sat up, squinting into the sun. Tsiala stood outside the invisible circle of runes protecting our cabin. She was dressed in black leather armour despite the heat.

"Neve sent me to warn you," she said. "Ivar's pissed. He was sure Tiernan would face the noose. So, y'know, don't go into any dark alleys."

"Hadn't planned on it," I said. "Is that all?"

Tsiala's mouth twisted. "Can we talk? Alone?"

I shrugged. Akohin pinched the air, disabling the protective runes, then headed into our cabin. Tsiala took his place under the chestnut tree. This grove was full of memories with her — water-calling and combat lessons, kisses, fights, our breakup.

"So, uh." She cleared her throat. "I talked to Alesso a couple months back. Told him he's my cousin."

That was the last thing I'd expected her to bring up. "How'd it go?" I ventured.

"Terribly at first. He's kind of racist, and defended his alliance with my shitty warlord father, but . . . he's learning. I figured if you could get through to Nerio, maybe I can get through to Alesso. I think he's glad to have another living relative."

"Huh," was all I could say.

"Anyway," Tsiala went on, "remember he and Síona got sentenced to teach Ferish at the university? They asked me to help. Once my sentence at the militia complex is done, we'll start preparing for the autumn semester. It won't pay much, but I can live in the dorms."

"Really? You're staying in Ingdanrad?"

"For a while, at least." She looked at me sideways. "What about you? I saw Geniod on my way here. He said he's moving back to the Kae gathering place."

"Oh." I picked at my nails. "We, uh, had a fight."

"About Tiernan? I heard the rumours."

My cheeks burned. "Whatever you heard is wrong."

"Is it?"

"What's *that* supposed to mean?"

"You wouldn't be the first girl to fall for an older itheran man, a powerful and respected soldier, then find out what he's really like. Know how that story ends? Dying in childbirth in a refugee camp."

"You're comparing Tiernan and me to your *parents*?"

Tsiala shrugged. "They were about the same age when—"

"You don't know Tiernan," I snapped. "He cares about me."

"So do I. And there were plenty of times you should've told me to fuck off, but you didn't."

She was right. Early on, it had been easy to tell her not to touch me. Once we became a couple, it got tougher to hold her at bay. Everything had felt so cloudy and confusing. I'd *wanted* to sleep with her, but she'd always been a step ahead, pulling me into things before I was ready.

"Listen." Tsiala laid her hand over mine on the grass. "I dunno what Geniod said, but . . . he loves you. I wish my father cared that much. If you're choosing between him and an outlaw mercenary, you better think damned hard about that choice."

※

At the hospital, Tiernan's breakout was all anyone could talk about. It was hard to forget with Clan Murragh's architect druids traipsing around the in-patient hall, fitting new glass into the window frames. Wanted posters went up offering a reward for Tiernan's capture. I felt the whispers and stares on my back. Some people sounded sure we'd plotted it together, while others clicked their tongues in sympathy for "that poor broken-hearted girl."

Janekke invited me to eat lunch outside in the relative privacy of the hospital gardens. "You know," she said, picking at a bowl of pickled cabbage and cold blood sausage, "I usually stay out of other people's relationships. But when one person's recovering from a coma, I think it's justified to offer a little help."

I looked up from my own bowl of freshly picked greens. "What do you mean?"

"History repeats itself. Years ago, I watched Tiernan fall in love with Marijka — a kind, patient girl who devoted her life to healing people. I didn't see their breakup, but I know why it happened. She wanted to settle down, have kids, make a home together. He didn't."

"But—" I blinked in confusion. "I thought he wanted to marry her."

"He thought so, too. He even proposed, but Marijka turned him down. It's . . . complicated." Janekke smiled wryly. "It's also not my story to tell. But if I can give you one piece of advice, talk this through with him. Figure out what you each want and whether it works together. Be honest, and trust he'll be honest with you. He's a good man."

"What if . . . what I want isn't actually what *I* want?"

She tilted her head. "You'll need to explain that one."

With a sigh, I explained the log cabin vision, how my love for Tiernan felt corrupted by strangers. Janekke listened in near silence, crunching away on her pickled cabbage.

"Firstly," she said, "the other Kateiko's parents aren't strangers. They were *your* parents until the worlds split. You were — what, ten or eleven? They might not know you well anymore, but I'm sure they love you. Secondly, that vision is up for interpretation. You're living alone in a log cabin with a teenage boy, but you view Akohin as a brother. So why did you interpret the Kateiko and Tiernan in the shoirdryge as lovers?"

I opened my mouth, then closed it. They hadn't kissed or anything, just laughed as they made tea. "I don't know. It was a few weeks after Tjarnnaast. Tiernan had held me as I cried, and . . . I felt close to him."

"Oh? Sounds like you wanted to get closer."

I smacked her arm. "Don't be gross."

Janekke chuckled. "I'm just saying, it seems like you had feelings for Tiernan before the vision. Sure, maybe it coloured those feelings, but they're still yours."

The rest of the week passed in a blur of packing and planning. Travelling with Tiernan's horse, Gwmniwyr, was unexpectedly complex. He was too heavy for kinaru to carry. If we went north through the tunnels under the Turquoise Mountains, then exited at Dúnravn Pass, we'd have to cross the sky bridge into Tula territory, and no horse could climb the narrow spiral stairs up to the bridge. If we kept going to the next tunnel exit, we'd come out in Rin territory — enemy land.

Begrudgingly, I got help from Neve, who arranged passage on a galleon hauling Clan Ríain's metalworks to Caladheå. Her cousin would take Gwmniwyr to Parr Manor's stables and our luggage to my home. In the meantime, Akohin and I would fly to Nettle Ginu.

The day I finished work for good, we had dinner with Círa, Finín, and Pádraig to say goodbye. I'd been so miserable and paranoid that it was strange to remember I'd occasionally enjoyed living in Ingdanrad. A tiny part of me wished I had more time here as a free woman — time to explore the city, to study medicine like a normal apprentice, to have control over my life.

Near dusk, I changed into a cottonspun shirt and leggings, slung a canvas rucksack over my shoulder, and strapped my and Tiernan's swords to my hips. Akohin and I climbed the mountain to a remote clearing in the woods. Once night fell, he folded his hands over his mouth and made a warbling, loon-like call. A kinaru descended through the darkness and crunched onto the dry grass. I climbed onto its back and wrapped my arms around its long neck.

The kinaru launched into the air. Its enormous wings flapped around me, catching a warm wind that buoyed us up. Ainu-Seru had brought clouds to block the moonlight and mask our departure. The flat black sky felt infinite, spilling over the edges of the world. As we flew northwest, I chanced a look back. Ingdanrad was breathtaking at a distance. The thousands of firelit windows looked like flecks of gold scattered across the mountainside.

Akohin cawed. The clouds split above him, letting moonlight spill over us. He was a black-sailed ship cutting a path through an inky ocean. I followed in his wake, my braid streaming behind me, my last ties to Ingdanrad snapping and falling to earth.

37.

A NEW WORLD

The sky turned purple in the east as we neared Nettle Ginu. Dawn revealed huge swaths of rust-coloured conifers across the slopes. Akohin had warned me about the dryness, but it was another thing altogether to *feel* it. My lips grew chapped, and dust kept blowing into my eyes. The rainforest was becoming more like the wasteland I'd seen in visions.

My kinaru mount sank through the sky, looking for somewhere to land. Akohin led us to a stump-filled clearing blanketed in woodchips. A dark-haired man was sawing a log, filling the mountain air with the scrape of metal on wood. As we got close enough to see his face, I gasped. *Tiernan.*

The kinaru hit the ground with a *whump*, sending up clouds of sawdust. I tumbled off, coughing. Tiernan straightened up from the saw. We drifted toward each other like we weren't sure this was real.

His once-gaunt cheeks were fuller, his skin kissed with a sunburn, the nullifying cuff gone from his wrist. Now that he could stand upright, he was again taller than me.

"You made it," he breathed. "Thank the gods."

"You're sawing wood?" I asked. "At *dawn*?"

Tiernan shrugged. "The pain makes sleep difficult."

"Pain? The runes didn't wear off?"

He pulled his tunic over his head. Black runes twined around his body, so dark they must've been freshly applied. The rest of him was filling out, too. A layer of muscle covered his chest and arms.

"Oh," I squeaked, definitely not imagining him picking me up and . . .

A raven cackled in the distance. It took off into the sky, followed by the kinaru.

Tiernan hastily pulled his tunic back on. "I, uh, wanted to be ready. For battle."

"Mm-hmm." My voice came out too high. "And what's all this? The logging?"

"Ah — clearing land for a rainfall reservoir. If a forest fire breaks out in this weather . . ."

"Right. That makes sense."

He peered at me, his expression softening. "Did you travel all night? Do you need sleep? Breakfast?"

"Nei. Not yet. We, uh . . ." I tried to fiddle with my medic's woolwrap, startled to find swords instead. I unbuckled his scabbard and passed it to him. "We need to talk."

"I suppose we do." Tiernan brushed sawdust off stumps for us to sit on. "I have spent this week going round in my head. You asked if I have feelings for you, and . . . I ask that you hear my entire answer. It will sound like the one you want, but it is not."

"Oh," I stammered. "Um — okay."

He leaned forward, elbows on his knees. "The truth is, I have fallen in love with you. The pain in my body is nothing compared to being apart from you. The relief at my freedom is nothing compared to *your* freedom. My dreams for the future feel hollow without you in them. But . . ."

Dread crept out from a dark pit, snaking around me. "But?"

"My feelings do not matter." Sorrow tinged his smile. "We cannot be together. I am too old for you, Katja."

The dread gripped my lungs. "You mean I'm too young. Is that . . . still how you see me? The broken girl crying on your shoulder in Tjarnnaast?"

"No. Gods, no. *You* are not the problem."

"Then what is? What matters more than loving each other?"

Tiernan rubbed a hand down his face. "We are in different stages of our lives. I have had time to discover myself, my hopes and dreams and values. You deserve the freedom to chart your own course. Not the course of a jaded mercenary taking advantage of your trust."

"You wouldn't do that. I *know* you."

"Not on purpose. Love complicates things, though." He rested his chin on his hands, examining me. "What if I said your hair looks better as its natural brown?"

I'd stop dyeing it was my first thought. Anything to be more attractive to him. Yet I liked dyeing it — making the herbal infusion, breathing the peppery scents of sage and cloves, washing my hair with it once a week. It felt meditative. I liked matching Akohin, my adopted twin brother. I liked having control over some part of my life.

"See?" Tiernan said gently. "Advising the military requires me to constantly speak over people, insisting I am right. I have grown so used to it that I have trouble holding back. Even Nerio is still learning to stand up to me. I am not saying you are weak, simply that you have not had enough practice."

"Then give me practice. I—" A lump formed in my throat. "I'll do it right now. It doesn't matter what you think of my hair."

He chuckled. "Good. Although to be honest, I *do* like the black."

Warmth flooded through me. "Couldn't we just . . . take things slowly? It's not like we have to get married tomorrow. Right now I'd settle for kissing you."

His gaze flickered to my lips, then he turned away like it hurt to look at me. "There is . . . another problem. Remember in the hospital, I said I needed to tell you something?"

I paused, thrown. I thought his love for me *was* the thing. "What is it?"

He glanced at the blush of pink sky over the trees. "People will be waking soon. We should go somewhere we will not be interrupted."

✳

Tiernan had brought flatbread in a handkerchief, so we made a quick detour through the huckleberry patch to complete our makeshift breakfast, then headed down the mountain. Dry, rust-red pine needles covered the wooden steps. The only vegetation growing well among the trees were the ever-present nettles that snagged on our clothes.

"You asked once," he began, "how I know there are parallel worlds. The answer is that I came from one."

I missed a step and stumbled. He caught my arm, steadying me. "You *what*?"

"Recall Iollan och Cormic's work? His theory that people can pass through rifts between shoirdrygen? It is not just a theory. I am living proof."

"Wait." I pulled away, backing into the nettles. "How did — what *are* you?"

"Human. Just an ordinary man with bad luck and too much curiosity." Tiernan held out his hands, palms up. "Would you like to make sure?"

I took his hands. They were warm and solid, already forming new calluses. I touched his chest, feeling his heartbeat. It thrashed like a fish in a net. Sunlight falling through the trees illuminated gold flecks in his grey eyes. I stepped back before I caved to temptation and kissed him.

"How?" I asked. "What happened?"

He started down the steps again. "Like I said, too much curiosity. I was born Tiernan Heilesson in a country called Ålkatt, roughly equivalent to northern Sverba. I grew up buried in atlases and history books. At nineteen I got a job with a renowned explorer. The man was investigating rumours of a mystical place in the ocean where ships simply . . . vanished."

"A rift?"

"Precisely. We spent months at sea searching for it. Near its supposed location, a terrible storm hit, sinking our ship. That must be the truth behind the rumours, I thought. No rift. Just bad weather. Another boy and I survived in a longboat, drinking rainwater and eating salvaged hardtack, but . . . we were already weak from scurvy. Sickness took him. Days later, I washed up on a cold rocky shore. A group of hunters, dark-haired and tanned like you, nursed me back to health.

"Up the coast was a village of pale-skinned fishermen who spoke something like my language. They showed me a world map, explaining I had reached the so-called new world — the eastern side of this continent. I recognized the geography, yet all the place names were different. Ålkatt was part of a Sverbian Empire.

Then I realized I *had* gone through a rift. I was, quite literally, in a new world."

"Wow," I said faintly.

"Indeed." Tiernan flashed me a dry smile. "All I had was my sword and some coins in a non-existent currency. So I melted my coins into raw gold, bought Gwmniwyr, and worked as a mercenary while figuring out what to do. No one wanted to come on a suicide mission to help me find the rift again. I had no way to cross back into my world. So when I heard of a druid who studied rift magic, I set out west across the continent to find him."

"Iollan och Cormic?" I asked.

"Correct." He paused to cut nettles back from the path with a folding knife. "Unfortunately, Iollan had no patience for seeking out rifts. He wanted to make one instead. I agreed to help, but over time my conscience wore me down. What right did we have to meddle with the world? What disasters might we wreak? So I quit as his acolyte, resigning myself to never returning home."

"You're *stuck* here?"

"So it seems. I have not seen my parents, brothers, or school friends in fourteen years and doubt I ever will again. No doubt they believe I am dead."

My heart cracked. Tiernan's medical records had said he lost "everyone and everything" in a war and fled here as a refugee. It must've been unbearable — grieving loved ones who were still alive, being powerless to soothe *their* grief, knowing their memories of him would slowly fade. No wonder he had combat neurosis. I touched his arm. He looked up from cutting nettles, apprehensive.

"I'm so sorry," I said. "I can't imagine how hard that's been."

Tiernan managed a smile. After a moment's hesitation, he lifted my hand and kissed it. Once he turned away, I kissed the spot where his lips had brushed my skin.

"That was only part of the problem," he said, continuing down the steps. "The shoirdryge you keep seeing diverged from this world seven or eight years ago. I came from a different one, an earlier divergence. By my reckoning, they separated six centuries ago."

"Six *centuries*?"

"Aye, when Sverba first invaded Gallun. In this world, they conquered the islands. In my world, our nations forged a truce. We intermarried to the point of becoming one ethnicity, speaking one language and practising one religion. Magic was commonplace. When I came to this world . . . nothing made sense. Some people saw me as Sverbian, some as Gallnach. I had to learn new languages, new customs, an entire new version of history."

"Then when you woke from a coma . . ."

"My mind reverted to my past life. I wanted desperately to speak to you, but I could not find the words."

"What about before then?"

"Before?"

"You didn't tell me any of this." I couldn't hold back the hurt in my voice. "You hid the most important part of your life. For *years*."

Tiernan sighed. "It is not just about me. The more you learn about shoirdrygen, the more your concept of the universe changes. Religion falls apart. What is life anymore? Identity? Fate? I did not tell Nerio until he was your age, either. But I know too many people have lied to you, so . . . I am sorry. Truly."

Part of me wanted to forgive him immediately, but Pádraig's lessons about processing my emotions had sunk in, and I was too exhausted from travelling all night to think clearly. We kept walking in silence. Wrens and waxwings sang from the foliage, greeting the day.

"What about Marijka?" I finally asked. "Is this why she refused to marry you?"

Tiernan winced. "In a way."

"What way?" I pressed.

He began flipping his knife in the air and catching it. "Maika thought if I found a rift, I would abandon her and return to my world. I promised not to, but . . . I had my own fears. Ones I was too scared to talk about. She thought my fear was about her, that I did not love her enough to commit."

"What were you scared of?"

"The unknown. I had only been in this world a few years and had no idea what it would do to my body and mind in the long run. No idea if my soul would go to Thaerijmur with hers after death. And, well . . ." His cheeks flushed red. "Maika wanted children. I am not even sure I can have them."

Heat rose in my cheeks. "You . . ."

"In a metaphysical sense, not a medical one. If I was not born in this world, am I truly alive here? Can I create life myself? If I do, does that violate the fundamental laws of the universe?"

"Huh," was all I could say. He'd certainly had more time to think about this than I had.

In a way, I saw what Tiernan meant about being too old for me. He'd lived two whole lives before meeting me — one in his world, then another learning to exist here. I'd never catch up. He'd always be older, more experienced, more knowledgeable. Still, that wasn't necessarily bad. It might keep us from making stupid mistakes like having a baby that could break the universe.

That wasn't a thought I felt ready for, so I turned to his other fears. After fourteen years here, his body and mind seemed fine, coma aside. As for where our spirits went after death . . . maybe all the afterworlds were linked like shoirdrygen. Maybe I could leave Aeldu-yan and find him wherever Ålkatt people went, just like I'd found him in the desert. And even if I couldn't spend death with Tiernan, I still wanted to spend life with him.

It seemed so simple put like that. I wanted to be together however we could, however made us both stronger. I didn't know how to strike that balance, though. I'd looked so pale and sickly after living with him in the hospital. I'd told him to cut my throat so he could escape. He didn't *need* to pressure me into making bad choices, since I kept making them anyway.

I stumbled again. Tiernan caught me just before I went face first into the nettles.

"Are you okay?" he asked, frowning.

"Mmm." I rubbed my eyes. "I need sleep."

"Någvakt bøkkhem," he muttered. "We should not have gone so far from the settlement."

"S'okay. There's a clearing just ahead near a brook. Unless that's been taken over by nettles, too."

"We shall see." Tiernan looped his arm around me, holding me up. "If so, I can burn them away."

❋

I dreamed of the cabin in the woods. Nettles crept up its log walls, biting the timber. Through the open window, I watched Tiernan and me inside, tangled in each other's arms. He pulled her braid aside to kiss her neck. *Wait*, I tried to call. Did she know where he came from? I grasped the windowsill, leaning in. Nettles scraped my hands. *Wait!* I pleaded.

My lashes fluttered. I sat up blearily in the shade of a cottonwood. Tiernan lay asleep, head on his arm. Waves of yellow grass eddied across the clearing, filling the air with a sweet, dusty scent. A bluejay hopped through the brook, cooling itself in the last trickle of water that hadn't evaporated in the midday sun.

Tiernan was so still I touched his lips to check he was breathing.

Aeldu save me, I wanted to kiss him. Yet that dream . . . I'd never thought much before about why the other versions of us were alone in the woods. She had a kinaru tattoo, so where were the Rin? Where were Tiernan's friends?

My mind drifted to Tsiala. On the spring equinox, I made her come inside to the festival so my family and Círa could watch over us. Whenever she pressured me to sneak off, it felt like how Neve had isolated me — asking me to meet her alone, hanging out with her family but not mine, arranging for me to live with her clan instead of telling me I could take refuge in the Kae district.

Geniod had said my parents didn't want that log cabin life for me. To some extent, I saw their point. Of course they wouldn't want me cut off from my family, friends, and culture. Tiernan had never tried to take that from me, yet he'd just done it by accident, taking me away from Nettle Ginu when I was too tired to think straight. He wanted to take me to Nyhemur alone. And if he ever found a rift back to his world, maybe he'd want to take me there, too.

I took my journal from my canvas rucksack and started writing. Like Janekke said, the other Kateiko's parents were once my parents. If they loved me, why had they shown me that log cabin vision? Maybe it was a warning. Maybe they knew Tiernan wasn't from this world. Or they wanted to show me another version of myself, a reminder that life had multiple paths. That I could chart my own course.

Pages later, I set my journal in the grass. *Right*, I thought, heart pounding. *I'm really doing this.*

I touched his shoulder. "Tiernan?"

He stirred. "Hmm?"

"I don't care that you're older. I don't care that you're from another world. I'm in love with you. And I heard you out, so it's your turn to hear me out."

He sat up blinking. In a strained voice, he said, "Very well."

"Know how marriages work in my culture? The couple's family and friends put their crests on a joining cord, showing their approval. If someone *doesn't* approve, it's a huge deal. That rarely happens, though. Usually people show their disapproval long before the engagement, and everyone gets together to figure out a solution."

Tiernan's dark brows knit together. "Where are you going with this?"

"If you start pressuring me, abusing my trust, my family and friends will let you know. So will Jorum and Nerio. If I start acting weird, giving into your influence, they'll let *me* know. As long as we're around people who love us, they'll keep us in check."

Leaf shadows played across his face. His expression shifted like a cloud, never quite forming something solid.

I took a deep breath. "Janekke said we should talk about what we each want. First of all . . . you just want to visit Nyhemur, right? Not live there?"

"Of course. There are many places I would love to visit with you, but this coast is our home."

"So you're okay with staying in this world? Forever, I mean?"

Tiernan nodded. "In the early years with Maika, I had little binding me here. Now I have brothers in Jorum and Nerio. I have Nhys at the Golden Oak. I love Hanaiko and Samulein like my niece and nephew, and I expect to feel the same about Dunehein and Rikuja's new baby."

"About that." My cheeks warmed. "You mentioned Marijka wanted children, but not if *you* do."

"Ah." Tiernan scratched his beard. "Hypothetically speaking . . . yes. Very much. What about you?"

"I think so. Not anytime soon, but one day."

"And if I cannot have them? Would that . . . bother you?"

"Nei. I already thought about it with Tsiala." My insides squirmed, but I pushed onward. "I don't know if I could handle adoption after everything we suffered with Hako and Samu, getting them back from the Sarteres, but . . . we could use a surrogate father. Would that bother *you*?"

Tiernan folded his hands in front of his face. We'd been standing beside a chasm and I'd been stupid enough to step forward, plummeting into the dark abyss. Of course he'd hate the idea of me bearing another man's child, of *course*—

"I should say it bothers me," he said. "Anything that would convince you to forget about me. But the truth is, I already thought about it with Maika. I could handle it."

A gust caught me in the chasm, bearing me back upward. "Really?"

"Katja . . ." He took my hand in his callused one. "I want you to have everything you desire. Not all of it can come from me, nor should it. And it is clear from seeing Jorum with Hako and Samu that a blood relation is not required to be a good father."

"So . . . are you saying . . ."

His mouth edged into a smile. "I am asking for a chance to give you the rest. Everything you want in life that I can provide. Starting with a kiss, if you still want that."

"Yes," I said faintly.

Tiernan cupped my jaw and leaned in. My breath caught. His lips were warm and firm, his beard rough against my skin. He smelled like fresh-cut wood and sun-baked grass. All too soon, he pulled away, his grey eyes searching mine. *Is this okay?* he seemed to ask.

I slid my hand behind his head, weaving my fingers into his hair, and drew him back into a kiss. After all this time, all my work to keep him alive, we were *together*. Lovers. The word sent tingles down my spine.

"Katja." He uttered my name like a prayer, like the most precious thing he could offer in votive. "I love you. Gods' sakes, how I love you."

"I love you, too," I whispered. "I love you, Tiernan Heilesson."

A soft groan escaped him. *Names have power*, he'd once told me, and we'd found their magic. He wrapped his arms around me, pulling me down into the grass. Colourful specks flitted across my vision. This time, though, I wasn't seeing another world. I was seeing him.

✳

Lying in the tall grass with Tiernan was so surreal I kept touching him to make sure he existed. It felt like meeting him all over again. I had a million questions about his old life in Ålkatt, which he answered with amused patience. This clearing was an apt place for the conversation. Last winter, when I came here to avoid people, it had been veiled by snow. Now I was seeing everything hidden underneath.

Drifting through the field of his life, I kept finding flowers that opened with new realizations. His accent seemed so strong because it wasn't from any itheran language I'd ever heard. He spent so much time with Jorumgard because he needed help passing as Sverbian — someone to practise the language with, to remind him of the customs, to answer questions about Sverba that Tiernan couldn't. He'd kept his first name even though it sounded Gallnach because it was all he had left of his old identity.

Whenever the conversation waned, we slipped into each other's arms, finding solace in each other's eyes and mouths and hands. The one time he began kissing my neck, I lifted my shoulder to nudge him away, remembering my dream of the nettle-covered cabin. He moved his lips back to mine without comment. No pressure, no need to explain myself. I hadn't known I could love him more, but being with him felt so . . . natural.

"Gods' sakes, you smell good," he murmured, nuzzling my braid. "Like herbal tea."

I laughed. "It's my hair dye. Sage and cloves."

The mention of food made us realize how hungry we were. Up the brook we found a thicket of raspberries. I plucked a berry and held it to Tiernan's lips. He bit it gently and kissed me, slipping it into my mouth. Fire streaked through my body, lighting up nerves I didn't know I had. I pulled back, blushing fiercely.

Casting around for a distraction, I said, "So, uh — how many shoirdrygen do you know about?"

"Only two for sure." Amusement tinged his voice. "Although folklore is full of ones that *might* exist. Worlds where this king won the crown instead of that king, or magic has been forgotten, or gigantic lizards roam the earth."

"Those just sound like oosoo." I drifted through the thicket, picking raspberries. "What's the weirdest one you've heard?"

"Oh, definitely the goat world. No humans, just mountain goats. Goat king. Goat priests. Goats herding other goats."

I frowned, not sure if he was teasing me. A smile played around his face. I flung a raspberry at him, which he caught and popped into his mouth.

At dusk, we returned to Nettle Ginu hand in hand. Thankfully most of my family and friends were away scouting Algard Island so we only had to deal with a few people. Grinning, Nili whispered that Tiernan *was* awfully lush for an itheran. In Tema's plank house, Emehein gave Tiernan a look that said he'd be watching, though it was hard to seem intimidating with toddlers wrapped around his ankles.

Geniod awaited us in Temal's plank house. His shoulders were drawn tight and he rubbed his palm anxiously. Akohin lingered nearby, looking sheepish. I suspected he'd been keeping Geniod posted on my whereabouts for the last week, but being constantly watched no longer annoyed me.

"Go on," Tiernan whispered. "I have something to discuss with Akohin, anyway."

I met Geniod near his bed. Everything I'd planned to say vanished from my mind. Instead, I dropped my rucksack and hugged him. "Sorry," I muttered into his shoulder.

He kissed my hair. "Apology accepted. Though I see you're not taking my advice about Tiernan."

I pulled back and took a deep breath. "We love each other. I want you and my parents to approve, though. I want your advice on doing it right. So . . ." I fished in my purse and held out the swan and mountain cat makiri.

Geniod curled my fingers over the figurines. "How about asking them yourself?"

Apprehensive, I sat cross-legged on his mattress, a figurine in each hand. I closed my eyes and imagined looking out the window. A ghostly swan landed on the sill. After months of lessons, I'd still never managed to coax it inside. *Please*, I thought. *I'm ready now. I need your help.*

Something moved sideways in my mind like a bolt sliding out of its lock. My imaginary plank house sharpened into the real one — mattresses on dirt platforms, glowing vellum lanterns, bark mats on the floor. The swan leapt off the windowsill and soared inside. It circled Tiernan and Akohin, deep in conversation, then circled my cousin Kotiod, talking to his oldest sister's husband. Two pairs of brothers-in-law.

Across the plank house, a ghostly mountain cat padded through the door. It turned, stretched, and ran a huge paw down the doorframe. Temal's and Geniod's fireweed crest was carved there among the house's other family crests. It was my fireweed, too, but Tiernan didn't have a crest to carve there at all.

The swan and mountain cat faded into mist. I opened my eyes, dizzy. It had worked. I'd reached my parents' spirits in Aeldu-yan. Breathlessly, I described the vision.

Geniod's brows furrowed. "Can I offer my interpretation? They're open to you being with Tiernan, but . . . they're worried. You belong here. He doesn't."

"He could," I said. "He can marry me and join the Tula-jouyen."

"Yes, but would he? Swearing loyalty to the Tula means giving up his mercenary work. If you have children, what language will you speak to them? Will Tiernan be buried in our grounds, or will he want an itheran funeral? These are serious discussions you two will need to have."

"I know." I ran my thumbs over the makiri's polished wood. "We will, I promise."

Geniod managed a smile. "For now, I have one condition. You and Tiernan sleep on opposite sides of the plank house."

38.

CRABAPPLE LAKE

First thing the next day, Geniod started looking for work to keep Tiernan and me busy. Kotiod jumped in and invited us to pick crabapples with him and Nili, who amazingly were still together. I'd expected that in nine months they would've gotten annoyed or bored of each other. It was shaping up to be a baking-hot day, so I rummaged through my girl cousins' trunks for summer clothes. I settled on an open-backed shirt and leggings cut high up the thigh, both of pale green cottonspun.

As we hiked down the mountain, Nili whispered with a giggle that Tiernan was staring at me. He seemed oddly distant, though, barely talking or smiling. Maybe he thought I was showing too much skin. Itheran women always wore long-sleeved dresses. Or maybe he was annoyed at being around teenagers, or . . . *This is stupid*, I scolded myself. I'd just ask him once we were alone.

We tossed wicker baskets into a pair of canoes and paddled down a stream to a lake. The turquoise water was surprisingly high, coming right up to the shoreline pines and crabapple trees. It probably meant the glaciers out east were melting. Once we tied our canoes, Nili and Kotiod took their baskets a stone's throw up the shore. I could hear them teasing each other but couldn't make out the words.

"What's wrong?" I asked, turning to Tiernan. "You were quiet the whole way here."

He blinked like he'd been caught out. "I, uh, need to tell you something. About the war. But it is hard to concentrate with such a beautiful girl around."

"Oh." I covered my mouth, hiding a grin. "Sorry."

"Do not apologize." He kissed my temple, grazing my hairline. "I will tell you while we work. Perhaps that will distract me."

I pulled off my boots and climbed into a crabapple tree. Straddling a branch, I started picking the small golden-red fruits and tossing them down to Tiernan. He caught them and dropped them into a wicker basket.

"Long ago," he began, "I told you that shoirdrygen are created by some terrible catastrophe. Something so terrible it rips apart time, forming two different versions of history."

"I remember. I asked what kind of catastrophe, and you said I'd be happier not knowing."

Tiernan smiled ruefully. "Theological scholars have many theories. Iollan och Cormic suspects it relates to temporal mages. Their magic warps time, making it as fragile as their own lives. If they teeter on the brink of death, two timelines form — one where they live, one where they die."

"Yan taku." I stretched forward to reach a cluster of crabapples. "You think Iollan's right?"

"I do. You know the story of Rånyl Sigrunnehl, first queen of Sverba?"

"Yeah. She murdered Gallun's druid assembly, then burned and pillaged her way across the islands. Róisín ó Conn said it launched six centuries of flames — *ohhh*."

"Now you see." Tiernan caught a crabapple and bit into its crisp flesh. He winced at the sourness. "Rånyl Sigrunnehl is history's most infamous temporal mage. In *my* world, mere months after she slaughtered the druid assembly, she was killed in battle. Her empire collapsed in its infancy, splintering into smaller regions like my home, Ålkatt."

"So who created the other shoirdryge, the newer one? Astra Måritehl?"

"It seems so. That is what I discussed with Akohin last night. Ainu-Seru's mercenaries stabbed Astra during their invasion of Brånnheå. In this world, she survived and rebuilt the Rúonbattai. In a parallel world, she died. Hence her oak crests there are powerless and forgotten."

"But then . . ." A chill crept down my spine. "What happens if we kill her now?"

He drifted closer, gazing up at me in the tree. "It will splinter the world again. Two different versions of us, two different futures. One pair may have a peaceful life, happily in love, free of the Rúonbattai. The other may go on chasing Astra Måritehl forever, killing her over and over, splitting the world again and again."

"Nei. No way. There has to be *some* other option."

Tiernan laughed softly. He curled his hand around my ankle, resting his cheek against my bare calf. "One of the many reasons I love you. Stubborn resolve in the face of endless suffering."

Weariness filled his voice. I was gradually realizing what it meant to be with him, both as a lover and a partner sharing unearthly burdens. My love for him felt like a cut jewel. The more I explored it, the more sides I found — some clear and glittering, some scratched and cloudy. Leaning over, I kissed the top of his head. I didn't know where to start thinking about this, but we'd always made a good team.

*

At midday we paused for lunch. I waded into the lake and used water-calling to pull a trout into my hands. We wrapped it up with crabapples in thick leaves and roasted them in a fire Tiernan built. It was handy to have a jinrayul around, and I certainly didn't mind when he caved to the heat and took off his shirt. *Wow*, Nili mouthed at me. Kotiod elbowed her, making her giggle.

It was too hot to work in the afternoon, so Nili and Kotiod went swimming. Tiernan and I stayed in the forest's shade. We sat together on a bed of moss, him leaning against a thick rioden trunk, me between his legs and leaning against his bare chest. I felt so warm and sleepy and content that it was hard to focus, but with Tula scouts away looking for Astra, we had no time to waste.

"Okay," I said. "Tell me everything you've already thought of. All the potential ways we can stop Astra and *not* split the world."

"Hmmm." Tiernan's deep voice resonated through my spine. "One, we capture and imprison her. Not ideal considering she already escaped prison."

"*Caladheä's* prison. Ingdanrad has better security."

"True, but people there have strong grudges. If they know Astra is the Rúonbattai commander, someone may murder her and split the world, anyway."

"Fair point," I admitted. "What else?"

"We kill her so thoroughly she has no chance of survival. I am not sure it would matter, though. Say we tear her limb from limb. Does that mean we are *already* in the timeline where she dies? Did the world split back when she foresaw her death, or when it actually happens?"

"Fucking hell," I muttered.

Tiernan chuckled and kissed the back of my head. "Method three is pure speculation. If we nullify her magic, her influence on time will lift. Her fate will not affect the world."

I twisted around to gape at him. "Really? That could work?"

"Maybe. I am not sure temporal magic *can* be nullified. Clerics say it is a gift from the Sverbian gods. That separates it from typical magic — fire- or water-calling, for example, skills that can be gained with practice — and aligns it more closely with attuning."

"Oh," I said, surprised. "Because it's a gift from our aeldu?"

"Right. In prison, I overheard guards talking. A viirelei prisoner with a nullifying cuff once escaped by shifting into a sparrow and flying out through the bars."

"Wait. So *I* could've attuned in prison?"

"Presumably. You would still have been a wolf in a cage, though. With a concussion."

"Hmm." I settled back against his chest. "Are you sure it's that similar to temporal magic? Astra spent years at a stavehall honing her skill. Our attuned forms are thrust upon us, often painfully and without warning."

Tiernan traced the bite scars on my forearm. "I suppose. But there are other parallels between Aikoto spirituality and temporal magic, yes? Such as makiri and Astra's oak crests?"

"Only because she copied us. She stole sacred knowledge from Olina Kae and bastardized it. *That* wasn't gifted to her."

His fingers stilled on my arm. "Then maybe none of it was."

"What do you mean?"

"Picture it. Queen Rånyl claims her magic is a gift from the gods, setting herself up as a divine leader. She builds an empire where clerics repeat her story, choosing a select few people to train as the next divine leaders. It would be one of history's greatest lies."

"So then . . . it *is* normal magic? Something we can nullify?"

A laugh rippled through him, vibrating my bones. "Gods help me. I have spent so long pretending to be Sverbian that I have stopped questioning their ways. But *you*—"

Tiernan wrapped his arms around my waist. He pulled my braid aside and started kissing my neck. My nerves lit up. *Oh*, it felt nice — but it was too much like my dream of the nettle-covered cabin. Heat rolled off him, making me dizzy.

"Wait," I gasped.

He stopped instantly. "Sorry. I—"

"It's fine. Just — *wow*, it's hot." I pulled away, fanning myself. "Feel like going in the lake?"

Tiernan's mouth quirked with a smile. I padded barefoot across the moss and waded into the blissfully cool water. Nili and Kotiod were farther up the shore, splashing each other. Her shrieking laughter carried throughout the valley. Tiernan pulled off his boots and followed me until we were both neck-deep. I dipped my head under the surface, came up, and blinked droplets off my eyelashes. I felt better here in my domain. More in control.

"Okay," I said, treading water. "So if we *can* nullify Astra's magic, then *how* do we?"

"Good question." Tiernan rubbed the runes dyed onto his chest, checking they weren't smudging in the lake. "It would be difficult to put runes on her directly. The other typical way is for the target to stand on runes. Again, difficult to get her into precisely the right spot."

"How much area can they cover? Like, could we nullify an entire battlefield?"

"Theoretically, yes. Though we would still have to lure her into battle there. How do you trap someone who can see the future?"

I lay back and floated, gazing at the brilliant blue sky. I'd led us into a trap in Ingdanrad even though Tsiala warned me. Finding Alesso and stopping the coup had seemed worth the risk. Astra didn't care what happened to anyone else, though. She'd murdered her mage allies to save her own skin.

Nei, I thought. *Not just hers.*

"Ivar," I said breathlessly.

"Hm?"

"We use him as bait." I twisted out of my float, finding the rocky ground with my feet. "Astra already lost one child, her still-born daughter. She helped Ivar escape the stavehall raid in Caladheå even though it meant she got arrested. She'll do whatever it takes to protect him."

"That ... could work." Tiernan's voice sounded odd. He rubbed his wet hand across his jaw, leaving sparkling drops on his beard. "Gods' sakes. We could really do it. No more war, no splitting the world, just ..."

"Us. Together in this world."

His gaze went to my lips, but he didn't move. I'd asked him to wait, so he did. The chokehold of my dream eased. I didn't need to be afraid. I wanted us to start learning each other in this new way.

I pushed through the water and lifted my face to his. He kissed me, gently at first, then firmer. I looped my arms around his neck, then kicked off the ground and hooked my bare legs around his hips. Tiernan inhaled sharply. He curled his hands under my thighs, holding me up.

"Katja—" His voice came out strained. "I would hardly call this going slowly."

I grinned. "One step at a time. How about that?"

"That, uh—" He cleared his throat. "What would you like the next step to be?"

I tilted my head, exposing my neck. "You can start there."

* * *

Once the air cooled, we reluctantly went back to picking crab-apples. While we worked, we tossed ideas back and forth, figuring out a battle plan. One problem was how to capture Ivar. Astra was watching over him through Olina's garden, and as a militia soldier, he had more protection than we did.

"Then we need someone above the militia," I mused, perched in another tree. "Someone like Neve."

"*Neve?*" Tiernan echoed from the ground. "After everything she did to you?"

"I know, I know. But she took my side over Ivar's. Opposing the Rúonbattai is the only thing she's ever been honest about."

"No." He sliced his hand through the air. "I will not make you deal with her again—"

"It's our best option. She's been getting close to him for months, earning his trust. Besides, if she can smuggle Gwmniwyr out of Ingdanrad, she can smuggle a soldier."

Another problem was Ivar himself might be a temporal mage. Ingdanrad's clerics could've been training him to become the Rúonbattai's next divine leader. That would explain how he knew *The Lilac Queen* was missing. He probably foresaw Tsiala taking it, figured she was stealing it for me, and searched my home. He didn't seem very *good* at temporal magic yet, considering his failed coup. Astra had struggled in her early years, too, accidentally driving the Iyo-jouyen out of the alliance her father had forged. As long as we warned Neve, she had a chance of outmanoeuvring Ivar — though we'd have to make sure that if he died, it was in a nullified zone, too.

Once we returned to Nettle Ginu, we took our plan to Naneko, the Okorebai-Tula. She discussed it with her advisors, and the next morning, she sent Tula scouts to start looking for suitable battle-fields near Algard Island. Emehein flew to Caladheå to tell Nerio, so he could try to keep Captain Valrose from killing Astra before we were ready. Akohin flew back to Ingdanrad to talk with Neve.

That left Tiernan and me to figure out the rune trap. The Tula had picked the lock on his nullifying cuff, so the runes were still intact for us to use as a reference. The stronger their effect, the better — Tiernan's plan was to reverse-engineer the healing runes dyed onto his chest, isolating the amplification components and adapting them to nullifying runes.

Naneko lent us the canoe-carving workshop to experiment in. I cut sheets of soft inner bark from pine trees to use as paper. Tiernan sketched his potential designs with charcoal, then we replicated them on the dirt floor with sawdust. We took turns standing on them and trying to call water or fire. I loved watching him work, the way his brows furrowed in thought and his scarred hands glided across the bark paper. His gentle touches left charcoal smudges on my skin like little shadow kisses.

We worked day in, day out. My family brought us food and helped us test the nullifying runes. Geniod sat cross-legged amidst the sawdust and tried to communicate with my parents' makiri. He described it as trying to think of someone's name and failing. Tiernan smacked his hands together in triumph. His theory was that since makiri-reading and temporal magic both took place in the mind, nullifying runes should work similarly on them.

On another searingly hot afternoon, Nili dashed in and said a scout was back with news. He and the others been flying over

Algard Island, struggling in the perpetual frozen fog, when the fog began to clear. No one knew why or how long it would last, but one thing seemed certain — it was our best chance to find Astra.

✳

Tiernan and I tossed supplies into canvas rucksacks. I took my fir branch blanket and healing supplies while he packed food and our rune designs. Neve had made matching gold bracelets and sent one back with Akohin. Each had an iron bead, etched with magnetic tracking runes that would guide us to each other, and a glass bead etched with trigger runes. I smashed the glass one, which would break hers in turn, signalling it was time to capture Ivar.

A kinaru arrived to carry us again. Geniod, Akohin, and Ainu-Seru came with us, flying west over a forested peninsula. We landed by a lake near the coast, just across an inlet from Algard Island. Tula scouts were living here in secret camps. Hardly had our feet touched the dirt when a goldeneye duck and a dove swooped down and shifted. Malana had javelins strapped to her back while her wife, Aoreli, had a bow and arrows. They looked windswept and exhausted, but Malana still wrapped me in a bear hug.

"What's this about you two hooking up?" she said with a grin, nodding at Tiernan.

"You heard already?" I said in disbelief.

Aoreli laughed. "There's not much to do out here except gossip. Speaking of which, do we have news for you."

Our kinaru waddled into the lake to hunt for fish while we talked. The Tula scouts had figured out what caused the fog. They'd spied Rin warriors flying all over Algard Island, smashing rocks and fallen logs carved with runes. Everywhere a rune sparked out, the fog began to fade.

Tiernan whistled. "That is astonishing magic. To cover that much ground, and for so long—"

"Sure," Malana said, sounding unimpressed. "What we care about is why they're destroying the runes. Did the Rúonbattai abandon the island? Or did the Rin-jouyen break their alliance?"

I glanced at Akohin. "We could ask."

Malana snorted. "The *Rin*? They'd never tell us."

A smile crept across Akohin's face. "No. But they wouldn't dare lie to a tel-saidu."

Aoreli and Malana traded a look. They hadn't asked who Akohin was, which probably meant they'd heard that, too.

Akohin took off, leaving the rest of us to wait. Twilight on the coast was refreshingly cool. We didn't want to draw attention with a campfire, so when I shivered, Tiernan slid his arm around my shoulders. Warmth flowed into my body as smoothly as poured water.

My gold bracelet still felt the same. The magnetic bead pulled ever so gently southeast. Its pull was meant to grow stronger as Neve got closer with Ivar, but I couldn't sense any change. I kept fiddling with the bead, twisting it on the chain, until Tiernan wrapped his hand around my wrist. "She will come," he soothed. "Have faith."

Past nightfall, as crickets chirped in the woods, Malana volunteered to take first watch while the rest of us slept. I cast Geniod a questioning look. His rule about Tiernan and me sleeping on opposite sides of the plank house didn't work here. Reluctantly, Geniod waved me on.

I dug my fir branch blanket out of my rucksack and snuggled up with Tiernan on a bed of moss. He kissed my cheek and draped an arm over me. For months now, I'd longed for someone to share my blanket with, a warm body to hold me through the nightmares. I couldn't ask for a warmer body than a fire mage.

39.

TIDAL FLAT

In the greyish-blue light of dawn, two birds appeared over the lake. I leapt up. My bracelet's magnetic pull was growing stronger, which meant Neve was on the move, but it wasn't her. Akohin landed first. The other bird, a storm petrel, shifted into a bare-chested young man with okoreni lines tattooed around his upper arm. *Fendul.*

For a long moment, we just looked at each other. When we last met, I'd bared my spirit to his family, confessing how much I resented them for sending me away from the Rin-jouyen. He'd left before saying a word to me. Now he swallowed hard like his words were stuck in his throat.

"We don't have much time," he got out. "Liet — Astra, I mean — is gone. So is my tema."

"*Gone?*"

"They vanished yesterday. We tore up our fog runes and scoured Algard Island. A Rin scout just found them on a ship down south.

They—" Fendul's mouth twisted. "Astra kidnapped my tema. She's threatening to kill her if we intervene."

"Oh, no." I felt an impulse to hug him, but my feet stayed rooted to the lakeshore. "I'm so sorry, Fen."

He flinched at the nickname. "It gets worse. The Rúonbattai captured an alatu."

I gasped. "From the legends? Astra has a sacred sea monster?"

"Held captive in a tank on the ship. She's going to smuggle it into Caladheå's harbour, then cut it open. By the time it bleeds to death, they'll be long gone."

"Yan kaid. And when it dies . . ."

Akohin finished my thought. "Every anta-saidu nearby will wake in a fury. They'll wipe out Caladheå in storms and tidal waves like we've never seen. A hundred thousand people dead, maybe more, and the Rúonbattai will claim the capital. Or what's left of it."

I covered my mouth, feeling sick. "Our family's there. My cousins, your uncle in prison—"

Tiernan wrapped his arm around my shoulders. "We can use that. We lay our trap as planned, then offer to trade Ivar for Fendul's mother and the sea monster."

Fendul rubbed his okoreni tattoo, studying us. "You'd really work with the Rin? After we've been at war for years?"

"Of course," I said. "Are *you* willing to kill Astra?"

He gave a dark laugh. "We don't have a choice."

❋

Astra was already so far south that none of our potential battle-fields worked anymore. Tiernan, who knew Eremur's geography best, drew a map in the dirt. We chose an uninhabited island for our new site. Aoreli rounded up Tula warriors while Malana flew to Caladheå to find Nerio. In case we lost the battle, they'd have to convince the city to prepare for an apocalypse — no easy task considering Captain Valrose didn't believe saidu existed. I wrote the hostage threat on a page torn from my journal.

Hello again, Astra. Remember me? I'm the girl who got your lover, Gúnnar Halvarind, executed for treason. I'm the girl who got your brother, Magnús Ainarind, killed in Tjarnnaast. Now I'm the girl who kidnapped your son. If you want Ivar back alive, bring Rumiga Rin and the alatu to me by sunset. The messenger will guide you.

Fendul left to dispatch the messenger and to gather Rin warriors. Akohin and Ainu-Seru came with Tiernan, Geniod, and me, summoning a strong wind to speed us along. Forested islands and glittering inlets passed below. We shot past ships, easily overtaking them. Rushing air stung my eyes and ripped my breath away. The fastest Rin and Tula warriors, mostly birds of prey and waterfowl, caught up on the way. My bracelet's magnetic pull kept growing, so Neve must've changed course to follow us.

At our chosen island, Tiernan pointed out a tidal flat. Our kinaru landed hard, splattering wet sand everywhere. Its webbed feet left huge prints that filled with water. Stomping happily, it wandered into the ocean to find lunch. Geniod took charge of the Tula, helping me haul driftwood and clumps of kelp off the tidal flat. Fendul and his Rin warriors used the debris to build defensive barricades along the shoreline forest.

Tiernan swept his arms through the air, drawing huge glowing symbols. They floated down and draped across the sand like gossamer, then faded away. He marked from the ocean to the barricades, then we tested the runes. Tiernan stood outside the nullified zone and tossed fireballs at it. They winked out in midair. I pulled tendrils of water from the ocean. Over the runes, they fell limp, splashing onto the ground. It was a dead zone. Astra would have no power in it, and neither would we.

In late afternoon, my bracelet pulled hard to the east. Two kinaru landed on the sand. Off slid Neve, wearing burlap robes belted with an iron chain. I barely recognized her. She'd smudged charcoal around her eyes, painted blue runes across her skin, and put her strawberry-blonde hair in a messy braid. Off the other kinaru came Tsiala in her leather armour, carrying Ivar's limp form.

"Did you kill him?" I asked apprehensively.

"Drugged him," Neve said. "He's just starting to wake. Aren't you, my stupid, handsome man?" She flicked Ivar's forehead, making him groan.

He was still in his red militia woolwrap, though his sword was gone. His hands were bound, and a nullifying cuff circled his wrist. To be safe, we tied him to a driftwood log in the nullified zone, then I flung seawater in his face. He gasped, spluttering.

"What . . ." he muttered, tugging at his bonds. He spied Neve and growled. "Lying bitch. What have you done?!"

Neve grinned, baring her teeth. They were dyed red. "Only what you deserve. Remember Kateiko?"

A laugh skittered from Ivar as he squinted up at me. "The undead freak of nature. Which god did you sell your soul to?"

I snorted. "A better one than you did, obviously."

"Yet you're still with *that* fool?" He nodded at Tiernan. "The idiot walked right into my trap."

Tiernan drew forward, hand on his sword hilt. "What trap?"

Ivar smirked. "The Nyhemur garrison. I used to serve there. A few hints that you and Jorumgard Tømasind are Rúonbattai spies, and . . . well, I hoped they would kill you, but the dungeon was enjoyable in its own way."

Tiernan looked as thrown as I felt. I'd spent so long looking for proof he fought in self-defence, and the proof was right here.

"Oh, yes," Ivar went on. "I took prison shifts just to see you. The infamous Tiernan Heilind, rotting in a dark hole. Gods' sakes, the things you said, thinking no one could hear."

"What things?" I asked.

Ivar leered at me. "Men get lonely down there, you know. They go mad from it. That's why I locked you up close by — a pretty little thing just out of reach. That's all he wanted. A warm, soft body to fuck."

I grabbed Tiernan before he lunged. Neve scooped a rock from the sand and smashed it into Ivar's mouth. He grunted in pain, rolled his jaw, and spat blood at her. She stomped on his crotch, making him howl.

Geniod pulled Tiernan and me aside. Quietly, he said Fendul wanted to speak with us. We met him by the driftwood barricades, out of earshot from Ivar. Fendul looked grim, rubbing his okoreni tattoo raw.

"We've been watching the ocean," he said. "Astra's not alone. She must've brought the entire Rúonbattai force here to seize Caladheå."

"Yan taku," I muttered. "How many of our warriors have shown up?"

"A dozen Tula and two dozen Rin. A few are still trickling in, but we Rin were scattered everywhere searching for my tema."

Tiernan looked to the sky. "What if Ainu-Seru slows the Rúonbattai ships down? That might buy enough time for help to arrive."

I will try. Ainu-Seru's hollow voice curled around us. *I am weak here, though. Saidu are not meant to stray this far from our homes.*

I slipped my hand into my leggings pocket, brushing my fingers over my parents' makiri. They'd sent me back to life once, saying it wasn't my time yet. Maybe this was finally our time. We just had to take Astra and Ivar down with us.

✳

As we waited, our shadows grew long across the sand. Neve perched on the log Ivar was bound to, tossing a rock from hand to hand. Tsiala looked bored like always. Fendul and Geniod paced back and forth, hands on their sword hilts. The setting sun reflected off rivulets of water, turning the tidal flat into a mirage.

A cool breeze rustled my hair. In the distance, a ship appeared. Then another, and another — their white sails formed a rippling line across the horizon. The Rúonbattai had always been so spread out, from Tjarnnaast up north to Brånnheå down south. I hadn't realized how many people they'd convinced to join their crusade against the Ferish.

Tiernan shifted his feet, hesitating, then whispered in my ear. "About what Ivar said—"

"Don't worry," I said. "I know he was lying."

"Katja . . ." Tiernan's mouth twisted. "Honestly, I have no idea what I said down there. I *was* losing myself. But I love you, truly."

We'd both lost ourselves this past year — him in his mind, me to grief. All that mattered was that we'd found each other. Maybe by some miracle, we would survive this battle. We'd get married, start a family, and take our children to Nyhemur to befriend windmills. Or maybe these last few days, precious and shimmering, would be the only days we'd ever spend together as lovers.

I kissed his cheek. "I love you, too, Tiernan Heilesson. Always and forever."

The ships dropped anchor. Each flew the Rúonbattai flag, a white raven and crossed swords on pale blue. One had a smaller crew flag of a raven on yellow, symbolizing the grain fields of Nyhemur. Mercenaries, probably. Another ship had a red-and-black crew flag for Gallun. Too many men to count swarmed across the decks.

So many, I thought faintly. We still only had a few dozen warriors hidden behind the driftwood barricades.

Soldiers piled into longboats and rowed toward us. Astra's white robes stood out among the armoured figures. Silver hair draped over her shoulders, stirring in the wind. An iron pendant of a nine-branched oak hung from her neck. After so many nightmares, it felt surreal to see her again in the flesh.

The longboats ran ashore. A few men climbed out to secure them. Astra stayed seated, scanning the tidal flat. I lifted her obsidian-handled knife in salute. Her face twisted with grim recognition. I wondered if she could tell something was wrong, or if she just thought this exchange was too unpredictable to see the future. Our hope was if she couldn't magically see into the nullified zone, then she couldn't see her potential death there — meaning the world wouldn't split simply from her looking upon the tidal flat.

"Send my son forward," she shouted. Her voice was strangely flat. "I want to see that it's him."

Tsiala drew a dagger and cut Ivar free from the driftwood. She pushed him forward, holding her dagger to his throat.

"Same for my mother," Fendul shouted back.

Astra beckoned to a soldier. He hauled a woman with bound hands out of a boat, using her as a shield. Her black braid and sharp features were that of Fendul's tema, Rumiga. The woman had once been like my aunt, helping raise me in our shared plank house. For all I knew, I'd condemned her to death.

I swallowed hard and managed to call out. "Release the alatu. Then you can have Ivar."

"Two for one?" Astra replied. "That's hardly fair."

"You can catch another alatu. You can't bring your son back to life."

"If you kill him, none of you leave this island alive." She lifted a crossbow from her boat and loaded it.

For a second, I was in Tjarnnaast, watching a swan fall with a bolt in its chest. Tiernan, Geniod, and Fendul drew their blades. Soldiers leapt out of the longboats, brandishing swords, axes, pikes, and shields emblazoned with their raven sigil. They formed a line on either side of Astra, filling the shoreline. Back on the ships, archers lined the bulwark, arrows nocked.

"Stalemate," Geniod muttered.

Neve dropped the rock she'd been tossing. She circled Ivar, still with Tsiala's dagger at his throat, and smiled sweetly at him. Quiet enough for only our side to hear, she said, "How about two for two? You can take me."

Ivar's sneer rang through his words. "I took you once already. You think I want to again?"

"No, honey. You want this." She placed a hand over her stomach.

The realization rippled through us one by one. Geniod flinched, Fendul froze, and Tiernan swore. Ivar stared at Neve, then crowed with laughter. Tsiala pulled her dagger tight, spilling blood down his neck.

"The gods have blessed us!" Ivar bellowed. "Look upon the mother of my child! Look upon your next divine leader!"

Astra leapt up, making her longboat rock in the shallows. A soldier whooped. Cheers and hollers streaked across their ranks like a grass fire, rising into cacophony. The men stamped their feet, fell to their knees, clanged their weapons against their shields, raised their arms to the sky.

That wasn't just loyalty. It was worship. If they were so sure Neve was carrying a divine child . . . maybe we were wrong. If temporal magic *was* a gift from the Sverbian gods, our whole plan to nullify it might be impossible. Maybe we were about to split the world again. I swung to Tiernan for reassurance, but he looked just as unnerved.

Astra lifted her hand. The cheers ebbed into silence. "Two for two," she shouted. "Rumiga Rin and the sea monster for my son and grandchild."

She signalled to a ship. The sailors on deck pulled the lid off a long crate. They tipped it over, sending a pale green, rubbery bundle spilling out in a cascade of water. A keening whine made my hair stand on end.

"Is that really an alatu?" I asked, aghast. "It's so *small*."

Sailors cut ropes around the bundle, letting the creature unfold. Its flippers and forked tail thrashed, knocking men over. Its head twisted on a slender serpentine neck. The men grabbed the creature and hauled it overboard. It splashed into the ocean and vanished.

Nei, I thought in horror. If that fall killed it, and every anta-saidu nearby woke in a rage . . .

"Nice," Tsiala said. "I always wanted to die in a big fucking typhoon."

The creature's head popped back up. It beat its flippers, splashing water, whining. The long neck, bobbing head, and gnashing teeth reminded me of a gosling searching for food.

"Yan taku," I said. "It's a *baby*."

"So much for our battle," Tiernan muttered. "If we hit it by accident—"

Allow us, came Ainu-Seru's hollow voice. *If I feign being an anta-saidu, I can lead it away. Akohin and I will go find its mother.*

A raven skimmed across the ocean, sending out ripples. The alatu's whining and thrashing faded. It slipped under the water. A moment later, it surfaced beyond the ships, following the raven. Tiernan and I traded an awestruck look. We'd just witnessed the world's oldest and deepest magic, the bond between all living things.

"There," Astra called. "Now let's finish the trade."

And with that, it hit. We'd prevented an apocalypse, but now we were facing battle without Ainu-Seru. Without any help at all.

Tsiala cut the ropes around Ivar's wrists. He grabbed Neve's chin and kissed her fiercely. She bit him. He laughed, his mouth bloody, and dragged her toward the ocean. The soldier holding Rumiga pushed her forward. She stumbled across the wet sand toward us.

Astra stayed in her longboat, gripping her crossbow. We needed to get her on land, in the nullifying zone, so we could safely kill her. Our window was closing. Once Ivar and Neve reached the boats, the Rúonbattai would leave.

Tiernan's hand found mine. We looked into each other's eyes for a second that lasted an eternity. We'd go together. A desperate surge into certain death, fighting through hundreds of Rúonbattai soldiers to reach Astra. Nothing else mattered. *I love you*, his grey eyes said. *May our spirits meet again on the other side.*

I thrust my sword into the air, signalling to our warriors hidden in the forest. Birds streaked toward the ocean. Arrows and javelins slammed into the Rúonbattai, downing men, striking the longboats. Splinters exploded across the water.

Astra flung out a wave of fire. It winked out at the water's edge. Shock covered her face. Like my nightmares, she lifted her crossbow and fired. Rumiga, halfway across the tidal flat, dropped with a bolt in her back. Fendul shouted and lunged toward his mother.

Tiernan and I charged. Rúonbattai soldiers flocked toward us. We cut through them, whirling, slashing. Birds tore at their faces. A man slammed into me, knocking me down. Tiernan hauled me back up. Everything was blood and metal and feathers. We had to reach the water — reach Astra and Ivar —

A soldier swung in front of me, sword raised. Tsiala stabbed a dagger into his back, yanked it out, and kicked him over. A pike bloomed through her stomach.

I felt myself scream. Tiernan yanked me onward. An eagle tumbled across the sky, trailing blood. It hit the ground and shifted to Geniod. For a second, his face was Temal's, telling me to keep running. I ran.

Tiernan slipped in a tide pool. I dragged him up. Swinging back toward shore, we found a wall of soldiers. No — a *ring* of soldiers around us. Tiernan and I went back to back, swords raised. Iron and steel pointed at us from every direction.

Not here, I thought. *Not yet.*

Huge black and white wings flashed overhead. A kinaru swooped low and knocked into the soldiers, scattering them like thrown dice. Tiernan and I dashed for the gap. More soldiers closed in —

Birds descended from the sky. They shifted in midair and plowed into the Rúonbattai. I knew the warriors' tattoos at a glance. Iyo dolphins, Kae herons, Dona seagulls. Beyond the frenzied fighting, whales, seals, and sharks surfaced in the ocean.

Tiernan seized my arm. "If they kill Astra in the water—"

We had to reach her first. I thrust my sword at Tiernan, cupped my hands over my mouth, and made a warbling loon call. The kinaru wheeled in the sky and dove toward us.

An arrow struck its head. It slammed into the ground and skidded, bowling over soldiers, leaving an enormous groove in the wet sand. The bird screeched, thrashing. I swore in horror. When it died, every tel-saidu in the region would wake in a rage, and Ainu-Seru wasn't here to fend them off. We had minutes, maybe seconds, until tornadoes and crushing gales demolished this island.

Tiernan pressed my sword back into my hand. We surged forward, swinging wildly, shoving past soldiers. Like a dam bursting, we broke through the fray into the open.

Ivar grappled with Neve, dragging her toward the longboats. She kicked and bit and dug her heels into the sand. Astra, standing in the shallows, lifted her crossbow. I'd had this dream too often. She looked me dead in the eye —

Neve unhooked her chain belt. She lashed out, knocking the crossbow from Astra's grip. Ivar backhanded Neve, making her stumble. He scooped up her small frame and tossed her into a boat.

A wall of flames erupted across the shoreline. On instinct, I tried flinging water at them. Nothing. Tiernan sprinted at them. As he crossed the threshold of the nullified zone, he swept out his hand, parting the flames like curtains. He shot through the gap. I ran after him, pushing through a veil of searing heat.

I expected a torrent of arrows from the ships. Instead, archers scrambled to the far bulwarks and fired at the open ocean. Ships with Eremur's naval flag careened toward them. One crashed into a Rúonbattai schooner with a bone-crunching sound, smashing open its hull.

Tiernan grabbed my arm, dragging my attention back to the shallows. Neve stood knee-deep in the ocean, hands in the air, burlap robes floating around her. At first I thought she'd surrendered — but

Astra and Ivar were writhing and shrieking in pain. Neve's lips curled back, exposing her red teeth.

"So much iron in the blood," she said. "Know what temperature it melts at?"

I drew back in horror. "Don't kill them — not here—"

"Oh, I know. Take her first." Neve jerked her head at Astra. "Her bastard son will be fine with me. Won't you, honey?"

The two Sverbians spat curses at her. Tiernan sheathed his sword and grabbed Astra. Fire swirled around them, reeking of singed flesh and hair. He hauled her back through the wall of flames. The second they reached land, the flames winked out.

"What is this?" Astra hissed. "What did you do?"

Tiernan pulled her against him, pinning her arms to her sides. "Remember, Katja. Make sure the runes work."

Gripping my sword, I met Astra's pale, furious eyes. "We'll either kill you or Ivar. It's your choice."

"Take me," she gasped. "Spare my son — please, I beg you—"

"You're absolutely sure?"

Astra twisted, searching for Ivar. Neve was still tormenting him. He was on his hands and knees in the water, shaking and sobbing with pain.

"Yes!" Astra cried. "Just make her *stop*!"

I clicked my tongue. "Wrong choice."

Tiernan shoved Astra forward. I lunged, driving my sword into her heart. Up close, her grey irises looked like molten iron, her pupils like infinite chasms.

"That's for my parents," I said.

I yanked my sword back. Blood sprayed across me. Astra collapsed at my feet, her white robes draping across the sand. Ivar's screaming wreathed us.

Neve blew a kiss at Ivar. "Your turn, honey."

"Bitch," he snarled, "I should've—"

She twisted her hand. Ivar's eyes rolled back as he screamed. Tiernan dragged the young man's limp, battered form out of the water. He hauled Ivar to his knees, holding him upright. I dropped my sword on the sand and drew my obsidian-handled knife. A laugh scraped out of Ivar, turning hysterical.

"Just you wait," he scraped out. "I already killed you once. I'll find you in the afterworld and—"

I yanked his chin up, wrenching a strangled cry from him. "I'll be ready."

40.

ABOVE WATER

Blood-soaked, we stumbled back from the dead Sverbians. The battle raged around us. Rúonbattai soldiers and Aikoto warriors fought across the tidal flat. Eremur's naval soldiers fired flaming arrows at the Rúonbattai ships, igniting their sails and timbers. The moment the windstorms began, those fires would become an inferno.

Yet the air remained calm. I scanned the tidal flat. The wounded kinaru lay in a heap of black and white feathers, twitching feebly.

"It's not dead," I said in disbelief. "It's not dead!"

Colourful specks flickered across my vision. I could rejoin the battle, protect my loved ones, tend their wounds. Save Geniod and accept his offer to adopt me. Make amends with Rumiga. Give Tsiala the life of freedom she deserved. Or I could run to the kinaru, tend *its* wounds, and keep a firestorm from devouring the island and everyone on it.

That's your wildfire, Tsiala once told me. I'd taught her that lesson. Run toward the flames. Extinguish them before they destroy everything.

I ran for the kinaru. Tiernan and Neve followed. We plowed through soldiers, stumbling, splashing through tide pools. I dropped to my knees by the bird. Blood pulsed from the arrow in its massive head, pooling on the sand. Up close, I realized how it survived. The arrow had lodged in the kinaru's skull, just shy of hitting its brain.

I worked my way along the bird's feathery bulk, checking for other wounds. It flinched and shrieked when I touched its side. Broken bones from the fall, probably. Punctured lungs, internal bleeding.

"I can't fix it," I said desperately. "It needs healing magic."

Tiernan caught me as I swayed. "Amja, amja," he soothed. "Breathe."

Neve put her fingers in her mouth and whistled. Three kinaru swooped through the sky and thumped onto the tidal flat, splattering out sand and seawater. Pádraig, Janekke, and Círa slid off the birds. They each had a canvas rucksack, presumably full of healing supplies.

"Aeldu save me," I said. "Where—"

"Akohin left me as many kinaru as I needed," Neve said. "So I brought help."

Their kinaru formed a protective circle around us, wings spread, snapping their bills at soldiers. We were still on nullified ground, and we couldn't move the wounded kinaru, so Tiernan lifted one of his glowing runes from the sand. It faded in midair.

Pádraig began mending the kinaru's internal wounds, focusing on the iron in its blood. It flailed and squawked. Neve pulled stone tendrils from the ground to bind its long neck and webbed feet in place. She and Tiernan held its wings down while Círa and I joined Janekke at the head.

"I need to remove the arrow," Janekke said. "If it goes in deeper and hits the brain, it could be fatal. Never thought I'd do surgery on a giant duck."

I stroked the kinaru's head. "You'll be fine," I soothed. "We're going to heal you. Akohin and Ainu-Seru will be back soon."

Círa and I froze water from a tidal pool and rubbed ice around the kinaru's wound. Once the flesh was numb, Janekke yanked out the arrow, showering us in blood. She used pliers to remove splinters of wood and bone, then placed her palms around the wound and closed her eyes in concentration. The pulse of blood slowed, then stopped. The bird squawked feebly, its breath easing and wings settling.

A warm breeze rolled over us. As if from very far away, Ainu-Seru's hollow voice spoke. *Thank you.*

❋

Emerging from our circle of kinaru guardians, we found the Rúonbattai had surrendered. We healers swept into action, triaging the wounded. By some miracle, my loved ones were alive — barely. Geniod lay with broken ribs where he'd fallen from the sky. Tsiala had collapsed with a stab wound in her stomach, bleeding into a tide pool. Fendul had been injured protecting his mother, Rumiga, who'd fallen with Astra's crossbow bolt in her back.

Navy medics brought supplies from the Eremur ships. We handled the mild cases while the mages handled the serious ones. Soldiers arranged the dead in rows under the darkening sky. There were too many, always too many. Yet it had paid off. Tiernan and Neve examined the tidal flat, searching for signs of a newly formed shoirdryge. They found none. By all evidence, the Fourth Elken War was over — not just for us, but for everyone.

I knelt by a young woman with a broken leg and was startled to realize it was Malana. She'd found Nerio in Caladheå, then flew on to Toel Ginu, where she told the Iyo-jouyen that the Rúonbattai were planning to murder an alatu and destroy the region. The Okorebai-Iyo had finally abandoned her neutral stance and sent help. She'd also sent messengers across the coast, rounding up every Kae and Dona warrior they could find.

Nerio had done his part, too. Knowing Captain Valrose wouldn't take the threat seriously, Nerio sent a courier to the naval training camp at Ile vi Dévoye. Captain Baccini had dispatched every crew stationed on the island to help us. I glimpsed the man across the bustling tidal flat. He smiled at me and touched two fingers to his forehead in salute.

The wounded were too weak to travel, so it was agreed that we'd camp here. The navy supplied food, blankets, and tents. They piled dead Sverbians into longboats, set them alight, and pushed them out to sea so their spirits would reach Thaerijmur. Flames filled the dark horizon. Tiernan insisted that any Rúonbattai with a Gallun flag on their armour get shipped to Innisburren to be buried in Gallnach catacombs.

For Astra and Ivar, Neve dug two graves in the forest with her earth-calling. If their lost spirits got captured by the god Bøkkai and taken to the barren flatlands, Bøkkhem, then so be it. All the harder for them to find us in the afterworld. Before their bodies were taken away, Tiernan and I drifted over to look at them, lying side by side on the wet sand. Neve joined us.

"I meant to ask," she said. "Why'd you tell Astra to choose between herself and Ivar?"

"We had to be sure the runes nullified her magic," I explained. "So ahead of time, we agreed on two possible paths. If Astra chose to spare Ivar, we'd kill them both. After everything she's done to protect her son, she would only tell us to kill him if she could foresee the *other* path. If she said that, we'd take them to Ingdanrad's prison."

"Ahhh." Neve grinned, flashing her red teeth. "Because if she could see the future, the runes didn't work, and it wasn't safe to kill them."

"I've got a question, too," I said. "Are you really carrying Ivar's child?"

"Mother of mountains, no. We never even slept together. I just got him blackout drunk, then talked about how amazing the sex was." She nudged his leg with her boot. "So handsome. So stupid."

"Gods help us," Tiernan muttered. "Can you imagine if after all this, there *was* a child?"

"Believe me, I'll be watching." Neve folded her hands among her draping sleeves. "Looks like that'll be part of my life forever. Keeping an eye on Ingdanrad's clerics in case they train another temporal mage."

✳

Deep into the night, Tiernan and I found a quiet sandy beach and collapsed together. We were soaked with blood, but I needed to be close to him. After so many months of drowning, I'd crested the surface, rising above water. This felt like the start of our lives together, the peaceful future he'd described at the crabapple lake.

Yet when I woke at sunrise, I found misery written across his face. "What's wrong?" I asked.

Tiernan brushed sand off my cheek and kissed my forehead. "Something happened last night while you were tending patients. A naval lieutenant tried to arrest me."

I jerked upright. *"What?"*

"Baccini intervened. He told me that Antoch Parr pulled some strings to find out why Valrose wanted to arrest Jorum and me. Apparently he thinks we are Rúonbattai spies. I can guess who started that rumour."

"Sacro dios." I rubbed sleep from my eyes. "Ivar only said he spread the rumour among Ingdanrad's militia."

Tiernan managed a grim smile. "We killed the one person who could clear my name. Now I am an outlaw in both Ingdanrad and Eremur."

"But Valrose let Jorum go. He wouldn't arrest you now, when we just won the war—"

"He might. Mages are dangerous in his eyes, and it would be a good excuse to get rid of me." Tiernan gazed out at the sparkling ocean. The sun illuminated the gold flecks in his eyes. "I already stared down the gallows once. I cannot do it again."

A cold feeling grew inside me. "What are you saying?"

"I will never be safe here. Neither will you, if we are together. I . . . made up my mind overnight. I am moving to Sverba."

"You're *leaving* me?"

"Not necessarily." Tiernan took my hand. "You could come."

I stared at him, aghast. "You mean — move to Sverba with you?"

"It will be new for both of us, somewhere to explore together. We can live however you wish. In a log cabin in the woods, or by the ocean, or in a city. A safe, peaceful life together like we talked about."

"But — we talked about having our family and friends keep us in check—"

"Your parents will. You've learned how to consult their makiri yourself. And . . . if we go, I want to do it right. I want you to know with your whole heart that I will look after you, that I will be faithful and loyal to the end of days. So . . ." Tiernan got on one knee, shifting in the sand. He held out a brass ring etched with delicate knotwork. His hands were shaking. "I love you more than life, Katja. Would you do me the honour of marrying me?"

✳

I didn't know how to answer Tiernan. I put the ring in my knife sheath for safekeeping, not ready for anyone to know about the proposal. Still, whenever I looked at my hands, I imagined the ring there, as if it was another shadow kiss Tiernan had left. He'd crafted it from the buckles on his sword sheath. A promise, he explained, to lay down his blade for good and take up a life with me. The etched knotwork was in the style of Ålkatt designs, as best he could remember them.

A navy schooner took us to Toel Ginu along with Akohin, Geniod, and the dead and wounded Iyo. Nothing seemed real — meeting Dunehein and Rikuja's baby boy, eating meals in their plank house, sharing a mattress with Tiernan. Dunehein teased us endlessly about being together. In private, Rikuja gave me a cottonspun bag of bloodweed tablets. "Just in case," she said with a pointed look at her baby.

It felt like looking into a glassy pond and seeing a reflection of the life I'd dreamed of. Everything seemed fleeting and fragile. Nothing made sense. If I married Tiernan, I was letting him chart our course in life, which meant I hadn't yet learned to stand up for myself. *Definitely* not ready to move overseas with only my parents' spirits to look out for me. If I turned down his proposal, giving up the love of my life for my own well-being, then surely I *was* mature enough to get married and move overseas.

While I battled that storm in my head, Yotolein and Jorumgard arrived with their kids. They had news. Riding on the triumph of the war ending, Jorumgard had proposed to Yotolein, who accepted. Tiernan and I shared a look no one else would've understood — wry amusement at the timing, overwhelming joy for our loved ones, and silent agreement to keep our potential engagement quiet a while longer.

The couple wanted a small wedding, something we could do before Hanaiko and Samulein returned to Caladheå for the next school year. Rikuja's family offered to prepare the feast. Kirbana, Narun, and their toddlers canoed down a few days later. Nerio came riding Gwmniwyr, returning Tiernan's beloved gelding. Nhys brought a wagon of his finest spiced mead, brånnvin, and ale from the Golden Oak.

We had the ceremony in a sunny meadow. Kirbana read aloud from a Sverbian religious text and Rikuja's mother did the Aikoto salmon-blood blessing, then the couple exchanged joining cords and did a handfasting ritual. An Iyo tattooist inked Yotolein's crowberry crest on Jorumgard's upper arm. On Yotolein, she inked juniper berries. Since Jorumgard didn't have a formal crest, he'd chosen a plant that reminded him of his homeland.

"What would your crest be?" I whispered to Tiernan. "What reminds you of Ålkatt?"

He touched my bare arm where the crest would go. "Rye, perhaps. I remember playing in the grain fields with my brothers."

The image of grain blowing in the wind stirred a thought. There was a way I could try married life with Tiernan, far from my family, before committing to it forever. I linked my arm into his and whispered into his ear. "We should visit Nyhemur."

❋

It was too risky for Tiernan to ride across Eremur as a wanted man, so we flew on a kinaru, soaring over the snowy peaks of the Turquoise Mountains and into the endless plains of northern Nyhemur.

Sparkling sapphire rivers threaded through fields of green and gold grain, blue flax flowers, sunshine-yellow canola, and wild purple fireweed. Seeing my family crest felt like a tiny bit of home.

We landed in the shallows of a vast lake. The kinaru splashed away in search of fish. Tiernan and I wandered up the shore hand in hand, skipping rocks and watching flocks of birds swirl across the immense sky. On the horizon, windmills turned with a slow, soothing rhythm. I'd spent so long dreaming of them that they already felt like friends.

"I never realized it before," Tiernan said, "but this place feels like Ålkatt. I think that is why I wanted to take you here."

"Really? I thought Ålkatt was mountainous."

"The lowlands are flat. Well, mostly. There are . . . island mountains, I think we called them. Lone hills and rock outcrops dotted across the plains."

I still knew so little of his old life. Just how different was Ålkatt from Sverba? Could he ever be happy there, pretending to be something he wasn't? Somewhere he knew the shape and smell of the earth but was foreign in so many ways? Could I be happy somewhere that was foreign in *every* way?

At night, we stayed up to stargaze, lying together amidst the tall grass. I pointed out familiar constellations. A kinaru, higher overhead than usual. The sword of the tel-saidu, a cross forming the hilt, hand guards, and blade. Orebo who tried to steal a moonbeam, but it shattered and formed the stars. Tiernan pointed out a caribou, the national animal of Ålkatt. It felt like looking six centuries into the past when our worlds were one and the same.

I sat up. "Tiernan?"

He glanced over at me. It was too dark to see the gold flecks in his eyes, but I knew they were there. I knew the important things about him. Or at least almost all of them.

"I . . ." My breath hitched. "This isn't a yes. Not yet. I just . . . need to know."

He pushed himself upright. "Know what?"

I kissed him. He pulled me close, slipping his arms around me. I bit his lip, slipped my tongue into his mouth, exploring. Learning him.

"Katja," he whispered. "Do you mean . . ."

I tugged his shirt over his head. The dyed runes had faded, but they'd done their job. I traced his muscles, his scars, the dark hair on his chest. His heart pulsed against my hand. I'd brought him back to life. Back to me. That felt like the old, deep magic of the world. Faint with nerves, I undid the ties of my own shirt, letting the fabric fall away.

Tiernan drew a sharp breath. He kissed my neck, sending fire shooting through my veins. His beard prickled my skin. Heat and humidity bloomed around us.

"Promise me one thing," he said. "If you want to stop, tell me. No matter what."

I wove my fingers into his hair. "I promise."

We started slowly, exploring each other. Our naked bodies folded together in the grass. Pressure swelled against my thigh, proving he wanted me as much as I wanted him. Dizzying heat rolled over me. As our voyage turned south, we turned breathless, desperate, craving. I gasped as he pushed into me, linking our bodies. Mist erupted around us and steamed away into the night sky. Finally, finally, we floated together among the clouds.

❋

Day by day, we made our way around the vast lake. Every moment with Tiernan felt sacred. I loved talking to him, sharing whatever stray thoughts passed through our minds. I loved sitting in silence, listening for the distant thrum of windmills. I loved tangling with his naked body in the grass. Taking bloodweed too often would be dangerous, but there were ways to connect that didn't require it.

On the fourth day, we found an abandoned log cabin. The roof had collapsed into splinters. I drifted around it, picturing Tiernan and me living somewhere like this in Sverba. Planting a garden. Building a lakeshore dock. Raising goats or chickens, then children. Having windmills as distant friends. It seemed peaceful but also . . . lonely. We moved on. That night, we camped on an island mountain, an outcrop overlooking the lake.

Birdsong stirred me awake. Tiernan lay asleep next to me, his arm draped over my bare stomach. Our clothes lay scattered across the dirt. I picked grass out of his rumpled hair. The dawn light softened the lines of his collarbones, the jut of his hip bone, the crook of his knuckles. Aeldu save me, he was beautiful. I kissed his nose and nuzzled against him.

He blinked sleepily and smiled. "Good morning, my love."

Four soft, radiant words. Part of me wanted to hear them every day for the rest of my life. But the other part . . .

I knew the truth now. My first thoughts in the morning were of Tiernan, but other thoughts surfaced throughout the day. Through their makiri, my parents showed me memories of our family, our plank house, our fishing grounds. My spirit belonged in the rainforest, in the soil my ancestors were buried in. That had always been home and always would be.

"Tiernan . . ." My voice wavered.

"Ah." His smile faded. "You made up your mind."

"I'm so sorry—"

"Do not apologize." He traced his rough fingertips along my jaw. "I have been so afraid you would say no, but . . . I have been more afraid you would say yes."

"Really? Why?"

"Because it is asking too much of you. I could never forgive myself if you regretted marrying me. If I pushed you into something you did not want to do."

I curled into him. None of this felt fair. I was trying to protect my spirit, yet it was breaking apart, escaping my body in every tear that slid down my cheeks. So many times, he'd comforted me as I sobbed, but this time he cried, too, which just made me sob harder. When our tears ran dry, we lay together in silence, listening to the wind.

"I think," Tiernan began, "I may try to go home. *Truly* home."

"To your world?"

"Aye. There is an explorers' guild in Sverba. Maybe I can launch another expedition to find the ocean rift I came through."

I kissed his fingertips. The thought of him leaving this world would've made me cry again if I had tears left.

"What will you do?" he asked, stroking my hair. "Where will you go?"

"I've been thinking about that. I settled in Caladheå to help Yotolein raise his kids, but he's got Jorum now. And I don't know about living in Nettle Ginu, but . . . I'm going to ask Geniod to adopt me."

"Good. He clearly loves you like a daughter."

"I know. Although I'm going to suggest he go live with Róisín on Innisburren awhile, see how things work out. As for me . . . after the tidal flat battle, seeing my family and friends and that kinaru on the brink of death, I felt so helpless. I don't ever want to feel that way again. So I'm going back to Ingdanrad to study medicine."

"Oh?" Tiernan propped himself up on one elbow to look at me.

"I passed the third-year exam, so I can start with the fourth-year apprentices. That's when they start learning healing magic. And I thought I'd have to swear neutrality in all future wars, but that's only for combat magic. I just have to swear to help people in need."

"What about the rumours there? That you are in love with an escaped mass murderer?"

"It'll be awkward," I admitted. "But I won't be alone. Pádraig, Círa, and Janekke will be at the hospital. Ako's moving back, too. He wants to start talking to the Kae saidu scholars about his bond with Ainu-Seru. They want to be open about it, to live as themselves."

"That sounds wonderful." Tiernan kissed my forehead. "May I give you something to put in your new home there?"

"What is it?"

He searched through our discarded clothes and produced a small caribou figurine, carved from golden pine. "I hoped we could put it in our new home together, but instead it will be a goodbye present. Something to remember me by."

I touched it in awe, admiring the points of its thick antlers, the dappled grooves of its fur coat. "It's beautiful. But . . . you know I'll never forget you, right?"

"Nor will I forget you." He smiled faintly. "I will think of you every time I put a berry to my lips. Every time I smell sage and cloves. Every time I touch the ocean."

"And I'll think of you every time the sun rises. I'll know you sent it to me, to this side of the earth, and every twilight I'll send it back to you."

In the distance, a white-sailed cutter drifted across the lake, leaving a wake of foam. For so many months I'd been following in Tiernan's wake — searching for him across the coast, in that endless dark rainstorm of my death, in the desert of his comatose mind. It was time to chart my own course. Time to lift my head above water and see what else lay ahead.

EPILOGUE:

EIGHT MONTHS LATER

Deep in the mountains, over the crux of four inlet arms, a crow drifts through the sky. Sunbeams claw at the western peaks. Defeated, they sink below the horizon. The crow caws. It has seen many sunsets, yet this one will be different. The crow has come to bear witness.

Far below, a creek valley tears asunder. Earth and sky shred like birch bark. A shockwave explodes across the crux, flinging the inlet arms away like blue silk cords, exposing beds of tangled seaweed. High in the sky, a swirling gust slams into the crow. It tumbles beak over tail, grasping, flailing, a flurry of black feathers.

The wind screams.

Night has fallen by the time the gusting fades. The battered crow alights in the creek valley, criss-crossed with splintered trees. Leaves float down the creek into a sliver of smoke, a hazy ribbon that rises from the water into the starry sky. Through the sliver, beyond the drifting smoke, is a wasteland of scorched earth and crushed rock.

All night, the crow watches the smoky rift, preening its broken feathers. Near dawn, a sooty man stumbles through the rift. The crow knows the man's face, yet not the man. He is a foreigner. One not born to this world.

In mid-morning, a girl arrives through the rift, paddling up the creek on a wooden raft. Once again, the crow knows the girl's face, yet not the girl. Her brown hair is cut to her chin and the roots are growing in white. The crow has seen that before. A boy with white hair, bonded to an air spirit.

The crow does not know this girl, but it knows what her arrival means. Its caw cuts through sun-drenched forest, spreading a warning.

Death is coming.

GLOSSARY

etymology: A: Aikoto, F: Ferish, S: Sverbian, G: Gallnach

Abhain: Gallnach sowing festival in spring

antayul: [A. *anta* water, *-yul* caller] viirelei who have learned to control water

attuning: shapeshifting into an animal; a rite of passage for viirelei adolescents

Battle of Tjarnnaast: a brutal battle in which an alliance of Tula, Haka, and Eremur soldiers razed the Rúonbattai village Tjarnnaast

bloodweed: semi-poisonous leaves; used as birth control by viirelei

Bódhain: Gallnach harvest festival and day of the dead in autumn

bogmoss: moss used for dressing wounds; antiseptic and highly absorbent

brånnvin: [S. *brånn* burn, *vin* wine] several varieties of clear rye
    liquor, including vodka

Cághain: Gallnach summer festival atop a mountain

céilídh: Gallnach social gathering with food, folk music, and dancing

Coast Trader: a pidgin trade language derived from Aikoto,
    Sverbian, Ferish, Gallnach, and others

duck potato: underwater root of arrowhead plants; ground up
    for flour by viirelei

Elken Wars: a series of wars fought between Ferish colonists
    and a Sverbian-Aikoto alliance for control of the coast and its
    natural resources

glissetto: Ferish bread rolls containing a stew of chicken offal

itheran: [S. *ithera* 'out there'] viirelei term for foreign colonists

Jinben: [A. *jin* sun, *benro* meet] Aikoto summer solstice festival

jinrayul: [A. *jinra* fire, *-yul* caller] mages who have learned to
    control fire

jouyen: viirelei tribe(s) typically belonging to a confederacy

Kånehlbattai: [S. *kån* royal, *-ehl* female, *battai* guard] Sverbian
    queensguard

laudanum: tincture made from poppy seeds; used as a painkiller
    and sedative

makiri: Aikoto guardian figurines carved in the shape of animals,
    which hold a fragment of a person's spirit after their death

mezcale: a clear, smoke-scented Ferish alcohol made from
    succulents

needlemint: evergreen-scented leaves native to Sverba; used as
    numbing painkiller

okorebai: political, spiritual, and military leader of a jouyen

okoreni: successor to an okorebai, typically passed from parent
    to child

Ólmhain: Gallnach winter rites held underground

pann: a denomination of the sovereign currency; 100 pann to 1
    sovereign
plank house: a large building and social unit of the Aikoto,
    housing up to ten families
rioden: massive auburn conifer trees used for dugout canoes,
    buildings, bark weaving, etc.
Rúonbattai: [S. *rúon* rain, *battai* guard] radical Sverbian militant
    group attempting to drive the Ferish out of Eremur
sancte: Ferish holy building
Sol vi Caladheå: [F. *sol* sun, *vi* of] a disreputable Ferish-language
    newspaper
sovereign: a form of currency introduced by the Sverbian monarchy
stavehall: Sverbian holy building
tulanta: [A. *tularem* a type of plant, *anta* water] hallucinogenic
    painkiller used by viirelei
viirelei: [A. *vii* they, *rel* of, *leiga* west] colonists' term for coastal
    Indigenous Peoples, including the Aikoto, Nuthalha, and
    Kowichelk confederacies
willowcloak: painkiller made from willow bark
woolwrap: a long skirt worn by Gallnach men and women
Yanben: [A. *yan* world, *benro* meet] Aikoto winter solstice festival
    when the worlds of the living and dead unite

GODS, SPIRITS, MYTHOLOGY

AIKOTO

aeldu: spirits of the dead
Aeldu-yan: land of the dead
alatu: sea monster sacred to anta-saidu and coastal Indigenous
    confederacies

Eredu-yan: land of the living

kinaru: giant waterfowl sacred to tel-saidu and the Rin-jouyen

oosoo: giant salamanders sacred to jinra-saidu and the Kowichelk
Confederacy

Orebo: legendary figure who accidentally broke a moonbeam into
shards and formed the stars

saidu: spirits that control the weather and maintain balance in
nature

> ANTA-SAIDU (WATER), EDIM-SAIDU (EARTH AND
> PLANTS), JINRA-SAIDU (FIRE), TEL-SAIDU (AIR)

FERISH

dios: the god above all

SVERBIAN

bjørnbattai: [S. *bjørn* bear, *battai* guard] legendary warriors who
shapeshift into bears

Børkkai: a god who steals souls

Børkkhem: [S. *Børkkai*, *hem* flatlands] a barren land of the dead

dúnravn: [S. *dún* pale, *ravn* raven] sacred white raven

shoirdryge: [S. *shoird* shard, *ryge* realm] parallel world that
splintered off from other worlds

Thaerijmur: an abundant land of the dead across an ocean

Thymarai: Lady of the Woods; goddess of fertility, love, beauty,
and juniper trees; accompanied by *bjørnbattai*

GALLNACH

Folk: dangerous spirits in Gallnach mythology, said to emerge
from the otherworld on Bódhain and Abhain

mother of mountains: Gallnach earth goddess who birthed
the world

PHRASES, SLANG, PROFANITY

cingari tia/sia mera: [F. *cingari* fuck (imperative), *tia/sia* your/ his or her, *mera* mother]

Elkhounds: slang for Caladheå city guards

hanekei: [A. 'it is the first time we meet'] formal Aikoto greeting

kaid: any insult to the aeldu, used as strong profanity by the Aikoto

kianta kolo: [A. *ki* golden, *anta* water, *koro* 'to flow'] Mikiod's mantra, lit. *the sap will flow*

má sí: [G. short form of *máthair* mother, *sídhe* hills or burial mounds] casual form of *mother of mountains*

någva: [S. 'to fuck'] highly versatile Sverbian profanity; adjective form is *någvakt*

sacro dios: strong interjection taking the Ferish god's name in vain

takuran: [A. *taku* shit] highly offensive slur alluding to Aikoto burial rites, referencing someone so foul they must be buried in shit because dirt rejects their blood

tema: Aikoto affectionate term for *mother*

temal: Aikoto affectionate term for *father*

yan taku: [A. *yan* world, *taku* shit] profanity with religious connotations

yonna: Kowichelk term for *grandmother*

CULTURES

Aikoto: [A. *ainu* mountain, *ko* flow, *toel* coast] A confederacy of nine (formerly eight) jouyen occupying a large region of coastal rainforest.

Ferish: Colonists from Ferland who landed on the west coast of the Aikoto's continent. Later, a mass exodus from Ferland of famine victims caused a population boom in Aikoto lands.

INDUSTRIES: wheat farming, manufacturing, naval trading.

RELIGION: monotheist.

Gallnach: Settlers from Gallun, persecuted by Sverbians. They fled to Aikoto lands and built Ingdanrad as a refuge to practice druidism.

INDUSTRIES: barley farming, sheep herding, smithing.

RELIGION: polytheist druidism.

Kowichelk: A confederacy of jouyen in the rainforest south of the Aikoto. Largely wiped out from disease brought by foreign colonists.

INDUSTRIES: fishing, textiles, jade carving.

RELIGION: animist.

Nuthalha: A confederacy of jouyen in the tundra north of the Aikoto. Largely isolated.

INDUSTRIES: whaling, trapping, bone carving.

RELIGION: animist.

Sverbians: Settlers from Sverba who landed on the east coast of the Aikoto's continent, migrated west, and later allied with the Aikoto against the Ferish.

INDUSTRIES: rye farming, goat herding, logging.

RELIGION: polytheist.

AIKOTO JOUYEN: NORTH

Beru-jouyen: *People of the sea.* Live in Meira Dael on the coast of Nokun Bel.

CREST: grey whale.

INDUSTRIES: whaling, soapstone carving.

Dona-jouyen: *Nomad people.* Live in Anwen Bel and on the ocean. Formed when members of the Rin and Iyo split off.

CREST: white seagull.

INDUSTRIES: fishing, transient labour.

Haka-jouyen: *People of the frost.* Live inland in Nokun Bel.

CREST: brown grizzly bear.

INDUSTRIES: fur trapping, tanning.

Rin-jouyen: *People of the lakeshore*. Live in Aeti Ginu in central Anwen Bel. Oldest jouyen in the Aikoto with significant territory and influence.

CREST: white or black kinaru.

INDUSTRIES: woodcarving, embroidery, fur trapping.

Tamu-jouyen: *People of the peninsulas*. Live in Tamun Dael on the coast of Anwen Bel.

CREST: orange shark.

INDUSTRIES: fishing, boatcraft.

Tula-jouyen: *People of the gateway*. Live in Nettle Ginu in southern Anwen Bel. A new jouyen formed by Rin defectors who disagreed with the Okorebai-Rin's alliance with the Rúonbattai.

CREST: slate blue kingfisher.

INDUSTRIES: boatcraft, embroidery, fur trapping.

AIKOTO JOUYEN: SOUTH

Iyo-jouyen: *People of the surrounds*. Live in Toel Ginu and Caladheå on the coast of Iyun Bel. Largest and second-most powerful jouyen in the Aikoto. Historic allies with the Rin.

CREST: blue dolphin.

INDUSTRIES: stone carving, textiles.

Kae-jouyen: *People of the inlet*. Live on the coast of Ukan Bel alongside Burren Inlet.

CREST: green heron.

INDUSTRIES: fishing.

Yula-jouyen: *People of the valley*. Live inland in Ukan Bel in a network of river valleys.

CREST: copper fox.

INDUSTRIES: weaving.

A BRIEF HISTORY OF EREMUR AND SURROUNDING LANDS

WRITTEN BY HANAIKO KIRBANEHL

-200   The Rin-jouyen constructs a shrine in Aeti Ginu, one of the oldest surviving buildings in the Aikoto Confederacy.

-60   Sverbian sailors land on the east coast of the Aikoto's continent and begin migrating west.

1   The Sverbian monarchy introduces a new calendar, marking the birth of an empire.

24   Rånyl Sigrunnehl, queen of Sverba, invades Gallun and massacres the druid assembly. Gallnach refugees flee to the Aikoto's continent and migrate west ahead of the expanding Sverbian front.

366   Gallnach druids build a refuge, Ingdanrad, in the mountains

bordering Aikoto territory. They establish trade with the nearby Kae-jouyen.

428   Sverba founds the province of Nyhemur across the mountains from Aikoto lands. The two groups begin trading.

487   Ferish sailors land in Aikoto territory. They clash violently with Aikoto and Sverbians over trade routes and natural resources. Ingdanrad declares neutrality and offers refuge to all mages.

492   Gustos Dévoye, a Ferish naval captain, builds a trading post on an island in Iyo-jouyen territory. He names the island Ile vi Dévoye. The post fails to last the winter.

513   Barros Sanguero, lord of the New Ferland Trading Company, builds the Colonnium stronghold in Iyo territory. He quickly dominates regional trade.

530   Dévoye's son, Gustos II, builds a stone keep on the peninsula north of Tamun Dael, taking advantage of local unrest caused by a historic land dispute between the surrounding Rin-, Tamu-, Beru-, and Haka-jouyen.

✳

533   FIRST ELKEN WAR

Sanguero and Gustos II join forces, prompting Sverbians and Aikoto to ally against them. Some Rin and Iyo refuse to go to war and instead split off to form the nomadic Dona-jouyen.

In the south, the Sverbian-Aikoto alliance kills Sanguero and captures the Colonnium. Iyo, Rin, and Sverbian settlers build a fort around it to ensure Ferish soldiers cannot retake it. They name the fort Caladheå.

In the north, the Sverbian-Aikoto alliance kills Gustos II and captures his keep, which they name Caladsten. The Rin, Tamu, Beru, and Haka let Sverbians occupy the disputed region on the condition they protect it from the Ferish. The Sverbians name the region Nordmur.

❋

535   Imarein Rin, traumatized from the war, abandons his jouyen. He climbs Se Ji Ainu and swears devotion to the air spirit Ainu-Seru, known by itherans as Suriel.

545   Sverba founds the province of Eremur in southern Aikoto territory, declares Caladheå the capital, and establishes a local military. The Aikoto Confederacy refuses to recognize these actions. Imarein briefly returns to the Rin-jouyen.

547   Famine hits Ferland. Thousands of Ferish immigrants flee overseas to Eremur and nearby lands. Caladheå blooms into an international trading port. Construction begins on a new district, Ashtown, to house Ferish refugees.

❋

Mardos Goyero, a Ferish naval captain, attempts to retake the Colonnium and claim land for new immigrants. The Sverbian-Aikoto alliance nearly defeats Goyero — until his soldiers raze Bronnoi Ridge, the Aikoto district in Caladheå. The Rin abandon the city and return north.

Sverba agrees to share control of Eremur with Ferland via an elected council. The Iyo surrender Bronnoi Ridge in exchange for land and housing in the Ashtown slums. Sverbian dissenters form the Rúonbattai, a radical militant group, and vow to drive out the Ferish.

❋

559   The war treaties prompt another immigration wave from Ferland. Wealthy settlers take over Bronnoi Ridge and the nearby town of Shawnaast, which later merges with Caladheå.

563   The Rúonbattai construct a hidden colony, Brånnheå.

573   The Okorebai-Rin and Okorebai-Iyo forge a secret alliance with the Rúonbattai, who gift lilac seeds to the Iyo as a symbol of the alliance.

❋

An influenza epidemic ravages Eremur, killing thousands. Ferish rebels, angry about treaties from the previous war, take advantage of the weakened military and stage a coup. The Rúonbattai have a resurgence of support and retaliate against the Ferish rebels.

The war-torn Rin and other northern jouyen refuse to come south and fight, breaking the Aikoto alliance. The Iyo temporarily abandon Caladheå.

The Rúonbattai leader is killed in combat. Their new leader, Liet, retreats and ends the war. The Caladheå Council regains control of the city.

※

606   Several Sverbian mages, accused of helping the Rúonbattai massacre Ferish immigrants, are murdered in Council custody. Ingdanrad cuts diplomatic ties to Eremur.

614   Antoch Parr is promoted to captain of the 2nd Royal Eremur Cavalry. He recruits Jorumgard Tømasind and Tiernan Heilind, immigrant mercenaries from Sverba, to fight the Rúonbattai.

616   Imarein passes away. Ainu-Seru's grief turns his behaviour erratic.

618   Ainu-Seru learns that Liet plans to wake other saidu as a weapon against the Ferish. He hires the Ombros-méleres, a

Ferish mercenary group led by Sofia Mazzina. They storm Brånnheå and massacre the Rúonbattai, but Liet and his cleric escape.

622   Rumours emerge that the Rúonbattai have reappeared in Nordmur. Captain Parr coordinates with Eremur's navy and storms the north in search of them, causing thousands of Sverbians and Aikoto to flee. Ainu-Seru hires the Ombros-méleres to find Liet, but they are unsuccessful.

623   Captain Parr's son, Nerio, takes a mercenary band to investigate Brånnheå. During battle with the Rúonbattai, they kill an oosoo and enrage a fire spirit, which triggers a volcanic eruption.

The Rin discover their okorebai's secret alliance with the Rúonbattai. Two hundred Rin defect in protest, move south, and build the settlement Nettle Ginu.

Akohin Dona follows the path of his great-great-grandfather, Imarein Rin, and becomes Ainu-Seru's new companion. Ainu-Seru calls off the Ombros-méleres' search for Liet.

✳

625   FOURTH ELKEN WAR

Tiernan Heilind steals a sacred Rúonbattai tapestry from a Caladsten stavehall. The Rúonbattai retaliate with a surprise attack across Nordmur, capturing towns occupied by Eremur's military.

Rin defectors storm Ivy House and capture a major Rúonbattai ally, Councillor Gúnnar Halvarind. Soon after, they form a new jouyen, the Tula.

An alliance of Tula, Haka, and Eremur soldiers lay siege to the Rúonbattai village Tjarnnaast. They raze it and kill Liet. His cleric, suspected to be the Rúonbattai's true leader, escapes.

ACKNOWLEDGEMENTS

My gratitude to the following:

Rob Masson, my life partner, for your boundless love and patience, especially during those busy weeks when deadlines loom. Like the Gallnach say, you're always my first thought in the morning.

Jen Albert, my editor, for your wisdom and talent. You see things I miss, and you push me to fix things I do notice but wish I could ignore. David Caron for championing this series. Jessica Albert, my art director, for developing another gorgeous cover. Everyone else at ECW Press who graced this book with your hard work: Sammy Chin (managing editor), Jennifer Gallinger (production and type-setting), Emily Varsava (publicity), and Emily Ferko (sales). Crissy Calhoun for copy editing, and Andrew Wilmot for proofreading.

Simon Carr for illustrating the stunning cover, and Tiffany Munro for illustrating the beautiful provincial map. Sera-Lys McArthur of the Nakoda for your incredible audiobook narration and for being a constant inspiration.

All my wonderful writer groups. Squid Squad: Roy Leon (THALL), Rochelle Jardine, Shannon O'Donovan, Lilah Souza, and Bo Jones for moral support and squiddiness. Cythera Crew: Michael Knudson for your insight and Jessica Smith #453 for your unwavering enthusiasm. The Last Wyrd: Dani, Julie, Karissa, Kayla B., Kayla M., Maddie, Nici, Selbe, and Sydney for bringing light into my week with our Discord calls. Jacklyn and Alli of the Bibliovert podcast for introducing me to a vibrant community of book lovers.

Kathleen and Douglas, my parents; Fletcher and Nic, my brothers. Special thanks to Fletcher for sensitivity reading. Extra special thanks for letting me use Vladimir Catimir's likeness for Og the Destroyer.

Jackson 2bears of the Kanien'kehaka (Mohawk) and Luke Parnell of the Haida and Nisga'a, my former art instructors, for teaching me how to blend old and new culture. Many, many other First Nations, Inuit, and Métis creative folk whose work I've learned from.

The Wurundjeri, in whose territory this novel was written; and the nations of the Northwest Coast of North America, in whose territory it's set.

Jae Waller grew up in Prince George, in northern British Columbia. She has a joint BFA in creative writing and fine art from the University of Northern British Columbia and Emily Carr University of Art + Design. She lives in Melbourne, Australia, and works as a novelist and freelance artist.